PRA
FEMAL

"*Female Fantasy* is a rompy g
it's a beautifully defiant love letter to the romance genre, with
a main character who wholeheartedly and unapologetically
believes in love in all its forms—and then learns that she deserves
it herself. Iman Hariri-Kia's writing is hilarious, razor-sharp, and
vulnerable when it matters most. She's also a legend who gave
readers not one but TWO addicting love stories, both of which I
inhaled in one sitting. I loved every second!"

—Jessica Joyce, *USA Today* bestselling author of *The Ex Vows*

"There is nothing more delicious than being seen as a romance
reader, and Iman Hariri-Kia's *Female Fantasy* does exactly that
and more, playfully yanking us into a page-turning caper filled
with hilarity, hope, and crackling banter. With an older brother's
grumpy best friend, a quirky clan of fanfic besties, clumsy kidnappers, and psychics—and the power of romance novels—Hariri-Kia
shows us that being your own main character takes more than
determination and verve. It takes knowing you deserve your own
happily ever after, full stop."

—Sierra Simone, *USA Today* bestselling author
of *A Merry Little Meet Cute* and *Salt Kiss*

"*Female Fantasy* is fresh, fun, and utterly bingeable. Iman Hariri-
Kia writes with a natural rhythm that makes me feel like I'm floating on champagne bubbles. Decadent and dreamy, this one is for
the romantics."

—B.K. Borison, *New York Times* bestselling
author of *First-Time Caller*

"I had the time of my life reading *Female Fantasy*. Iman Hariri-Kia's writing is equally whip-smart, introspective, and hilarious."

—Hannah Bonam-Young, bestselling
author of *Out of the Woods*

"Clever, delightfully chaotic, and a total joy to read! *Female Fantasy* is truly a one-of-a-kind novel. Hariri-Kia has crafted a magnetic story that is both fantastically mystical and deeply relatable. As a lifelong romance reader, this is the type of book I'm looking for—a book that makes me feel seen, adored, and brave enough to hope for something bigger. Absolutely stellar."

—Lyla Sage, #1 *New York Times* bestselling
author of *Wild and Wrangled*

"An unapologetic ode to all of what we love in the genre. Iman's love for romance and romance readers shimmers on every page of this fresh-feeling rom-com!"

—Tarah DeWitt, *USA Today* bestselling author of *Left of Forever*

PRAISE FOR
THE MOST FAMOUS GIRL IN THE WORLD

"If you found yourself all the way down the Anna Delvey rabbit hole like I did, then *The Most Famous Girl in the World* is the perfect book for you. There's such a relatable bite to Iman Hariri-Kia's voice, a surprising vulnerability in her guarded characters, and a clever construction to this game of cat-and-mouse that will leave you guessing. I was completely immersed in the world of this book!"

—Alicia Thompson, *USA Today* bestselling
author of *Love in the Time of Serial Killers*

"Outrageously fun but also sharp and clear-eyed, *The Most Famous Girl in the World* is the perfect novel for our scammer-obsessed age. Iman Hariri-Kia has given readers an unapologetic satire filled with surprising humor and heart."

—Laura Hankin, author of *The Daydreams* and *One-Star Romance*

"Reading *The Most Famous Girl in the World* is like riding a roller coaster through the dark. Iman Hariri-Kia takes readers on a thrilling, fast-paced adventure, where you know the twists are coming but you're not sure when they'll happen or what they'll entail. Iman's sophomore novel is incredibly fun and deliciously chaotic. I loved it and couldn't put it down!"

—Carley Fortune, #1 *New York Times* bestselling author of *Every Summer After* and *Meet Me at the Lake*

"No one's voice sparkles with camp and au courant humor like Iman Hariri-Kia's. Combined with this gasp-inducing, galloping plot centering on female celebrity obsession, Hariri-Kia has penned a thrilling romp you'll down in just a couple of scrumptious sittings."

—Amanda Montell, *New York Times* bestselling author of *The Age of Magical Overthinking* and *Cultish*

"*The Most Famous Girl in the World* is a razor-sharp satire, twisty mystery, and smoking hot romp all wrapped up in one compulsively readable package. I devoured it!"

—Ava Wilder, author of *How to Fake It in Hollywood*

PRAISE FOR *A HUNDRED OTHER GIRLS*

"Noora is a perfectly flawed, expertly crafted protagonist, and a highlight of her character arc are the explorations of her Iranian American identity and of the meaning of family. The distinct and vivid narration, especially the electrifying descriptions of NYC, makes this debut engaging...relevant, witty, and easy to devour."

–Library Journal

"Noora's personal journey will resonate with millennial and Gen Z readers, and it's also a good choice for fans of dishy workplace dramas like *The Knockoff* and *The Devil Wears Prada*."

–Booklist

"Witty and winning, *A Hundred Other Girls* announces a new writer of immense gifts."

–BookRiot

"A refreshing take on the classic media-insider novel, championing the value of passion and thoughtfulness over career."

–Kirkus Reviews

"The most delightful, absorbing, and hilarious book I have read in ages! An automatic favorite–there is nothing like this anywhere. Iman Hariri-Kia has that rare talent that comes along once in a decade."

–Christina Lauren, New York Times bestselling author of *The Soulmate Equation*

ALSO BY
IMAN HARIRI-KIA

A Hundred Other Girls
The Most Famous Girl in the World

FEMALE FANTASY

A Novel

Iman Hariri-Kia

COSMO
READS

Published by Cosmo Reads, an imprint of Sourcebooks
1935 Brookdale RD, Naperville, IL 60563-2773
(630) 961-3900
sourcebooks.com

Cataloging-in-Publication Data is on file with the Library of Congress

The authorized representative in the EEA is Dorling Kindersley
Verlag GmbH. Arnulfstr. 124, 80636 Munich, Germany

Manufactured in the UK by Clays and distributed by
Dorling Kindersley Limited, London
001-355567-Oct/25
10 9 8 7 6 5 4 3 2 1

For the romance community.
The readers and authors and fan girls
and annotators and theorizers.
I see you. I am you. I love you.

AUTHOR'S NOTE

I still remember being told that I couldn't do my book report on a romance novel. My teacher encouraged me to find a book that was more "serious," more "substantial." She dismissed my favorite series, the characters who taught me how to exist in the world, as frivolous "chick lit." As a teenager, I felt embarrassed. Ashamed.

Around this time, I also started to search for answers about my changing body, information that my sex-ed class failed to teach me. I was having thoughts and feelings and urges but had no one to ask, nowhere to turn. As a first-generation Middle Eastern American child, I wasn't comfortable talking to my parents about intimacy. But my body felt totally and utterly alien. As my male peers snickered and made jokes, and my female peers sneered and laughed at said jokes, my sense of isolation soared. I'd never felt more alone. But I didn't realize that we were all falling victim to a broken system that pitted us against one another, siloing women and marginalized people in the process.

When I arrived at university and started learning more about America's puritanical roots, I realized that so much of our daily social discord can be traced back to our flawed sex education. As children, we learn about sex from a penetrative, heteronormative lens but aren't taught about our sexual pleasure, sexual health, sexuality, consent education, and so much more. As a result, straight, cis-gendered men are able to form community around sex ("locker room talk"), whereas women and marginalized people are further isolated, encouraged to associate an interest in sex with fear and shame. As their collective power grew, ours diminished.

After becoming a sex and relationships editor, I committed myself to publishing accessible, nonjudgmental articles about everything from sex, relationships, and dating, to sexuality, gender identity, sexual health, sexual autonomy, and more. As of 2024, only eighteen states mandate that sex education be medically accurate. That means that millions of young adults are graduating high school without the ability to make informed decisions about their bodies. And I knew, from personal experience, that there was only one source they would trust to turn to for answers. The same place women and marginalized people have always looked to, for centuries: the written word. Reading. Whether that be magazines or novels.

Throughout this entire period of my life, I continued to privately read romance—despite my teacher's ill-fated attempt to coax me away from of my interest. I devoured anything I could get my hands on: rom-coms, romantasy, erotica, fanfic. Dark, paranormal, historical. Mafia, cowboy, hockey. You name it, I've read it. By reading romance, I was learning so much about my body, desires, and preferences. I was unlocking kinks and unpacking traumas, studying how to communicate my wants and needs, redefining my standards for intimacy and partnership. Romance gave me a cipher with which I could finally decode my psyche. I was learning to trust myself for the first time. Reading romance made me feel strong, capable, and in control.

Then something incredible happened: Readers started to become loud and proud about their love of romance. The romance community began using supply and demand and word-of-mouth marketing to swap romance recommendations and form real community. As romance book club numbers grew, members could finally ask questions and expect candid answers in return. Romance readers were healing together in real time. And by gaining more and more knowledge about their wants and needs, they began to take their power back.

And yet, there are still those, like my teacher, who are patronizing toward the romance community, the billion-dollar industry that publishing relies on to remain afloat. People who call the writing weak and predictable, who dismiss the readers as delusional and perverted. People who condescend to romance readers think that by under-estimating and undermining us, they can diminish our power. But they have always been wrong.

I'm not telling you that every time you read a romance novel that you are taking part in a radical act. Sometimes, you need to pick up a light rom-com just to feel a shred of hope and happiness as the world is burning or a steamy, smutty novella to get off at the end of a long day. But I am telling you that when you do select a romance novel from your TBR, you are just one thread in a much larger tapestry that is slowly chipping away at patriarchal social structures, one sentence at a time. And I think that's fuck-ing amazing.

Friend, when I first told people that I wanted to write women's fiction in the romance genre, they looked at me like I'd officially lost it, but this novel is a true labor of love. In these pages, I use satire and camp to tell a story about a young woman who refuses to give up on hap-pily ever afters. I also parody a romantasy novel, with the utmost reverence and respect, as a lover of the subgenre. Please know that there are also mentions of domestic abuse and that I worked with sensitivity readers and copy editors to tend to that storyline with precision, integrity, and care. Please prioritize your own comfort and health. I hope you love these characters, this world, and their message as much as I do.

Thank you for being a part of my happy ending.

An excerpt from
A Tale of Salt Water & Secrets

It was never my intention to steal the conch.

Ever since my husband's accident in the mines, the rules have bent where they once were ironclad. My moral compass has been askew, the colors I once knew in songs and sleep, as clear as glass spires, turned to graying ash. Unable to walk, my husband has been sentenced to a lifetime in proverbial chains. He now spends his days in bed, shouting orders. He is unable to work or help with the household chores. The corners of each room remain undusted. The kitchen is coated in residue. We have been unable to fill our cupboards for a fortnight. Our table is barren, our stomachs empty. We cannot afford to pay for food or cloth or the upcoming tithe to the clergy. And one night, as my husband drank and his condition worsened, my own temperament grew desperate. I knew I had to do something to change our luck. To make our own luck.

The creek cottage has been empty for a millennium, or so say the village folk. A house perched on the water's edge, its walls made entirely of glass, its wooden roof partially caved in. No one goes in, and no one comes out. As children, we were told ghost stories about the dwelling. We were warned against exploring the deserted grounds at night when we were young and restless. In the lore, the house used to belong to an old sailor who met a helpless maiden out on the cliffs one night. She did not speak the native tongue, lacked clothes on her back or a morsel in her belly. He took her home, fed her supper, and dressed her in the garments of his late wife. She, in turn, made music for him. Music of the sea. Beautiful, terrifying enchantments. They grew comfortable together, but then one day, he woke to find her missing. The villagers claimed that she had run off with the stonemason's son, but the sailor refused to listen. He believed that she had returned to the river. Each day, he swam out and held his breath before the current grew too strong. One morning, the undertow pulled him under, and he was never seen again. But it was rumored that his spirit still haunted the house, mourning his beloved, humming her song. He waits for her to return even now. Today.

I have never been one for silly stories. To me, there is nothing more terrifying than having our home seized by the church, and that includes love-stricken spirits and water nymphs. The neighborhood miscreants have always been too afraid to pillage the house and risk angering the old sailor's spirit, but not I. While I have never learned to swim, I have always been drawn to the water.

Mustering my courage, I slip into the house in the dead of night, unsure of what I will find. I hope to stumble upon a sack of gold, safely hidden away beneath an unstable floorboard. Something to help fend off the wolves while my husband makes his recovery…if he ever makes his recovery. But as I take my first steps into the house, hearing the floor creak beneath me and the earth start to shake, I peer into the dusty foyer and spy a shape catching the moonlight. Smooth like a seashell, looking both hand carved and whittled by sand and time. Adorned with gold and carvings in a language I do not understand. A horn, an instrument of some kind.

Suddenly, the air in the room shifts. Some current of electricity, or perhaps the strings of fate, pull me toward the horn. I wrap my hands around it—soft as the skin of a babe, shining like the sun. Startled by my own yielding, I grab the instrument and begin to run. But some force of nature pulls my feet, which sink beneath the air like sand, planting me firmly on the ground. Unable to fight the temptation a second longer, I raise the conch to my lips and blow. And the sound that permeates the atmosphere, the song that rings out of its tendrils, is the most marvelous, magical noise I have ever heard. For a moment, I am in a trance, unable to think or move or even feel. At the absolute whim of the instrument, suspended in time.

And then I hear the clearing of a throat, like the hoof steps of a fawn. Like that, the spell is broken, and my body returns to this world. And in the doorway of the creek cottage, a stranger stands, applauding slowly, each clap of his hands a bolt of thunder. I remain frozen in place, unsure of what has happened, what has befallen me, until I realize with horror the truth of my situation. It dawns on me slowly, then all at once: I have been caught red-handed with the horn. And this stranger, with his dark hair, tanned skin, and glimmering eyes as golden as the sunrise, is its rightful owner.

I try to run. I sprint as fast as my legs can carry me, all the way up the riverbend and through the drunken forest, and past the corporeal keep, until I reach my husband's hovel. Barely three minutes pass before the stranger breaks down the door with the heel of his boot, then looms above me as I double over, panting, winded.

The stranger's upper lip curls. He watches my husband hunch over the fire, fighting the urge to vomit. I remain steadfast, shielding his body by standing in front of him, meeting the stranger's eyes. He snarls at my defiance, my refusal to show cowardice or submission. But I feel my insides melt to milk, my bones deteriorate to dust.

My husband attempts to stand and limp his way to my side, his forehead creased with concern but his eyes lit with rage. "Who goes there?" he wheezes.

The stranger barely raises his voice above a whisper, the sound deep and rough as aged ale. "Your ward has taken something from me."

My husband looks between us in a panic. "Is that true, Merriah?"

I shake my head defiantly, the horn digging into my lower back.

In an instant, the stranger is behind me, one arm wrapped around my neck and the other around my abdomen. "How sweetly you lie to me," he leans down to murmur in my ear. Each hair on the back of my neck stands in anticipation, betraying the fear in my gut.

Unable to fight him off, he releases the horn into his hand. He chuckles darkly, and I fall to the ground, gasping for air and trying to regain control of my senses. In one swift movement, he takes out a silk pouch, buries the horn inside it, and tucks it beneath his cloak. Then he turns back toward me.

"You have attempted to take a priceless possession from me. A penance must be paid."

My husband's face drains of color, and his fists clench so tightly that his knuckles turn white. "Kind sir, my sincerest apologies for the actions of my wife. You see, she is unwell. Ever since my accident, we have struggled to maintain decorum. We have nothing to offer to make up for this offense."

The stranger dusts a layer of invisible dirt from his pant leg. "Allow me to explore your home, to judge your assets as I see fit. Should I find an object of equal value, I shall take it and let you go unharmed."

I watch my husband make a quick calculation. If the stranger lingers too long, opens the wrong drawer, he could seize the last of our estate. We would starve in earnest. My husband would wither away in this shack we call a home, his lost pride chipping away at his sanity long before his empty stomach does.

"No," he says. "Do not bother with my assets. Take her."

I watch in horror as he points to me.

"My wife is of little use to me. Take her and be done with it."

My husband. The man my father betrothed me to at seventeen. For four years, I have lived at his beck and call, nursing his wounds and preparing his meals. I have bent to his standards and welcomed him into my bed. Done my duties as a wife, though never as a partner. He rarely looks me in the eye or speaks directly to me. Not once has he doted on me. I am no beauty, but to him, I am a wilted weed. I once dreamed of experiencing a great love, one that could bring the gods to their knees and spin the Earth off its axis. But by now, I have learned that those wishes are the deceptions of fairy tales. I have accepted a life of cold beds and empty words.

"Is that what you want, little minnow?" the stranger whispers. "To come with me?"

I think of the life I have lived since the day I entered this world. Confined to this village. To a family of little means, to a marriage that lacks warmth and compassion. A life of skipped meals and broken promises. Of curses and angry rants. I watch the flames dance in the stranger's eyes, and I am horrified to hear a single thought echo through the cold chamber of my mind: Can it get any worse?

Not once do I turn to look at my husband, the man who would sell me for a sack of silver.

Instead, I tilt my head up toward the stranger and breathe in his scent.

Ash and salt water. The beginnings and ends of new worlds.

"Yes," I say. "I will go with you."

CHAPTER ONE

S o, let me get this straight: You're breaking up with me to be with someone who *doesn't exist?*"

A dribble of Busch Light trickles down Job's chin like a loose tear. Sighing, I pick up my napkin and dab at it. "Not to be with him," I explain for the zillionth time. "*Because* of him."

The line cook calls out an order from the back of the house. A baby emphatically flaps his arms, knocking over a large Sprite. Job tugs at the bottom of his THE SPICE MUST FLOW! T-shirt, a nervous tic I picked up almost immediately upon meeting him. At first, I found it kind of endearing. I mean, if I made him uncomfortable, that must mean he really liked me, right? But after a couple of weeks, I came to the unfortunate conclusion that it was just another coping mechanism, one that allowed him to avoid confrontation (and eye contact) for as long as humanly possible.

In total, Job and I have spent about three months dating, but so little of that was quality time that it might as well have been three minutes—which is, coincidentally, about how long he lasts in bed.

If I'm being generous.

"I don't get it," he whines. "That's make-believe. This is reality. You do know he's not going to come to life, right?"

"Yes, I know he's not going to come to life," I snap. "And quite frankly, the implication that I can't distinguish fact from fiction is both misogynistic and idiotic. So congratulations—you're not only sexist, you're a tool, too."

Job pulls at his wheat-like hair, his face flushing tomato red. "If you know that he's not real, then why are you leaving me?"

I roll my eyes. *Because I am looking for a great love, one that could bring the gods to their knees and spin the Earth off its axis,* I recite by heart. "And Ryke has taught me that I don't need to settle for less than I'm worth. That there are men out there who will put in the work, the time, and the effort to get to know the real me. To be there for me. To really fall in love with me."

Job snivels, and I fight the urge to cringe.

Honestly? I can't believe I ever thought Job "Space

Travel Is the Next Frontier" Pesce could possibly be my one true love. Sure, when I came across his dating app profile last fall, I found him mildly attractive. Between his wisps of yellow hair, pale complexion, and five-foot-eleven stature (five-foot-nine, I'd come to discover; predictably, he lied about his height in his bio), he looked nothing like Ryke. But he had a niche Jonas Brothers lyric in his profile and a mysterious closed-mouthed smile in his photographs, one that compelled me to swipe right.

That smirk screamed *danger*. I wanted to know all his secrets.

On our first date, he took me to the planetarium, where I immediately began spotting red flags. He didn't hold the door open for me: red flag. When I told him what I'd studied in college, he cut me off before I could finish: red flag. I asked him his favorite Taylor Swift song, and he said "Shake It Off": red fucking flag. But then the lights went out, the ceiling lit up, and Neil deGrasse Tyson's voice began booming from the speaker system. Hundreds of constellations glittered overhead. The Earth spun hypnotically. And as we watched a detailed recreation of the Big Bang, an event that literally created the universe as we know it, Job put his arm around me and leaned down to whisper in my ear. "You remind me of a star," he said. "You shine so bright."

I mean, *cringe*.

Still, my breath hitched. Despite the extreme corniness,

the sentiment reminded me *exactly* of something Ryke might say.

Suddenly, the red flags I'd noticed before started to look kind of pink.

Before I could overthink it, I leaned over and kissed him. He opened his eyes wide in surprise as I crashed my lips into his. For several seconds, nothing happened. I held my breath and waited for the room to spin and time to stop. For my heart to explode out of my chest and my vagina to grow a pulse. For *something* to happen.

Anything.

But all I felt was his semihard boner pressing up against my leg.

The relationship should have ended then and there. And it would have, had I not promised my brother, Tey, that I'd give the next guy I dated a serious chance. So I stuck it out for a few months, hoping the tide would turn, that I'd have an "aha" moment when everything clicked into place. But the bond never solidified. I got tired of laughing at his borderline-offensive jokes and faking orgasms when I could have been at home. Reading. Writing. Spending quality time with Ryke.

Now tears—actual tears—well in his eyes. I exhale, preparing myself for what will inevitably come next. All of them do this when I break up with them. Every single goddamn one. They cry. They scream. They call me names. I usually just wait it out, like you would with a petulant toddler throwing a tantrum. They reel from the familiar sting of rejection. But the funny thing is, none of them actually want me either. Not the real me, anyway. It's companionship they're after.

What really tickles my fucking pickle? Not a single one of these men ever expects to be dumped! Isn't that absolutely baffling? Even when they've done literally nothing to deserve a relationship. They're not looking for a partner, just someone to make them feel special. A woman who is willing to thank them for doing the bare minimum—with a smile, to boot. And that's not me.

Not anymore.

"But I treat you like a queen," Job complains.

Now I really have to laugh. "Job. Be fucking real. You never text me first. Whenever we go out, I have to take the initiative and make a plan. Your phone background is a picture of you and your mother…that your ex took. Oh, and you never go down on me."

"I'm Italian!" he cries.

I shake my head sadly. "No, Job," I say. "You're a pussy."

"You bitch!" Angry now, he slams his fists down on the table and stands up suddenly, causing a scene. Everyone else in the room turns around, taking note of us. Him, sweat circles under his armpits and steam coming out of his nostrils. Me, legs crossed and fingers laced on the table. I'm the picture of composure, which only serves to underline and escalate his hysteria.

The line cook pauses to listen in.

The baby quiets and sucks his thumb.

Job's forehead vein begins to throb.

"Those dumb romance books you read have given you unrealistic expectations. And it's not like you ever have time for me, anyway. Always writing your dumb flip-flops—"

"Fanfics," I correct him.

Very popular fanfics, at that.

"Whatever."

We're in the final stretch now. I can feel it. He's about to cut his losses and go home. Later, he'll call his mother to cry and complain. If his friends ask what happened, he'll tell them he ended things because he realized that he's out of my league. I'm not hot enough. He can do *so* much better. Etcetera.

Good.

I'm fucking starving. The sooner he settles on this course of action, the sooner I get to eat.

Job takes one last swig of his beer, then attempts to look me dead in the face. Unfortunately, he's pissed, so he's a bit cross-eyed. I choke on another laugh.

"Face it, Joonie. There were always three people in this relationship: you, me, and Ryke."

"No, Job," I stand up and pat him gently on the head like a wounded animal. "There was only ever Ryke and me."

That about does it.

Job blinks once.

Twice.

Everyone else returns to their own crises, bored with our antics. My phone buzzes in the palm of my hand. I think about the laundry I left unfolded on my bed, how many episodes of *Love Island* I need to watch before I'm caught up.

Job gives me one last desperate, pleading look.

I shake my head.

And he walks out the door.

Relieved, I sit back down and open up a menu. Minutes later, I flag down the waiter.

"Can I please have an order of fries and a carafe of wine?"

He nods, scribbling away on his notepad. "That was quite the show."

"Sorry about that." I wince. "Some guys just can't take a hint, you know?"

The waiter smiles. I know exactly what he's thinking.

I'm in on this joke. I am not like other guys. I am the exception to the rule.

I drink him in. The lean lines of his torso beneath his apron. The dimple in his left cheek. His sandy curls. He's cute, don't get me wrong. First-love-interest material.

But he's no Ryke.

"Dining alone, then, miss?" he asks.

I smile and shake my head. "I've got company."

The waiter walks away, confused, his brows furrowed and his head hanging low.

And I take out my book and begin to read.

I open my eyes to find myself surrounded by the sea. Waves crashing, wrestling for control, the sound thrashing in my ears. Pulling me under, wrapping my body in an ice-cold, deadly embrace. I jump, gasping, fighting to fill my lungs with even a morsel of air. That is when I realize my skin is dry and my blood warm. I am huddled in a mass of silent blankets, a fort of goose-feather pillows and plush quilts. The four walls around me are glass. The floorboards are crystal, too, but tinted black so that I cannot see what lurks underneath. Heaven knows what watches me. No cousin to the creek cottage. And the water comes from all directions, humming a chantey that's all its own. This is a submarine of sorts, then. An underwater ship nestled in the sea.

My exhale of relief is short-lived. I look for an exit, some way of getting out, and find none. No rowboat or sailboat tethered to my sanctuary. How in the devil's name did I get here?

And more importantly, how will I escape?

The events of the previous day replay in my mind like a three-act opera.

My foolish decision to break into the creek cottage.

The force that compelled me to touch that horn, to stow it away under my cloak, to slip its beak between my lips.

And the stranger who came for me. Who took me. Claimed me as his.

Take my wife. She is of little use to me.

Bastard.

My recollection of the evening's events ends soon after that. Did I faint from the shock? Or did the stranger knock me out cold? Somehow, the mere thought sits upon a lump in my throat. I remember his eyes, dancing like sunrays at dawn. I recall his lips at the nape of my neck, his hands on my abdomen.

And now the stranger has imprisoned me in some kind of glass box in the middle of sea, levitating in an in-between place. I'm far enough below the waves that I can no longer see the sky, but far enough from the bottom of the ocean that I cannot rake my fingers through the sand. It is as if time does not exist here. Wherever "here" may be.

Where has he gone?

Did he bring me to this place?

As if my thoughts alone have summoned him, I hear a latch sliding free beneath the tinted floorboards of the glass sleeping chamber, and then a panel opens, and the stranger lifts himself up and into the room. There appears to be a shallow pool, a wading room, hidden below my feet. He drinks me in slowly, as if checking to make sure all of my parts remain unbruised, unbroken.

"You are awake," he says.

He, too, is dry, no sign of the tides except for the moisture that drips from his dark locks.

Odd.

"From where have you come?" My voice rings truer than my heart. "Is there a house below this hollow box? A glass castle buried deep beneath the sea? A coffin?"

He cocks his head, the corners of his mouth curling up with amusement.

"So many questions," he muses.

"By what method did we arrive? I do not see a boat or ship."

"We had no need for one."

My eyes narrow. "Do not mock me. I know not how to swim."

"Oh, but I do, little minnow." He lowers his voice to a whisper. "All too well."

Frustrated, I throw up my hands. The chamber has no

mirrors—no furniture at all, in fact, with the exception of the pile of plush bedding—so I am unable to lock eyes with my own reflection. But I catch a glimpse of myself in the glass. My hair is wild, curling every which way. My dress is torn at the leg, revealing an unseemly sliver of flesh. The stranger follows my gaze, and his own darkens.

"I do not have a change of clothes," I tell him.

His eyes lift to meet mine. "If you prefer, you may remove your clothes and go without."

A shyness takes over my composure. Uneasy, I cross my arms in front of my chest.

"Do you mean to keep me imprisoned here forever?"

His brows shoot upward. "You followed me here by choice. You are no prisoner."

"Sir, I do believe—"

"Ryke."

The name catches me off guard. "What?"

"Ryke," he repeats, running a hand through his hair, his expression almost sheepish. Embarrassed. "My name is Ryke."

I pause for a moment, getting my bearings. "Merriah."

"Tell me, Merriah. What possessed you to attempt to steal my conch?"

Blood rushes to my ears as I remember that feeling. The strong pull, the siren call of fate, urging me to declare the horn my own, to devour the noise whole.

"I am quite unsure," I confess. "I felt drawn to it. As if phantom hands had reached inside of my body, hooked my chest with an anchor, and tugged."

He looks up, alarmed. "A pull? Of this you are certain?"

"I do not see why I should have to answer your nagging queries when you refuse to address my own."

The stranger—Ryke—chuckles. "Fair enough, my minnow. We are at my home, my true home, at the bottom of the sea. Here you are no prisoner but a most cherished guest. You may come and go as you please. Say the word, and I shall deliver you back to the rock-strewn shores."

My breath hitches as I take in his candid words. "You missed a question, Sir Ryke," I say. "You have not confessed how you delivered me to your glacial haven. This room lacks windows and doors. I see no floating tavern. We are trapped, you and me. Here, I am but a bird in a glass cage. And yet, you ascend from below."

He nods once. "I told you already: we swam. Well, I swam. You slept."

I nearly let out an imprudent sound. "And how, pray tell, did we move against the current, our heads beneath the surface, for so long? I have looked toward the coast. We must be miles from shore."

Ryke smiles then, a warm, glowing grin that bathes me in light and sends sparks through every ash and ember in my body, toward my very soul.

Against my better judgment, I return the look with a smile of my own. "You will not tell me, then?"

A shake of his head. A smirk of his lips.

"No," he says. "But I can show you."

Ryke leans down to open the trap door.

I watch in horror as he dives headfirst into the ravenous current of the sea.

And nearly hits me with his tail.

CHAPTER TWO

As two lucky lovesick idiots swap saliva while hovering over a melting ice cream cone, I ponder why God gives his toughest battles to his strongest soldiers. I mean, I've done my time, haven't I? I've used more dating apps than cats apparently have lives. Gone on so many first dates that I've had dinner with three—no joke, *three*—different men named Marrion Chad. (And not just Chad or Marrion. Marrion Chad!) I've learned to play the banjo to appease a bluegrass musician, gone halal and kosher, and joined fantasy football leagues and Dungeons & Dragons games. Not to mention becoming proficient in Mandarin and a black belt in tae kwon do! And all of this for what? The mere chance of falling deeply, passionately in love with a good-for-nothing, borderline-disgusting, small-brained man who doesn't even come within ten feet of my favorite fictional character? In fact, comparing Ryke to these imbeciles is like looking at a Picasso next to a finger painting done by a ten-year-old. It's practically obscene.

The lovebirds pull their mouths apart long enough to turn their attention to the drawbridge. At a hundred years old, Mystic Drawbridge is one of the main attractions of our quaint little tourist trap of a town—that and Mystic Pizza. (Damn you and your million-dollar smile, Julia Roberts.) Several times a day, as boats pass along the canal toward safe harbor in New London, the brass bells chime and the bridge splits down the middle like a cracked spine. For those few minutes, time stands still. It's like the Earth ceases its rotation, like someone hits pause on the universal remote. Us locals are used to the maddening stagnation, often grunting our annoyance that we have to wait to cross over to the other half of town. But visitors usually react with glee, sometimes even breaking into applause once the boat is finally through. While they wait, they often treat themselves to ice cream from the nearby shop, which is about as old as the bridge itself and sells only treats made in-house. A hot fudge sundae and a picture or two later, the tourists are off on their merry way.

Life here goes on as usual.

I've lived in the small fishing town of Mystic all my

life. Settled by whalers in the eighteenth century, the town feels like a small slice of New England history, a virtually untouched time capsule. Well, except for the new glossy details. A nautical-themed inn sits on one side of the harbor, complete with an adjoining candy shop. There are a few scattered boutiques that cater to customers from out of town, a shack run out of an old mill that claims to serve the best lobster in the Northeast (Portland, Maine, can suck our dick), and a couple of local bars with dedicated regulars, one of which hosts a popular karaoke night on Tuesdays. My favorite spot on Main Street is an independent bookstore run by an old-timer named Cece, a local whose family has owned the joint for several generations. She still orders all the books herself and selects each month's fiction picks. Sometimes she hosts reading nights themed around a specific genre or decade. There's a donation rack full of free used books and a rotating glass Little Free Library that sits outside. Most people in town have a close connection to Ends Whale Books, but mine is personal. After all, it's where I first discovered Ryke.

And it was love at first sight.

Some adults find it somewhat suffocating to live in the small town where they grew up, but I've never really felt that way. First of all, there's a steady stream of outsiders with second homes in nearby beach towns who drift in and out. Most come with money burning through their pockets and steam to blow off, which, in my experience, can make for a pretty good cocktail party anecdote. And then there are the tourists, who see the townies as extensions of the quaint New England experience. That can be fun, too, if you're down to play a part. Sometimes I'm in the mood to give the performance of my life. Other times I make an excuse and head straight for the door. Either way, you get to reinvent yourself daily.

Second, I take comfort in the fact that Mystic feels like a real community. I love that Terrence at Young Buns Donuts starts making my coffee order the second I walk through the door, that I used to babysit the waitress at the seafood restaurant down on the docks when she was a kid. Plus, it helps that my family is part of the small business scene—they own a Kabob shop up by the old church, across from the parking lots. My father leased the space before I was born and bought it when I was in high school. For years, I was teased for showing up to class reeking of lemon chicken and lamb. It wasn't enough that I was sporting a full unibrow and skin the color of sandpaper, a far cry from most of my fair-skinned public school peers. No, I also needed to smell like I'd been roasted on a spit so I could receive the maximum amount of mockery. Of course, I now accept that those kids were just trying on cruelty for size. Most of the students didn't like the look and feel and ended up hanging it back on the rack. When we see each other now, we're cordial. Acquaintances. Growing up, the people I felt closest to were my older brother and his best friend. But I've never had too many close friends.

In fact, I've never seen most of my favorite people in the flesh—but more on that later.

And then there's the fact that said older brother, Teymoor, comes across as a tad overprotective. (It's not his fault; his eyebrows are just really thick.) For a while there, he scared off all my potential friends *and* suitors. Not even by doing anything, really—he's just so damn tall, and those thick brows are always furrowed in a way that makes him look angry. He's working on that, though. Apparently, scaring away strangers is bad for business. And ever since Tey took over Kabobs 'n' Bits, he's been taking customer service very seriously.

I guess that's the third reason I don't feel suffocated here: Once my parents reached retirement age, they decided to sell our childhood home and live on a house-boat. They didn't consult us kids first, just sent us a text demanding we pack up our remaining possessions in the house and say goodbye to sentimentality. That's life in the diaspora for you: Once your parents have had to pack up and go several times, they won't hesitate to do it again. And they might even pass on that same underlying panic to you. I inherited all that and more from my mom and dad: furry eyebrows, thin lips, and generational trauma.

But I didn't get the short end of the stick in the same way Tey did. They all but tossed him the keys to Kabobs 'n' Bits before motoring off in the direction of Maine. Not that Tey seemed to mind all that much. He studied business at the local state school and likes the responsibility. Classic firstborn, golden-child stuff. Now my parents communicate with us only via a WhatsApp group, where they send selfies from the high seas. Who knows when we'll next see them. Probably Nowruz, if I had to guess. I usually text the group distasteful jokes that I know will piss my parents off, partly because it's funny and partly because, as the baby of the family, I'm entitled to seek attention. Tey always tells me to can it, though. He doesn't like getting in hot water, pun intended. See? Despite the Bigfoot stature and the scary-ass stare, once you get to know him, he's an absolute muffin.

Speaking of muffins, I turn my attention back to the pastry I'm nibbling on and the hot apple cider smell that's wafting out of the back room of Sift. With freshly baked goods each morning and a line that's often out the door, Sift boasts the title of best bakery in town, if not the state. I love that only a panel of glass separates customers from the kitchen so we can watch the maestros work their magic. My mouth salivates as one chef uses a tiny pointed instrument to impregnate a flaky puff pastry with some sort of milky filling.

Fuck. My body often confuses hunger with horniness. I shake it off. I need to snap out of the delusion before my date arrives. The last thing I need is to be sporting rock-hard nipples under my fuzzy striped sweater and scare him off before he's even ordered a beverage.

I look at the time in the corner of my laptop screen. This dude still has fifteen minutes to show before I send him a passive-aggressive text and never contact him again. The employees at Sift would take my side. After all, I'm one of their best customers. Plus, every time I reach the register, I do, like, five minutes of free improvised stand-up comedy. And I'm moderately hot! The general manager would probably kick my date's ass on my behalf.

My Google Doc word count stares me down, reminding me that I'm still no closer to my goal than yesterday. When I'm not writing fanfic (or *flip-flop*, as Job called it), I pay the rent by copywriting, both for local businesses and virtual clients. Right now, I'm attempting to come up with a slogan for a suppository company. So far, the best I've been able to muster is "VIPussy" and "Put the *But!* in Butthole," both of which, I think, are a little bit too rock 'n' roll for my sixty-year-old white conservative clientele.

I let out a long sigh of despair.

Sometimes I feel like Wonder Woman or Hannah motherfucking Montana or something. By day, I write for people who barely appreciate me, taking the straw they send me and spinning it into pure gold. But by night, I'm revered, beloved by a niche community of online freaks just like me. My latest fic has hundreds of thousands of saves. Sure, nobody knows that StepOnMeRyke432 is me, but the validation those numbers give me? More than I could ever ask for. Honestly, who needs parents or a partner when you have virtual fame?

Oh, right.

Me.

Your online readership, in my experience, won't stroke your hair while you sleep. Or take care of you when you're sick. Or threaten to kill anyone who touches you.

I shudder.

Just then, my phone rings, breaking me out of my erotic daydream. I look down at the screen and feel the equivalent of a cold shower soak my senses.

It's my brother.

"What up, what up?" I can hear the clanging of plates and utensils behind him. "What are you doing on Main Street? You're two minutes away, and you can't spare a second to come say hello to your big bro?"

I roll my eyes, annoyed. "For the very last time," I say, "stop tracking me on Find My Friends, Tey. Or I swear to God I'll turn off my location."

"But what if you're kidnapped by an ax murderer?"

"Then my blood will be on your hands," I laugh. "Anyway, I'm at Sift. Getting a little work done."

I can practically hear his eyes narrow on the other end of the line. "But you hate working at Sift. You always say the smell distracts you from being productive."

Damn. He's good.

"Fine," I acquiesce. "If you must know, I'm going on a first date."

There's a leering silence on the other end. Never good.

"Joonie." His voice teeters between gentle and stern. "What happened to Job?"

"Um…" I search for an excuse but come up with squat. "He died?"

"You promised!" my brother groans. I picture the look of desperation on his face as he preps the *polo tahdig* and fights back a grin. "You swore you'd give this one a real shot!"

"I did! I really did, Tey. You don't get it. This guy was capital-*w* the Worst. He told me that if he had daughters, he would name *every single one* after his mother, Elizabeth. So, like, one daughter named Eliza. Another named Beth. One named Liz. One called—"

"Okay, enough. I get it," he says, cutting me off, but he's not quite ready to let me off the hook. "Sure you aren't exaggerating? Who the hell is pumping out four daughters, anyway? You?"

"I'm sure." I choose to ignore that last comment. "He was okay at first, but he was no—"

"Ryke," my brother says, finishing my sentence.

"Right." I swallow, preparing myself for what comes next.

"And how many men have you ended things with prematurely because they didn't hold a candle to Ryke?" he asks, treading carefully. "Twenty? Two hundred?"

I gasp. "Teymoor Saboonchi, are you slut shaming me?!" I feign horror. "I thought you were raised better than that. What would Oliver say?"

Tey groans, and I grin, knowing I've won this round.

Oliver is Tey's partner and a public defender. He has bought Tey more books on social justice than he has room for. Every time I call my brother a bad feminist, even in jest, Christmas comes early. For me, anyway.

"Speaking of Oliver, I want you to come to Sunday dinner this week," he says. "At the restaurant."

"Done." Even though my parents have fled town to become pirates or whatever, my brother and I have maintained our weekly Sunday dinner tradition. I, for one, am a huge fan. Free food and making my brother uncomfortable at work? Who doesn't love dinner and a show?

"And Nico is coming," he adds as quickly as possible.

"Tey!"

"Gotta go, bye!"

He hangs up the phone, leaving me to fume alone in front of the baked goods.

Nico is Tey's best friend, my childhood crush, and the current bane of my existence. Tey met Nico playing Little League, where they failed to impress their coaches and ended up benched for the majority of the year. Those two instantly became an inseparable duo. Legend has it that Nico once beat up a kid for making a terrorist joke about my family. Tey told the coach, and that racist kid was promptly kicked off the team. He was the first friend my brother came out to, and they're still tight.

Can't say the same about me.

I didn't always find Nico to be as unbearable as listening to an off-key children's choir. In fact, there was a time when I found his chiseled frame and buzzed blond hair appealing. Back when I was having trouble at school, Nico was one of the few people who stuck up for me. I looked up to him in so many ways.

I guess he acted that way because I was an extension of Tey and all that. But it felt good to have someone in my corner—a cool older kid, at that. I might have even developed a small middle school attraction to Nico. Okay, fine. When he started defending my honor, it felt like my favorite TV character had actually listened to my ship request. I fell hard.

The hopeless romantic: That's me.

To a literal fault.

But it all came crashing down like the stock market after tenth grade.

Now I go out of my way to avoid him. Tey knows that.

Why is he torturing me?! Because I couldn't make it work with a guy who once compared my birth control prescription to his preventative Rogaine?

"Hi! Are you Joonie?"

And it's showtime.

I look up into a pair of deep-blue eyes the color of the

nearby harbor. The owner of the eyes has hidden them behind round wire spectacles and floppy black hair. His ears are studded with small silver hoops, and he's wearing black nail polish on his thumbs. A tote bag from a foreign bookstore hangs off his right shoulder. There's a Bernie 2020 button pinned to the handle.

Underneath all that hardware, he kind of looks a little bit like a blue-eyed Ryke.

Like always, the highlights of the life we could have together flash before my eyes like a movie trailer.

The stolen kisses in public.

Trips to faraway lands.

The moment when he gets down on one knee and—

"So, where are you from?" he asks, taking a seat across from me.

"Oh, I'm from here—Mystic born and raised," I say, wiping the drool from the corner of my mouth. "You're from Groton, right?"

"No, where are you *really* from?" he asks, his eyes moving up and down my torso appreciatively. "You don't see a lot of caramel-colored people in these parts. Your beauty is totally exotic."

I suddenly feel the muffin churning in my stomach.

Hipster boy might read like a sensitive soul on-screen, but in person, he's just as bad as the rest of them. Maybe even worse, because he's got the righteous superiority of someone who thinks of himself as an ally.

Silly me.

"Can you excuse me for a moment?" I say as sweetly as possible, shoving my laptop into my purse under the table and throwing my coat over my shoulders. "I need to use the restroom."

"Sure thing!" His tone is cheerful. Oblivious. "It'll give me a chance to order. Do you know if the beans here are ground sustainably? I'm trying to reduce my caffeine footprint."

"You know, I'm not sure," I tell the dude. Mike, I think his name is. Maybe Matt? "Why don't you ask and I'll pee?"

I make a beeline for the bathroom, but at the very last second turn into the kitchen.

"Back door?" one of the pastry chefs asks with a half smile.

"Back door," I confirm.

Then I sneak out of the bakery, get into my car, and don't look back.

I know what you're probably wondering. Do I feel any remorse, an ounce of guilt, for abandoning the well-meaning Neanderthal while he's pestering that poor barista about her coffee beans? Honestly, no. I do not. I've saved us both a hell of a lot of time. Had I been honest with him, he'd probably ask me what he did wrong. Then I'd have to explain, and he'd get angry, and we'd do that whole song and dance where he cries and calls me a bitch three months early. There's nothing more fragile than a man's ego. Well, maybe his masculinity.

It's tied. Fifty-fifty.

By the time I pull into the parking spot outside my apartment complex, I am totally and utterly emotionally exhausted. Not ideal, considering I still need to come up with a slogan for this femcare company other than "Take It Up the Ass!" The second I unlock the door to my studio, I flop facedown on my bed and exhale. My apartment is tiny but cozy. I've decorated it with vintage movie posters, corny book quotes, wacky wallpaper, and colorful furniture. My bedside table resembles a corncob and my sofa is polka-dotted. I absolutely detest minimalist apartments. Why would I pay to live somewhere with no personality? I'd rather sleep in my car than in a white Scandinavian box cosplaying as an IKEA warehouse.

My phone pings. I look down.

The Bernie Bro has left me a voicemail.

I inhale sharply, shut my eyes, and prepare myself for the worst.

Then I press play.

"How could you do that to me, Joonie?" he wails. "Running out on our very first date? Seriously? That's really shitty behavior, even for some guy you don't know. I waited for you. For, like, ten whole minutes. You're probably used to getting away with this sort of stuff because nobody ever calls you out. So I'm putting an end to that cycle. You're selfish, Joonie. You're judgmental and cruel and—"

I really need to stop dating all these loser boys. Where can I find a real man in eastern Connecticut?

Maybe I need to date a dad. But whose dad? And how does one procure a dad?

"If you had just gotten to know me, you would have seen that I'm a really good guy," the dude continues, monologuing. "I was a Boy Scout. I'm registered to vote. I attended the Women's March *and* the Black Lives Matter protests! And I'm an incredible lover. If you asked my ex, she'd tell you—"

Oh, who am I kidding?

As my date continues to drone on and on over the speaker, I pull out my laptop and open up the last chapter of the fic I'm writing. Smiling to myself, I reach for a throw pillow to prop myself up and open my bottom drawer.

Then I touch myself to the idea of Ryke until I fall asleep, sated.

Ryke appears in the shallow pool, a shining mirage of a man.

First the top of his head.

The tip of his tail.

Then the rest of him.

I sink to my knees, ever so unbecoming of a lady, and stare at him, mouth agape. He is beyond my comprehension. A miraculous sight. Dark heavy locks glued to his head by thick beads of water. His golden eyes flicker like falling stars. He is nude from the waist up. I drink in his strong forearms, his sculpted chest. Dark and defined, all of him. The vision is almost too much to take in all at once.

And then my gaze wanders below his abdomen.

My mouth dries up.

A glorious tail the color of squid ink, practically obsidian, but shimmering as he moves like the sunlight reflected on the crest of a wave. The texture appears sturdy, like the skin of a dolphin or whale. But the whisper of small scales, similar to pearls strung together on a necklace, robs me of my next breath. He is magnificent.

And utterly terrifying.

I open my mouth to speak, but words fail to fall from its trapdoor.

Ryke throws his head back and laughs.

I am in disbelief.

A shock so pure it is chaste.

"You," I try again. "You are a…fish."

His upper lip curls up at the corner as if dragged by a hook.

"Mer," he corrects me. "I am mer."

But it is not possible.

It cannot be.

"Mer," I repeat. "Like the sea monster? From our bedtime stories?"

He shakes his head. "I am no monster, Merriah. In this world, I am but a man, same as you. I walk among you. Eat as you do. Drink as you do. Fuck as you do. But in the next…"

His explanation lacks sense.

Even as every hair on my body stands up straight.

"There are multiple worlds?"

"So many—"

"So many questions?"

He grins.

Behind him, his tail slaps against the pool of water, splashing me.

But somehow, I do not mind getting wet.

"Little minnow, there is so much about this realm that you do not yet understand. That you have not dared allow yourself to dream about. There is a world that sits above the clouds in the sky. And one nestled beneath the ocean floor—that is where I reside. Or, rather, where I once lived."

I raise my hand to my forehead, as if to check for a fever, and wipe away the ripples of water falling to my lips.

"Do you mean to tell me that beneath the sand beds and dunes, in the darkest depths where salt water meets seaweed, there is a hidden species of man with…tails?"

The entire notion sounds so ridiculous, I could convince myself it was but a ruse if not for the evidence in front of me.

Taunting me.

Flesh and blood and water.

Ryke shakes his head. "The sand is but a false floor to ward away visitors who mean us ill. But there are rifts in the ground. Doors to another world. And if you know how to uncover such passages, you will enter a land of light and sound waves where breathing grows inconsequential. Cities more advanced than those on the shore. Jewels more refined and colors more brilliant. Languages you have never heard and art so revered you would think the world had seen the last of it. A society full of culture and cuisine fresh from the tide. Seahorse-drawn carriages and raucous beach balls. Yes, my people are the muses of your stories. But we are not the monstrous krakens you fear. The objects of beauty you admire."

My breath catches.

I allow myself to dream of it all.

A secret world beneath the sea, ruled by the mer.

A land free of poverty, where splendor reigns supreme.

I can practically taste the oyster delicacies, smell the fresh caviar.

"It sounds wonderful." My voice comes out strained—with desire, I realize. Longing. "Why in the devil's name would you and your people dwell in our world, passing among us as mere mortals, when you could lose yourself in time and space beneath the sea?"

What I dare not say—what I whisper in my mind—is that I would abandon my world entirely if I could.

Escape my own life.

Become one of the mer.

But such things are not possible.

I am nobody.

Nothing but a sack of blood and bones and salt.

Ryke's eyes grow stormy. With trouble clouding the skies and the long scaled appendage cascading from his torso, I find myself short of breath in his presence. He is a stranger once more.

"Our world has been marked by a predator, one unknown by those who dwell above the watery graves. Its name is rarely uttered but always feared. For generations, we took to the shores, living next to rivers and creeks, bodies of water that kept us sheltered from discovery. The members of the rebellion were in hiding, plotting our return, all the while fearing what would happen if our presence was discovered before we were ready. Until now, that is."

Thunder crashes in Ryke's complexion.

I gulp, then force myself to speak with a strength I did not know I possessed.

"Until?"

As lighting flashes in those twin tide pools of gold, a shiver runs down my spine.

And I swear my soul knows his next words before he says them aloud.

"Until you blew the ancient Conch of Hippios," he says, "and called the mer to war."

CHAPTER THREE

When I was thirteen, I was in homeroom with a super popular but utterly average white girl named Sam. She had warm brown eyes that crinkled in the corners when she smiled and long blond hair that she wore French braided down her back. And she played lacrosse, one of the most American sports there is—short of football, of course. I used to sacrifice good study time to sit up in the nosebleed bleacher seats of our high school and watch her run around holding a net on a stick. (The rules of the sport never really sank in, but the BO of the rest of the crowd sure did. Literally ew.) Anyway, she sat behind me in biology. Whenever an exam question confused her, she'd absentmindedly play with my hair. One day, she asked if she could give me a braid that matched hers. I said yes, and later, she invited me to hang out at her place after school.

Up until that point, I had been a bit of a loner. No girls wanted my smelly food near their perfectly packed lunches in the cafeteria. So I jumped at the opportunity to make a friend. To know what it felt like to be accepted. To be understood. My test scores suffered after that, of course. Worth it, though. Or so I thought.

After a few weeks, Sam and I started doing everything together. I went to all of her games to hoot and holler. She invited me to sleepovers at her house, but my strict Iranian parents never said yes. In between classes, I walked with her down the hall—always several steps behind her, but still, I was there. We exchanged friendship necklaces from Claire's; I wore BEST FRIENDS, and she rocked FOREVER. She invited me to my first ever boy-girl party. I went over to her house beforehand, and she straightened my hair and lightened my skin with foundation. And even though I didn't look like myself, I felt pretty enough. For the first time in my life, I wasn't on the outside looking in.

Then one day when I arrived late to class, she wouldn't make eye contact with me. There was an unreadable expression on her face. After the bell rang, she tapped me on the shoulder.

"Hey," she said. "Can I ask you a question?"

I nodded, praying to whatever God she believed in that she couldn't hear the pounding inside my chest.

"The war."

"The war?"

"In Afghanistan. Whose side are you on?"

I blinked. It was common knowledge in our small town that Sam's older brother had been deployed. Her family had hosted a big tear-filled send-off party. But I wasn't sure what that had to do with me.

Carefully, I responded, "I'm American, Sam."

She shook his head. "Not really, though. You're one of them. Right?"

My cheeks started to heat. "My family is Iranian," I said. I willed my temper to remain in check.

"So?"

I tried to reason with her, to get her to see that I was still me, Joonie—the same Joonie I'd always been—but I could tell she'd already made up her mind. She told me that she needed space, a "break" from our friendship. A day turned into a week turned into a month. Texting 24-7 became forced smiles and curt words in passing, as if we were strangers.

When Tey found out, he told me to keep my head down and not cause trouble. He'd learned the hard way what could happen when you made a scene in a small town. But then I told Nico, and he lost his shit. Showed up at Sam's house and had a little "talk" with her parents—who, unsurprisingly, were the source of her vitriol.

But after that, Sam never bothered me again.

My "best friend" also never spoke to me again.

I'll never forget the way Nico sat me down. Held both of my hands and told me that I deserved better. That not all people would treat me like I was a foreign object instead of a human being. Nico made me swear that I wouldn't let an over-tweezed idiot like Sam dull my sparkle. That I would keep romanticizing life, believing in happily ever afters. And I promised him.

Looking at Nico, how could I not?

The proof that good people, true protagonists, existed was right in front of me.

Until it wasn't.

But that was a huge wake-up call, a lesson about how other people in town saw me and my family. Other than Nico, of course. He always stayed the same—loyal to a fault. But to everyone else, we were Other. Alien. Even, in some circumstances, dangerous. A threat. I spent hours walking aimlessly around the streets of Mystic after school, searching for distrust in the eyes of passersby.

One day, I decided something had to give. If the town wasn't going to change for me, I'd have to step up and change myself. And change always required sacrifice.

So when I went away to college, I decided to take a new approach. I'd suppress the louder, more colorful parts of my identity and do my best to fit in with my peers. If I looked, spoke, and smelled like everybody else, maybe I could go four years without anyone bothering me. I could finally blend into the background, melt into the floorboards.

I began straightening my hair every morning, just like Sam had taught me, and lightening it so it was no longer midnight black. I plucked and threaded my eyebrows and lathered my skin in a whole-ass protective layer of sunscreen each morning to keep my complexion as pale as possible. Abandoning my vibrant, expressive wardrobe, I focused on dressing the same as all the other students: leggings and oversize sweaters and sneakers, all in dark colors.

The mission was to look ordinary. Mundane. Average.

And for the most part, it worked. I made surface-level friends and got invited to terrible parties with milquetoast music and white-people dancing. Sure, I was no longer myself, but no one called me names or asked invasive questions about my cultural heritage. I ate sushi and watched *The Bachelor* and pretended to love Disneyland. (To this day, I have an irrational fear of Disney adults. Shudder.)

Then, as a consequence of my deception, I was rewarded.

The impossible happened.

I caught the eye of a boy. A quiet, sensitive English major named Kyle.

We met at a 1975 concert. He wore tortoiseshell glasses and had a slight lisp. The next day, he offered to carry my books to class. I knew he was smitten with the artificial, watered-down version of me, but by the time I was ready to expose myself to him, both metaphorically and literally—my life prior to college had been sexless as hell—I was too afraid to jinx it. To scare him away.

Plus, he was kind to me. Well, kinder than most people.

He held my hand before the plane took off and always paid for our movie tickets. I didn't notice that he always chose our seats and what we watched until much later.

Little by little, Kyle started to restore my faith in happy endings.

To piece together what Sam had cracked.

And what Nico had fully broken.

Then we graduated college, and the nature of our relationship changed. He got a boring desk job that he hated in New Haven. We moved in together. When he arrived home each day, he expected me to dress and behave a certain way. And he started taking out his stress on me—little by little, then all at once. If dinner was cold, he refused to eat it. If I cried in response, I was *purposely trying to guilt him.* The real world hardened him. Or maybe he had been hard to begin with.

Perhaps he'd been putting on a show, too.

Kyle began casually controlling every single aspect of my life. When we were out with other people, he treated me as a punch line rather than his partner. And things at home weren't much better. Although I was normally the one to cook dinner, he began dictating what we ate, controlling how many calories I consumed in a day. When we'd started dating, I had stopped seeing my college friends as frequently, so our social group now consisted mainly of his own buddies, which meant he decided who I saw on the weekends. My girlfriends, mostly the partners of his friends, often reported our conversations to him. Nowhere was safe. He told me what I could and couldn't wear, even going so far as to call me names if I went outside in something he deemed too revealing. When I questioned him, he told me he was behaving this way because he loved me so much. He was worried about me. He wanted what was best for me.

For a while, I was naïve enough to believe him. I was afraid to say anything, to fight back. The truth was, I thought I'd found my soul mate, my one true love. Admitting I was wrong felt terrifying. I thought that if I left him, I'd never get another chance at love. I'd be alone forever. The possibility paralyzed me.

Cruelty, I resolved, was better than excommunication.

I let all of the sunshine drain out of me, a slow, steady, depressive drip.

Kyle had let the light back in, then shut the blinds. His explosive declarations had actually been love bombs. He lit candles inside of me only to snuff them out on a whim. I was tired of fighting tooth and nail to hang on to my optimism.

Sam. Nico. Kyle.

They were all the same.

Happy endings had never felt more like a myth.

And then one day, I came home to find Kyle reading my diaries. He was tearing out entries, page by page. With a terrifying, manic look in his eye, he informed me that I was not allowed to write anything down ever again. That was the last straw. My writing was my one solace, the only truthful part of my life. Those journals were the only things that were 100 percent mine and no one else's. I stormed out the door, even as he yelled after me. He warned me that if I left, he'd lock me out.

I could never come back.

It's funny. I now recognize his behavior as emotional abuse. But I couldn't tell how bad it truly was until I had some distance from the relationship. I had never wanted to call it the *A*-word. To admit how I had allowed him to treat me. Our time together had felt like waiting out a passing storm. I kept thinking, *Well, maybe it'll stop raining soon and I can go outside.* But I had been stuck inside the hurricane for far too long, seconds away from being struck by lightning.

I didn't tell Tey until after I'd already left. My parents were off doing their own thing. When they'd met Kyle at Thanksgiving, they'd declared him charming and well mannered. I did not want to pop their bubble of delusion, to let them down that way. They were happy for me. After years

49

of watching me suffer from bullying and assimilation, they could finally exhale. How could I pull back that curtain, depriving them of the fantasy that everything was okay?

That's the thing about being the child of immigrants. When your parents risk so much to give you a better life, you feel like the least you can do is pretend said life truly is better, even if the reality is so much darker.

Nico had never liked Kyle, though. When I told him, blinking back tears, that we'd broken up, he muttered only two words: "Good riddance."

But he had lost the right to care a long time ago.

The day that Kyle kicked me out of our shared home, I found myself back in Mystic, wandering the streets just as I had after Sam revealed her true colors back in middle school. Just as I'd always done as a kid. And my feet pointed me in the direction of Ends Whale Books. As I lost myself in the stacks, hiding from the realities of the outside world, I heard a rustle. I shut my eyes and held my breath, preparing myself for the possibility that Kyle had found me. That he was going to let me have it in front of all of my favorite authors.

Instead, I came face-to-face with Rona, the owner. She placed a slender hand on my shoulder, then rubbed my back until my breathing slowed and my body stopped shaking.

"Oh, honey," she said, each syllable full of concern. "What's the matter?"

I didn't want to tell her. I couldn't. I did not yet have the words.

"I need a book rec," I blurted out instead.

She studied me, apprehensive. "What kind of book?" she finally asked.

I chewed on the inside of my cheek. *Yes, what kind of book, Joonie?*

"One that will restore my faith in love," I said. And then, in a quieter voice, "And maybe myself."

She nodded, offering up a sad smile. "I've got just the thing."

I expected her to bring me a classic. Austen, maybe. Or *Jane Eyre*.

Instead, she returned moments later with a thick hardcover novel from the fantasy section. I eyed it curiously.

"What's this?" I'd never read fantasy as an adult before. In my head, it was a genre that children escaped into, then grew out of. A phase. Something frivolous.

"Welcome to the world of *A Tale of Salt Water and Secrets* by Evelyn Grace Carter," she said. "I'm so very excited for you to meet my friend Ryke."

I sighed and graciously accepted the book, thanking Rona, fully believing I wouldn't read past the first chapter. But that night, hidden inside a fortress of cotton quilts that Tey had lent me while I crashed on his pull-out couch, I devoured the entire novel. And began the second. The next morning, I staggered down to the restaurant with red eyes, bad breath, and damp underwear, a changed woman.

The books followed a badass human woman in her early twenties named Merriah and her ancient all-powerful love interest, Ryke. But the story was so much more than a romance. Merriah has suffered verbal abuse from her husband. Her shimmer has dulled, and she has lost sight of herself. But as the story progresses, she grows resilient, stepping into her power. At its heart, the series is about Merriah learning to trust herself, owning her strength and her femininity, and the way her potential grows alongside her confidence. I see so much of myself in her journey. She inspires me. Makes me feel seen. Less alone.

And then there's Ryke.

Ryke, with his dark hair and amber eyes and flirtatious smile. Yes, Ryke is part mer (as in, cousin to Ariel). Sure, he can grow a sparkling onyx tail. And fine, it's *heavily* implied that the size of said tail correlates to the size of his, um, appendage. But that's not what makes Ryke so special. He not only cherishes Merriah's beauty but respects her agency. He never tells her what to do or how to think. Instead, he listens to her and supports her. He asks for consent and allows her to take the lead. He always gives her a choice, even when it isn't advantageous to him.

And he loves her. Oh, how he loves her.

With every ounce and fiber of who he is.

Even more than his good looks, dirty tongue, and

perfectly defined torso, that true, unrelenting, all-consuming love is what makes Ryke the world's most perfect fictional man.

Written by a woman, of course.

In other words, I fell head over heels in love.

The day I first read that book, I vowed never to settle for anything less than I deserved. A man who is as charmed by my intellect as he is the slope of my neck or the arch of my back. A partner who will ask me to remain by his side as we chart the course of our lives together instead of leaving me behind. Someone who makes me blush and flush with pride in equal measure. Who believes that my flaws are strengths and that our differences are what make us special.

A lover and a friend and a true equal.

A great love, one that could bring the gods to their knees and spin the Earth off its axis.

I've been searching for him ever since, to no avail. But I refuse to give up, to believe the Ryke to my Merriah isn't out there waiting for me. I can't allow my mind to go there, to slip into old habits, even for a second. I have to have faith. To trust the process. Even if that means spending my nights alone, snuggled up with words on paper instead of skin and bone.

Because if I can't have the real thing, at the very least, I'll always have Ryke.

I gape at Ryke, awaiting an explanation.

What is the Conch of Hippios? I have never heard the name before. Is the horn I attempted to steal some sort of religious artifact sacred to his people?

And what of war?

I was born during peaceful times. My father had never been summoned to war, nor had my wretched husband. I knew not of blood-soaked glass, of dull cleavers. Of swaths of fabric tied on doorknobs or haunted spirits.

But before I have a chance to pose my many queries, a sound rings out from all four corners of the glass oratory, shrill and shrieking. The most horrible noise I have ever heard, loud enough to wake the devil from his slumber, sharp enough to fill the banshees with envy. It vibrates through the walls until they shatter, and water begins to flood our hallowed hall.

"What is happening?" My voice is shot through with tremors.

Ryke is already moving about the room. He has lifted his body from the hatch below, his scaled black tail once again transforming into muscular legs. When I realize he is undressed, I look away quickly, my face undoubtedly red. But there is no time for such inconveniences as bashfulness.

Something is deeply wrong.

The sound continues to pulse through my eardrums as Ryke's haven in the middle of the ocean begins to sink. He is collecting hidden items, I observe, nestled in the ceiling and within trick panels in the tinted glass floor.

He is preparing to make a swift exit.

"We are under siege," he answers. "Our location is compromised. There has been a breach in the waters surrounding this fortress. We have but minutes to make our escape before they arrive."

"Before who arrives?" I cry, wishing I could help him prepare.

"The sirens." His lips are pursed, his expression grim.

"Sirens," I repeat. "Are you referring to that sound?"

He shakes his head. "Sirens are mer," he explains. "Well, they were once mer. Now they are more of a subspecies, one that rules over all of Atlantia. They are power hungry and greedy. It is not enough that they have overthrown our sovereign and conquered the land. No, they also insist on hunting down every mer who poses a threat to their rule to ensure that the rebellion never sees the light of day. Or rather, the light of the seven seas."

"So your war is civil?" I say, piecing things together. "Brother fighting brother?"

If such is the case, then the mer are truly no different from the men who dwell on the shore. Impetuous and powered by greed. Hot-tempered, allowing their emotions to overthrow their logic until the only way to work through a disagreement is through violence and conflict. I have read the histories, heard the stories whispered around campfires. Neighbors becoming enemies over a border dispute. Friends becomes foes because of a love match gone wrong.

People are feebleminded and shortsighted, whether they lack the ability to walk a day in each other's shoes or swim a mile in each other's tails.

"In a sense, but the sirens have a wholly unnatural asset that gives them an unfair advantage, a strength that the mer lack no matter our numbers: raw magic in its purest form. We call it life force. True energy."

Magic.

Magic is…real.

Magic exists.

The truth hits me like a thunderbolt. I am unsure why

it takes me by surprise. After all, I have seen Ryke's flesh turn to fin before my very eyes. But I realize I was waiting for some sort of scientific, logical explanation. I have always been ruled by fact.

Rarely have I been asked to believe in anything.

"And there is no way for the mer to acquire this forbidden magic and even the playing field?" I ask. "After all, the sirens were once mer. Surely it can be done."

Before I can react, Ryke is right in front of me, covering me. So close I can feel the heat of his body warming mine. I will myself to not look down, to ogle at his form. He hooks one hand beneath my chin and forces my gaze upward. I look directly in his gleaming eyes, now darkening with the threat of danger.

My pulse skips. I grow lightheaded, faint.

"Not without becoming monsters ourselves. You see, little minnow, the mer might be as strong in mind, body, and spirit as their siren kin, but they have a weakness. One they are unwilling to sacrifice. A weakness the sirens willingly exploit."

His breath ghosts across my lips.

My toes curl against the glass floor.

"What is this weakness you speak of?" I whisper.

"Not a what. A who."

Ryke looks at me pointedly.

My stomach flips.

Then the sound swells, somehow growing louder and

more urgent. I lift my hands to my ears, expecting to feel blood smearing across my palms. Ryke collects his objects in a sack made of an odd soft, malleable material and turns back to me.

"There are many questions you have yet to ask, Merriah." My name falls from his lips, sweet as honeysuckle. "And much I must tell you. But not now. That conversation must wait until we reach the underpass."

My eyes widen. "You cannot possibly mean…"

"I am taking you home," he confirms, his head hanging in resignation. "To Atlantia."

"But I cannot swim!" My panic bleeds from each syllable.

For the first time since the alarm began to sound, Ryke offers up a coy smile.

"That is no issue, my minnow," he says.

All at once, I am consumed by the rush of a riptide.

And then the world around me grows still.

CHAPTER FOUR

I 'm sitting upright in bed, avoiding working on my latest copywriting assignment by looking up NSFW fan art, when I hear my computer ping. Groaning, I say a silent prayer that it isn't yet *another* text from last week's Guinness World Record holder for shortest date. Or Tey, once again confirming details for Sunday dinner. With He Who Shall Not Be Named.

But it's neither. In fact, it isn't a text at all.

Curious, I scan the one billion tabs I have open in my browser until I notice the little red notification bubble. I discover it's a message from my Evelyn Grace Carter fanfic group with the subject "A Tale of Salty Girls."

About three months after I finished *A Tale of Salt Water & Secrets* (or *ATOSAS* for short), I was insatiable.

I'd absorbed as much of the world of Atlantia as possible, so much so that it practically coursed through my veins and characters had begun appearing to me in my dreams. I'd read and reread all six books in the series, underlining and annotating, tabbing my favorite parts. (Pink for swoon-worthy moments. Blue for heart-wrenching, sad quotes. And red for passages that required one-handed reading.) I'd joined Reddit subcommunities and littered message boards with fan theories and oral histories, memorizing and cataloging every detail of the lore mentioned throughout the books and bonus chapters. I'd even ordered custom throw pillows from Etsy with fan art of Ryke's face plastered on them in sequins.

Still, it wasn't enough.

I was a woman obsessed. Possessed. I needed more content to feed the fangirl inside of me. The thought of waiting another *two years* to read another ATOSAS book made me want to stick my head in an air fryer. How was I supposed to live through a miserable 730 days without knowing what Ryke was up to? Without confirming that he was alive and well?

That was when I found my Salty Girls.

There was a fanfic community dedicated to writing Ryke into everyday scenarios as well as expanding upon the world of the book. Want an alternate ending? The community had written many. Hungry for a Ryke POV? You could literally read the entirety of ATOSAS written in his voice, from his perspective. I was in heaven. I mean, these stories are basically novellas catering to the female gaze. In one chapter, you could find conflict, romance, and sex, written by people who had read so much EGC that they had the voice down pat. It was practically impossible to separate their writing from the author's. In one story, Merriah watched Ryke compete in a competitive kelp ball game against his archnemesis before visiting him in the locker room to deliver a spicy surprise. In another, Merriah was kidnapped by a jealous sea nymph, and Ryke tore apart the ocean in order to find her before making sweet, sweet love to her in an underwater cave. The best part? All of the stories were self-insert, so the reader could pretend to be Merriah, whether that meant going grocery shopping with Ryke or fighting off underwater aliens with his Upper Shoal.

Or, you know, dry humping and stuff.

Just girlie things.

It took me a while to work up the courage to write my own fanfiction, but after a whole lot of encouragement from the community and a desire to read stories that hadn't yet been penned, I finally caved. And thus my alter ego, StepOnMeRyke432, was born. At first, my writing was pure unadulterated shit, a smear on EGC's good name. But with practice, I got better. I began truly nailing her voice. My first story to go viral was a thousand-page epic in which Ryke and Merriah were spies recruited during the Cold War who had to monitor Russian forces through underwater passageways. At first, I was apprehensive about posting it—was it too historical, lacking in fantastical thinking? Then the comments started trickling in. First by the hundreds. Then by the hundreds of thousands. They were overwhelmingly enthusiastic. Everyone wanted more, and I began to pump chapters out faster. I was elated. The internet *loved* me. Nobody knew that StepOnMeRyke432 spent her days writing copy for prescription eczema cream and her evenings going on lackluster dates with man-children.

But I'm between chapters right now. My readers know my posting schedule. There's no reason for anyone to be pinging me or for the message boards to be active.

Something must be wrong.

Swallowing down the bitter taste of an oncoming panic attack, I click into the conversation and am instantly greeted by links and 911!!!! messages written in all caps.

MERderMe71: JOONIE!!!! Have u been hit by a bus?
LilMinnow69: If she has, dibs on her special edition Ryke & Merriah collectible dust jackets
SoManyQueefs: Seriously WRU!!! Ur missing EVERYTHING!!!

I giggle at the frantic DMs from my virtual friends— Angel, Roya, and Kalli, all of whom I would I give a kidney to in a heartbeat despite the fact that we've never met in real life. Then I follow the URL down the rabbit hole, which is how I come face-to-face with my hero, the woman who changed my life forever, the legendary Ms. Evelyn G. Carter.

She's giving a live-streamed interview.

But why?

I check my calendar.

According to my calculations, it isn't the anniversary of the release date of any of the books, nor is it the birthday of any of the characters. EGC isn't scheduled to give an interview until next June, six months from the release date of the next ATOSAS book.

My heart races.

Could she be releasing a surprise special edition cover for her fans?

Perhaps an unscheduled novella?

The possibilities are endless.

Face flushing, I put aside all of my responsibilities and crank the volume up to ten before taking out my sketch pad and preparing to take diligent notes.

"As many of you have most likely guessed, we're gathered here for a very special Q and A," she begins. "There are twenty-six letters in the series title. And if you divide twenty-six by six, since there are six books, you get four point three. Today's date is April third."

I curse, chastising myself for not paying closer attention.

She's been posting Easter eggs all over her social channels. I should have gotten the letters thing, goddammit!

"As a treat for eagle-eyed readers, I've decided to answer the first ten questions submitted in the chat forum below."

All at once, a million questions flood my head like the basement of a beach house. I shut my eyes and try to focus on one but find the task impossible. Now that I have the opportunity to ask any question of the woman who has permanently altered my outlook on love, I can't possibly pick.

"Done," EGC announces. "The portal is now closed."

"Fuck my fucking life!" I shout out to no one in particular. "Get it together, Joonie! You're better than this!"

EGC begins addressing the queries methodically, one by one. She answers a few painfully obvious questions ("Did Oceania really die in book three?" Give me a fucking break. Locals.) She dodges some interesting queries about the space-time continuum and the rules of the universe. I find myself itching to abandon my work project, open a new blank document, and start drafting a fic that features Ryke and Merriah on an intergalactic mission, soaring through space.

I'm seconds away from acting on my fantasy when EGC clears her throat.

Stilling right away, I sit up straight.

"Thank you so much for tuning in, dear readers," she says, as if addressing each of us individually. "You know how much I appreciate your devotion and patronage. The final question is: *What celebrity was the blueprint for Ryke?*"

EGC laughs, but I roll my eyes. What a dumb waste of a question. Couldn't that reader just look up a few fan edits and call it a day? Jesus Christ.

"Funnily enough, the character of Ryke wasn't based on any of my celebrity crushes. While I did do a lot of mythological research to construct his backstory, the actual character dossier was fully inspired by my old college friend, Ryan. They even look alike. And he's single, ladies!" She pauses for a second, her eyes growing wide. "You know what, I don't think I've ever revealed that before! Shoot. He's *so* going to kill me."

She breaks out into giggles before bidding viewers goodbye and ending the live stream. In my fanfic forum, the Salty Girls are blowing up my notifications, freaking out about her comments and allusions to time travel.

But not me.

I can barely breathe, let alone think about the implications of an underwater wormhole.

Ryke.

Real.

Ryke is *real*.

Evelyn G. Carter just revealed that there is a living, breathing man out there whose chivalry and good looks inspired the character of Ryke.

A man whom I have never met.

Have not yet properly thanked.

A man who doesn't even know I exist.

My pulse grows erratic. Hands shaking, I reach for my phone.

First, I Google the names Evelyn G. Carter and Ryan together.

Nothing.

Irritated, I pull up her Instagram account and search her followers for the name Ryan. But that yields seventy-two results. Ugh. I don't know what I was expecting. The woman has over a million people following her.

Refusing to be deterred, I begin clicking on each profile, one by one. Until finally, I find one user with the words "Kenyon alum" in his bio.

Do you know who else went to Kenyon?

One Evelyn G. Carter.

She called him an old college buddy. This *has* to be him.

Hello, Ryan Mare.

The bad news? His profile is private.

The good news? I've never let a little security stop me before.

A more intensive search leads me straight to his LinkedIn.

While his profile is relatively barren (no profile picture, zero hobbies listed, definitely no endorsed skills), I deduce that Ryan Mare is about thirty-two, based on his graduation date.

The best part? According to his employment status, he's worked at an environmental start-up for the last three years.

In New York City.

Only one hundred and fifty miles away.

Would it be crazy to…?

No.

I can't possibly try to meet him.

That would be crazy.

Right?

Look, I'm not an idiot. I fully understand that Ryan Mare and Ryke are *not* one and the same. I mean, the latter is more fish than man, for fuck's sake! And nothing drives me further up the wall than when people, especially straight, cisgender white men, act like romance readers can't differentiate between reality and fiction. It's beyond condescending and totally misogynistic—we all know they only say this because women are the main consumers of the genre. Like, would those same men accuse thriller-lovers of being more likely to murder their friends and family? Probably not. Not to mention the double standard: Tons of fantasy and sci-fi franchises with majority-male audiences feature incredibly graphic sex, but no one is accusing fans of George R. R. Martin of being brainwashed, you know? There's nothing more frustrating than having to constantly defend the merits of romance to naysayers. Women, especially marginalized women, deserve more credit. Period. We're not frivolous and *delusional.*

I brush off a buried memory from the past, of Nico muttering that word with a finger to my temple.

But there's this nagging voice in the back of my head.

One that whispers, *What if you and Ryan Mare are star-crossed lovers?*

What if everything is happening for a reason?

What if my past with Sam, with Nico, with Kyle, the doubt that led me to pick up *ATOSAS*, was all an elaborate way for destiny to lead me to meet my soul mate, Ryan?

What if we are truly fated?

In that case, *not* pursuing this, strictly for the plot, would be like depriving us both of a chance at happiness.

And the truth is, I'm tired of meeting up with the boys on dating apps. Of dating like I'm training for an Iron Man. I'm ready to meet The One, and I need a sign to keep me from giving up.

What if this is my sign?

I shut my laptop and get to work. For the first time since I left Ends Whale Books with my copy of *A Tale of Salt Water & Secrets* in tow, I make a decision that I'm positive is going to change the course of my life.

It's time to go get my man.

"We are here."

My eyes fly open, and I'm greeted by a thick blanket of darkness, swirling layers of shadow and brine. I gasp for air, then come to the realization that I can breathe the atmosphere freely, just as I did on land.

I can barely make out the shape of Ryke's body beside me.

We are in some sort of stone quarters, a bare-bones room collecting dust and decay. And the darkness—that murky, dull depth—is not, as I first believed, an absence of light. No, the blackness is its own entity.

And when you listen carefully, you can hear it hum. A heavy baritone.

The ocean floor. The end of all life, all creation. A great

wall where neither the sun nor the moon can break down its defenses. The fortress of the sea.

A false door.

"I have brought you to a cavern wedged between your world and mine," Ryke explains, his amber eyes the only source of luminance in the grotto. "You are essentially in what your kind would call the crust of the Earth but what mine would rightfully identify as a false bottom. This tunnel blocks out all outside light and sound. It exists somewhere between time and space. You are safe here, little minnow."

He points out into the abyss, into the darkness.

"But if we travel past these hallowed walls, into Atlantia, you will be introduced to a reality your kind was never meant to know exists. The sirens are looking for us. They will hunt you down with a harrowing precision. But in Atlantia, we will have aid. Protection. You will no longer be alone."

My ribs tighten around my heart at his final words.

You will no longer be alone.

How long have I waited for those words to be strung into a sentence directed at me?

I nod once, resolute. "Show me."

Ryke's hand brushes against mine in the shadows, tentative. Our fingers touch, his presence a comfort.

Then the stone beneath my feet begins to rumble, the earth quaking, an angry giant awakening from his slumber. A crack begins to form in the cave, the rift between worlds. I stand on one side of the fissure while Ryke remains on the other.

A portal.

Light pours from the crevice, temporarily blinding me. A gust of phantom wind knocks me off my feet. I gulp, preparing to hold my breath as water rushes in, but find that I am suspended in some sort of air bubble, delicate as the beads of soap I might find at the bottom of a bathing bucket. And when the fog clears and the light dims, my ground is someone's sky, and I am floating above the land like an angel.

Ryke has transformed before me, his obsidian tail flexing beneath him, strong with muscle and movement. His dark hair billows in the water like tendrils. There are ancient symbols carved into his skin, starting at the nape of his neck and continuing over the ripples of his back.

"Do not be afraid, Merriah." His use of my name shocks me awake. "Look down."

And so I do.

The darkness is banished, replaced entirely by a world colored in shades of teal, azure, and aquamarine. Sky that is not sky at all but bright glittering water, shining like gemstones, somehow both clear as day and pigmented in blues and greens. Glowfish strung like twinkling lights and clouds of jellyfish. My breath catches as I take in the great underwater mountain range made of mud and rock and salt, a volcanic seamount larger than any I have ever seen above the surface. And nestled into the cliffside, castles of densely packed sand, decorated with pearls and gemstones. Grander than the royal palace on land, larger than any residence I have ever laid eyes upon. There are great columns outside each entrance, statues of unknown mer in the courtyards. Gardens made of seaweed and kelp, finely cut hedges and extraordinary mazes.

Beside the village is a marketplace. Stalls of fresh halibut and cod, deep-sea clams and freshwater oysters. A stand boasting hand-dyed silk and scales carved in compelling patterns, sewn together into corsets and armor. Combs made of shell and utensils that appear to be made of sanded-down teeth from great extinct beasts. The smells waft upward toward my nostrils, and I inhale, my senses hungry. The scent is sweet as algae and briny, sulfur mingling with sea air. I want to bottle it and smear it upon the nape of my neck. There is something more precious than just life down here. Joy. Unadulterated delight that permeates the water molecules, creating a palatial utopia.

And in this underwater paradise, people can fly.

Well, not people.

Mer.

And not fly.

Swim.

They are scattered everywhere. Traveling in hordes, laughing like ringing bells, carrying scrolls and parcels, perhaps on their way to school. Alone, talking rapidly into shells glued to their ears, as if the objects could possibly transmit sound—an advanced technology that humans have not yet invented. There are mer shopping for underwater antiques scavenged from sunken ships. Mer dining in underwater caverns, drinking wine from chalices made of cockles. Mer playing checkers with ancient coins and riding seahorse-drawn carriages. Living their lives, oblivious to the troubles above the water.

Famine and fire and flooding.

The woes of humanity.

"It is glorious," I breathe, my voice snagging.

Ryke watches me as I take in Atlantia from above, a dove on the wind.

"It is home," he answers.

My eyes wander over to an outdoor amphitheater made of carved stone and coral. There are mer of all ages hovering above the stands, their eyes fixed on the performance happening in the center of the circular stage. The players seem to be acting in a tragedy. I watch in awe as false blood is spilled from the chest of a thespian, dissipating into the water around him instead of leaking into a puddle by his tail. The opposing player holds a sword made of sharks' teeth. He glowers, delivering his lines with gusto.

"Atlantia belongs to the siren race now!" he proclaims.

I suck in my cheeks. The play must be a reenactment

of the first war, the battle between brothers, when sirens turned on their rulers and colonized the mer.

As the bloodied actor seizes his chest and pretends to die, he cries out his final words to the crowd of steel-eyed spectators.

"Never," he swears. "By these watery graves, Prince Ryke will rise again."

I turn to my traveling companion in shock.

He shrugs. "Guilty."

CHAPTER FIVE

Well, well, well. Look who finally decided to show up."

I walk—honestly, more like saunter— into Kabobs 'n' Bits on Sunday night to find Nico and Oliver huddled in a corner, talking about sports or politics or whatever else guys talk about when they're alone. The former barely looks up to heckle me for being late. While it's true that I'm tardy by American standards (fifteen minutes, give or take), I'm actually early according to Persian Standard Time (PST). Nico just needs to hate on me regularly. You know, the same way other people need to drink water and shit regularly to survive.

"Sorry to keep you waiting. I know how hard it is for you to socialize without me."

I pull up a chair and take off my jacket, haphazardly slinging it across the back. Nico takes in my colorful seventies-inspired printed pants and matching cropped cardigan and scowls. As if the explosion of patterns and sliver of exposed midriff personally offends him.

"What was it your sixth-grade teacher told your parents again?" I ask. "That you lacked interpersonal skills? Or was it an active imagination? I believe the terms he used were *underdeveloped* and *pathetic*."

"Loving the bags, Joonie," Nico replies.

I narrow my eyes, waiting for the catch. Yes, my micro purse and ironic boat tote embroidered with I LIKE TO READ, BUT I'M ALSO HOT are objectively adorable. But the day Nico compliments me is the day hell freezes over. Or the Swifties forgive Jake Gyllenhaal.

"The ones under your eyes?" he clarifies. "I had no idea the sleep-deprived conspiracy theorist look was in this season. What did you do, spend all night debunking the moon landing? Oh, wait, I know! Zooming in on photos of Harry Styles, searching for signs of Dunamis?"

I smile sweetly. "No, actually. I had that dream again. Well, nightmare. Terrible nightmare. You know, the one where you're singing ABBA, covered in whipped cream, butt-ass—"

"Behave, children!" Tey calls out from behind the counter.

"Oh, God," Oliver murmurs under his breath.

"How funny! That's exactly what Nico kept saying last night in my nightmare. Over and over and over…" I sing-song with glee, watching his face flush crimson.

Just as Nico opens his mouth to sling another insult my way, Tey arrives at our table with red plastic trays over-flowing with Persian goodies: *polo*, *khoresht*, and *joojeh*, and *kubideh* Kabob. Oliver immediately shovels a piece of chicken into his mouth while it's still hot and practically moans with appreciation. He looks up at my brother, his eyes wide with admiration and affection.

My stomach drops an iota.

I hate being jealous of my brother, but I'm brave enough to say it.

Nobody has ever looked at me like that.

"*Morg. Khoob*," Oliver says proudly.

He's been learning Farsi using Duolingo, to minor success. As in, he knows about five words. And three of them are food items. Roughly translated, his statement means, *Chicken. Good.*

"Well done, Ollie!" I tease. "Next, why don't you try saying *tokhmeh sag*—"

"Do not listen to my delinquent sister," Tey says, shaking his head and taking the seat next to me. "If she isn't the center of attention twenty-four seven, she deflates like a flat tire."

I laugh and stick out my tongue but don't bother to argue. Because, like…yeah. He's not wrong. But that doesn't stop me from grabbing a piece of *tadik* off of his plate while he protests. In our family, vengeance is a plastic dish best served piping hot.

Oliver smiles, taking our dynamic in stride. He's a good fucking egg. He and Tey met a couple of years ago, when Ollie was overseeing a discrimination dispute a town over and dropped by the restaurant for lunch. Oliver tried to order Kabob without rice, claiming to be on a cleanse or some shit. Tey told him he was crazy and gave him a side of rice anyway, on the house. And Ollie practically licked the plate. It was love at first bite. When he was done eating, he realized that Tey had written his phone number on the bottom of the basket. They've been together ever since. Long distance, though—Oliver is from right outside of Chicago. A very nice Midwestern boy. If I'm being honest, a bit too buttoned-up for my taste. But perfect for my control freak brother.

"Have you heard from Maman and Baba lately?" I ask mid-bite, my mouth full.

"Ever heard of chewing?" Nico mutters.

"Ever heard of fucking yourself?" I retort.

He looks at me with twisted lips and slowly shakes his head.

"Oh, wait. Of course you have. That's what you do every night. Alone. With a bottle of lotion for extra-dry skin. While watching anime—"

"Big words from the girl who apparently just broke off her hundredth relationship in six months," he smirks.

I snap my head around to glare at Tey. "You told him?"

Tey shakes his head slowly, like he can't believe the hand he's been dealt. "No, Joon. I didn't tell him. The whole town saw Job Pesce crying into his ice cream on Main Street this week. Apparently, you really did a number on him."

I frown. Job couldn't be a little more discreet?

"And to answer your earlier question, Mom FaceTimed me this morning. They just reached Cape Cod last night."

I nod, but my dinner churns in my stomach. Why didn't they call me? Are they disappointed that yet another one of my relationships was a failure?

In a sense, I've long since accepted that Tey is the favorite, the kid my parents trust. I'm the baby of the family, the child they always worry about. But sometimes I worry that they see me as more of a burden than an adult. They've never gotten over the childhood bullying, the unflappable optimism as a coping method, so they sort of coddle me. If Tey knew I felt this way, he'd tell me I'm being ridiculous. So I keep that intrusive thought locked deep inside my brain in that box I only tap occasionally, when I need writing inspo. *It's nestled between body-snatching narwhals and* High School Musical, *but everyone's gay.*

"So, Nico. What's new with you? Still making money off of hurricane survivors and tragic house fires?" I ask, my voice casual. "Hey, when we enter hurricane season, do you cream your pants? Or just hear *cha-ching*?"

Nico works in crisis insurance, which Tey has repeatedly told me mostly involves crunching numbsers in Excel and making conversation with geriatric men. But I still like to make fun of him for it, mostly because it's *so* him. I've never met anyone as cynical as he is, as anxious, as disaster-obsessed. Forget glass half-empty. In Nico's head, the glass has shattered on the carpet and he has stepped on it with bare feet. He's been that way ever since we were kids. I call him a pessimist; he calls himself a realist. One time, when we were in middle school and high school, I told him that our parents were considering letting us get a puppy. He informed me that most dogs have lifespans of ten to thirteen years and that I should avoid getting too attached.

Naturally, I started to cry.

"And you, Joonie? Still LARPing inside a romance novel day in and day out?"

I clench my fists. He has successfully struck a nerve.

"First of all, it's a *fantasy* romance series. Romantasy. Big difference. Second of all, romance is a billion-dollar industry. Publishing relies on romance readers to make ends meet. But sure, make fun of romance because the majority of its readers are women. Everyone loves a misogynist, right? Hey, I have an idea! You should join my book club!"

"Sure thing. Do you guys actually read books or just drink wine and scroll on Reddit?"

"All three! Plus, I bet the genre could teach you a few useful skills. Like open and honest communication. Boundary setting. Empathy. How to please a woman."

His eyes narrow. "Believe me, I don't need an instruction manual for that."

Once again, my stomach stirs. But this time, I don't think it's the food.

Why am I suddenly picturing Nico in a very compromising position?

Tearing my gaze away from his, I desperately try to change the subject. Anything to take attention off of Nico, his nighttime activities, the color spreading up my neck.

"Tey, I need to borrow your truck," I blurt out. "I mean, please. Please may I borrow your truck?"

"Wow. Nice attempt at manners!" Tey cocks his head. "And why is that?"

"I have to drive to New York next week, and my car isn't going to make it. You were right. I should've asked that Craigslist guy who sold it to me more questions. You remember the dude with the top hat? Anyway, it'll never survive the trip. So, pretty please, can we car swap? Just for a few days?"

"Sure." Tey shovels another spoonful of *khoresht* into his mouth. "Why do you have to go to New York?"

I freeze.

Fuck.

I totally forgot to come up with a good excuse for my New York trip. There's no way I can tell my brother, *Oh, so you know that fictional character I'm obsessed with? Well, as it turns out, he's based on a real person. His name is Ryan, and he lives in New York, and I'm curious about whether or not he's my soul mate. So I'm going to drive to the city, track him down, and try to seduce him. I promise I'll pay for gas!*

Yeah, I don't think that'll work.

Instead of committing, I'll get committed.

"I got into a creative writing workshop," I lie. "Yup, a prestigious one. Run by NYU. It's a three-day intensive course. Full of lectures and workshops. I'm finally going to take a stab at writing that novel. You know, turning my fanfic side hustle into something legit."

"Really? That's awesome, Joon!"

Tey beams, and I swallow the acidic bile of guilt in my throat. My brother is always encouraging me to take my writing to the next level, to put myself out there more. It's not that I don't want to. But between my copywriting gig, my Salty Girls community, keeping up with ATOSAS, and dating a few times a week, my schedule is pretty packed. But I hate lying to him about this.

Nico, on the other hand, doesn't look convinced. "What's the course called?" he asks, an eyebrow raised.

"Um…Write Guy, Wrong Time," I fib like it's my calling. "It's specifically for aspiring romance authors."

"Is that so?" he says. "Well, if you're headed in that direction, I might as well join you. I was planning on going into the city that week anyway. Now I can avoid fighting tooth and nail for a seat on the train."

I try and fail to hide my panic. "What? No!"

"That's a great idea." Tey nods. "Nico can keep you company. And, um, make sure you stay alert on the road."

Jesus Christ. "I checked my phone at the wheel one time for a quarter of a second!"

"And almost swerved off the highway."

"Emphasis on *almost*. That was the day advanced reader copies of *A Tale Of Sand and Cannon Fire* were released. I got the shipping notification from the publisher!"

Nico stares blankly at me. "The fact that you think that's a reasonable excuse is seriously concerning."

"What do you even have to do in New York? Planning to cut the cord at the Empire State Building?"

"Americans will do that themselves, given the direction the energy crisis is headed…"

"Or, wait, I know. You're going to kidnap Eloise."

"If you must know, I have to see about a woman," he says, silencing me.

Woman? What woman? Nico doesn't date. He hasn't dated since…

Since the incident. In fact, he famously believes starting a relationship is irresponsible when the future of the planet is at risk.

83

"And for the last time, I'm not the villain in some story, so stop making me into one, okay? Get your head out of your ass and join the rest of us in the real world, Joonie."

The real world. Whatever that means.

You're living in a fantasy.

His words push on a broken bone that never healed quite right. One that brings back the sound of a squeaking shoes on a dirty gym floor. Thumping bass. Quiet laughter and pointed looks. Nico's glazed eyes—

I blink rapidly, pulling myself out of the memory.

This is why I avoid Nico at all costs.

"Why is he here again?" I whine to my brother. "Doesn't he have adoptions of orphans to stop or something?"

"He's just helping me out with some business stuff." Teymoor scratches his ear, exchanging a look with Oliver, then Nico, before dropping his gaze to the ground. "I needed to get his opinion on some projections. You know. Crunching numbers."

"Right."

The second someone says the word *numbers*, I basically black out.

Oliver gives Tey a stern look, which he very obviously avoids meeting.

Weird.

I clock the silent conversation and make a mental note to return to it later.

"So, what do you say, kid?" says Nico. "Meet here tomorrow at eight?"

Kid.

I absolutely detest being called a kid.

The word reeks of condescension.

I'm a grown woman, goddamn it.

"Maybe I'll get here at seven fifty-five and hit you with his car," I mumble.

"Oh, Joonie," he says, getting irritatingly close to me. Determined to have the last word. "It's adorable that you think you'll be the one behind the wheel."

I groan.

This is going to be a long fucking trip.

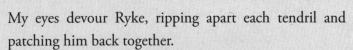

My eyes devour Ryke, ripping apart each tendril and patching him back together.

His stature: shoulders back, neck long, head raised.

The dip of his lips, his straining Adam's apple.

Strong, defined muscles.

Dark, lost eyes.

Dominance and confidence radiating from every inch of his body, from the top of his head to the tip of his tail.

Royal.

"So, you are no simple mer," I state, my eyes narrowing.

He sucks in his cheeks. "It would appear not."

"You are a prince."

"So they tell me."

Beneath our bubble in the sky—the sea—applause

breaks out among the spectators in the amphitheater, and the performers bow. Instead of rose petals, the mer throw pieces of algae and coral in appreciation. Thick braided ropes pull the set pieces from the stage, and the audience disperses, swimming in all different directions.

Ryke moves his body slightly in front of me, a show of protection.

Even though he is meant to be in hiding himself.

I take a deep breath.

"Start at the beginning, my prince."

He turns back to me and smiles, the corners of his mouth twisting as my stomach knots.

"As you wish, princess."

"I prefer *minnow*."

That smile stretches into a grin wider than the four corners of the Earth.

"Our tale begins as most do: with the creation of man. The Great Furnace carved its clay and let the fire burn, giving form to man, maecena, and mer, all in the same breath. Then he carved into thirds. The maecenas would rule a star in the sky, hidden from sight by a thick layer of cloud. Men would prosper in the in-between, dwelling on land where all things grow, good and bad. They would harvest crops and dig their heels into the earth. And the mer would rule a realm beneath the ocean floor, concealed by the sandy false bottom. A valley of seaweed, a haven of salt water. Our bodies evolved to allow us to survive in our separate terrains."

"*Evolved*?" I dare to ask. "So your tail is not, then, a product of this magic you speak of?"

"No, my minnow. Man, mer, and maecena share certain attributes. We all begin life through our lungs, chant our prayers through hopeful lips, and hold our loved ones in our arms. But man was born with formidable legs to walk upon the Earth's surface. The mer were given great tails with which to navigate the tides. And the maecenas? Well, they sprouted white eagle wings so they could soar into the atmosphere and look upon the planets. Now, the Furnace made us so, forged these worlds in an attempt to keep us separate but powerful. And for good reason. But of course, over the millennia, curiosity got the best of a few wayward travelers. Mer met man. Man met maecena. And a few mated, giving the children of certain—but not all—bloodlines the ability to shift, as I can."

All the blood rushes from my brain to the organ in my chest.

My dream.

The sacred wish I dared not whisper aloud.

To be mer. And have the chance to swim away from my reality to a utopia below.

Could it be?

A lump forms in my throat.

"So there are certain humans who have the ability to grow a tail or sprout wings?"

Ryke grimaces. "Correct. But most elders who bear that secret have joined the underworld without passing on their knowledge. At this time, the majority of humans who do have mer or maecena in their ancestry have such small amounts that they lack the ability to shift. The ones who do have the ability might not be aware of it, so that power sits dormant inside of them. There is no way of knowing, of sensing who has the gift."

What a waste. Rage fuels me as I think of those missed opportunities.

"How tragic," I whimper.

Ryke reaches out for me, then pauses. My air bubble is blocking him out, I realize.

"Perhaps in some ways," he says. "But not in others. For we soon realized that there was a reason the Great Furnace left our kind on different planes. A motive for our dissociation. When men, mer, and maecenas breed, there is a cost. A deadly one."

"Deadly," I repeat. "Deadly how?"

Ryke blows out a tight breath. It's clear to me now that he is nervous.

How odd to see this great man so visibly uncomfortable. Brought down by something as mundane as apprehension.

"During the act," he says, gesturing vaguely, "a subset

of mer discovered that if one party takes life by way of creating it, the entirety of the slain creature's energy transfers to the surviving partner. For when two come together to form one body, for fleeting seconds, they combine souls, energies. If one light is snuffed out, the other grows brighter, stronger, more powerful. It is a dark magic."

My mind races, attempting to understand the subtext beneath his cryptic message.

"Are you telling me that if a mer murders a man during a coupling, they have the ability to become some sort of super mer?"

He gulps. "In not so many words, yes."

"Why would anyone ever agree to that?" The words burst out of me.

"So many questions," Ryke whispers. "Different reasons. To bless their line by siring a child with the ability to shift. For love. And of course, it can happen by force. When ancient humans began to catch on, they avoided the waters, refusing to leave their ships. But mer are able to manipulate sound waves in the same way that maecenas can fiddle with air currents. There are certain frequencies we can hit that humans are not used to hearing. Sounds we can make. Songs so seductive to humans that they know not what they are doing until they are already dead."

My heart rattles against my ribs. I think back to the stories I grew up hearing. Tales of missing townspeople.

Warnings to avoid the creek cottage. The old wives' tale of the sailor who yearned for his missing maiden so much that he drowned in that love. Is all the folklore true, then?

Have all my nightmares come to walk in the light?

"And these mer are the sirens? Those who use their song to drink the life force from their human prey like fine wine?"

"Yes." Ryke's eyes grow dark, his voice dangerous. "After my family outlawed such practices, preferring to mate with humans in peace, a small group of transgressors banded together and developed a plot to continue the ritual in secret. Eventually, their numbers grew, and their magic became so strong that they staged a coup. They slaughtered my mother and my father. I can still see my sister's child limp in my arms. I barely escaped and went into hiding in the only place I knew where only those with the ability to shift could find me."

"On land," I breathe. "At the creek cottage."

"Hidden in plain sight," he confirms. "Now the sirens rule beautiful Atlantia, this utopia you see around you, with fear and malice. They recruit innocents and force them to sing. So bigoted that they routinely hunt down mer with the ability to shift, with human blood in their lineage, and deliver the killing blow. My land has become segregated, stagnant. We are under a dictatorship. But I have long been plotting my vengeance with my brethren hidden above."

I look at this man—no, this mer—who carries the weight of the underwater world on his shoulders. And I wonder why he would waste his breath on a commoner like me.

"And are you ready?" I ask instead. "To fight?"

His lips curl. "No, little minnow. Not yet."

"Then why are we down here?" It takes everything in me to stifle a scream. "Aren't you risking your life and the lives of those in the resistance? The future of Atlantia?"

Ryke sighs long and hard and turns to face me fully.

"This is where you come in, Merriah." My name. He has called me by my given name. "When I escaped to shore, I was able to bring along something very valuable. An artifact that has been in my family since the first cinders of creation. An ancient conch rumored to have once belonged to the first mer king, Hippios. My greatest ancestor. When someone blows the conch, an alarm of sorts sounds—the primeval war cry of our people, calling all mer to battle. By blowing into that which you called a horn, my minnow, you accomplished three things. You instructed my troops to ready themselves for a fight. You alerted the sirens to my location. And you instilled hope in the hearts of Atlantians. You are both a hero and a curse. Though of course I cannot blame you. The conch creates a whistle of the highest frequency, one barely discernible to the human ear—which is why, I presume, you were unable to hear it."

A shiver runs down my spine.

I can barely murmur the truth.

"But I did hear it," I confess. "And what's more, the instrument called out to me. It was as if we were shackled to each other by the bonds of fate."

My entire body shakes as I ask my next question. "Why did the conch sing to me, Ryke?"

I watch as he clenches his fists, his knuckles turning white.

Fighting, it occurs to me.

Fighting the urge to burst through my air bubble.

"That, little minnow, is your very best question yet."

CHAPTER SIX

Good morning, sunshine!"

I'm leaning against Tey's truck, holding two cups of coffee, feeling chipper. The morning sun is beating down on the top of my head, causing my curls to expand. All around me, bells ring and keys jingle as businesses begin to open for the day. I love Mystic mornings. You can hear the water stir, the seagulls chatter away to each other. I've always been at my most calm right when I first wake up, before the rest of the world comes rushing in to invade my head.

Nico, on the other hand, looks like roadkill.

His clothes are wrinkled, and a golden shadow lines his chin, like he was in such a rush to get ready that he forgot to shave. His shirt is inside out with the tag showing, the fly of his jeans unzipped. He's got an old Jansport back-pack in one hand and a pair of aviator sunglasses in the other. When I speak, he shuts his eyes tightly, as if my voice grates on his eardrums.

"Still not a morning person, huh?" I ask, handing him a cup of coffee.

"Morning people are government plants," he growls. He studies the coffee intently. "Did you poison this?"

I roll my eyes. "That depends on your sugar tolerance. I dumped, like, a year's supply of Domino packets into these."

He looks up at me, taking a long sip just as our gazes lock.

"I like sweet things," he says.

I swallow. "Good to know. Out of character, but duly noted."

"When are you going to get it through your head, kid?" He grabs the keys out of my hand and unlocks the doors. "I'm not a character. That means I'm going to go off script."

I purse my lips. "If you think I'm going to let someone who barely managed to get dressed this morning drive a vehicle"—I throw my duffel in the back of the truck—"you are seriously deranged."

The vein in Nico's forehead pops. "Joonie. Give me a break. We both know you can barely drive."

My hand flies to my mouth in mock horror. "How

dare you! Must I remind you that of the two of us, only one actually owns a car?"

"Fine." He opens the passenger door for me. "Never mind that forty-six thousand people die in car crashes every year. Have you ever even handled something this big?"

"That's what she said." It slips out, almost like a reflex. I feel my face instantly turn tomato red.

He smiles smugly. "That's what I thought."

"Fine. Shotgun," I grumble. "And I'm controlling the music."

Minutes later, we hit the road. Mystic Village shrinks from a bustling ecosystem to a tiny dot in our rearview mirror. A familiar wave of anxiety washes over me, the same panic I usually experience whenever I leave home and embark on a new adventure in the great unknown. But I shake off the uncertainty, choosing instead to focus on the changing leaves outside my window, the autumnal foliage our quaint New England enclave is known for. I close my eyes and belt out the lyrics to the road trip playlist I put together, full of bangers by my favorite pop girlies: Sabrina Carpenter, Chappell Roan, Charli xcx.

Female vocalists who stay in their feelings for a living.

I hit a particularly loud high note incredibly off-key, and Nico bursts out laughing.

"How do you sound exactly the same as you did at thirteen?" he asks, bewildered. "You've somehow managed not to age at all."

I shrug. It's not my fault that I have a youthful exuberance. In fact, I thrive on my silliness, my ability to find joy in things that are mundane. After Kyle, I honestly consider that a win. There was a time where I'd go days, if not weeks, without laughing. Now I make it my personal mission to put myself first, to take myself out of situations that don't serve me and put a smile on my own face.

Pulling out my phone, I fire off a quick message to my Salty Girls to update them on my mission. When I told my group chat what I was planning, they were understandably skeptical but supportive. That's the nice thing about having best friends who could basically be bots: they're in it for the voyeurism, for the adventure. They'll never, say, platonically love-bomb you for months, then ghost you over a misunderstanding. If you crash and burn, it's no skin off their backs.

Right?

StepOnMeRyke432: The mer has swum out of her cave. I repeat: THE MER HAS SWUM OUT OF HER CAVE.

SoManyQueefs: Shit...new york doesn't know what's coming.

MERderMe71: Pls be careful!!! And update us every step of the way. We DEMAND pics

MERderMe71: Of his face. Not his...you know

SoManyQueefs: Dick?

MERderMe71: ok fml

LilMinnow69: You know I live in nyc right Joon??? If u have time, hmu :)

I close the chat so fast I get whiplash.

Don't get me wrong: I love Angel with a fiery passion. But meeting them in person would make our relationship a little too...real. Through a screen, it's impossible to disappoint someone. Or allow them to disappoint me. Relationships feel more intentional. I can take time to think about what I say and how I say it. There's a certain level of imagination at play. I can world build the person I want to be. And the people I want them to be.

What if they meet the real me and I fall short?

What if I meet them and they let me down?

Everyone lets me down eventually.

Sam. Kyle.

The heathen currently behind the wheel.

Then I'd lose my only real friends for good. I can never let that happen.

Nico grabs my phone out of my hand and changes the music to some sad boy emo rock. I grunt my disapproval, and he gives me a triumphant grin.

"So, what's the real reason you're heading to New York?"

I snap out of my spiral, his question catching me off guard.

"I have no idea what you're talking about." I force myself to fake a smile.

Nico gives me the side-eye. "Yes, you do. I Googled the name of your creative writing program. Turns out it doesn't exist."

"It's very underground. A Sprouse twin started it. The pretentious one."

"Sure. And I secretly moonlight as a pop star."

I feign shock. "You too?!"

"Come on, Joon. Fess up."

"You first," I try to deflect. "Who's the girl? I thought you didn't date. Anymore."

There's an awkward silence that lasts about twenty seconds.

"Her name's Hannah. And we don't date. We fuck."

In the window, I see my ears turn crimson.

"She's a friend of a friend. We meet up a couple of times a year in the city. It's a mutually beneficial arrangement."

I snort. "Does she know that?"

Nico frowns. "What's that supposed to mean?"

"Well, I'll bet you a hundred dollars that she has feelings for you and is hoping you'll change your mind. It's a classic trope: friends with benefits to lovers. One party—in this case, Hannah—falls first. And when you realize you've lost her, probably because she's met someone who wants to date her, you'll grovel. And then you'll live happily ever after."

Nico throws his head back and laughs. "A classic trope? You really do live in some kind of magical pretend land, don't you?"

I grit my teeth, blinking back the anger pulsing in my forehead. Nico always does this: instantly makes me feel infantile, like a delusional toddler. He's done it since we were kids acting out skits in the backyard. He did it that night when he broke my heart. Yes, I know that everyone confused my optimism with naivety when I was little. As a kid, playing pretend was a way for me to cope with the real world, with the way people saw me. Treated me. As an adult, I've realized that reading can provide the same escapism. Most days, my imagination makes me feel more creative and confident. There's just this one single person who has the ability to snap his fingers and darken the sky of my mental utopia.

I smack his shoulder. "You know, I'm getting really sick of hearing you shit-talk romance. It's seriously overplayed and small-minded. Let me guess: You only read dystopian novels about the end of the world. Flesh-eating diseases, the Earth running out of natural resources, etcetera?"

"Hey, it's not my fault that society is on the brink of collapse. Excuse me for wanting a good seat on the first shuttle to Mars." The muscles in his jaw tense. "I read apocalypse porn. You read porn-porn. We're two sides of the same coin."

I shake my head. "You still don't get it, Nico.

Romance…it's about more than happily ever afters. More than smut or spice. It's about people. Relationships, connections. Communication. You know you can be asexual or aromantic and still enjoy romance, right? Reading the genre isn't a means to an end. In my opinion, it's about righting a wrong, a power imbalance. You see, it all comes down to the patriarchy."

Nico rubs his budding beard. "I don't follow."

"Well, from a young age, girls learn about our bodies through a patriarchal framework. Boys learn about what to expect during puberty. Kids and teens only learn about penetrative sex, which robs women of agency. Women get pregnant; men don't impregnate women. Women lose their virginity; they don't exercise their sexual autonomy. And the act culminates whenever the man finishes, but women are never taught about how to chase their own pleasure. Combine that with the fact that there's little conversation about hormonal changes, sexual urges, and consent, and women are left scared, confused, and ashamed of their feelings. They're afraid to talk about sex with each other for fear of being labeled or oversexualized. So they have to search for answers somewhere, the ones they don't get in health class.

"And one of the ways that women learn about what they want—from a partner, out of a sexual encounter, in a relationship—is through reading romance. It's women giving other women a literal helping hand. As they gain more knowledge about their bodies and themselves, they grow more confident and begin taking back that power from the patriarchy. That's why men like you enjoy making fun of women for reading those books, why you trivialize their impact and liken them to trash. It's why men guilt women into hiding their desire to read the genre, calling it a 'guilty' pleasure. Because you know that once women start swapping book recommendations and discussing their standards for love and sex, the jig will be up. And you'll lose your power for good."

Nico stares at me, mouth agape like a fish.

I reach over and close it.

"I had no idea your connection to those books was so…deep," he finally says. "Honestly, I was just busting your chops. Shit."

I blink a couple of times, caught off guard by his earnestness.

"Listen, I'm sorry, Joonie. Honestly. I don't want to be one of those guys who mocks women for liking what they like. I'll stop."

I squint, waiting for the catch.

Asshole Nico, the one who calls me names? I know what to do with that Nico.

This genuine, pensive Nico? Not so much.

"Thanks," I say, apprehensive. "Maybe I can lend you a book sometime."

"I'd like that."

We sit in the truck, stewing in silence. My words hang heavily in the air. I snatch back my phone, my hand accidentally brushing against his leg. He jolts as if I've shocked him with a live wire. I lean against the truck door, putting as much space between us in the nineteen-foot-long monstrosity as possible, then crank up the air-conditioning. It's suddenly insufferably hot in here.

I check my phone and look at Waze. Our driving time has shot up. How is that even possible? There must be roadwork or something forcing cars into a single lane. Great. Only six and a half more hours to go. I wish I could just put on an audiobook, soothe myself with the sound of Ryke's voice. But letting Nico hear that feels…wrong, for some reason. It's like the two just weren't meant to meet.

"You never answered my question," Nico says, disrupting the quiet. "Why are you actually going to New York?"

I don't know why I do it.

Maybe I'm feeling emboldened after the warm reception of my tirade.

Perhaps I experience a moment of temporary insanity.

For whatever reason, I say, "I just found out that Ryke, my book boyfriend and the love of my life, is kind of, sort of real. So I'm going to the city to find him. To meet him. And then maybe our love story can finally begin."

Nico doesn't give me any time at all to gauge his reaction to my confession. Instead, he steps on the brakes, jerking us forward.

And I have a single second to process what's happening before the car behind us collides with the back of the truck and we go flying.

"Fight with us."

Ryke's eyes search mine, bright and urgent.

"What?" I ask, sure I have misheard him.

That I have misunderstood.

"Join the resistance, our fight against the sirens," he says once more. "And together we will liberate Atlantia."

My mouth falls open, slack. A tiny guppy worms its way into my air bubble and down my throat. I begin to cough, embarrassed.

"You cannot be serious."

"As a shark attack," he says.

I regain my ability to breathe and huff out a laugh of disbelief. "But Ryke, I have nothing to offer."

"Nothing to offer?" he repeats, incredulous.

I nod. "I am just a woman, Ryke. Weak. Feeble. I have spent the last few years of my life catering to a man who never met my eyes, who never spoke my name with an ounce of kindness or gratitude. I spent my days caring for a house that would never be my home, polishing spoons that could never properly feed me, cleaning corners that boxed me in. And I never fought back—did not dare question my position—until you walked through my door and demanded that I go with you. Challenged me to change. So you see, Ryke, I am a liability. For without you, my instinct was to submit. And when I could not take it anymore, I left without argument. I never put up a fight. I simply gave up."

Before I understand what is happening, the air bubble around me begins to move. I float, turning head over heels, spiraling like a spinning wheel through the ocean's sky, and Ryke swims beside me until we reach some sort of underwater cove. Another hidden cave, but this one is filled with light, sound, and vibrant life.

Scrolls upon scrolls documenting years of Atlantia's history.

Knickknacks and artifacts from his travels all over the world, on land and beneath the sea.

Watercolors of a young mer with dark hair and golden eyes.

This is Ryke's private hideaway, I realize. His haven.

Then he swims toward me, swiftly popping my air bubble.

I puff out a sharp breath, afraid to move.

He leans forward and tips my chin up to meet his face.

"Let me be frank, little minnow," he says. "When you left that wretched man, you didn't give up anything. You *gained* everything. Walking out of that house, quitting your unsanctimonious union—that was no act of weakness. No, there is only strength in leaving a path that leads to harm. In walking away. You are strong, Merriah."

My heart waltzes about in my rib cage.

My eyes flicker from his own to his lips. If I were to angle my head just slightly, to lean in and shut my eyes, I could feel his mouth against mine. Soft and firm. Warm and wet.

He grits his teeth. "Have I made myself clear?"

"As a wading pool."

"Good," he says, backing away slowly. I feel the absence of his body heat immediately.

I swallow my disappointment at the lack of contact.

"Besides, I hope to keep you close. At the very least, until we learn why you have such a powerful connection to the ancient Conch of Hippios."

Of course.

That is why he is keeping me at his side.

Not because he has developed an attachment to me.

He needs to study me.

To understand what makes me, a human waif, so special to the horn.

I have been a fool to hope otherwise.

"I do hope you still stay and join our cause," Ryke says, his voice clipped. "But the choice is yours. I mean it, Merriah. My desire to keep you safe is stronger than my impulse to take my next breath. But I will remain true to my word. You can leave at any time. Say that is what you want, and I will find a way to return you to the shore, by the water's edge. And I will watch over you from below. But if you do choose to stay and fight, know that you will have a fierce protector in me. No, not a protector. A partner. An ally."

Bewildered by his words, I take him in.

His obsidian tail is black as ox blood and his kingly stature makes me feel like a member of his court, adjacent to royalty. He holds his posture with honor, readies his locomotion with a kind reverence I admire. But it is his eyes that truly undo me. It's as though he can see every thought and feeling that moves through my body, and he treats them all with both honor and respect. And I believe what he said. I trust that while he would like for me to work alongside him, to help unravel the true purpose of the conch, he would never pressure me to do so. To give up a life onshore for a life beneath the depths. And regardless of my growing attachment to him, despite the fact that I yearn to match my lips with his, to share one breath of life, I want to make that choice.

To choose him.

To live side by side with him, a child of the tides, fighting for a people I have never known.

I have spent so much of my precious time on this planet thinking of myself as a weak woman. Maybe it is high time I step into my own strength.

"Okay," I tell him.

"Okay?" he asks.

Hope is a steady spring in his eyes.

"Okay, I will stay and fight with you. But there is one problem."

In this moment, Ryke almost looks childlike. Youthful and exuberant, giddy with pleasure. He looks down at me fondly, as if I am the most precious gemstone beneath the sea. And for a split second, I am worried my insides might well and truly burst.

"Any problem you might find," he says, "I am certain we can fix it together."

"Well, you see, sir…" I drawl. All around us, bubbles rise like stars. "I do not know how. To fight, I mean."

"Little minnow, your training begins tomorrow."

Ryke leans in, his lips barely brushing against my cheek.

Beneath my pebbled flesh, a phantom tattoo looms.

"We shall make a mer out of you yet."

CHAPTER SEVEN

I smell the smoke first.

Thick and heavy, wafting into my nostrils like a dark cloud of gasoline.

Then I hear him call my name.

Urgent, panicked.

Like there's gravel stuck in his throat.

"Joonie? Joon, are you okay?"

My eyes flutter open. "Nico?"

The truck is nestled in a shallow ditch on the side of the road, all but totaled.

My head is resting on the airbag that has mushroomed in front of me, and my seat belt is seconds away from cutting off my circulation.

Nico sits next to me, a thin gash on his forehead. His eyes are wild with worry.

"Wh-what happened?" I ask.

My brain searches for answers, swimming against the current of pain. The faint throbbing in my temples. A churning in my gut, threatening to give way to waste.

We were arguing about the validity of romance as a genre.

Nico wouldn't stop calling me kid.

I checked the ETA on the Waze app, and it said six hours.

What else?

"I think I'm concussed," I mutter.

Great. I get so close to finding the love of my life, and this is how I go out: in a ditch in middle-of-nowhere rural Connecticut with only my nemesis at my deathbed.

"You don't remember?" Nico's eyes search my body, frantic, looking for injuries.

"Wait, it's all coming back to me." I squeeze my eyes shut. "There was a loud crash. A sound like the cymbals. Then a bright light. I can see it now. And you were there, dressed all in green. Like Kermit the Frog. And you were singing 'Bananza' by Akon…"

"Okay, you're fine," he snaps, but there's a hint of something else in his voice as well.

Relief?

"That asshole just hit us and kept going," Nico says.

"Well, no. He paused for a second to make sure we were still alive. Then he kept going. God, I hope he steps on a Lego."

I choke on a laugh. Is that some kind of Millennial version of *go fuck yourself*?

"Did you get his license plate number?" I ask, sniffing the air. Something smells like it's on fire. Not the best sign.

Nico glares. "I was a little busy seeing double after *hitting my head on the dashboard*."

"Hey, now, don't take this out on me." I throw up my hands. "And if I recall correctly, this little fender bender was not all that dude's fault. You did kind of step on the brakes like you were playing DDR."

"DDR?"

"*Dance Dance Revolution*," I explain.

"Well, you had just shared some startling information. You know that you're heading to New York to stalk a stranger."

"Not stalk! Meet. It's only stalking from a distance, I think."

Nico just shakes his head. "Were we even just in the same car crash?"

Before I can come up with a clever comeback, I feel a vibration in my pocket. My phone's buzzing.

Teymoor is calling, now of all times.

"Hold that lackluster thought," I tell Nico.

Tey greets me, skipping the pleasantries. "Why haven't you moved in the last twenty minutes?"

"What ever happened to *hello, how are you?*"

"Are you stuck in traffic? Was there an accident?" he asks, ignoring my question.

"Yeah, you could say there was an accident." Shit. I haven't even thought about how Tey's going to react when he learns we fucked up his truck. "You don't happen to, uh, have Triple A, do you? Or does Oliver, maybe? He's, like, super boring and responsible, right?"

"Ollie always flies or takes the train when he visits. I'll have to check with Baba, but I doubt he coughed up the money for that when he's already insuring the truck." He pauses. "Holy shit, Joonie. Did you—"

"Before you finish this sentence, just know that Nico was driving."

"It was her fault!" Nico calls from beside me.

I narrow my eyes at him.

He smirks.

"Wait a second. How did you even know we were stalled?" I raise my voice a little in an attempt to sound intimidating. "Teymoor Saboonchi, are you *still* tracking my location?"

Silence on the other end.

Crickets.

"That's it. I am *so* blocking you on Find My Friends!"

"Call a tow truck in case your phone dies and I can't reach you," Tey manages to say before I hang up.

Nico stares at me for a second, his eyes flitting between the frown lines on my forehead and my pursed lips. "He's only looking out for you. You know that, right?"

"Shut up and call a tow truck." I pause for a second and reconsider my words. "Wait, that was rude. *Please* shut up and call a tow truck."

Nico straightens his clothes and opens the car door. "So polite. Fine. I'll go assess the damage."

I sigh, then kick up my feet up on the dashboard and busy myself by updating the group chat, then opening Find My Friends and turning off my location.

There. That will show Teymoor what happens when he insists on treating me like a child instead of the fully grown twenty-five-year-old teenage girl that I am.

I take in our surroundings. We're on some sort of hidden path, a dirt road instead of the larger route that leads straight to the highway. An ill-conceived shortcut, no doubt.

Classic man. Always trying to find the easiest path forward. Forgetting that when something looks too good to be true, it usually is.

To the left of the road, there's nothing but forest. Red maple trees taller than buildings, older than the majority of the houses in Mystic. They're starting to shed their leaves, baring their speckled spines before the harsh realities of winter. To the right is abandoned farmland. Grass that's brown and overgrown, mixed with dirt and debris. A tumbleweed blows by, innocent to what it's stumbled upon. This is the last place anyone would want to be in an accident. The odds of someone finding us feels like close to zero. We could easily die out here from starvation or dehydration, whichever comes first.

That is, if one of us doesn't kill the other first.

Nico knocks on my window, startling me. I roll it down an inch.

"Password?" I quirk a brow.

"Go ahead. Laugh it up. You won't be smiling in a minute."

My face falls. "That bad, huh?"

"Do you want the bad news or the bad news first?"

"Um." I pretend to think about his question really, really hard. "The bad news, please."

"The tailgate is dented and there's something leaking from the bottom of the truck. We need to get it to a shop ASAP."

My heart sinks. If this little fender bender takes more than a few hours to fix, we'll have to look into alternate ways of getting into New York.

If we make it today at all.

"And the bad news?" I'm almost afraid to ask.

"We're about an hour and a half from the closest body shop. The mechanic says it could take double that for a tow to show up. We could be waiting here for a while."

I stick my head out the window and let out a primal yell. "Furnace, help me!" I shout. "Why did we break down in the middle of Guam?"

Nico scowls. "Next time, I'll try to crash the car somewhere more convenient."

"Thank you," I say. "Preferably near a Starbucks or something."

"Also," he says. "Furnace?"

I roll my eyes. "ATOSAS reference," I say. "Duh. Read a book."

Nico studies me for a second. "Don't worry, Joon. I'll get you there. Promise."

"Yeah, well…" I glare up at him. "Your promises don't mean much to me these days."

He stares at me for a beat, confusion etched into his forehead. Then he pulls out his phone and opens up an app before groaning softly. I watch as he refreshes it over and over again, to no avail.

"Do you have service?"

I check. "Only a single bar. Probably just enough to call someone, but not to Google or stream or whatever. How is that even possible? I literally just checked the ATOSAS message boards."

"There must be an outage or something," he says. "This is a nightmare. What are we supposed to do for three hours?"

"We could play I Spy."

"No."

"You could tell me your deepest, darkest secrets."

"Tempting. But no."

"I could read to you?"

The corner of his mouth ticks up at that suggestion. "You haven't memorized those books of yours by now?"

"I could probably freestyle the first few chapters."

He chuckles. Then his expression darkens, a shadow passing over it. "Can I ask you a question without you doing that thing where you get all mad?"

I roll my eyes. "That's like saying, *Don't be offended*, before saying something offensive."

"Well, then, don't be offended."

The smoke outside of the truck begins to dissipate, wafting off into the forest. Nico sits back inside. He leans over in his seat, throwing an arm around the steering wheel. I try to ignore the way his biceps casually flex. The sight is practically NSFW.

Nico sucks, my brain reminds my body. *We do not have dirty thoughts about Nico.*

Unfortunately, it appears to not matter who the arm in question is attached to.

Sexy is sexy.

"Why are you going after this guy?" he asks.

And just like that, I'm dryer than the Coachella Valley.

"That's none of your business," I say, crossing my arms.

"You understand that thirsting over a fictional character

isn't the same thing as doing it in real life, right? Have we learned *nothing* from the Great Leviathans Incident of 2023?"

I glare. "We don't talk about that. Besides, I have no plans to harass him. I would never make anyone uncomfortable or do something they don't consent to. I just want to meet him."

"Seriously, Joonie," he pushes. "I never see you get sad after you break up with any of these dudes. You just get all businesslike. It's like you dissociate or something. Cut your losses and move on as quickly as possible. Why don't you take a break from dating instead?"

"Because," is all I have to say.

"Because what?"

"Because." My tone is biting, like a rabid dog. "Everyone needs something to believe in, Nico. To give their life meaning. Some people believe in a god that I personally don't think exists, but if that's what gets you through the day without being hateful, who am I to judge? Other folks believe in their favorite musician or astrology app. But not me. I believe in love. In soul mates and happy endings—if you make an inappropriate joke right now, I'll scream—and *a great love, one that could bring the gods to their knees and spin the Earth off its axis.* That belief? It grounds me. It gives me purpose, something to live for when my thoughts get dark. Do you think it's been easy for our family, settling here? In the, like, Vineyard Vines capital of America? I need my faith, Nico. The few times I've come close to losing it—after the Sam drama in high school, after Kyle turned on me, after—" I almost say *after you*, but I cut myself off just in time. "Anyway, I've very nearly lost myself before. Do you get that? Giving up on love almost meant giving up on myself." My lower lip starts to wobble. "So no, I'm not going to take a break from dating. I'm going to keep on believing that my one true love is out there waiting for me. Call it eternal optimism or naivety or whatever. But there is value in believing in love. Power in the idea that I am worthy of someone who loves me for exactly who I am."

For a split second, Nico's eyes carve a hole through my skull.

The air thrums between us, thick with tension.

The words I left unsaid hang around us like an unsung limerick.

The hint at the abuse I suffered.

The mark Sam left on me.

Nico's own betrayal. Scabbed over, but still etched into my skin.

"Joonie," Nico says. "You know you don't have to be a romantic heroine to have a happily ever after, right?"

Don't cry, I will myself. *Not in front of Nico.*

"I know that," I whisper. "But it's hard to heal a wound all alone when it's in a place you can barely reach."

"But you are already loved for exactly who you are. By so many people."

We stare at each other for another moment, our breath intermingling and fogging up the windows. Nico swallows. I watch his Adam's apple bob, and a shiver works its way down my spine.

"You're cold," he says.

"I guess." I shrug. "Can we turn on the heat?"

He shakes his head. "It's too dangerous to start the engine now."

"Right," I say, not bothering to correct him. "Want to snuggle for warmth?"

I expect him to hit me back with his usual *I'd rather be skinned alive.*

Instead, he gestures for me to come closer.

The moment my head hits his chest, every muscle in my body relaxes. He feels both hard and soft in all the right places, like a human Tempur-Pedic pillow. I inhale the scent of sawdust and sandalwood.

"Did you just sniff me?" He chokes on the accusation.

"Maybe," I admit. "This is weird, right?"

"Can you not make it more awkward than it already is?" He groans. "I just can't have you turn into a human ice sculpture on my watch. Teymoor would kill me. Believe me, I'd rather be anywhere but here."

"Took the words right out my mouth," I agree, choosing to ignore the way his body stiffens, then melts beneath mine in answer. "Let's never acknowledge that this happened, okay?"

"I have no idea what you're talking about."

Then I close my eyes for a second. Just one.

My training starts at the very next sunrise.

Or roll tide, as I have come to learn the mer are fond of calling it.

Ryke meets me in the underwater cavern right outside of his private safe house. I am securely locked in my air bubble, floating around in the water with little to no ability to control my movements, a situation that frustrates me beyond belief. Ryke watches me flail my arms around, attempting to turn left, then right, but the pull of the Earth and the moon works differently down here.

He laughs, and I let out a growl of irritation.

"For a minnow, you move through the water with the grace of a hippo," he teases.

I have the urge to pop my bubble and punch him right in the center of the chest.

Then I realize how absurd that concept is. Me, Merriah, assaulting the prince of the mer?

"I hope none of today's training requires the coordination of my arms and legs," I reply. "As you can see, my trainer will be sorely disappointed."

The corners of his lips pull up. "There are ways for us to condition your body without the gravity of land to hold you in place, little minnow. The key is to strengthen your core, that place in the center of your stomach that tightens every time danger is near. Learn to control your core, and you can control that danger. Do you understand?"

I reach down and pinch the skin of my stomach. "I cannot seem to find the muscle," I say, frowning.

Ryke reaches out a hand, his touch a ghost on the outside of my bubble.

"One day soon, I will teach you how to swim. And when that day comes, with your permission, I will place my hands on your body and help you locate every muscle."

My heart constricts, but I nod. "I have always wished to learn how to swim," I admit. "It was not considered ladylike in the village, becoming of a wife or a would-be mother. But I have always felt a call to the water. It is hard to admit, but the river has always given me a sense of comfort. As if the waves were offering a blanket of safety instead of a watery grave."

Ryke watches me, listening with an eel-eyed intensity. "Fascinating," he marvels. "So many secrets lie inside this flesh palace, distilled in your blood."

I laugh nervously. "I do not have any secrets. Only hidden desires."

Perhaps I imagine it, but I think his eyes heat at the sound of the word *desire* on my lips.

"The training." I swallow. "Tell me more of the training. What else will we do?"

"Well, after we work your core"—his pupils are dilated, his irises molten lava—"I shall tie you up with a sailor's rope. Teach you how to escape."

I blink rapidly. "I cannot tell if you are jesting, my prince," I say, my laughter nervous.

He shakes his head. "Not in the slightest. We will strengthen every inch of your body, teach you to swim, explore your potential as a mer warrior. And then, once you are no longer sore and are able to move with agility and ease beneath the waves, the real work will begin: battle preparations."

My mouth forms a tiny circle. "You will carve me into a weapon to wield in the war?"

He nods. "We will work on both offensive and defensive strategies. You shall learn to throw a punch. To bind your legs together with the inner muscles of your thighs and kick as if you have a tail. I will gift you the finest underwater javelins and a seafarer's spear, and we will learn combinations and study technique. You will learn how to hold a shark's-tooth knife, how to strike an enemy in the right place and gut them like a fish."

I shut my eyes and attempt to picture myself brave and strong. Gripping a javelin in one hand and a shark's-tooth shiv in the other, battling amongst the ranks of the mer, Ryke by my side.

For the most part, I fail.

But when my eyes open once more, my cheeks feel flushed.

"And the defensive strategies?" I ask.

The fire in Ryke's eyes dims. "There's a chance, little minnow, that we are betrayed below the tides. Every mer with loyalties to the siren cause is looking for me. Even a prince can sometimes place his trust in the wrong people. If that happens, I want you to be prepared."

Understanding washes over me like the salt in the water. "The ropes...you think I might one day be captured."

He bobs his head in confirmation. "Merriah, I will do everything in my power to keep you safe. I would rather lose my own eternal life than see yours cut short."

He swears this oath to me with so much sincerity that even beneath the salt water, my eyes sting.

"But if a day ever comes when you find yourself in enemy hands, I want you to be able to hold your own and escape. To fend for yourself. I will teach you how to evade ropes. How to outsmart even the cleverest of locksmiths, the wisest of riddlers. You will become a masterful spy, a savant of seduction and manipulation. No bonds will be able to hold you, do you hear me?"

His next words make the hairs on my arms stand up straight.

"You have spent too much of your life living in fear, Merriah, believing yourself to be weak. Let me train the fear right out of you, my warrior. Allow me to show you just how strong you actually are."

And then, just then, I feel guppies swimming around in my abdomen.

A fluttering feeling.

Followed by a clenching

I think I have found my core.

I look up at him, eyes defiant.

"Enough talk, Prince Ryke," I tell him. "Let us begin."

CHAPTER EIGHT

J oon, are you awake?"

My head is nestled somewhere soft and warm. Safe. All at once, I'm overwhelmed by a familiar yet foreign sensation. I'm transported back to winter mornings growing up in Mystic. Tey shoveling snow outside my window. Fresh *barbari* bread baking in the oven. Coming inside after a cold day and heating up by the fire. Sighing, I lean deeper into my pillow, mussing up my hair.

Then the bedding below me shifts. Moves out from underneath me.

And that's when I realize that the cotton is no bedsheet.

It's a living, breathing organism.

A man.

Odd. Normally, my dreams about Ryke are less snug

and secure and more pulse-racing, body-jerking fantasies. Regardless, I nuzzle into his chest, desperate for the three more minutes before my alarm goes off and I have to get up and start writing.

Wait a damn minute.

I recognize that voice.

That isn't Ryke's voice at all.

And this isn't Ryke's cold, wet, chiseled body.

No, these arms belong to someone way more dangerous than the prince of the mer.

My eyes fly open.

The light around us has dimmed, the sun starting to sink beneath the bony silhouettes of the evergreens. The trees now look like ghostly shadows haunting the abandoned field. Daylight Saving Time came and went mere weeks ago, so I'd put the time at around 2 p.m. But that must mean—

Holy shit.

Did I fall asleep for fucking hours?

Worse, did I fall asleep on *Nico's shoulder* for hours?!

"Oh my God," I say, backing away as if every point of contact between us is singeing my skin. "Get off, get off, get off!"

"Me?!" He rubs his hands on his jeans like they're stained with ink. "You're the one who passed out practically the second we started—"

"Don't you dare finish that sentence," I warn, unable

to bear hearing the word *cuddling* fall from those swollen, sleepy lips.

How could I have allowed this to happen? I guess the late nights updating my current work in progress (combined with all the research I've been doing on Ryan Mare, plus the hours of conversations I've been playing out in my head and then transferring to my Notes app) are finally catching up with me. What with our early-morning departure time and the fact that I had only one coffee, I must have crashed.

Hard.

Ironically, that was the best sleep I've had in weeks, if not months.

But Nico certainly does not need to know that.

"Holy Furnace," I whine. "What is wrong with me? I definitely have a concussion or something. How dare you take advantage of a poor defenseless girl with a concussion?"

Nico shakes his head like he's trying to dislodge water from his ear.

"One of these days, Joon, we're going to have to get to the bottom of why you hate me so much."

I snort. "As if you don't know."

His face deflates, a sorry sack of skin. Hurt lines mark the corners of his eyes.

"No, Joonie. I don't."

My brows knit together in confusion. How is that

remotely possible? Sure, he'd been drinking when it happened. And yeah, he apologized at the time—sort of. And it's not like any of it was ever real. But that night is etched so deeply into my psyche that I replay it every time someone laughs at me, every time I read a hateful comment or receive a dirty look. Nico's red eyes and slurred words that night played a significant part in my villain origin story. It never occurred to me that for Nico, I'm just a side character. That the moment I lost trust in him, in our friendship, was barely even a plot point for him.

I look up at him now, understanding dawning on my face.

He has no idea why I treat him this way, does he?

I understand why I hate him.

But if he doesn't resent me for the same reason, then why does he hate me?

Does he even hate me? Or is the way he treats me just a reflex?

I rub my temples, trying to soothe my oncoming migraine.

Then a faint rumbling noise sounds from behind the truck.

"Wait, do you hear that?" Nico asks.

I nod, drawing shallow circles at my hairline with my fingertips.

"This is the first time I've heard another car in four

hours," Nico mutters. "It must be the tow truck. Thank sweet Jesus."

"I thought you only worshipped science."

But really, I'm secretly relieved to be given an out.

"Life, death, and taxes," he agrees. "But we were kind of headed toward the death part."

He rolls down the window just in time to lock eyes with the driver of a red sports car passing along the back road we're on. A man sits behind the wheel, wearing a maroon velour tracksuit, complete with gold hardware and a nondescript logo stitched to the breast. Pieces of some sort of melting wax are falling from his hair. His face is friendly, his exaggerated smile a red crescent against his pale skin.

Stranger danger?

My stomach churns.

Next to him, a younger woman with gloriously bright blue hair, dressed head to toe in black, smokes a vape.

From the radio, death metal swells like an ambulance siren.

Nico's relief falters. Definitely not a tow truck, then.

"Howdy, y'all," the man behind the wheels calls out. "You folks in a lick of trouble?"

Nico regards the man apprehensively, taking in his off-duty track coach getup.

I lean over his body and jump into the conversation. "Hi! So nice to meet you. Thank you for stopping! We were rear-ended—a hit and run. Emphasis on the *run*. We've been waiting for a tow for, like, five hours."

My pulse quickens as I remember what that means for my mission. Even if help arrives in the next five minutes, it'll take *another* ninety minutes for us to get to the shop. That means I'm not making it to New York until at least sunrise—if I end up going at all. I can only afford to take a few days off from work. After all, that campaign slogan for Clever Fox's Fungal Cream is not going to write itself.

This was so *not* part of the plan.

"Is that so?" the man coos, clocking our damaged truck.

His eyes rake over my colorful printed seventies retro set before snagging on the vintage watch hanging off of Nico's left wrist. It's a white gold antique that belonged to his great-grandfather. Nico seems to notice and casually places his hand behind his back, pretending to stretch.

"You see, we were just on our way to the county fair up by Hartford. We're traveling salesmen, Clarisse and me. We do local carnivals, the Renaissance Faire circuit, sometimes farmer's markets, if you can believe it. Selling trinkets and knickknacks. Specializing in rare objects. Y'all would be surprised by what people find valuable these days. Like to travel up and down the coast, setting up at as many fairgrounds on that circuit as we can find."

I wrinkle my nose. Why is this man speaking like some kind of old-school game show announcer?

He extends his left hand out his window and toward Nico's. "Thomas Milford, at your service."

Nico stares at the hand but doesn't move the arm he's hiding in order to shake it.

Thomas chuckles to himself. "Smart man right here." He turns his attention to me. "And what might your name be, darling?"

I smile apprehensively. My parents warned me against making nice with random white men by the side of the road, especially when they look like they're in costume. And I've watched an absurd amount of *CSI*. Despite what Nico thinks, I'm not naïve.

But for circus freaks, these two seem relatively harmless.

Eccentric, but harmless.

"Joonie." I take his hand and give it a firm, no-nonsense shake. "And this is Nico."

Nico glowers at him.

"You two make a handsome couple," Clarisse coos, her voice lined with a smoker's rasp.

"We're not a couple," Nico says quickly.

I nod. "We barely tolerate each other."

Clarisse lets out a full belly laugh. "Well, hon, I hate to break it to ya, but you've got what looks like your enemy's drool all over your forehead."

Gasping, I take out my phone and check the front

camera. Sure enough, there's a sticky, wet patch of slobber all over my brow and left cheek. I wipe at it manically with my sleeve, as if it's a virus.

Great.

As if this day could get any worse.

"Where are you two heading?" Thomas asks.

"Nowhere," Nico says.

"New York City," I say at the same time.

Nico gives me another one of his looks. This one says, *I don't like this one bit. Stop talking right now before I make you.*

I shoot back one of my own: *Don't tell me what to do, jackass.*

Thomas scratches his chin, then interrupts our silent conversation. "Tell you what: Why don't we give you a lift? Get you two a little closer to your destination? It's getting dark, and all kinds of dangerous things can happen to a pretty girl like you under the cover of nightfall. Monsters lurking in the dark and all that."

His words are delivered in a sugar-sweet fashion but leave a bitter aftertaste.

"Thanks, but no thanks," Nico says firmly. "We're waiting for a tow. Should be here any second."

Thomas lets out a dark chuckle. "Fella, the odds of a tow getting here before sunrise feel as low as the Jets winning the Super Bowl. And I wasn't talking to you and only you. Why don't we let the lady decide for herself, huh?"

FEMALE FANTASY

I smiled warmly, liking that I am being given a choice.

"Thanks, Thomas," I say, hopping out of the truck and grabbing my overnight bag. "A ride would be wonderful. Nico, you don't mind waiting with the truck, do you?"

Nico's answering glare is sharp and cutting. I can feel it all the way down to my toes.

I gulp, preparing for a verbal lashing.

Instead, his next words come out lethally soft, a killer's caress.

"Joonie, if you think I'm about to let you hitchhike to New York alone with a couple of strangers who picked you up off the side of the road, then you don't know me at all."

He surprises me by grabbing his own backpack and following me to the car.

I raise a brow. "What about the truck?"

"It's headed to the shop anyway. We can pick it up on our way back to Mystic. Tey will probably have my head, but better me dead than you."

Better me dead than you.

He settles into a protective stance, putting his towering frame between the car and me. I swallow my surprise, then try to slap on a happy face. No need to trouble our new travel companions with our antics just yet.

"Great!" I shout. "Shall we hit the road?"

Thomas and Clarisse cheer as a grumpy-as-fuck Nico and I cram into the back seat. We have so little room that

135

our arms and legs are pressed together, every inch of his side touching every inch of mine. When our hands graze each other, we both jerk them back.

I scoot as far over as possible and lean against the door. Neither of us is too keen on acknowledging the Great Nap Incident of 2025.

Clarisse and Thomas start chatting in hushed tones in the front seats, giggling like lovestruck teenagers. The former removes her vape from her mouth just long enough to blow a big pink bubble with her gum, allowing it to explode all over her plumped lips with a loud *pop*.

She turns to face us but addresses only me. "So, what takes you down to the Big Apple? Business or pleasure or pleasurable business? A dead rich aunt? Fancy job opportunity? Collecting lottery winnings?"

Her eyes glow in the dark, bright and serpentine.

"Love," I announce. "We're both going to attend to matters of the heart."

"I wouldn't really say my heart's the organ I'm following," Nico mutters under his breath.

Clarisse draws her hands to her chest and sighs. "How romantic! Ain't that romantic, Tom?"

Thomas grunts in agreement.

"So, you two are able to just up and go like this? With nothing and no one back home missing you, worrying about you, wondering where you've gone? Not, say, your brother, Joonie? Your friend, Nico?"

Next to me, Nico's nails dig into the leather seat.

I puzzle over that question. "Guess not? I have my own business. And most of my friends are online."

Wait. Did I mention having a brother?

Clarisse hums. "Y'all would make good salesmen. Fair folk. True vagabonds. Maybe you should join us. Become a part of our shtick."

"I'd love that." I beam, imagining myself in a tight, sparkly getup and top hat.

"Though it'd be a mighty big shame if one of you were to go missing," Thomas adds.

The air in the car seems to shift slightly, growing colder. I move closer to Nico.

"What exactly did you say you sold again?" he asks. "Trinkets and knickknacks?"

His question drips with aggression, maybe even a bit of accusation.

"Nico, chill," I whisper. "Don't be weird."

"I'm just wondering what kind of traveling salespeople drive limited-edition red Jaguars down dirt roads that don't even appear on most maps."

Thomas and Clarisse stir silently.

I bite my lip. I mean, when he puts it like that, the whole thing does seem kind of suspicious.

"You guys said you specialize in rare and valuable objects, right?" I ask, trying to remain optimistic. To believe the best about people. "What kinds of things do you sell at Ren Faires? Like, handcrafted jewelry and leather goods? Turkey legs and mead? Ooh, those pendant lockets with cutout silhouettes inside always seemed like pure magic to me. Any chance I can buy one off of you?"

"Our goods aren't really the kind you can just buy," Thomas says.

"They're free?"

"In a sense." Clarisse cocks her head toward me slowly. "You see, we work for specific people, specifically one very peculiar man. And he caters to what you might call a unique kind of clientele. Thomas and me, we're professional dealers. But only for the people who pay to be dealt in, you feel me?"

"Joonie," Nico says, something like understanding dawning in his voice. "Stop talking."

"We're hunters, too," Thomas adds. "Collectors."

I shake my head. "I'm not quite sure I understand."

"Joonie. Please." Nico's voice is hoarse, strangled.

"It's real simple," Clarisse says. "Thomas and I do a lot more than wheel and deal. We also play finders keepers. Sometimes people have the audacity to steal from us, to take what's ours. And our boss hates it when someone makes off with what's his. So sometimes he sends us out on little missions. We go retrieve things for him. His products. His commodities."

Just then, the music goes off, and the radio lets out the sound of a man breathing heavily.

"Thomas, Clarisse—do you copy? I repeat, do you copy?"

Nico face goes pale. "That wouldn't happen to be your peculiar boss right now, would it?" he bites out.

Thomas and Clarisse make eye contact, a silent conversation taking place between them.

"No, no," Thomas says. "That's just our favorite podcast."

"A true crime podcast," Clarisse adds.

"Pick up, you idiots!" the voice barks. "Do you have the boy? And his girl?"

My next breath gets trapped in my throat.

"Boss, you're on speakerphone," Thomas mutters. "I'm going to have to call you back."

"What?" I stutter. "But...I thought you were salespeople!"

"We are, in a sense!" Clarisse says, bursting into laughter. "Tell me, you two: Have you ever heard of Harry 'the Hug' Lester? Well, I know you have, Nico."

Harry "the Hug" Lester. Why does that name sound so familiar?

"Nico," I whisper, "what is she talking about?"

Clarisse jumps-scares into my face, and I jerk backward into the leather seat.

Nico reaches for his phone, but Thomas stops him by twisting his body at an inhuman angle, placing one hand around his neck.

"Now, what do you think you're doing, son?"

"Calling the police."

Thomas shakes his head slowly, making a hissing sound. "A little late for that, don't you think, boy? Should've thought about that before you made a bet you couldn't back up, huh?"

A bet? What bet? Nico doesn't make bets. Nico is the *antithesis* of a bettor. He is risk averse. The literal definition of *playing it safe*.

"Joonie," Nico murmurs. "I'm so sorry."

Thomas's hands twitch, gripping the wheel. He isn't panicking, I realize. This is all going according to his plan.

Which means that none of this was a coincidence.

These two didn't just stumble upon us on the side of the road.

They've been following us. Tailing us.

We are the precious cargo they've been after.

But just who is this Harry "the Hug" that we're being sold to?

"Take their phones, sugar," Thomas orders Clarisse.

She turns, reaches into my pocket, and pulls out my iPhone, a smug look on her face. I feel something cold and hard press against my abdomen, wedging its way beneath my top.

A gun. I've never even seen a gun before.

Unless you count Comic-Con.

I see Nico reach for the car door handle. Unfortunately,

so does Thomas, who turns on the child locks, then leans back to elbow Nico in the temple.

Nico's head rolls back, and I stifle a scream.

"Let us out," I plead. "Please."

Clarisse's head snaps around to stare at me. "Let you out?" she clicks her tongue. "But sweetheart, we're only just getting started!"

Nico grabs my hand and squeezes it hard.

This time, I don't pull away.

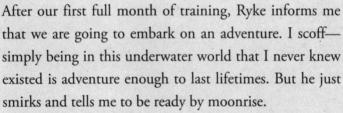

After our first full month of training, Ryke informs me that we are going to embark on an adventure. I scoff—simply being in this underwater world that I never knew existed is adventure enough to last lifetimes. But he just smirks and tells me to be ready by moonrise.

I stagger over to the stone dresser in the cavern, barely able to remain upright. Every muscle in my body aches from holding planks and balancing on one foot. My legs shake. My core has turned to jelly. Even my brain hurts, my temples throbbing from solving logic problems, riddles, and puzzles of the heart and mind. I am exhausted, shredded and stuck back together again.

And yet, I feel myself growing stronger.

More sure of myself. And my ability to help the mer.

From the closet, I select a wet suit made of a reflective turquoise fabric that stretches to fit my form. As the garment contorts to cover my curves, a gasp catches in my throat. The sight is practically obscene. Every part of me is hidden yet exposed, and the blue-green nylon shines like the scales of the fish. With my hair loosened from its braid and cascading down my back, I do not look like a mere woman.

I look like the mer.

My breath quickens.

There is only one reason Ryke would have instructed me to dress in a suit this tight and elastic.

He appears at the archway, ridding my head of all thoughts. He is wearing a vest of a similar material, the same obsidian color as his tail. His dark hair is slicked back out of his golden eyes, which twinkle in the moonlight.

"Ready?" he asks.

I start. "You mean…"

He nods once. "Yes. We shall swim to our next location."

"But I am not—"

"You are ready, little minnow."

For weeks on end, Ryke has been following through on his promise to teach me to swim. At first, I was terrified that I would panic outside of my air bubble and sink to my death. But Ryke's hands gripped my waist, and he vowed not to let go until I felt ready. His confidence in me allowed me to start kicking my legs and moving my arms.

And then I was swimming.

Like a babe, a guppy.

But still.

He hands me some sort of contraption, which he then helps me place over my head.

"Whenever you need to breathe, do so through this tube," he instructs me. "This device operates like a miniature air bubble. It will allow you to draw breath from the water as you swim like the mer do."

I follow his instructions, inhaling through the tube. Clean oxygen floods my lungs, sending a wave of shock through my body.

"It is miraculous," I declare.

He grins at me. "Follow my lead. It is a short swim, but do your best to stay close to the surface. Remember, it is imperative that we stay hidden."

I do as he asks, flexing my tender core and flipping my feet as if they were fins. We swim silently, side by side, passing over a reef of pink speckled coral. I let out a squeal of delight around the tube between my lips. Ryke surprises me by reaching out and taking my hand. And I surprise myself by accepting it.

Together, we swim the rest of the way in each other's grasp.

Finally, we come upon a grand castle of sand, complete

with a moat guarded by two great horses of the sea, their manes as golden as Ryke's eyes.

"Welcome to Fort Caspian," Ryke says. "One of my family's ancestral homes, long abandoned by my kin and forgotten by the sirens. We shall be safe here."

My eyes widen, though I'm unable to speak around the contraption. Instead, I follow him down a narrow path of crystal-covered sand, past the grand sand columns and double cork doors. Once we enter the magnificent hall, complete with stained-glass windows and fresco-covered ceilings, I feel Ryke's hands at the back of my head. He removes the breathing device, and my heart starts to hammer, my hands immediately flying to my mouth.

"It is all right, my minnow," he says softly. "The entire castle was built in an air pocket, intended to allow the mer shifters in my family to take their human and maecenean forms as well. You can breathe here."

I let out a literal breath of relief.

"Well, well, well. Look who finally decided to show his face," a mer calls down from the spiral staircase, his voice rolling like thunder.

His eyes are a pale gray and his skin dark as smoky quartz. But it is his dragon-red tail, long and thick behind him, that causes my heart to skip a beat.

Put plainly, the mer is beautiful.

He looks at me and winks. "Before you ask, yes," he says with a smirk. "It really is that big."

I feel my neck start to heat.

"Play nice, Kai," Ryke grunts. "It is not like I was in hiding. Or exile."

Kai rolls his eyes. "Prince Ryke, ever the martyr."

The two grin at each other for a beat before embracing.

"Good to see you, old friend," Kai says.

"You too, brother," Ryke says, his voice choked. "Where are the others?"

"Whoever could you possibly mean?" A high-pitched voice rings out from the other direction. A pale-skinned mer with short blond hair emerges from the left wing. She wears a bustier of rose-colored pearls, which matches her narrow tail. When she spots me, her eyes twinkle. "Ryke, you disappear on us for years, then emerge with…a date? And here I thought you were saving yourself for me."

Ryke laughs heartily. "Sorry to disappoint you, Mira. This is Merriah."

I offer up a meek smile, but I am distracted by the pretty mer's words.

Decades.

She said Ryke had been gone for centuries.

But these mer look no older than thirty and two years.

Just how old is Ryke?

"Merriah! What a lovely name. Welcome, welcome to Caspian. My name is Mira, and this scoundrel here is Kai. Do not sit by him at supper unless you wish to have your appetite disturbed."

I stifle a giggle.

"Might I suggest he dine in the kitchen?"

Another male appears behind Kai, his skin pale like Mira's but his locks a fiery orange color, the same as his tail. With an earnest grin and shaggy brows, he appears friendlier than the others. Approachable, even.

But I know all too well that looks can be deceiving.

"Oh, shut it, Dylan," Kai growls. "You shall scare off poor Merriah before she has her dorsal fin soup."

The female mer claps. "My favorite!"

Dylan saunters over to Ryke and pulls him into a hug. Ryke practically collapses into his arms, I note. The two must be close.

"Good to have you home," he says. "Where you belong. Come, there is much to discuss. I need to hear about your travels into the human world. And you owe us an explanation. We all heard the conch, Ryke. Was it you?"

Ryke winces. "That story requires many glasses of ale indeed."

Kai lets out a chuckle. "Then follow us outside. We thought we'd dine on the balcony this fine evening. The water is just the perfect temperature. Not too hot, not too cold." The mer then turns his head, gesturing to me. "Why don't you shift and join us, little one? I cannot wait to hear the tale of how you melted our ice prince's heart."

I freeze when I realize that they know not what I am.

147

Ryke's friends believe me to be a mer shifter in my human form.

"I—" I stumble over my words. "I cannot."

Dylan raises a brow. "And why is that?"

"Because she is not mer."

The voice sounds from the entryway behind us. I turn around to find a petite mer with hair as black as night sliced in a sharp line above her shoulders, the sandy skin of both of her forearms and her torso covered in dark inked designs. She wears what resembles a cowhide vest. And her tail, her tiny but magnificent tail, is the hue of a deep green jewel, matching the color of her eyes.

She squints at me, her stance mildly threatening.

"Guinn," Ryke says, his tone a warning.

"She is not mer," Guinn continues. "No, not at all. Can you not smell it on her?"

Her nose scrunches as she sniffs the water around me.

"Tell me, human. How did you come to be below the ocean floor?"

CHAPTER NINE

The first thing Clarisse and Thomas do is place brown paper bags over our heads.

Next, they tie our wrists with what feels like a thick, coarse rope—softer than fisherman's rope but rougher than a jump rope. I feel Nico struggle against his restraints next to me, flailing around like a dying fish.

I, on the other hand, choose to sit still, taking this time in the dark to recalibrate and calculate my next move. An unexpected wave of calm washes over me, as if I've been in this situation many times. Strange, considering the worst crime I've ever committed is stealing a Juicy Tubes lip gloss from the mall as a middle schooler in order to feel alive. And I felt so guilty afterward that I went back the next day and returned it. But now that I've essentially been "taken," it's almost like some deeply buried reflexes have kicked in. I have settled into the comfort of muscle memory.

Bizarre.

"Why aren't you freaking out?" Nico whispers to me, his words muffled by the flimsy layers of paper separating us.

I shake my head, then cringe. Nico obviously can't see me. Idiot.

"I'm sorry," I say instead.

Nico inhales sharply, incredulous. "What could you possibly have to be sorry about? You didn't kidnap us."

"No," I agree. "But I did get into this car even when you clearly didn't want me to. You knew it was a bad idea. We're in this mess because of me."

Nico is silent. For a minute, I wonder if he has fainted due to the stress.

"Joonie," he finally says. "You're not responsible for the bad actions of others. You know that, right?"

"I know," I breathe.

But do I?

I've spent so much of my life feeling like I had to over-compensate. To make up for the way others saw me. To be the best kind of Middle Eastern American—white passing and well behaved, always the optimist—to accommodate my peers. To devote myself to the romance genre even after the romantic leads in my own life turned on me, broke my heart and my spirit in so many ways. I even posture to Nico to show him how little I need him after he disappointed me. I rarely do anything just for myself, simply because I want to. I'm always trying to prove something to someone.

To get rid of this knot in my stomach telling me that if I end up alone and miserable, it will be all my fault.

Maybe that's why this trip to New York is so important to me. In a way, this is me attempting to choose myself.

Or at least it was.

I clear my throat, my airways clogging with unshed tears.

In the front seat, Clarisse and Tom are laughing, shouting the lyrics of a rock song I don't recognize. The car is cutting through the air with ease, accelerating as if it's packed with jet fuel. The police scanner hasn't come on again, but static blares from the radio every so often, threatening to deafen us.

"What do you want?" Nico calls out. "You said you were here to collect. So do it. Looking for money? I have some cash in my wallet. Let me pay you and let us go."

Clarisse clicks her tongue. "After you tried to call the pigs? So you can run off to the nearest station and ID us? I don't think so, baby. We'll take that sweet piece on your wrist, though. All in due time. You just sit tight and wait for Harry."

I feel Nico's body start to shake, causing the seat beneath us to vibrate.

He's panicking. And I don't blame him. This is objectively scary as fuck.

But he's losing his cool, and quickly. This is where his pessimism really has the potential to slow down our escape.

Me, though? I'm getting out of this alive. I have a date with destiny. I can't allow myself to think of any other outcome.

I inhale for three, exhale for six. Somehow, the strategy works. I focus my attention once more.

"What's the plan, then?" I ask casually. "If you're not planning on robbing us, what good are we to you?"

Thomas scoffs. "As if we're going to give you a villain monologue. Nice try, sweetie. This ain't no action movie."

Nico bristles, shifting back and forth in agitation.

I sigh, spittle splattering the inside of my brown paper bag.

It was worth a try.

Suddenly, the car stops and the radio shuts off. I hear the front doors open, then slam shut. The tapping of heels on the pavement, followed by the muffled sound of raised voices.

Our assailants must be arguing about what to do next. This is clearly their first kidnapping.

I shift to the right slightly and reach out with my tied hands, trying to find Nico's fingers. Unfortunately, I scrape something else with my nails instead.

"Hey!" he whisper-shouts. "Watch your hands!"

"I'm sorry, do you have a hard-on?"

"It's an involuntary reaction to adrenaline. Sue me!"

For the first time since we met Thomas and Clarisse, I stifle a laugh.

Then the door next to me flies open, and two strong arms loop under my armpits and haul me out of the car. I smell burned cinders, cheap liquor, and gas station perfume. I groan as my assailant throws me over their shoulder, my torso dangling down their back and my legs in front. Without thinking, I start to kick. Like Merriah learning to swim.

But Clarisse is prepared. She begins binding my legs with the same material she used to tie my wrists.

"Hey, careful with the pants," I tell her. "They're one of a kind!"

She chortles. "You're a riot, girlie."

She treks across what sounds like a gravel parking lot. When we finally pause, I hear her press some kind of button, resulting in a repetitive beeping sound. After a few moments, gears rotate and metal clangs. I shut my eyes and try to place the noise.

A garage door. She's brought me to a garage.

The draft hits my bare stomach, and goose bumps spread across my midriff. Clarisse struts forward, dumping my body onto what feels like a wooden chair before adjusting my restraints. Seconds later, I hear the beeping sound again, and heavier footsteps join Clarisse's.

Based on the wiggling and grunting, it sounds like Nico is still fighting back. Hard.

I roll my eyes beneath my bag.

Men—all struggle, no strategy.

Once Nico is safely secured to a chair that I assume is right next to mine, Thomas huffs, clearly out of breath. "What?" he asks, his tone defensive. "That boy is heavier than he looks."

"Sure," Clarisse snorts. "You get the watch?"

He whistles a high-pitched tune. "You know it. This little baby should make for some sweet pocket change at the pawn. Just need to file off the serial. You ready to make the exchange?"

"Got all the dominoes in a line. There's nothing left to do but blow. Harry wasn't happy, but he was heading in this direction anyway. I'm sure the crew will find a way to make it worth our while."

Harry.

Who the hell are these two dummies working for? I figured them for two idiots running petty schemes like pickpocketing and shoplifting. I mean, it's clear that kidnapping is not exactly their forte. But they know what they're doing to a degree. It just never occurred to me that they could be small cogs in a much larger machine.

Well, until they singled out Nico. And brought up some mysterious "bets" I seem to be the only one to know nothing about.

Thomas lets out a whoop, and then there's the shuffling of feet, followed by wet slurping sounds. The sliding of tongues and the nipping of lips. A soft moan followed by a much louder groan.

I try not to gag into my paper bag.

"If you two are going to do it right here, at the very least take off these bags and let us enjoy the show," I taunt.

"You've got a mouth on you, girl," Thomas snickers.

Seconds later, the bag is ripped from my head.

Holy Furnace, he's easy to goad.

I blink several times, blinded by the light. As I predicted, Nico and I are strapped to two wooden chairs, our wrists and ankles bound with what looks like hemp rope.

Clove hitches, if I'm not mistaken.

Tricky devils to escape from.

But not impossible.

We're in a dimly lit, bare-bones garage. There are a few brown boxes stacked up by the door, along with some gardening supplies: shovels, tools, pots, bags of soil. A long loose hose uncoils on the ground like a snake. There's a lawnmower parked in the right-hand corner, a long extension cord, and a sparkly pink tricycle.

I note all the sharp, pointy objects, and it takes every bit of effort not to smile.

And these two said they specialized in valuable cargo?

Puh-lease.

"All right, you two. Behave, you hear?" Clarisse says,

her red lipstick now smeared all over her face. "This will all be over before you know it."

"Thanks again for the company," Thomas calls out as our kidnappers turn to leave. "It's been a real treat. I hope you both eventually find love in the big city!"

Clarisse reaches up to tug on a rope hanging from the ceiling.

The lights go out.

Seconds later, the garage door starts to close behind them.

The minute we're alone, Nico loses his shit. "Okay. It's going to be okay. Right? Right. They wouldn't take us here to kill us. I mean, they said they were just kidnapping us. That's all this is. A nice straightforward kidnapping. And hypothetically, if they were going to murder us, wouldn't they just get it over with? Unless they're serial killers who enjoy torturing their victims. Do you think they're serial killers? Oh my God, no one will ever find us here. No one is looking for us. And they took my watch. My great-grandfather's watch. They'll have nothing to identify our bodies with. Except for our teeth. Fuck, what if they knock out our teeth?"

I wait patiently for his panic to subside. How come there are no book tropes about hysterical men?

"Breathe, Nico," I command. "Slow down your heart rate. In through the nose, out through the mouth. Here, watch me."

I demonstrate meditative breathing for him. He follows my lead until color returns to his cheeks.

"Thanks," he says. "You're being weirdly chill about all of this. Unless…" His face brightens. "Oh my God. Of course. I can't believe I didn't realize it sooner. Tey has you on Find My Friends, doesn't he? Oh my God, he's probably on his way here right now. Right? That's why you're not bugging out. We're saved!"

I bite my lip. "Um. About that."

His jaw drops. "You didn't."

"Well…"

"Joonie!" He groans loudly.

I give him a sympathetic look. "But if you think about it, Tey was totally right. About the ax murderer thing. So that's cool."

Nico looks up at the garage ceiling.

"So." I clear my throat. "Do you have something you want to tell me?"

He looks away, guilt-ridden.

"Oh my God, I knew it," I say. "Tell me exactly what we're doing here, Nico. Who the hell is Harry 'the Hug' Lester? And what does he have to do with you?"

Nico clears his throat. "Um, has Tey talked to you about how the business is doing?"

I stare at him. Hard. "What are you talking about?"

"He swore he was going to," he mutters under his breath.

Crunching the numbers. That's what Tey said Nico was doing at Kabobs 'n' Bits before Sunday night dinner.

Oh no. Oh God.

"Ever since your parents left…" His voice trails off. "Things haven't been going too well. You know how Abbotts opened that outpost. And then there's that Michelin-starred oyster bar down the street. People are just…less interested in fast casual Middle Eastern food, I guess."

This baffles me. Kabob is timeless!

"Anyway, when the books started to look really bad, Teymoor asked me to take a look. I promised I'd help him get back into the black, but I made a miscalculation that resulted in Tey taking out a loan…using the shop and his apartment as collateral. I felt so bad, Joonie. So fucking awful. I mean, he trusted me with this, and I let him down in this massive way. So I made another really stupid decision. I thought I was helping. I truly believed I was doing what I had to."

I stare at him, letting the silence between us grow thick.

"I went to Mohegan Sun."

My groan must be audible in New Jersey. "Nico! *Nothing good happens at Mohegan Sun casino.* Everyone and their mother knows that!"

"You think *I* don't know that?" he asks. "I was desperate, Joon. Come hell or high water, I needed to pay off that loan. So I chose hell. I had a fair amount of savings, and I ended up placing some risky bets—"

"But you detest gambling!" I interrupt. "You once told me that I played poker like a reckless child!"

"I studied blackjack for *weeks*," he retorts.

"Watching *Casino Royale* doesn't count."

"Well, I thought I was prepared. I had a plan. Play a few hands, make the money I needed, pay off the loan, save the business. Except…"

"Except that's not what ended up happening. You lost. Big. To Harry the Lobster."

"Harry 'the Hug' Lester," he corrects me. "And now I owe him an ungodly amount of money. Money I don't have. Money he gave me a few weeks to come up with, but the deadline has passed. I never thought he'd actually come after me like this. Come after you. Joonie, I would never, ever, ever intentionally put you in danger. I swear on my mother's life, I had no idea he was Mafia. Otherwise I never would have played that hand. He told me he worked in waste management."

"If you had ever read a Mafia romance in your damn life," I practically snarl, "you would know that's practically *textbook code for the Mob*!"

"Well, as we've established, you've read a lot more books than me."

I huff. "You bet all the money you had to save Kabobs 'n' Bits? Why would you do that? Why put yourself at risk?"

He looks at me pointedly. "Why do you think, Joon?"

We stare at each other for a single heated moment, but it's too much. I look away first.

"What kind of name is Harry 'the Hug' anyway?" I ask.

"He's known for starting every conversation with, *Where's my hug at?*"

"Jesus Christ," I say. "And I thought this couldn't get worse."

"We're dead," Nico agrees. "We're completely and utterly dead."

I pound my bound feet against the pavement to get his attention.

"Listen to me very carefully. We are *not* dead. These guys? They're clearly amateurs. Pretty terrible bad guys, in my opinion. They may have taken our cell phones, but they placed us next to each other. Rookie mistake. *And* they didn't bother to tape our mouths. That's, like, kidnapping 101. This is a totally workable situation."

Nico stares at me, unblinking.

"Who are you, and what have you done with Joonie?"

I grin. "Now, do exactly as I say. Okay?"

"Yes, boss."

My cheeks flare with heat. "Pull your hands in close to your chest. Splay your elbows out wide, creating space between your wrists. Good. Now, I want you to start stretching the rope by twisting your wrists."

Nico starts frantically contorting his wrists. I watch as his forehead beads with sweat.

"Like this?"

"Yes, but easy. It's a dance, not a fight. Now, bring your elbows back together. See that slack? Take it in your teeth and work one of the loops over your hands. Then get back to wriggling. And repeat."

We both work in silence, twisting our wrists to loosen our ropes' grip. Over and over again, until our skin is red and sore.

After what feels like years of trying, we finally break free.

I let out a silent cheer before getting to work on the knots around my ankles.

When I look up, Nico is gaping at me as if he's never really seen me before. "How on earth did you know how to do that? Are you secretly a spy or something?"

I waggle my eyebrows. "You don't think the only thing I learned from *A Tale of Salt Water and Secrets* is what I deserve out of a romantic relationship, do you?"

Nico's mouth widens another degree.

"You learned how to escape from restraints by reading a *fantasy romance series*?"

I free my ankles and fight back a grin, satisfied by the flabbergasted expression on his face. "I learned how to be strong and independent from reading my silly little fantasy series. Physically agile and mentally tough. I've trained. Practiced. Just like Merriah. And I'm saving your ass, so I better not hear any more complaining about the *fairy-tale world* I live in. Now, hurry up and untie your feet, *kid*. We need to keep moving."

I run over to the gardening tools, grabbing a shovel and a rake. When I hand the latter to a newly liberated Nico, he looks at me quizzically.

"We'll need weapons," I explain. "Do you know any hand-to-hand combat?"

"Do *you*?" he asks, shaking his head.

"Not much. Just some judo. And I have a black belt in tae kwon do."

"I'm a crisis insurer, not the Karate Kid."

I stifle a laugh, then look around the mostly empty garage. "So, here's where I'm stuck. Even if we can open the garage door, that loud beeping sound will give us away—although I'm sure off-brand Mr. and Mrs. Smith will black out pretty soon from whatever cheap booze they've been drinking. They reek. Breaking a window will set off the alarm, too."

Nico follows my gaze, both of us sweeping every inch of the room for an escape route. Finally, he points at a small hatch at the bottom of the right-hand wall, by the stacked boxes.

A doggy door.

"You think you can fit through there?" I ask.

"Not really," he says. "But I can try."

We don't waste time.

I go first, dropping to the floor. First I push my

shovel through the tiny door. Then I silently roll onto my stomach and slither my way through. I pull myself onto the gravel on the other side of the wall with a grunt.

"Okay, your turn," I whisper.

Nico whistles in response. Moments later, his hands shoot through the door, gaining purchase on the sidewalk, followed by the crown of his buzzed blond head.

"The miracle of childbirth," I murmur.

"Shut up," Nico's head says. "Joonie, I think I'm stuck."

He's about halfway to freedom, his lower abdomen partially through.

And the door is clamped down on the round curve of his ass.

"Okay, you clench." I bite my lip. "I'll pull."

Nico's calloused hands latch on to mine. I shut my eyes tightly, mustering up every bit of inner strength I have, and pull him forward. When I open, I'm disappointed to discover that he hasn't moved an inch.

"One more time," he says.

He squeezes my hands, and I nod.

We count to three, then hang on for dear life.

And his body snaps like a rubber band, landing next to me with a thud.

"We did it!" Nico pulls us to our feet and wraps his arms around me. My heart thuds loudly as I exhale. My entire body is vibrating. "Joonie, *you* did it."

My stomach twists, constricting tightly. For a second, I think I'm having a heart attack.

"Well, we're not home free yet," I say, pointing to where Clarisse and Thomas's car remains parked in the lot.

Our bags are still stowed in the back seat.

Dumbasses.

"They took the keys," Nico says. "How are we going to get the car running?"

"I have a couple of ideas."

He shakes his head in disbelief. "Let me guess. You know how to hot-wire a car, too?"

My answering grin tells him everything he needs to know.

"Man," he says. "I've got to read these fucking books."

It is silent for the space of a rolling wave.

Then all the mer begin to speak at once.

"Human?" Kai paces back and forth, his tail swishing behind him. "But that is impossible. How did you get a human past the barrier?"

"I have been hiding her in air bubbles," Ryke says calmly. "And in my private chambers."

Kai curses in a language I have never heard before.

Dylan studies me closely, as if I am an endangered species.

I suppose in some ways, I am.

"But humans are not allowed in Atlantia," he says. "A human has never set foot in our world. Not once in thousands of years. If the sirens catch you, they will kill you."

Ryke shrugs. "They want to kill me regardless. At least this way, we get to have a bit of fun, no?"

Dylan grins, his face full of mischief.

Without warning, Mira pokes my thigh. I wince, jumping backward.

"I apologize," she says, her eyes wide as saucers. "But I have never seen a real human up close before. Your legs are so much softer than I imagined."

I frown. And here I thought I was building muscle in my training sessions.

"We are working on it," Ryke says, the corners of his mouth turning upward.

Guinn circles me like a predator, concentrated and menacing. I shrink under the heat of her gaze. "You still have not explained what she is doing here, my prince," she says, her voice cold and measured. "Unless you have finally broken your vow of chastity and taken a lover?"

I blink hard, shocked.

Vow of chastity?

Ryke?

Kai lets out a deep belly laugh. "Trust the prince of the mer to be ruled by his cock like any common guppy."

Ryke elbows him in his side, shutting him down for the time being. "So many—"

"Questions?" we all sing in unison.

The mer and I exchange looks of surprise. Then we all burst into laughter together. And it feels so wonderful to laugh freely in harmony.

"Before I expose every one of our secrets, perhaps you lot would like to be polite and introduce yourselves to our guest?" Ryke's words are a suggestion, but his voice is a command. "Merriah, I would like you to meet Kai, Mira, Dylan, and Guinn, my friends since childhood and my most trusted guards. I call them my Upper Shoal, or the Shoal for short."

The group and I study one another. Then Mira pulls me in for a hug. I stiffen, unsure of what to do with my arms. I am not accustomed to being held even by those I know, let alone strangers.

"It is so nice to make your acquaintance, Merriah," she says. "You can call me Mir."

Her smile heats my cheeks. I nod once.

"Merriah is no bystander in this whole affair," Ryke continues. "But that is not my cross to bear. Little minnow, would you like to tell the Shoal why you are here?"

I stare at him, shocked that he would have me reveal my hand to those I have never met.

"You are scaring the poor girl," Dylan says. "Ignore him, Merriah. He has never had a way with females."

Ryke glares, and I stifle a laugh.

But it is Guinn who speaks next.

"I do not know you," she says, the harsh lines of her

face softening. "But I trust Ryke. I have trusted Ryke since he found me at the bottom of a ravine and gave me shelter in this very fortress. I trusted Ryke when he fought back against the usurpers, and I trusted Ryke when he fled to the human lands and promised to return one day. He has earned my faith in him."

Guinn locks eyes with Ryke, and they share a private smile. Their intimacy causes a hot rush of jealousy to flood my veins.

She turns back to address me once more. "And Ryke trusts you. Therefore, we trust you, and you can trust us in return. On the ancients and the unborn, the moons and the tides, the current and the bay, I swear it."

Guinn reaches out to touch me, and it's like making contact with an electric eel. So different from the warmth I felt from Mira or the rush of excitement I get from Ryke.

She is not like the others.

Mer, yes.

But something else, too.

I cannot put my finger on it. And I cannot ask.

Not yet.

"Trust does not come easily to me," I tell her, then turn back to face all of them. "I have never found comfort in the company of others. My whole life, I have kept my thoughts and dreams under lock and key. The love you have for each other, unconditional and unwavering? It is as mysterious to me as this new world."

The Upper Shoal listens to my every word, their beautiful faces twisting in pain.

Empathy.

For me.

Even though I am no one.

Then, one by one, they make the same oath as Guinn.

On the ancients and the unborn.

The moons and the tides.

The current and the bay.

They swear fealty to me and my secrets.

When they are done, I blink back tears and clear my throat.

"It was I who blew the Conch of Hippios," I admit. "The immortal instrument. It called out to me."

Guinn's jaw drops. "Holy Furnace, it cannot be," she says.

Ryke furrows his brows. "Speak, Guinn."

She looks me dead in the eye.

"Amphitrite," she says. "She returns."

CHAPTER TEN

I keep driving.

Past the dirt back roads, the deserted fields and empty farmland, eerie at the witching hour, haunting as a spirit.

I keep driving in silence with only the moon to guide us.

I keep driving when I hit the highway, picking up speed along with the other late-night roadies, each traveling toward or escaping from something.

All the while, Nico watches me, his forehead scrunched and his eyes narrowed.

Contemplative.

In awe.

After the fifth exit sign, I take a sharp right, pulling into a Denny's parking lot.

"What are we doing here?" Nico asks. The first words he's spoken since the great garage escape.

"Get your bags," I tell him, turning off the car. "We're leaving the car here."

I rummage through my purse for a packet of tissues and a small bottle of hand sanitizer. Dabbing a little bit on a Kleenex, I start wiping down any surface we may have touched, from the back seat to the steering wheel. Nico stares at me for a second before grabbing the sanitizer and getting to work.

Once we're done disinfecting the leather, I let out a tiny sigh of relief.

"I think we've put enough distance between ourselves and that garage. Once Thomas and Clarisse—or whatever their real names are—wake up from their drunken stupor and realize we're missing, it'll take them a hot second to find us," I explain. "But that doesn't change the fact that we're in a stolen vehicle. Which means the police will be looking for us as well."

Nico rubs at his beard in distress. "Wouldn't the police finding us be a good thing? I mean, shouldn't we call them anyway? We need to report what happened to us. Unless…do you think the Mob has the police in their pocket? No, what am I saying. This isn't *The Godfather*."

I let out a strangled laugh, shaking my head.

"Nico, as a self-described cynic, you should know better than to trust the cops with something like this. I hot-wired the car. You really think they're going to believe that some guy in a tracksuit picked us up on the side of the road and tried to kidnap us and that's how we ended up lifting a Jaguar? Come on. That sounds totally made-up."

"But we can point them to Tey's truck," Nico says, exasperated. "We can tell them about the garage!"

I roll my eyes.

White men.

"Nico. We have zero idea where the truck is. We don't have our phones, so we can't check maps. Even if we were to return to the garage, there's zero chance those two are still hanging around. It'll just look like we broke into some stranger's garage, stole their gardening tools, and commandeered a sports car. We'll look totally guilty."

"So, what? We're just going to pretend this never happened? That we were never *kidnapped*?"

"Who is there to tell?"

"Um, I don't know. Your brother?"

"Tey? He'll just worry. Maybe Ollie can give us some legal advice. But why bother?"

His eyes widen as he processes everything I'm saying, his face growing red.

"Are you okay?" I ask, my voice soft, as I realize I haven't checked in on him yet. "That was…traumatic, to say the least. I don't blame you if you need a beat to process."

He stares vacantly at me, as if the word *traumatic* is

floating around in the space between us. After a minute or two, he nods, more to himself than to me.

"I'll be okay, boss. I don't know if it's the adrenaline or what, but I want to keep going. What's our next move?"

I smile at my new nickname.

Boss.

So much better than *kid*.

"For what it's worth," he adds, "I'm really, really, really sorry. Like, really sorry. I'm in total denial that any of it even happened. I don't know how you're not furious at me right now."

"Nico," I say. "You know you're not responsible for the actions of others, right?"

He smiles, just a little. "Even if my moronic actions led to their actions?"

I look at him for a moment. "You did something monumentally stupid and out of character," I finally say. "But your heart was in the right place."

"*Out of character*, huh? Would you say I went a little bit off script, Joon?"

I roll my eyes. "We'll figure out what to do about the money you owe and Kabobs 'n' Bits later. First we need to dump the car here. Tomorrow, we'll get some burner phones from a gas station, and then we'll take a taxi to the train. Wait, do you still have your wallet?"

He checks his Jansport. "They took all my cash but left the cards."

"Same. Probably because they knew they'd be easier to track." I scrunch my nose, slightly impressed. I thought they were too dumb to realize something like that.

"So, that's tomorrow," says Nico. "What do we do tonight?"

I point into the distance. If I squint, I can make out a flashing red sign covered in a shroud of mist. "We walk to that motel over there and get some rest."

He snorts. "I doubt I'll be able to sleep after a night like this."

"Tough shit. You'll need the energy. You're no good to me grumpy."

"I'm always grumpy," he mutters, the corners of his lips tugging upward.

My heart does that twisting thing again.

We grab our bags and begin the trek over to the motel, walking on the side of the highway like two nomadic travelers in a coming-of-age film. Every once in a while, I'm startled by the sound of brakes behind me, convinced that Clarisse and Thomas have found us. That we'll be forced into the trunk of a brand-new car and shuttled somewhere no one will ever find our bodies. But it's always just a passing delivery truck or late-night road-tripper.

"Here, switch places with me."

Nico moves past me so that he's walking on my left side instead of my right, closer to the road. Keeping a lookout.

Ensuring that, if push comes to shove, he'll take the brunt of a hit.

"What are you doing?" I ask.

"Don't worry about it," he says.

I didn't realize Nico fancied himself a gentleman.

All at once, every hair on my body stands up straight. Because this?

This is something Ryke would do.

"You don't have to do that, you know," I tell him. "I can take care of myself."

"I know," he says quietly. "But just because you can doesn't mean you should have to."

The Lonely Hearts Motel stands proudly near exit 17 on I-95, its bubblegum-pink paint chipped all over. The motel is two stories tall, stretching along the highway. Its railings are slanted, nails hanging loose, a single storm away from falling over. There's a latched gate leading to a pool out back, which is littered with cigarette butts and crumbling leaves. The neon sign features an ace of hearts playing card and two flamingos kissing, leaning on one another for support.

We step inside and ring the bell.

A woman in her late thirties comes rushing out of the back, her eyes red from working the night shift and crusted with melted mascara. There's a plastic fork stuck in her messy bun and a crease on her left cheek. She's speaking loudly on the phone in Mandarin.

"Hello, ma'am," Nico says.

Her eyes flit over to his before she returns to her call, flat-out ignoring him.

Nico sighs, exasperated.

"*Can you please hang up the phone and help us?*" I ask in near-perfect Mandarin.

Behind me, I hear the sound of Nico choking on his own spit.

I smirk. I knew all those lessons would come in handy one day.

The woman's pierced brow flies up, but she clicks a button and places her cell on the counter. Then she takes in our disheveled appearance and the matching red marks on our wrists and grins, unfazed.

"Long night?" She tucks a curl behind her ear.

"Something like that," I grumble. "We need two rooms, please."

"Two? That a kink of yours or something?"

Nico starts coughing.

The lady's knowing expression makes me giggle. I smile and shake my head. "You don't know the half of it."

"Unfortunately, no can do," she says. "There's some kind of fidget-spinner convention up the road this week. We're booked solid. Only got one room left. The paradise suite."

"We'll take it," I say before Nico can object.

"Fabulous."

She hands us the keys, leaning over the desk. "And a little pro tip: If you're planning on securing yourself to the headboard, I suggest you use handcuffs. Those mother-fuckers are too slippery for ropes."

She winks, and I get the distinct pleasure of watching Nico's face turn the same color as the dying grass.

He follows me up to our room, dumbfounded. I throw open the door to find a heart-shaped waterbed, complete with a leopard-print duvet, floral wallpaper, and a full-size jacuzzi with some questionable brown marks at the bottom.

Honestly? I have to laugh. This room looks like the backdrop of a really corny porno.

"I'll take the floor," Nico says immediately.

"Don't be stupid," I say, dropping my duffel on the floor. "There are literally red stains all over the carpet. And something tells me they aren't ketchup."

Nico gags. "I thought that was just an artistic pattern or something."

"Sure," I say sweetly. "Splatter paint. Bloody red splatter paint."

I sit down on the waterbed, and it dips beneath me, almost causing me to slide off onto my ass on the Furnace-forsaken crime scene floor.

"Come on. I need your weight to balance out the oil in this thing anyway."

Nico begrudgingly approaches the waterbed and takes

a seat before stretching out beside me. I try to ignore the way his arms flex as he stretches them above his head, his abdomen taut and clenched as he yawns. We both lie there staring up at the speckled ceiling. I replay the day's events over and over in our heads.

Literally occupying two sides of the same heart.

"Do you think that's black mold?" I whisper.

Nico grunts, which turns into a fit of giggles.

Before I know it, we're both on our sides, our bodies shaking as tears stream down our faces, our cackles all-consuming. After a while, I can't tell if we're laughing or crying.

Most likely both.

"I can't believe we got kidnapped today," Nico says. "That shit just doesn't happen to people like me. I don't get kidnapped. I go to work. I go to the gym. I go home. But I never get kidnapped."

I snort in agreement. "For someone who loves playing out worst-case scenarios in your head, you were oddly unprepared for the worst-case scenario."

He turns to face me. "But you weren't. You're being surprisingly calm about the entire thing. Like, you're not *traumatized* at all."

"Maybe I'm dissociating." I shrug, uncomfortable with being complimented by Nico.

"You were incredible."

Blood rushes to my head. "I just read a lot is all."

His eyes are fixed on me, unwavering and sincere. "I think you were right. Maybe I do need to start believing in the power of love. Maybe then the universe will stop kicking my ass."

A beat goes by before I fully process what he's saying. "Wait. I'm sorry. You don't believe in love?"

He shakes his head. "My parents made sure of that."

I rack my brain for more information. Nico's parents got divorced when I was in middle school. Before that, they always seemed enamored with each other. I remember them holding hands at Chowder Fest at Olde Mystick Village and making out like teenagers at Clyde's Cider Mill. But I don't remember too many details of their breakup.

Nico was a quiet kid. Reserved. He and Tey always hung out at our house or at Kabobs 'n' Bits. It never occurred to me that there was a reason he didn't want to go home.

"They were high school sweethearts, right?"

Nico nods, but his eyes are somewhere far away.

"Next-door neighbors. Childhood friends, too. There are pictures of them together as toddlers. Celebrating birthdays. Trick-or-treating. Playing in the tub. Their mothers were best friends and decided that they were destined to be together. They never had a chance to love anyone else. Falling in love with each other was just this accepted thing, as easy to them as breathing or eating or sleeping. It sounds corny, but their families really believed that fate had placed their houses next to one another. My dad always said it was love at first sight, that once he set eyes on her, he knew he'd never want anyone else."

A frog catches in my throat. "That's beautiful," I croak.

"Sure." His laughter is clipped. "Right up until he cheated on her. He'd been cheating on her, in fact, ever since they were teenagers. With her girlfriends. With his classmates. With her own sister, my aunt. My mom never saw it coming. Christmas was pretty awkward that year. The family kind of fell apart after that."

My heart drops as he sucks in his cheeks, trying to mask his emotion.

I have the strangest urge to reach out and touch him.

To comfort him with the warmth of my body, the strength of my arms.

My hands clench and unclench.

"Fuck," is all I can think of to say. "I can't believe I never knew."

"Not your fault, since I never talk about it." He shrugs. "It's kind of hard to believe in happily ever afters when the best love story you've ever heard turns into a tragedy."

I think back to all the comments Nico has ever made about my love of romance. The quips about living in a fantasy, refusing to face the harsh realities of the world. His cold demeanor when I told him about my breakup with Kyle. His obsession with preparing for a crisis. His pessimistic worldview.

In order to avoid getting hurt, Nico has been steering clear of vulnerability.

He'd rather feel nothing at all.

"Thank you for telling me," I say. My hand hovers over his like a drone. "For what it's worth, I get it. I don't agree. But I do understand."

Nico doesn't respond.

He just reaches out without looking at me and takes my hand in his.

Electricity immediately shoots up my arm, setting my whole body aflame.

We lie there in silence. And this time, when my mind settles on that night all those years ago—what I witnessed, what Nico said—it stings a little less. I'm sure my outlook on life, my blind optimism about love, has always triggered him to a certain degree. I've always believed he looked down on me. But maybe he was just protecting himself.

Maybe there's more to that story from all those years ago.

I must drift off, because hours later, I come to. The room is dark, the bedside lamps turned off. I'm still lying on top of the waterbed in my clothes. But Nico is awake, propping something up against his knees, a glowing orb of light glistening from the heart's other atrium.

I hear the thumbing of paper, the rustle of a page as it turns.

I open one eye, curious.

And my pulse stumbles.

Nico is huddled over a reading light.

And in his hands?

My copy of *A Tale of Salt Water & Secrets*.

"I do not understand what that means," I repeat to Ryke.

We sit together under a dome made of sea glass, lit by a string of glowing orbs overhead. All around us, colorful fish move in unison, a staccato dance. Art in motion. We are seated at a cement table covered in ancient carvings, sipping small cups of ale and dining on oysters. The moon hangs heavy tonight, shining past the false bottom of the ocean, all the way to our sea-washed skies. At the edge of the orb, a tiny mer plays the sea organ. Its melody drifts over us like the fog of a new day.

Across the table from me, Ryke smiles. He has shifted back into his human form and is wearing a navy-blue fitted suit that hugs every toned, expertly carved inch of his torso. In the glow of the orbs, his eyes shine bright like molten gold, and his dark hair falls into his eyes. He glances up at the moon, then back down at me, shaking his head in wonder as if I am responsible for its presence.

I lean forward and groan. Every inch of my body is sore from our training sessions. My abdomen is taut, my legs liquid. I can feel my pulse in all four quadrants of my body. Even my eyelids hurt each time I blink. But it is working. Every day, I feel myself grow stronger and more capable. Earlier this morning, I came close to disarming Ryke with a sword. My hand-to-hand combat needs more work, but as soon as I perfect my punch and stop leaning so far into my left knee, I should be able to use more force. Ryke has taught me how to escape from the most difficult sailor's knots, to pick the lock of any treasure trove. Each night, I go to bed exhausted but with a sense of excitement for what is to come the next day.

If my husband were to see me now, he would hardly recognize me.

And the idea sends a shiver down my spine.

"Fifteen hundred years ago, Amphitrite was a hero to our kind—part mer warrior, part goddess of the sea. She fought for our people in the primary wars, when the mer had to reclaim the oceans after they were captured by creatures who claimed it to be their territory. In the lore, she distracted the godlings with a dance before slaughtering them all. She was our salvation, but she died shortly after her final battle, succumbing to her wounds. But it is rumored that her lineage lives on in a human bloodline. She was a shifter, you see. While recuperating on land, she took a human lover, a sailor. The two fell in love, and she went to live with him, but when the time came to call the mer to war, she had no choice but to leave him. She did not even have a chance to bid him farewell."

"How awful," I say, my mind drifting back to the creek cottage. To the story I had been told as a child about the sailor and his lover. "He must have been heartbroken."

Ryke nods. "As was she, but she knew her duty. The Conch of Hippios belonged to her. It is blessed with the holy water of the gods. She was the first and last to blow it. When she passed away, it fell into the possession of the ruling sovereign of the mer. But her descendants are its rightful owners. I am beginning to suspect that her blood might flow through your veins."

My pulse begins to race. "Does that mean I can shift?" I ask, perhaps too eagerly.

"So many questions," Ryke laughs. "No, my minnow. If my suspicions are correct, your blood would be far too diluted to hold any true mer properties. Any connection to Amphitrite would be distant. But still, if you are her kin, you are more valuable to the cause than I could ever be. Worth protecting with armies and weapons. More precious than your weight in gold."

My stomach drops.

Valuable to the cause.

Is that all I am to Ryke?

Precious not because of who I am, but what I am?

I swallow my disappointment.

"And why is that, my prince?"

Ryke grins wickedly, and I trace the muscle working in his throat with my eyes, wishing I could do the same with my tongue.

"Because only you can wield the objects in her treasure trove."

I raise a brow. "There are more magical objects besides the conch?"

"There are four, to be exact," he says. "Unfortunately, I could grab only one when I fled Atlantia. The others are hidden in the palace, guarded heavily by the sirens. Which is why tomorrow night, I plan to go undercover to retrieve them. The mer are having a ball in honor of the annual Eve of Sinking Stars, an important holiday to our people. They will be distracted, providing me with a perfect opportunity to steal the treasure trove."

I surprise myself by standing suddenly, slamming my hands onto the table.

"You cannot go!" I practically shout. "It is far too dangerous. You are going to get yourself killed."

"Now, now, minnow," Ryke says with a smirk. "I am flattered that you worry so much for me. But Dylan, Guinn, Kai, and Mira will all be in attendance. They will ensure my safe return."

My heart races as I imagine Ryke, my Ryke, in the belly of the beast.

Not that I have the right to call him that.

"Take me with you," I say.

"Absolutely not."

"I have been training for this. I am strong enough to maintain an air bubble on my own now. I will no longer be swayed by the current. Mira can dress me so that I fit in with the mer. No one will even be able to tell that I am human."

"Were you not listening when I told you how valuable I believe you to be?" Ryke snaps. "It is too dangerous, Merriah. I cannot lose you."

"And I cannot lose you!"

We stare at each other, out of breath.

Our chests rise and fall in unison.

Heat flares between us. This time, I'm certain it is not just my imagination.

Ryke knows how my husband treated me.

Trapped me.

Took away my agency and ordered me around like a common whore.

And yet he still expects me to submit?

"Please, my prince," I whisper. "None of the sirens know what I look like. I am your best bet, your secret weapon. Use me."

Ryke shuts his eyes for a moment.

When he opens them again, his expression is one of reverence.

"I do not want you to go," he says, blowing out a short breath. "But I will never force you to stay behind. The choice will always be yours, my minnow. The decision will always lie with you."

I reach for his hand and squeeze it tightly. "Does that mean…"

The next time he smiles, the roguish expression reaches his golden eyes.

"Merriah, will you please escort me to the Ball of Sinking Stars?"

And though I cannot see myself, I know my face matches his.

"It would be an honor."

CHAPTER ELEVEN

The next time my eyes flutter open, light is flooding into the motel room, coloring every inch of the space a majestic golden hue. Both of us must have fallen asleep before thinking to draw the hideous paisley curtains. I yawn, reaching over to the nightstand and feeling for my phone. When I can't find it, the truth dawns on me.

My phone is gone.

It was taken by Dumb and Dumber last night.

They're probably halfway to Panama right now.

I cringe at the memory of the paper bag over my head, the sight of Nico tied to that chair…

Nico.

Everything he did for my brother. For my family. For *me*.

Misguided, to be sure. But brave.

I suddenly become aware that Nico is all over me, everywhere at once. Somehow, in the middle of the night, we became entangled. His arms are wrapped around my waist from behind, the scruff on his chin scraping the juncture where my neck meets my collarbone. One calf is folded over my knees, his chest against the small of my back. He's breathing softly against my skin, eliciting involuntary shivers. And I can feel the shape of something harder, something growing, digging into my backside.

Even weirder, the revelation does not repulse me. If anything, it makes my body react. I fight the temptation to arch my back, to squirm against him, not wanting to wake him up and ruin this rare moment of quiet.

"What time is it?" he whispers against the shell of my ear.

"No idea. No phone."

He hums for a moment, and then his body freezes as he realizes where he is and who he is holding. I wait for him to panic, just as we both did in the truck less than twenty-four hours ago. But instead, after a second of uncertainty, I feel his tension melt away. The muscles in his body relax once more, as if settling into the decision to not make this weird.

The memory of waking up in the middle of the night and seeing him hunched over my annotated, dog-eared copy of my favorite book comes rushing back, faded and blurry, like a dream within a dream.

I blink as a novel emotion invades my senses, causing the blood in my brain to thrash violently against my ears.

"We should get going," I tell him, breaking the spell.

Begrudgingly, he untangles his limbs from mine. I feel his absence immediately, missing the heat of his body, his breath against the nape of my neck.

"To New York," he says, a bite of bitterness in his innocuous words. "Your soul mate awaits. Right?"

I swallow, staring at the floral wallpaper, which distorts in front of my eyes like a kaleidoscope. "Right."

What in the siren's name is happening to me?

Ever since I mustered the courage to walk away from Kyle and serendipitously discovered *A Tale of Salt Water & Secrets*, Ryke has been my dream man. Beautiful, attentive, supportive Ryke. Nico is the polar opposite of Ryke in every way. Stubborn to a fault. Pessimistic like he's paid to be. For my entire adulthood, he has treated me like some naïve, starry-eyed kid with no knowledge of what it's like to survive in the real world. He has tested my belief in happily ever afters, stolen away my childhood and its innocence. Nico has always refused to take me seriously. That's one of the only facts of the universe I can count on.

So why am I sitting in the center of this heart-shaped waterbed with a fresh face of makeup, dressed in a coquettish baby doll dress and tights, actively trying not to think about the fact that Nico is currently in the shower, presumably very naked?

I really need help.

And to keep my eye on the prize.

Today, I get one step closer to Ryan Mare.

New York City.

The bathroom door opens, and Nico walks out, steam from the shower wafting into the room. There's a faded towel hanging low on his hips and droplets of water weaving their way down his bare chest.

All coherent thought leaves my brain.

I can't help it.

Like, I straight-up gawk.

Nico smirks. "Did you talk to the front desk lady?"

I dig my nails into the palm of my hand, attempting to snap out of it. "Yup. I paid the bill—you owe me twenty dollars, by the way—and asked her to call us a cab to the nearest Metro-North station. We need to be downstairs in ten."

He nods. I don't miss the way his eyes rake over my outfit. Quickly, as if he's scared of looking too closely and burning his retinas.

"Can I have a minute?"

"Oh my God, of course," I say, slapping a hand over my eyes. "I'll go wait downstairs."

Mortified, I get up and grab my duffel, then shuffle toward the door, all the while avoiding his gaze. I don't exhale until I get downstairs, the color in my cheeks rosier than the motel walls. I need to get my shit together before this spirals out of hand.

The same concierge lady as last night is waiting at the entrance. She takes in my red face and throws me a wink. I wish, and not for the first time, that I could blow the Conch of Hippios and be spirited away.

Minutes later, a fully clothed Nico comes downstairs and joins me. "You look nice," he says without looking at me.

"Go to hell," I reply.

He bites his lip, fighting a grin. "I'm serious."

"Me too."

Holy Furnace, this is awkward. I don't know how to act around him anymore. Trading insults and smart quips? My bread and butter. Chatting up unimpressive men? I'm practically licensed. But talking to someone who launched a crusade for my family's honor *and* inside my panties this morning? That's uncharted territory for me.

And I'm learning that I'd actually rather go back to being held hostage.

A crush.

Is this what this is?

God, I haven't had a legitimate crush on someone since...

"Remember when you had a crush on me in middle school?" Nico asks suddenly. As if our minds are in exactly the same place.

"Did not," I retort halfheartedly.

"Did too," he teases. "I remember catching you writing our names inside a heart in your notebook with one of those pink gel pens you loved so much. I thought it was so cute."

"Must have been another Nico," I insist.

Outside the motel, a car honks. Our taxi. I exhale in relief, then thank the front desk lady and book it outside to avoid continuing this conversation.

"The closest train station, please," I tell the driver.

"That'll be New Haven," he says.

I let out a startled laugh.

"Oh my God. Those shitheads actually did it. They kept their word. They got us closer to the city." I shake my head. "I wonder what they planned to do with us."

"About that…" Nico rubs his chin. His nervous tic, I've realized. "I have a theory."

I quirk a brow, waiting for him to continue.

"So, you know how Clarisse told Thomas she was ready to *make the trade*?"

"Yeah."

"Do you think maybe that trade was…us?"

I think about it for a second. "You mean, like, for ransom?"

In the rearview mirror, I see the taxi driver frown. Nico lowers his voice.

"I'm saying, what if Harry 'the Hug' Lester was coming

himself to finish the job? What if he hires idiots like Clarisse and Thomas to round up people who owe him money, and when they can't pay up, he…takes them out? What if they've done this before?"

I bite my lip, remember their hushed words. References to a *he*. That could make sense, of course. But our kidnappers seemed like petty con artists. Thieves at most. Not cold-blooded killers. But maybe they've gotten involved with some bad guys who do much worse?

"What makes you think that?" I ask.

Nico pulls out a notebook, a cheeky smile on his face. "They left their ledger in the car, and I kind of took it."

My jaw drops. "You stole their ledger?!"

I open the book and begin flipping the pages. Scribbled numbers and data tables, notes about accounts and IOUs. Gambling numbers. Some kind of code I can't understand.

"Not sure what most of it means or if it proves anything," Nico says. "But I figured if we could make sense of it, it would give us leverage. You know, if they try to come after us again."

I drop my head into my hands. "Nico. Now there's no way they're *not* going to come after us."

His brow furrows. "You mean…"

"They're *definitely* going to want this back." My voice cracks. "Which means they'll definitely come looking for us. Sooner rather than later."

Nico's face pales. "Should we ditch it? Burn it or something?"

I shake my head. "It's too late for that. Let's just keep moving. The more distance we put between ourselves and them, the better."

Minutes later, the taxi pulls up in front of the station. I reach into my duffel and pull out a scarf, a hat, and two pairs of sunglasses. I drape the scarf over my hair and hand the hat and one pair of glasses to Nico.

He gives me a look.

"Come on, we need disguises. No arguing. Put those on."

He grumbles, then dons the bedazzled oversize spectacles.

I burst out laughing. "Oh, this is too good. If only I had my phone. I can't wait to buy a burner in New York."

The train is already waiting for us on the tracks. We get on at the café car, and I position us by the bathrooms so I can watch as people get on and off at each stop. My stomach grumbles so loudly that several passersby look up and shoot me dirty looks.

"I'll go get us breakfast," Nico offers, "before your body makes a sound so offensive that we're thrown off the train." He gets up before I can say thank you and approaches the counter.

I sigh, wishing—not for the first time—that I could check the Salty Girls group chat. I miss my friends, my community. But on the bright side, if I don't update my latest fic by the end of the week, there's a 90 percent chance my readers will send an actual search party out looking for me. I smile, thinking about 911 texts and police dogs.

It's nice to be noticed.

To be missed.

Too bad they don't even know my real name.

Someone clears their throat. I look up just as an older woman slides into the seat across the table from me. She has gold bangles on both her wrists, henna tattoos swirling up her inner arms. A long, tentlike skirt drapes across her body, and there's a scarf adorned with gold coins tied around her waist. Large black curls fall down her back. Her skin is cracked with age, but her eyes crackle with fire.

She looks in my direction. Not directly at me, but through me. I feel every inch of my body ignite at once.

"Um, hello," I hear myself say.

The strange woman stares. "I was called to you."

I squint, looking around. "Nico called you?"

"No." She shakes her head. "Your spiritual energy. I feel pulled toward you, as if propelled by a force larger than myself. By the universe. Do you know what I mean?"

My hands turn ice-cold. "Just like Merriah and the conch," I whisper.

"What?" The woman tilts her head.

"Never mind," I say quickly. "What's your name?"

"Veda. I am a psychic, the greatest in the tristate area. I have true ties to the prophet."

I frown. "Which prophet?"

"All of them. None of them. It does not matter, child. I come bearing a message for you and your traveling companion. A prophecy."

My heart races. As a lover of fantasy romance, I am obviously very fucking familiar with prophecies.

I lean forward across the café car table. "Tell me everything."

"Uh, uh, uh." She shakes her head. "What will you give me in return?"

I frown. "I have no cash. See?" I take out my wallet and turn it upside down, shaking it. Nary a cent falls out.

She lifts an eyebrow. "Venmo, then?"

"No phone."

She sighs, long and hard. "Okay, girl. Then this one's on the house. But listen carefully, as I will not be repeating myself. I will say this only once, and then the words will evaporate, never to be uttered again. Okay?"

I nod fervently, then shut my eyes, prepared to commit her prophecy to memory.

"Three men emerge from a shallow pool of damnation. One is made of tree sap and ink. The second, hallucinations and the fog of the mystic. And the third, flesh, fire, and the truth of the histories. When the squatting bird chants twice, go forth to the fallacies of your heart. Do not use your mind or your eyes to guide you. Follow the moonlight of your heart. Beware the goat dressed as a lamb. Only then will you defeat the fool and the red-painted maiden, and land in the arms of the steady tide. For what you seek, you hold in the marrow of your shrouded words."

"What the fuck does that mean?"

But when I open my eyes, the mystic is already gone.

The night of the ball, Mira dresses me in a skintight, serpentine skirt that resembles the tail of a fish. Made of brightly pigmented rainbow scales in the colors of royalty, it swishes around my ankles as I walk. Upon my bosom, I wear a similarly shaded brassiere made of thick mud pearl. It fits my curves like a corset, emphasizing the tops of my breasts and the flat of my abdomen, now toned with muscle. My thick brown hair has been braided down my back with combs of coral, and sea glass jewelry hangs from my neck and ears. Mira insisted on rubbing some kind of serum into my skin so that every time I catch the moonlight, my entire body shimmers.

For the first time in my life, I feel remarkable.

Until, that is, Ryke knocks on the door to my room.

He swims in front of me, his onyx tail strong and thick, swishing behind him. He is wearing a matching long-sleeved shirt that looks like a second skin, the material coarse, like embossed leather. It highlights every finely honed inch of him, from his pectoral muscles to the V shape of his torso, which forces my eyes to trail down his chest. His dark hair has been combed back with a material that looks slimy as squid ink, and his face is hidden behind a gold mask. A disguise, but not one capable of hiding those beautiful golden eyes, sweet as honey and bright as the sun.

When he sees me, those eyes immediately darken.

"You look…" His voice trails off.

I cannot help but blush. "As do you, my prince."

He offers me his arm, and I accept, careful not to burst my air bubble. But my core strength has vastly improved in the last few weeks. I am now able to control the direction in which I swim without popping the force field around me that allows me to breathe.

Ryke watches me closely. "I am impressed," he says.

Color creeps up my neck.

"Wait until you see me dance," I say. "I have been practicing."

I watch the muscles of his throat work as he swallows.

"I look forward to it."

As we swim toward the palace, Ryke and I review our plan. We are to enter together, two foreign travelers visiting Atlantia from a faraway sea. To avoid suspicion, we are to do our best to speak to no one. I am to resist the urge to acknowledge Dylan, Guinn, Mira, and Kai. They are known former associates of Ryke's who had to publicly denounce the royal family in order to survive. Communicating with them out in the open could put everyone at risk. We will do a round of the ballroom and dance once, after which I will create a diversion while Ryke sneaks into the throne room and steals the treasure trove. He doubts that the mer have moved the priceless artifacts from where they were laid to rest by Ryke's family, under lock and key.

Lucky for us, Ryke still has a copy of said key.

"Are you nervous?" he whispers.

His breath tickles the back of my neck and makes me shiver.

"Not at all," I lie.

Ryke chuckles darkly. "You lie so sweetly, little minnow."

The sand castle is so grand, it resembles a tiny town more than a home. Looking down at it from above, I count six towers, three of which are connected by arched bridges carved with ancient symbols I do not recognize and illustrations of mer using pronged instruments to maim sea beasts with eight tentacles and big teeth. There are spiral staircases leading between the entryways, a moat with a beautiful fountain shaped like a dolphin, and stained-glass windows made of sea glass similar to what I wear around my neck. Flags flutter above each spire, each featuring a mer with blood running from their fanged teeth.

The symbol of the siren.

"Okay, now I am nervous," I whisper to Ryke.

"Just squeeze my hand," he says. "I will not let anything happen to you."

The doors to the ballroom fly open, and we are immediately greeted by the sound of glorious music, a band of merry mer playing an upbeat melody I have never heard before on instruments I have seen only in my dreams. On the floor, pairs of mer clad in finery and riches move to the rhythm, their tails hovering above the sand-paved floors. They dance mainly with their abdomens and hips, a sensual mating ritual of sorts. Couples maintain eye contact, practically gyrating against each other, seducing one another with their movements. The sight sets off a tingling between my legs that I am not meant to have.

I press my thighs together to contain the sensation.

In the corners, mer are gathered, laughing loudly and drinking ale. I spot Dylan, Guinn, and Kai doing just that, the latter's gaze glued to the dance floor, where Mira moves in time with a mer with long auburn hair. When she throws her head back and shimmies, Kai clenches his teeth and downs his entire glass.

Interesting.

And above the dance floor sits a golden dais supporting a throne made almost entirely of reconstructed rare shells. Its painted edges threaten to cut anyone who dares get too close, but its alluring textures and colors simultaneously invite strangers in. And hovering above the dais are three menacing mer.

Not mer.

Sirens.

Ryke has prepared me for this, too.

In the center is Talassa, the false queen.

And on either side of her are Naia and Nix, her younger twin sister and brother.

At first glance, the three creatures are beautiful. Their skin is deeply tanned, as if they have spent their days sunning upon the shore instead of buried deep beneath its secret surfaces, their hair white as untouched sand. But upon closer examination, their eyes are vacant and bloodred, a reminder of the lives they took to gain their strength.

Above all, they feel wrong. As if their bodies have been poisoned, taken apart, then put back together.

I shudder as the sensation creeps over my skin and caresses my flesh.

"Do not look at them," Ryke commands. "Follow me."

The musicians are now playing a fast-paced jig that demands the mer dance as a group, divided into two clean lines. When they join forces by linking arms, they look like a blooming flower, gorgeous and organic. We approach them quietly, but the second we take our places in the lines, the music changes to something slower.

More enchanting.

Seductive.

My heart begins to race. I have never moved this way before, even in private, let alone in public. When I was married, the joining was for the sole purpose of procreating, birthing life. I have never experienced lovemaking or pleasure for pleasure's sake. When I shared my deepest desires with my husband, admitted to the fantasies I harbored and the curiosities I allowed my mind to linger on in the dead of night with my hand between my thighs, he called me a whore and refused to speak to me for a week. I have never worn my sexuality on the outside before.

I do not know where to begin.

So when Ryke locks his brilliant eyes with mine, lowers his thick lashes, and starts to move to the music, I allow him to take the lead.

We circle each other like great white sharks smelling blood in the water. Ryke juts out his chin in a silent question, and I nod, granting him permission. Then his hand is on my lower back, right above the curve of my backside, the other lightly ghosting across my collarbone. I feel all the air rush out of my lungs at once. The madness around us seems to momentarily still. And when Ryke's hardness brushes against the softness only he knows lies at the apex of my thighs, all thoughts vacate my brain.

And then he begins to move.

Slowly at first, grinding his hips against mine.

A light friction.

A tiny moan escapes my lips.

And at the sound of my desperation, Ryke growls.

His movements become feral. He holds me, practically thrusting his hips against mine to the leisurely, tantalizing beat. Our bodies join together, and we become one on the dance floor. I feel his pulse race below my fingertips, his breath lavishing my mouth. My eyes linger on his lips for a second, and his grip on my lower back tightens as if he is in pain.

"Merriah," he whispers. "What are you doing to me?"

I dare not answer, only close my eyes and allow myself to feel him. All of him. His desire flooding my senses, making me his without ever truly claiming me. The beat, a tantric rhythm of persuasion, possessing me until I have no choice but to swerve my hips from side to side, to arch into Ryke's touch, to tip my face up toward the moon and sigh.

And then there is a tiny pull.

It feels like an anchor in my chest, leading me somewhere I cannot see, only sense. An invisible thread in a larger tapestry, forming a picture I cannot yet comprehend.

The same tug that led me to the conch.

Fate is now hauling me toward the treasure trove, begging me to grasp the objects in my hands and give in to their magical properties.

The trove can control armies.

And I am destined to control the trove.

My eyes fly open, and when they do, Ryke is staring right into them. His red mouth is slightly parted, his nostrils flared. I bite my lip, and his gaze rakes over it, indicating what he'd like to do with his tongue. He reaches out and traces the bow with his fingertips.

But I know I should tell him about my revelation.

"Ryke," I start to say.

And then he swallows my voice as his mouth crashes into mine.

CHAPTER TWELVE

I must have left my wallet over here, but it's cash only anyway, so it doesn't matter," Nico mutters, sitting down across from me.

Then he notices my ashen, confounded face and startles.

"Whoa. What happened to you? Did EGC discontinue the series in the five minutes I was waiting in line to buy stale chips?"

I shake my head. "There was a woman."

"A real one?!"

"Very funny." I roll my eyes. "She was a mystic. A psychic."

"So not real, then."

"She shared a prophecy with me. It was for both of us, actually."

Nico throws his head back and laughs. "Now I know you're fucking with me."

I glare at him, scanning the other passengers, looking for a glimpse of the woman with golden bangles and cunning eyes. But the fortune-teller has seemingly evaporated into thin air. Maybe she's hiding in the bathroom a la *New York Minute* or something.

"I swear on Teymoor's life."

Nico cocks his head. "You're going to have to do better than that."

"Fine." We lock eyes, the stale air around us growing charged. "Then I swear on Ryke."

Nico's eyebrows fly up. "Shit. What was the prophecy?"

I rehash the prophecy to the best of my ability, trying my best to repeat it word for word. When I'm done, Nico's forehead practically folds in half.

"The red maiden? A goat dressed as a lamb? Squatting birds? What the hell does any of that mean?"

"Zero idea. Prophecies don't typically spell things out for you."

"Well, you're the fantasy expert," he says, scratching his chin. "Surely you have the tools to decode this bad boy."

I blow out a frustrated breath and wish for the millionth time that I had access to my fanfic group. They would have this prophecy annotated in seconds. A heroine like me isn't supposed to go through a story arc like this without her inner circle. At least I'll be with my love interest sooner rather than later. But what role does Nico play in this narrative?

"I'll think on it," I tell him, pulling my notebook from the back pocket of my purse. "Let me play around with it a little bit while I put off writing this advertising copy."

"She was probably just nuts anyway," he says. "What are you working on now? Another diaper rash ad?"

I shake my head. "Better. Anal fissure cream."

He groans dramatically, banging his head on the table like a cartoon character. "How is this even your life?"

I shrug. "Easy. I want to pay my rent with my words. That doesn't always mean writing the next great American screenplay. For me, it's raising awareness about foot fungus by day and writing viral fanfic at night."

"Have you ever thought about writing totally original stuff?" he asks. "A novel, perhaps?"

Maybe. It's not that I haven't thought about it—Tey is always bugging me about pushing myself, putting my original work out there more. "I guess it scares me," I admit. "Being exposed like that. As a fanfic writer, I get to hide behind characters and a world that aren't my own. Plus, I use a pen name. What if I create a universe and no one wants to live in it? Then it isn't just StepOnMeRyke432 who fails. It's Joonie."

Nico uses his nails to tap against my notebook as if he's knocking on a door. Asking permission to be let in. "Trying and not getting it right the first time wouldn't make you a failure, Joon," he says gently. "Do me a favor, okay? If you really don't want to write anything but fanfiction, don't do it. But make sure you aren't holding yourself back because you're afraid of not doing it perfectly and being rejected. Because the people who love you? They're going to stick by you no matter what."

I stare up at him, searching his face for a sign of sarcasm. For any indication that he's teasing, pulling my leg. I wait for him to say, *Gotcha!* or follow up his speech with a backhanded compliment. But instead, he just blinks back at me, allowing me to process his words in my own time.

Is Nico right?

Have I been holding myself back from trying to write something else all this time because I'm afraid of people abandoning or turning on me? Like my parents?

Or Sam?

Kyle?

Nico himself?

Holy hell, I need a new therapist.

"The thing is," I whisper, "I haven't let anyone read my original writing since her."

"Her?"

"Sam."

Nico looks at me for a long second, his forehead scrunched in pain.

I'm unable to bear the weighted silence for even another millisecond.

"Joon—"

"What are we going to do about Kabobs 'n' Bits?" I blurt out, desperate to change the subject. "If the bank forecloses on the property, what's going to happen to Tey?"

Nico opens his mouth to answer, then closes it.

My heart starts to hammer.

An hour and a half later, I'm still attempting to come up with the best-case scenario to soothe myself when the conductor announces that we're about to arrive at New York's Penn Station.

I wait for my heart to flutter.

For my pulse to race.

I'm hours away from meeting Ryan Mare. From looking the real-life Ryke dead in the eye, right into his very soul. After years of waiting for my happily ever after, I'm about to grab it by the balls.

But all that's on my mind are the words of the blond-haired boy who broke my heart when I was fifteen.

Nico clears his throat. "So I guess this is where we part ways, huh?"

Right. I'd totally forgotten that we only made plans to road trip *into* the city together. "You're staying in Harlem, right? With your lady of the night?"

He wrinkles his nose. "She's not, you know, a sex worker. Not there's anything wrong with sex work. But yeah, she lives in West Harlem. And your hotel is in Brooklyn?"

I nod. "Near the botanical gardens. They're supposed to be beautiful this time of year. Maybe if we both have time before we head back to Mystic, we can…"

I trail off as I feel around in my purse and come up empty.

"Wait a second." I attempt to steady the panic in my voice. "Nico, my wallet is missing."

"Okay, let's not freak out," he says, swinging his backpack off his shoulder. "You probably just left it in the taxi. Once we get new phones, we can call the motel and ask for the name of the cab company they called."

Nico yanks open the zipper of his Jansport and begins to throw objects onto the table in front of him, cursing under his breath.

"Shit. Mine's gone, too."

I suck in my cheeks. "How is that even possible?"

If neither of us have our wallets, that means we don't have a photo ID or credit card between us. We won't be able to check into our hotels, let alone buy new phones. Not to mention that we won't be able to buy any food or tickets back to Connecticut.

This is a category-four disaster.

"Are we cursed or something?" I wonder out loud.

Then something clicks in the back of my head.

"Holy shit. It was her. The psychic."

"No way," Nico counters. "You were across from her the entire time, right? How could she have stolen both our wallets when you were looking at her?"

"Well…" I bite my lip, guilty. "There is a teeny-tiny chance that, um, I closed my eyes for, like, a millisecond. To, you know, focus. On the prophecy. And committing it to memory…"

Nico gawks at me, dumbfounded. "For once, I literally don't know what to say."

The train pulls into the station. All at once, passengers get out of their seats, shoving each other aside to grab their overhead luggage and line up by the exit signs. Nico and I remain seated amidst the chaos, both of us in shock. I keep an eye out for a splash of color, the jangle of bangles, in the madness.

But Veda the fortune-teller is gone, and with her, my chance of completing my mission. Of meeting Ryan Mare. Of making it to New York and back safe and sound.

"How is it that two crazy kidnappers weren't able to take us down, but one crappy con artist was?" Nico asks with a dry laugh. "I have no idea what Nadia's number or address is. We're going to have to sleep on this train tonight."

Nadia.

I try not to let the sound of her name falling from his lips bother me.

Wait. Wasn't it *Hannah* before?

"Unless…"

"Unless?" Nico's eyes bug out as he waits for me to finish my sentence.

"How much do you trust me?"

"About as far as I can throw you."

"Well, that tells me nothing. You're very strong."

"I trust you, Joon."

"In that case, there is one address in New York that I have memorized. The apartment of a good friend. I've actually always wanted to visit but could never work up the nerve. In fact, I sent a framed fan art print of Rykiah there just last month! But there's, um, a catch."

Nico stands up and grabs his backpack, preparing to get off the train. Without asking, he grabs my duffel and throws it over his defined shoulder. The oxygen evacuates my lungs at the show of chivalry, and I attempt to get my feminism in check before it flies out of my body completely.

"Please don't tell me it's the home of one of the men you ghosted or something," he says as I follow him off the train and onto the platform.

A rat runs across the yellow line, barely missing my feet.

"Nope," I say. "It's just that we've never actually met."

Ryke's lips meet mine, and every nagging voice in my mind goes silent.

I can no longer see the bodies spinning around me.

Ryke's Upper Shoal watching from the corner of the room.

The sirens holding court on the dais.

My entire body, mind, and soul is invaded by him.

Him.

Him.

I open to the kiss like a water lily in bloom. His tongue runs over my teeth, and then he devours me whole. Worshiping my mouth, as if I am the one who belongs on the dais.

My senses are on fire. Beneath my scaled skirt, my toes

curl as my fingers find purchase on his body. Every hair on my neck rises, and my breath comes fast and hot. I submit entirely to this moment as Ryke makes this declaration of…what?

Surely not love.

But passion.

Desire.

Pure, unadulterated want.

A want that I fully reciprocate.

But our moment is interrupted by a sharp, taloned tap on my shoulder.

And when I turn around, I find myself face-to-face with Talassa.

The false queen of Atlantia.

"Sorry to interrupt," she coos. "I was so enjoying the show."

Every muscle in my body freezes. This is not part of the plan. We intended to fly under the radar until it was time for me to create a diversion. If Ryke moves, if he utters a single syllable, she might recognize him.

So I lift my mask, akin to Ryke's, and do what I did every day of my sorry marriage.

I pretend.

"Then kindly leave us to our second act," I sneer, turning up my nose. "Your Majesty."

She gasps, narrowing her eyes. "I have not seen you at court before."

I swallow the lump in my throat. "I am but a visiting sentry, my queen."

Her head tilts slightly toward Ryke. "And your dance partner?"

"My steward. A lowly mer from the swamplands."

I watch, frozen, as Talassa's bloodred eyes rake over Ryke's lips, swollen from my kiss.

"Why is he masked?" Her talons scrape the gold ornament.

I force my voice to remain steady. "A sandstorm grossly disfigured his face several years ago. And I wish to look upon only pretty things, wouldn't you?"

Her laugh is a throaty, vile poison. "Absolutely," she says.

Then she sniffs me. Wrinkles crease her nose.

"Your scent wafted all the way to my dais. It is most peculiar—ancient and foreign. Almost…human. But not entirely so."

"I have shifter blood in my lineage," I tell her.

"Hmm." She turns to Ryke. "And you, sir? Are you a shifter as well?"

I open my mouth to answer for him. "He is—"

"He can answer for himself," she snaps at me, her fanged canines breaching her bottom lip. She leans in, her lips a mere breath away from the tendons in Ryke's neck. "Can you not, princeling?"

Before I can process this turn of events, Ryke has

Talassa flipped, his forearm braced against her neck like a restraint, his other hand holding a dagger to her heart.

"Bold of you to assume I would forget the scent of your blood when I tracked it for more than a century," she snarls.

That is when I see it.

The bead of crimson decorating his bottom lip.

I touch my teeth. Did I put it there? If so, I may have accidentally ended my lover's life.

"Bold of you to speak so brazenly when my knife is at your chest," Ryke retorts.

Faster than the speed of sound, Naia and Nix are at our side, their teeth bared at Ryke. From every corner of the room, siren soldiers emerge. They are carrying green-tipped spears, painted in something that resembles the venom of a viper. Eyes as red and vacant as the queen's mar their otherwise-exquisite faces.

"You did not think you could take me alone, did you?" Talassa taunts. "Your time rotting away in hiding has clearly impacted your judgment, prince."

She says *prince* as if it is a curse.

"You did not think I would come here alone, did you?" responds Ryke with a grin.

Dylan, Guinn, Kai, and Mira drop their pretenses and line up behind us.

Kai cracks his knuckles, his sullen mouth twisting into a menacing grin.

Mira twirls her hair, as if bored by our antics.

But that is not all.

Other mer join our friends, linking arms. Members of the resistance, making themselves known to the sirens.

From what Ryke has told me, this can end only one way: with bloodshed.

"Have it your way then."

Suddenly, the water around Talassa starts to boil. Angry, tempestuous whirlpools explode, pushing everyone in her vicinity back until they are meters away, an invisible circle of protection around her.

I gasp. Are these the powers Ryke has spoken of? The special abilities the sirens gain from taking human lives? Do we even stand a chance against them?

"Do you know the easiest way to expose a false prophet?" Ryke asks, raising a brow.

Talassa only squeezes her hand closed, causing a tidal wave that strikes fear into the hearts of all the guests watching. Around us, mer flee the ballroom in terror, their tails flashes of brilliant color.

"Introduce her to her gods and watch them deny her prayers," Ryke continues.

With one brutal slap of his tail, he cuts through the chokehold of the water. Then his huge calloused hand is around the false queen's neck.

"Any last words?" he whispers.

Fighting breaks out in earnest then. The sirens' stolen

magic clashes with the mer's natural strength and finely honed skill. Battle cries ring through the air, each more high-pitched and beautiful than the last. The sound sends my body into a state of stasis. Blood begins to spill, clouding the water so that I can barely see.

I blink several times, trying to find Ryke in the fog of the fight.

If I can get to him, I can help him.

I have been training for this.

All I need to do is—

A male picks me up and throws me over his shoulder. "You are coming with me," Dylan says.

I bang on his back with my fists but fail to break free of his clutches.

"You need to find somewhere to hide until the sirens retreat."

"Ryke wants me to fight," I wail. "He has been readying me for war. The prince has given me a choice, and I choose to fight to free Atlantia."

"Are you mad?" he asks as he swims. "Do you not understand what you are? This room is teeming with sirens looking for a magical pick-me-up. If one of them realizes that you are human, your neck will be between their teeth so fast you will beg for a quick death. And if Talassa somehow discovers that the blood of Amphitrite pumps through your veins, she will destroy us. Not just you, but the whole resistance."

He dumps my body in a dark room. "Stay here."

"I can do more than stand idly by while people die," I protest.

"Fine. Then life will be your gift. I will be back for you once the battle is won."

Dylan turns to leave, locking the door behind him.

Tears immediately fill my eyes. All the air in my bubble seems to evaporate, and I feel like I can't draw in enough. My head spins as the space begins to shrink. Memories of my husband locking me in our house, refusing to let me leave, weaken my resolve like the blood of the dead mer.

I try my best to steady my breath, but it is all too much. Pictures of Ryke drained of life fill my mind. His dark lashes closed, that golden sunlight drained from his face. That strong obsidian tail limp in the sand. Wetness pricks my vision, rendering me blind.

And in the darkness, I feel it once more.

The pull.

The quiet request urging me forward. Singing to me.

Tugging me up off the floor and into the darkness.

I gasp at the realization.

Could Dylan have inadvertently led me to the treasure trove?

I follow the invisible string like a sailor's rope, and it guides me toward a heavy metal object in the shadows. My fingers skate over its ridges, discovering ancient lettering, the hard edges of gemstones.

A chest.

My eyes begin to adjust to the dark. There is a latch in the center, an elaborate cipher that I do not have the time or the language to open. My shoulders droop in disappointment. I attempt to lift the chest, but it is so heavy that even my newly muscled forearms quake with the effort. I am forced to put it down.

But then the tether between us begins to vibrate.

My entire body shakes, every organ so taut, I feel as if I am about to snap.

Take me, it seems to say. *I am yours.*

"Mine," I say out loud.

The latch snaps open.

Inside the chest are four objects.

Instinctively, I reach for the first: a three-pronged spear made of solid gold.

I expect I will struggle to lift it, but it feels light in my hand.

Right.

There's a rushing in my ears, the sound of water crashing at the bottom of a waterfall. Then a loud, violent clap of thunder sounds, followed by a blinding burst of lighting that explodes from my body. I begin to levitate above the ground, as the mer do. But I am not swimming. I am floating, tiny droplets falling from my skin.

I am a rain cloud. My tears of wrath are a summer storm.

And then it stops.

I fall to the floor with a thud, and everything goes quiet.

But the door to the room is now open.

A tall shadow appears in its frame overhead.

I point the strange spear in that direction.

"Minnow," someone says.

Ryke.

I go sprinting, the spear still in my hand, into his arms. His mask is gone, and there is a gash upon his defined cheekbone, another along the left side of his tail. He swims with a slight asymmetry, as if in pain.

"You are hurt," I whisper.

His eyes search mine, tiny embers of hope floating in them.

"You saved me," he says.

I choke on my laugh. "By hiding like a coward?"

"Come see for yourself."

He carries me back to the ballroom. The blood misting the air has now settled, painting the sand a dark maroon. There are dead mer and sirens scattered all over the room.

But the siren queen and her siblings are nowhere to be seen.

Ryke looks down at me, his eyes wide.

I realize with a sick feeling that the crown prince of Atlantia is afraid.

"Merriah," he whispers. "What did you do?"

CHAPTER THIRTEEN

The taxi pulls up to a three-story townhouse on Washington Park, a quiet, tree-lined street in the Fort Greene neighborhood of Brooklyn. A few residents of the block have already begun to decorate for the holidays, and I can see the glimmer of star-adorned Christmas trees and unlit menorahs through the uncurtained windows. Giant fluorescent snowflakes hang from traffic lights overhead, welcoming us to the community.

I take a look at the cerulean-blue door and swallow hard. "I'm so sorry, but do you mind waiting a minute?" I ask the cab driver, who grunts in response.

Nico trails behind me, holding our things in one hand and an old-fashioned paper map from a tourist information stand in the other. Navigating New York without an iPhone has proven absolutely impossible. Of course, we asked several pedestrians if we could quickly borrow their smartphones to figure out our subway route. Two didn't stop walking, one told us to go to hell, and the last spat at us.

Yep. We're definitely not in Mystic anymore.

Slowly, I make the trek up the stairs and knock three times.

No one answers.

I try one more time, a bit louder.

But I'm greeted by silence. No shuffle of footsteps on the other side of the door.

Oh well. I guess coming here was a long shot anyway.

Sighing, I turn around and prepare to tell Nico that plan B is a bust.

And then the door swings open.

A middle-aged femme with dark skin and long thick graying braids stares at me. Glasses sit on the bridge of their nose, and a fraying cardigan hangs loose past their wrists. A tiny orange cat nuzzles their ankles, scowling at me.

"Angel?" I blurt out.

They cross their arms in front of their body, pulling their sleeves over their fingertips. "Do I know you?"

"It's Joonie." I tuck a piece of hair behind my ear.

They blink at me, suspicious. As if I'm a ghost.

"You know. Um. StepOnMeRyke432."

"StepOnMeRyke432 has never shown interest in meeting up with me before," they say slowly. "How do I know it's really you and not some catfish?"

I wince slightly at their disbelief. Not that it's their fault, really. The Salty Girls have organized Skype sessions in the past, but I've always used some flimsy excuse to bail, afraid to show them my face. To make all of this real and accidentally ruin a good thing. I wanted to preserve the fantasy of friendship.

But now I'm standing here, unannounced, in Angel's doorway.

It doesn't get much more real than that.

"Let's see," I reply. "I know that you're a Pisces. Your mother's name was Shanti, but you called her Titi. And this little devil right here"—I nudge at the feline at my feet—"is Purrtha Mason."

There's a glint of mischief in Angel's eyes. But they refuse to budge. "All of that information is readily available online," they argue.

So I go in for the kill.

"I know that your favorite chapter in the ATOSAS series is in book two, when Ryke and Merriah are finally reunited and he teaches her tail play. I know you especially like it when he uses the tips of his fin to—"

"That's enough," they say, cutting me off, their wide grin finally reaching their eyes. "Joonie? Is that really you, girl?"

IMAN HARIRI-KIA

They cross the threshold and pull me into a huge bear hug. After a moment, my body melts into their softness and I exhale, all the anxiety of meeting my longtime friend in person dissipating. In truth, it feels like I've known them my whole life. The cotton of their T-shirt is butter soft beneath my fingertips. I inhale their scent, a lemon-infused, fresh-out-of-the-laundry smell. Having them in my arms feels like going through the cardboard boxes hidden away in my parents' attic and finding an old favorite.

Familiar.

Right.

"Holy shit!" they squeal. "Come in, come in! God, I have to tell the gang. We were worried you were dead in a ditch or some shit. You haven't responded to our messages for almost forty-eight hours. We thought you'd eloped with the real-life Ryke!"

"Actually," Nico says from behind me, reminding me that he's here, "any chance you could lend us cab fare? It's a long story, but we come to you on bended knee with empty pockets."

"I look forward to hearing that story, and I doubt I'll have a problem with the bended knee portion." Angel's eyes rake over Nico's body, lingering on his toned torso and taut behind before landing on his face. "And who might you be, handsome?"

Before Nico can answer, Angel sniffs me and makes a

228

face. "Oh, honey. You need a shower more than MMCs need to stop ripping their girls' panties off—I mean, honestly, do they think lingerie grows on trees? Let me take care of this taxi. Why don't you two get yourselves set up in the guest room? Freshen up, settle in, take your time. You're staying here tonight. Then you can tell me everything over dinner. Any dietary restrictions? Please don't say nuts."

"*You're* nuts." I laugh, feeling truly safe for the first time since leaving home. "That would be great. Thanks, Angel."

Nico nods. "You're a lifesaver. Can we help in any way?"

"Sure," they say. "By getting out of my sight and staying there until seven p.m. Wait, is that just dirt under your nails? Because it kind of looks like blood."

Three and a half hours later, Nico and I make our way downstairs, showered and changed. My normally straightened-to-perfection tresses are damp and curly, painstakingly combed down my back and tucked behind my ears. I'm wearing an oversize sweatshirt that says **Property of the Prince of Atlantia** and soft, worn-in jeans.

For someone who's used to performing 24-7, I look and feel oddly like myself.

Angel's house is filled with completely random objects. There appears to be no common theme to their eclectic decor except for the fact that everything here caught Angel's eye. There are deer antlers above the grand fireplace in the living room next to a vintage DRINK GUINNESS poster and one of those wooden plaques with a fish that comes to life and sings for you at the press of a button. The runner going up the wooden stairway is a red plaid, but the rugs in each room are colorful woven designs that remind me of the Persian carpets my parents had in my childhood home. Gaudy gold-framed oil portraits of Purrtha Mason hang all over the walls, and there's a room where every object is painted slime green and an old grandfather clock that plays Dolly Parton on the hour. But the pièce de résistance is the tiny library, which features Angel's massive collection of books on spiral-shaped bookshelves that look like the ancient carvings of the old mer language from *A Tale of Salt Water & Secrets*. They must have been specially made for the space.

"How do they stay put?" Nico wonders out loud.

He's dressed in a plain white T-shirt and black jeans. Ever since we arrived, he's been oddly quiet, studying me whenever he thinks I'm not looking. When I got out of the shower, I peeked through the crack in the door and caught him reading my copy of *ATOSAS* again.

He's about at the halfway point.

Ryke and Merriah are totally about to fu—

"Magic," Angel whispers from behind us.

We both jump.

They throw their head back and cackle. "Y'all are too easy to startle. Now, follow me."

Angel leads us down the hall, past a tiny kitchen with a checkerboard tile floor and all the cabinet doors removed. I inhale, basking in the scent of fresh dill and rosemary.

"I can't believe you live here!" I gasp. "I thought you were an executive assistant!"

"Oh, I am," they say with a shrug. "But my parents are multimillionaires. You know how the ends of your shoelaces have those little hard tips? My great-great-great-great-great-grandpa came up with that. I'm a total nepo baby. Attended Bernhardt Academy and everything."

I gape at them. "Do the rest of the Salty Girls know about this?"

They shrug. "Why don't you ask them yourself?"

Angel throws open the door to the dining room to reveal a long curved table shaped like a kidney bean.

And around the table, two eager sets of eyes trained on Nico and me.

A woman with a bleached bob and eyebrows throws her clawed hands over her mouth.

Next to her, a man wearing a fuchsia velvet double-breasted blazer and matching eye shadow shrieks.

"Joonie!" Pushing back his chair, he runs up to me and throws his arms around my waist; the top of his head comes to my shoulders. "I can't believe I'm finally hugging you."

I peer down at the gel coating his hair. "Kalli?" I ask.

The stunning blond vixen chortles. "That would be me," she says. "That's Roya."

He pulls back his head and gives me a bashful grin. "Roy A., actually. And please don't ask me what the *A* stands for. But you probably know us best as MERderMe71 and SoManyQueefs."

A snort of laughter sounds from where Nico is leaning against the doorway.

I just grin.

Truthfully? This isn't how I pictured them at all.

It's somehow better.

"Wait, *so many queefs*? Is that a riff on how Ryke always says, *so many questions*?"

Slowly, all of my friends turn to look at Nico.

"Who the fuck are you?" Kalli asks. Quite rudely, I might add.

"This is Nico," I explain. "Remember, I told you he was driving me into the city?"

"Your brother's best friend!" Roy cries. "Wait, but don't we hate him?"

A twinge of hurt passes over Nico's features.

Angel catches it and waves everyone toward the table. "Come now, children. Take your seats. I hope you like French mustard chicken and mashed potatoes, because that's what I'm serving tonight."

We all settle into our seats and pass around the

home-cooked dishes they have brought out. Once all of our plates are full and our mouths are watering, Angel takes their seat at the head of the table.

"Holy Furnace, bless this meal for human, mer, and maecena," they say.

My friends and I break into fits of giggles.

Nico raises an eyebrow.

"So, have you found your Ryke yet?" Kalli asks. "Start at the beginning."

"Um, no," I tell her. "We actually just got to the city."

Angel narrows their eyes. "Without your wallets or phones, looking like sad, lost puppies? Didn't you leave yesterday morning?"

This time, Nico interjects. "Well, we did take a quick pause to get kidnapped. Then, you know, we got pick-pocketed by a psychic. But we got here eventually."

Roy's eyes practically pop out of his skull. "Tell us everything. In detail. This will be incredible for my method seminar." He winks at Nico. "I'm an actor. Remember my name, pretty boy."

I start at the beginning, with our car crash in the middle of nowhere and our friendly neighborhood kidnappers. With my voice low, as if the goons might be able to hear us, I recount the call from Harry "the Hug" Lester, the garage Thomas and Clarisse left us in while they went to get drunk, Nico's misguided chivalry and misplaced bets. I pull out the notebook he stole and show them all the senseless scribbled numbers. Then I tell them about our escape to the Lonely Hearts Motel in the stolen Jaguar and the peculiar ride on the Amtrak. Finally, I end with the prophecy that resulted in our temporary poverty.

When I'm done, my friends stare at me, their eyes wide with horror. They look like I've just told them that EGC uses a ghostwriter.

"Um, okay. Main character moment much?" Kalli says. "You literally sound like Merriah training to confront the sirens at the Ball of Sinking Stars. And Nico's sacrifice to save your family's business? Sorry about that, by the way. But so swoon. *So* Ryke. And the way you escaped from your restraints? Badass. My pain tolerance isn't even that high, and I'm a freaking tattoo artist."

"And the fact that this all happened on your way to meet the love of your life?" Roy interjects. "So romantic. Ryan Mare is probably your fated mate. Your loch. This entire fucked-up quest is probably some kind of divine trial."

I beam, just as Nico shoots Roy a glare that could freeze a Flamin' Hot Cheeto.

"Y'all are ignoring the best part: the prophecy!" Angel cries. "Give it to us again, would you? You've got three of the best fantasy theorists on the planet in one room. I bet we can crack it together." My friends whip out their phones and get ready to write it all down.

There's a crash of utensils hitting a plate, causing us all to wince.

"I'm sorry, are you guys suggesting that this shit is normal?" Nico asks. "We were almost traded like cattle, and you all are taking *notes*?"

"Baby." Angel reaches out and places their hand over his. "You're new here, so I'll forgive the raised voice if you pay attention to this lesson: Sometimes the truth is stranger than fiction."

That shuts him right up.

"Now, let's hear that prophecy."

I recount from memory: "*Three men emerge from a shallow pool of damnation. One made of tree sap and ink. The second, hallucinations and the fog of the mystic. And the third, flesh, fire, and the truth of the histories. When the squatting bird chants twice, go forth to the fallacies of your heart. Do not use your mind or your eyes to guide you. Follow the moonlight of your heart. Beware the goat dressed as a lamb. Only then will you defeat the fool and the red-painted maiden, and land in the arms of the steady tide. For what you seek, you hold in the marrow of your shrouded words…* or, uh, something like that."

All three of my friends type furiously on their phones like they're taking the SAT and are concerned their time is running out.

"Well, it's obvious who the three men are," Kalli says, sounding bored. "Ryke, Ryan, and this dude." She nods at Nico, who looks disturbed. "The shallow pool of damnation is your love life. Ryke is made of tree sap and ink, because he's just words on paper. Ryan is hallucinations and fog, because he's the man of your dreams, a fantasy. And this man right here, who is obviously living and breathing, is flesh and fire. Not sure what *the truth of your histories* means, though. What's the deal with you two?"

"Nothing." I laugh lightly and take a sip of wine. The heat of Nico's gaze practically burns the side of my face. "He's my brother's best friend, like I said."

"Is that all I am?" Nico's voice wraps around my throat and squeezes. "We were friends once, too, weren't we?"

"Yes," I say quietly, not wanting to make a scene in front of my Salty Girls. "But that was before."

"Before what?"

"Come on, Nico. Let's not do this now."

But Nico pushes. "No, Joonie. I think now's the perfect time to get into this."

"Please…"

"Before what?"

"Before you stood me up and humiliated me in front of the entire school!" I snap. "Before you broke your promise. Before you shoved the one person you knew would hurt me in my face."

"Wait," he says, his eyes growing wide. "What? This is what you've been upset about all these years? That night at the dance? But—"

"But I'm delusional. I live in a fantasy and can't handle the real world, right? I am way too naïve for believing that someone like you could ever care about someone like me, is that it? Well, fuck that. You knew I had a crush on you. And I never forgot what you said. I vowed to spend every day trying to prove you wrong. And though you nearly succeeded, I will never let you kill my belief in love, no matter how hard you try."

The room falls silent. I hear my friends taking shallow breaths, afraid to make a single sound. Nico holds my gaze, his blue eyes like living flames, only brighter.

"Joonie," he says quietly. "You've got it all wrong."

"Really?" I challenge. "Then why did you do it?"

"I wasn't trying to hurt you. I was trying to protect you."

I clutch the golden spear with both hands, as if it alone holds the answer to Ryke's question. Underneath me, the muscles of his arms spasm, and he struggles to stay upright.

He is weak, I realize.

Weak—a word I have never once associated with the mer prince.

I did not see the battle play out, only heard the cries from the other side of the door, felt the energy in the palace drain as the ballroom emptied. Is Ryke injured? I scan his body for broken bones, but all I can find are those gashes. Deep enough to bleed, but not to do serious damage.

He places me gently on the ground, in an empty space amidst the dead and dying, with reverence.

"Where is everyone?" I croak.

Ryke does not respond. Instead, his eyes drift to the ancient artifact in my hand.

"Minnow," he breathes. "Do you know what you wield?"

The spear hums against my palm, thrumming with power.

"A weapon," I say. "From the treasure trove. It...called to me. From the moment I entered these hallowed halls. Dylan locked me away with the chest for my own protection, and I somehow...unlocked it. I have no idea how. It is almost as if I forced the trove to obey me. To bend to my will."

Ryke lets out a primal sound from the very back of his throat. I stir in his arms, startled. The stench of spilled guts reaches my nostrils. I fight the urge to heave.

"Dylan would not let me fight," I continue. "I tried to stay. I wanted to defend the kingdom. But he thought it was too much of a risk. I loathed feeling so useless."

Ryke's eyes flash as they meet mine. "You are anything but."

He closes his eyes for a second as he raises two fingers to his forehead in concentration. He looks as if his temples are throbbing, the room spinning.

"Merriah, you are holding the Trident of the Gods, Hippios's immortal weapon. Laced with ether, forged by the Furnace, and blessed by the spirit of the tides."

239

I look down at the weapon in my hands and frown. "It is quite filmy for such a powerful object."

Ryke throws his head back and laughs. "Only you could make light of a situation like this and still manage to bring a smile to my face." His gaze meets mine once more, and warmth starts to spread across my cheeks despite the tragic scene unfolding all around us.

"All I did was lift it," I confess. "And this current of energy just…moved through me. I began to levitate. For a moment, I even thought I might be shifting. Into a mer."

I turn away from him then so he cannot bear witness to the disappointment I know I wear on my face.

"Little minnow, you may be something much more powerful than a mere mer. No one has commanded that trident for thousands of years. It is spelled to ward off imposters. Only those with the blood of the gods in their veins can master that instrument, learn to play her most secret notes until she sings for all to hear. Do you know what that means?"

My heart pulses.

"That it is true," I murmur. "I am the descendant of the goddess of the sea. Amphitrite born again."

Even as I say the words, they do not feel true. How can this be real? How can I hold such importance in the lives of creatures I did not even know existed until recently?

He nods. "Merriah, I will not hide the truth from you. Tonight we were in danger of yielding to the sirens, who outnumbered the rebel mer ten to one. Kai took a brutal slash to the fin, and Guinn was briefly suffocated by one of the queen's whirlpools. You see, the sirens are able to control the water in certain ways because of the blood of the humans they have consumed. Talassa is the most powerful, as she continues to feed, addicted to the potency of life in death. She now possesses the abilities of a god. She can manipulate water molecules, turn liquid to ice or vapor. The whirlpools you saw earlier? That was the greatest display of her power that I have ever seen. I had heard rumors, of course, of what she could do. I am sure exerting herself to that degree left her relatively vulnerable. But even my brute strength is no match for that kind of omnipotence."

Ryke lets out a shaky breath, grimacing as he clutches his abdomen. I reach out and run a hand over his torso. He shivers under my touch, as if even the slightest pressure is painful.

"But then a miracle occurred," he says softly. "Just as I accepted our defeat, a rumble roared from the hall. It was the sound of thundering seahorse, the messengers of the apocalypse, come to deliver our fate. There was a roll of thunder, followed by a flash of lightning. Then all the waves, the elemental weapons at the queen's disposal, fell still, melted into the water we breathe as if they had never existed at all. The sirens began to turn red in the face, their bodies vibrating uncontrollably. I could not believe my eyes. Could not make sense of it. The queen and her siblings let out guttural screams and fled the palace, leaving the rest of the guard to collapse."

He gestures at the bodies scattered all around us. My eyes linger on a male siren. His bloodshot eyes are wide open, frozen in horror, his fangs bared. Just as Ryke described, his face is flushed as with fever.

"Feel his forehead."

I lean down and set the back of my hand against his face. Then I jump back with a yelp.

"He is burning hot," I tell Ryke.

His eyes dance as we did earlier that night. The memory makes my lower lip tremble.

"Did you know that the body is sixty percent water?"

My jaw drops. "Do you mean to tell me that something made the water trapped beneath their skin begin to boil?"

"Something." The corner of his mouth pulls up into a menacing grin. "Or someone."

The very blood stirring in my veins stills.

"Me?" I whisper. "You believe I burned the sirens from within? By wielding the trident?"

"According to legend, the trident had the ability to control any body of water, create water elementals, and command the tides. All at the will of the wielder." He stares down at me from under his dark lashes. "Merriah, you saved us."

"I—"

"Thank you."

He attempts to lean toward me, then groans.

"Are you wounded?" I ask, unable to bear his pain.

He shakes his head. "The battle drained me. I used the full extent of my strength, and now I have very little left. Eventually, my body will heal. But it will take time."

Panic begins to course through my veins. "But we do not have time! I have no idea how I used the trident. My actions were accidental. I do not know if I can replicate them."

"Hush, little minnow," Ryke says. "We have the trident and the rest of the treasure trove. And best of all, we have you. You have given me hope. Restored my faith. My minnow, my savior. My Merriah."

Tears fill my eyes. "I cannot do this without you," I cry. "There must be something I can do to help you heal."

He mumbles to himself, his eyes half closed.

I think back over all the information he has shared with me. The history of his people, all the lore of the gods of the sea. My ancestral claim. I remember our training, the preparations we have made for war. There has to be a way for me to help him. For Ryke to heal faster and be ready for the fight to come. For me to share my newfound power with Atlantia's one rightful ruler.

And then the riptide in my mind quiets, and all becomes clear.

When two come together to form one body, for fleeting seconds, they combine souls.

Power sharing.

I know what I have to do.

I take the first prong of the pitchfork and use its sharp edge to slice a thin line in my wrist. Red droplets immediately start to bead at the wound.

"Ryke," I whisper, caressing his cheek.

"Mm-hm?"

"I want you to kill me."

CHAPTER FOURTEEN

Even on a clear night in New York City, you can't see the stars. The buildings are too bright and blinding, lit up like Christmas trees no matter the hour of the night. Fluorescence drowns out the Milky Way, overshadows the constellations that I know hang above. Then there's the air pollution, a general fog of man-made mist. The air feels heavier here, nothing like the uplifting breeze that wafts in from the Mystic River. Back home, inhaling feels like taking a dip in the Atlantic Ocean right after sunrise—crisp and refreshing.

A constant state of renewal.

The view from Angel's roof, however, is breathtaking. To the west, I can see the tip of the Freedom Tower, lit up in holiday colors. Bridges connecting Brooklyn to Lower

Manhattan arch over the East River. Fort Greene park, stretching over several city blocks, the trees barren and the grass yellowed. New York feels almost peaceful from above. Organized chaos. I could manage a city like this if I were to lurk above it, like Merriah when she first arrives in Atlantia. Floating in an air bubble above everything.

I hear footsteps behind me.

Without turning around, I already know who it is.

Who decided to follow me after I escaped upstairs after dinner.

"Your friends are nice," Nico says.

He joins me, our hands inches apart on the railing as we look out at the city.

"They understand me," I tell him. "Angel, Roy, Kalli... we fell in love with each other when we were just pixels on a screen. They interact with my work. We theorize together. I share pieces of myself with them, details of my life that I could never trust anyone else with. I know it sounds weird, but sometimes I swear they know how my brain works better than I do. But for some odd reason, I was still...I don't know. Nervous to meet them in person? I was so worried I'd disappoint them somehow. Or that they'd disappoint me. And I couldn't stand to lose them. Not after what happened with Sam. Not after..."

The way I lost you, is what I don't say.

"So I guess I just clung to this romanticized idea of them rather than take a chance on the reality." I bite back a laugh. "Turns out they're even better in person. What a waste, huh?"

"They're your Upper Shoal," Nico says, his voice sheepish.

My response is a single raised brow.

"I've been reading. *A Tale of Salt Water and Secrets*, I mean. There are no apocalypses or zombies or anything in it, but it's not half bad. You might be onto something."

My belly does a cartwheel.

"Wow, what a compliment. Not half bad."

"Okay, fine. It's good. Really good. Great, even. I just got to that part where Merriah wields the trident from the treasure trove. The way she boils those dudes alive and they totally explode? It was fucking badass."

I can't help myself. "Even though it's a stupid romance?"

Nico's posture stiffens. When he moves to face me, his expression is solemn.

"I never should have said those things to you, Joonie," he says. "First of all, you were right. *ATOSAS* has much more to offer than people give it credit for. Than *I* gave it credit for. Yeah, the tension between those two is hot, don't get me wrong, but that's not all. I get it now. It's really a book about healing. About Merriah learning to trust herself, to master her power and understand her own strength. Her relationship with Ryke is obviously an important part of that, and I shouldn't have been so quick to dismiss it. I can see how much her story has impacted you. In more ways than one."

I pretend to be distracted by a passing plane. "Because I proved I how to escape from restraints and steal a car?"

Nico's eyebrows knit together. "Because when shit hit the fan and I fucked everything up and began to panic, you remained calm. You held me together and got us out of a bad situation. Your strength amazes me, but so does your softness. Because you and your friends sat at that table and made meaning out of that crazy vision from the fortune teller. Because you trust them even though you've never met in person before. And because you keep yourself open to the idea of falling in love no matter how many times people disappoint you. And how often cynics like me try to convince you that love doesn't exist."

My hands grow clammy. I turn to face the other direction, my back to Nico.

I don't want him to see what his words have done to me.

How much they mean.

"Why did you say that thing before?" I ask the night sky. "About protecting me?"

Nico is quiet for a moment.

"What do you remember about that night?" he finally asks.

"Everything. For years, it's played on a loop in my mind. After Sam stopped talking to me, I sank into a dark place. I barely left the house. Maman and Baba were so worried. I thought they'd bribed you, at first, when you asked me to be your date to the formal. That it was a pity invite. I mean, I knew you didn't think of it as a *real* date. But I liked you so much that a part of me didn't care. You knew that. I think everyone in town knew that."

"I liked you," he says quietly.

"Right, as your best friend's little sister. Not a potential love interest. But you said, *It's a date.* I remember because I had only ever read those words in books before, had never heard them spoken out loud. Not in person. I told everyone. Maman took me to Rochelle's to pick out a halter dress. She helped me tame my curls and let me wear red lipstick for the first time, and you know what? I felt pretty. Then I sat on the front steps at five forty-five, waiting for you—fifteen minutes early because I was that excited. I felt like I was on the precipice of something big, like my whole life was about to change. Then six rolled around. Six fifteen. Seven."

Nico looks aghast. "Joonie. I had no idea you did all that."

I gulp, hating reliving this as much I hated experiencing it the first time.

"Eventually, Tey convinced me to let him take me. He told me you were going through a hard time and to cut you some slack. He didn't have a date, wasn't planning on going. And my parents had already spent money they didn't have on that dress just to get me out of my room. So."

"So," he says. "You went."

"I went. And do you know what I saw when I got there?"

He stares at the skyline like he can't bear to meet my eyes. "Me."

"You," I repeat. "You, in the center of the dance floor. You, sloppily making out with girls left and right. You, grinding up on anything with a pulse. You were dancing with *Sam*, Nico. Sam! After everything she did to me. After you went to her parents and told them she was a bigot. She laughed at me, Nico! She saw my face fall and she *laughed*. Made fun of me for being there with my brother."

Nico doesn't say anything. He just shakes his head in disbelief.

"But it's what you said when I confronted you that really haunts me. *Did you think this was a real date? That's delusional. You're just a kid.*"

"Joonie."

"No, wait, here's my favorite part: *You're living in a fantasy. It's pathetic, Joon.*"

He lets out a small yelp.

"Like I was so silly to believe that you cared. Not only did you try to kill my faith in happily ever afters, you made fun of me for having hope in the first place."

Nico winces, singed by my words. He rubs his jaw, visibly distressed.

"God, I am so sorry, Joonie. I don't remember doing—don't remember saying—any of that. The next morning, all I could see were your eyes, how wide and teary they were. That sobered me right up. That was why I apologized to you the next day. I thought we'd put the matter to bed, that everything was okay between us after that. I was so confused when you started ignoring me. There was no part of me that realized you were still holding on to that night. But now that I know what I said, what I did to you, it all makes sense. Jesus Christ, what a fucking asshole I was."

"Yeah, well…" I huff out a breath. "You apologized for standing me up. That was it. I could have gotten over that part. It was all the other stuff that…" *Totally and completely crushed me.*

He takes a deep breath and continues. "Joonie, I never told you the full story about that night. The truth is, that was right in the middle of my parents' divorce. My dad wouldn't stop shit-talking my mother. Saying these awful crude things. Calling her names right in front of me—right in front of Tey, even. They'd been fighting nonstop. And you were this little ball of optimism, bright and vibrant as the sun. You were everything good and innocent, Joon. My parents had this perfect fairy-tale love story. And then one day, it disintegrated before my very eyes. I didn't tell you any of that. I didn't want you to know the truth, that love was just this big fat lie. I wanted to shield you from it."

"Shield me from it," I repeat, as if tasting the word for the very first time.

I wanted to protect you.

"Yes. And I knew how rough school had been for you, how mean that fuckface Sam had been. I didn't want you to miss out on anything else. My idiotic plan to take you as my date, even as friends, was meant to preserve your feelings, not hurt them."

Fake dating. Like the trope.

God, my head hurts.

"But that night, when my family split apart, something inside of me just cracked. A light went out. I'm broken, Joon. I think I have been ever since. Anyway, I drank half a bottle of gin that I stole out of my parents' liquor cabinet. I had never touched alcohol before. After that, the entire night is hazy. I sort of recall knowing I had somewhere to be but not being able to figure out where. When I showed up at the dance, I could barely remember my own name, let alone who Sam or any of those other girls were. And I sure as hell don't remember telling you that you were living in a fantasy for thinking you could rely on me or calling you delusional or pathetic. But when I woke up the next morning with a hangover from hell and realized that I'd forgotten you, I knew I needed to stay the hell away from you from then on. Because I'd let you down, and I knew I'd only continue to let you down. That's what I was apologizing for and why I thought you hated me all these years. For disappointing you, then walking away. I just didn't want to break you, too. I couldn't handle the idea of leaving you in pieces."

I say his words out loud again, this time with a different intonation. *You're just a kid.*

Nico nods. "You *were* a kid, and you deserved to be one for a little longer. God, I was such an idiot. But I was drunk and sad and angry with my parents. And you have to know I wouldn't do anything like that to you now, Joonie. I would never break a promise. If I could do that night all over again, I'd come clean to you about my family. Let you decide for yourself what you could handle."

My next breath gets lodged in my throat.

"I thought *you* had started to hate *me*," I tell him. "I never understood why you said all those things, and it broke my heart. Because you had always stood up for me. For our family. And then you stood me up instead. Confirmed all my worst fears. So I started to hate you, too. For being the first person to really let me down. All of my bullies, the people who poked fun at my appearance or my last name…I never expected much from them. But I thought the world of you."

"I never hated you, Joon," he says quietly. "Quite the opposite, actually."

When I turn around to face him once more, his eyes are wet and red. He wipes his nose with the back of his hand.

"I should have known that you were still looking out for me in your own way." I offer him a sad smile. "You really don't believe in falling in love, huh? Not ever?"

Nico shakes his head slowly, his eyes never leaving mine.

"Do you want to know why I do?"

He nods. Just the once.

"Do you remember Kyle?"

Nico frowns. "That pretentious asshole you dated for a little while?"

I bite my lower lip. "We were together for years, Nico. We lived together."

"Never liked him," he growls. "I didn't like the way he talked down to you."

"When I first got to college, I felt really lost. After being totally misunderstood by my classmates in high school and rejected by Sam and, well, you—"

"I never rejected you," he interrupts.

"Well, I thought you had," I snap back. "Anyway, in college, I focused on being the woman people wanted me to be. Blending in as best as I could. Basically just being… less. The 'right kind of girl.' And it worked, to a certain extent. That was the version of me that Kyle fell in love with. And for a while, nothing tasted sweeter than his love. Until it went sour."

Nico clenches his teeth. His narrowed eyes are seething with anger, and I can practically see smoke coming out of his nose. "What did he do to you?"

"He never physically hurt me. Well, he threw a plate at me once, but he missed. Mostly it was emotional abuse. He liked to control how I dressed, who I spoke to, where I went when I wasn't with him. It all got to be too much. I slowly started to disappear, Nico. Like I had never existed at all."

Nico clenches his fists. Then he unfurls one hand, reaches out, and places it on my cheek. Tenderly, he strokes the skin there with two fingers.

I close my eyes and lean into his touch.

He hums.

"The day I left him," I continue, "I felt the way you did—like the promise of love I'd been fed since I was a child was a lie. That I'd never find anyone who would accept me for who I was. But then I discovered *A Tale of Salt Water and Secrets*, and I realized the truth: that I'd never learned how to ask for what I wanted in a relationship or to communicate my desires. Through Ryke and Merriah, I had the revelation that men like Kyle wanted to own women, to possess them. But there were other men who saw women as their equals, their partners. And when I found my Salty Girls, I finally found community. I was no longer siloed. And I was able to ask questions openly, freely, and honestly. So I believe in love because of them. Because of EGC. And because the alternative, giving up on love, would mean accepting a world devoid of happily ever afters. And I can't do that ever again."

Nico's left hand joins his right, and he cups my face. "I hate him for making you feel that way for even one second, let alone years," he says softly. "I'll kill him if I ever see him again."

"I don't need you to fight my battles for me," I say. "I know my own strength now."

His eyes meet mine. "Of course, you do. You're a force, Joonie."

I shudder as his breath tickles the tip of my nose.

My forehead.

My lips.

"You keep talking about looking for love outside of yourself," he whispers. "But I think you *are* love, Joonie. Unrelenting, all-encompassing, pain-in-the-ass love in its purest form."

"Love, huh?"

"*A great love, one that can bring the gods to their knees and spin the Earth off its axis.*"

Holy shit. Did he just…?

Did he just quote my favorite line from my favorite book?

"But you don't believe in love." I blink up at him.

He stares at me, a myriad of emotions coming and

going, passing through his eyes like the debris of the dying stars overhead, hidden by the New York smog.

"I don't believe in love," he finally says. "But I do believe in you."

And then he kisses me.

Ryke's body tenses in my arms, his head falling back as if I have struck him across the face.

"I cannot believe," his says, looking grievously offended, "that you would dare ask me to do such a thing. That you believe I would even consider risking your life, let alone taking it."

I take a breath, then lean forward.

He flinches in response.

"My prince, listen to me," I explain. "I have a theory."

Even in his weakened state, he looks intrigued, his eyebrow rising. "A theory."

"Yes," I continue. "You told me once that the way sirens gain their additional power, their dark magic, is by seducing men, then drawing out their energy while they are joined together as one. Dimming life as they create it. Gaining strength through sacrifice."

"*Taking* life, Merriah," he spits. "Not dimming. Taking. In order for me to heal my body using that kind of sorcery, I would have to drain you of your life force while you were at the precipice."

"A human," I correct him. "You would have to drain a human."

He pauses for a second. Considers my choice of words. "Yes."

I hold my breath for a moment, then continue. "But I am not purely human. I am the descendant of Amphitrite, goddess of the sea. I command the treasure trove. Who knows what lies beneath my skin, inside my bones?"

Ryke studies my face as if it holds the secrets to the eighth wonder of our worlds.

"That may be true," he admits. "But your power is untested."

"Perhaps even a sprinkle of my life force would be enough," I say, "for you to quickly grow strong again. Perhaps I need only visit the entrance to the underworld, then return of my own accord."

He takes my face in both hands. His thumbs stroke my temples, tender and reverent. "I will not take that risk."

A flame flickers in my chest, angry and indignant. "It is not your risk to take."

"There is one thing you have not yet considered, little

minnow." His lips brush my ear, his breath tickling the sensitive skin with each syllable. "What if, once I find myself unraveled in your warmth, I am rendered mindless?"

I swallow, my mouth suddenly dry. "Mindless?"

He nods. "The sirens crave human life for a reason. When I have your very life at my fingertips, what if I am unable to stop?"

Understanding dawns.

I reach out and take both of his hands, now cold and pale, in my own.

"Ryke," I tell him, my tone firm and unwavering. "I trust you."

His eyes darken, a shiver working its way through his entire body.

"My minnow," he says, shaking his head. "That might be the biggest mistake you have ever made."

Then he leans forward and captures my lips with his own.

Light explodes behind my eyelids, so blinding that I worry the trident has caused another explosion. So vibrant that I fear I am already dead, floating in a watery grave, suspended before the heavens.

This kiss is different from the one he bestowed upon me while we danced.

There is no question, no trepidation in the way he presses against me.

Instead, his mouth devours me whole. His teeth nip at

my lower lip, his tongue running along the seam. Once it enters my mouth, we are a mess, biting and tangling and fighting for the upper hand. It is as if my training for war has prepared me for this moment: trying and failing to challenge him, then succumbing entirely.

Yielding to him, my prince. Until I am wholly at his mercy.

"Merriah," he groans, his words vibrating against my throat. "Are you certain?"

"More certain than I have ever been about anything." My fingers are greedy, combing through the dark locks of his hair with abandon, pulling and scratching like a banshee.

"You are a desperate thing, are you not?" he chuckles. "This is not exactly how I imagined our first time, my dear."

I gasp at the mental image of Ryke, sprawled out on his waterbed, touching himself to the idea of us joined in this way. "Have you imagined it before?"

"More times than I can count," he says. "But in my fantasy, you were spread out in front of me like a feast, one we could both enjoy in a leisurely fashion."

My entire body heats.

"I want that," I tell him, biting my lip. "Badly. But there will be time for pleasure for pleasure's sake once you are well."

Without warning, Ryke rips off my brassiere, the pearls

falling like teardrops to the sand-covered ground. Under the heat of his gaze, my nipples harden into two shell-like points. He reaches out and caresses them, then uses two fingers to capture each, pulling hard.

"Well, perhaps some pleasure now," he says before leaning down and nipping at one mound in his mouth.

I cry out, clawing at the second skin on his chest until it is in shreds. As I allow my head to fall back and my eyes to close, I touch every inch of skin I can find. Ryke's body is made up of hard ridges, smooth surfaces, and hard-earned muscles. He is built like a warrior, but he carries himself like a royal, the essence of composure. The mere thought of bringing that force to its knees is enough to make me rub my thighs together.

My hands drift lower, and I am surprised to find an absence of scales. In their place is an expanse of strained skin. Abs in the shape of a V point like an arrow toward his manhood. My eyes fly open in shock to find his tail gone, shifted into firm legs. And between his legs, an unspeakably large member has sprouted, seemingly from thin air.

Ryke laughs. "You did not think I would take you with my tail, did you?"

I feel my cheeks turn red.

He clicks his tongue at my bashful nature. "One day soon, minnow"—he lays a kiss in the space between my breasts—"I will teach you tail play. One day soon, I will show you the spots where my scales are most sensitive, the places between my fins that hold the key to barriers unknown to your realm. But today is not that day."

Before I can process his words, his fingers leave my bosom, moving lower over the dip of my waist, the indentation of my navel. Until finally they reach the top of the fabric sheathing my legs like a tail. We lock eyes as one finger dips beneath the skirt, running through my folds.

When he finds the wetness pooled there, Ryke moans.

"Did I do this to you?" he whispers. "Or does your command of the water extend to the high seas between your thighs?"

The muscles in my core spasm at his words. "You," I gasp as his torturous fingers circle my entrance, never quite giving me the relief I seek. "It is all for you, my prince."

Ryke's finger plunders me like a pirate, reaching the very back of my canal, rubbing against a spot in my body as soft as sea glass. I cry out as he works up a steady rhythm, adding another finger, then a third, wringing pleasure out of my body like a wet cloth.

"Too much," I choke, as his hand retreats and begins tracing slow circles around the spot that aches for his touch the most. "I cannot."

"You can." His voice is confident, cocky, and domineering.

Every bit the prince that he is.

That command is my downfall. I come apart against his palm, a tidal wave of emotion and sensation. My entire body shakes, rogue waves of pleasure crashing against my shore until I am a limbless, quivering mess.

"Look at you," he says fondly, raising his hand to his mouth and licking each finger, one by one. "Mere moments ago, you were ordering the tides, sending sirens to their knees begging for mercy. Now, you are entirely at *mine*."

"Yes," I tell him, before I can overthink it. "Yes. Yours. I am yours."

Something dangerous flashes across his face as his hands tighten on my body. "Be careful what you wish for, Merriah." He lines himself up at my entrance. "A mer like me could destroy you. And the sound of that sacred word falling from your lips pleases me a little too much."

The tip of his member teases my bud of nerves, and I let out an unseemly whimper.

"Please," I beg. "Do it. Ruin me."

And so he does.

We both watch as he enters my body, little by little, until he is seated. I look down at where we have become one and bite my lip.

"You feel…" Ryke closes his eyes. "Like mine."

Then he begins to move.

Slowly at first. Then fast, faster than I thought possible, his weakened muscles far stronger than those of any human man I have ever come into contact with. Beads of sweat start to form on my forehead, and he leans down to lick them off, groaning at the taste.

Without warning, his mouth opens, letting out a primal noise. "What was that?" he chokes. "What are you doing to me?"

"Nothing, I swear it." I sit up, alarmed.

He looks at me, curious. Then his eyes widen.

"Merriah," he says, a hint of playfulness returning to his voice. "I believe you are using your power to create— how should I put this—the most exquisite suction?"

My jaw drops. "I can do that?" I bite my lower lip.

"You are capable of more than either of us ever thought possible, my little minnow. My miracle."

With his tongue, he coerces me to release my lower lip from the confines of my teeth before sucking it into his own mouth, kissing me with animalistic ferocity. His ministrations start again, hard and fervent. I feel the whispers of another climax beginning to build in me. But Ryke's breath is growing shorter with each stroke, and I realize, to my horror, that our passion is weakening him.

Pulling back to break our kiss, I raise my bleeding wrist to his lips. "You need to drink," I plead.

He shakes his head. "I cannot. I will not risk you."

"Please." I arch into him. This time, I can feel the pressure constricting around his length with purpose, forcing his hand. He pants against me. "You will not hurt what is yours."

His molten gold eyes latch on to mine, and he nods once.

"Mine," he repeats.

Prince Ryke of Atlantia lowers his mouth to the trickle of red wafting from the skin of my wrist, darkening the water. His pupils dilate as he watches the blood float around us, clouds in a sky full of ocean. As his lips pull back to reveal his incisors, I wonder if there is a better way for us to bring me to the brink of death—perhaps for him to wrap his hands around my neck and cut off my airway as he pumps into me from below. As his lips come into contact with my skin, there is a tinge of pain, a slight sting. Then my blood starts to swim down his throat, mixing with his own, until I cannot tell where I end and he begins. And I know there was never another way. My life becoming his, belonging to him completely.

Until we are one in body and spirit.

A groan escapes me as the pain turns to pleasure. Ryke drains me—the energy in my body, the power of my muscles. The walls my husband has built around my heart. He takes it all until everything left in me clenches, pulling taut, then releases like a stream into a river.

"You are perfect," he murmurs against my wrist, full of awe, blood dripping from his chin. "Merriah, I—"

His roar of release is the last thing I hear before my vision blurs, fading to the darkness of the ocean's bottom.

CHAPTER FIFTEEN

Nico's lips gently brush over mine in a silent question. I shut my eyes and open my mouth, deepening the kiss in answer.

A groan wrestles its way from deep within Nico's throat, vibrating against my lips. Our tongues tangle together, giving and taking. Pushing and pulling. When he runs his hand through my slightly damp hair, wrapping the locks around his fist and tugging my head back to give him better access, I let out a gasp of surprise. But he devours the sound, and the quiet moans that get trapped between my lips. His teeth and tongue trail down my neck. Exploratory at first, then desperate.

"Can I touch you?" he mumbles against my ear.

"Please," I pant, grabbing a fistful of his T-shirt.

He flips us around so I'm facing the New York City skyline. My back is arched against Nico's front. I feel his hardness press against me, firm and imposing. He nips at my neck, running his hands along the curves of my body. His calloused fingers caress the sides of my breasts, the softness of my waist, before kneading the roundness of my ass. Nico lets out a little growl, cupping both cheeks before giving each one a playful smack.

"Perfect," he whispers.

"Is that right?" I attempt to tease.

Until Nico's fingers land on my breasts, giving each nipple a sharp tug.

My thoughts turn fuzzy.

"Yes, Joonie. That *is* right." He leans down to run his tongue and teeth over fabric-covered peaks. "You have no idea, do you?"

"No idea about what?"

"What you do to me. How often I've thought about this. About you."

My hands reach around, under his shirt, feeling the toned muscle there. The wisps of body hair and defined, earned lines. "Since that night in the motel?" My fingers move over his chest, down his abs. Lower.

"No." He lifts my sweatshirt over my head in one swift motion, covering every inch of the skin he finds with kisses. "Guess again."

My pulse races, my breaths coming fast and shallow.

"Oh God," I whisper as his hands migrate to the inner seam of my jean-clad thighs. "The accident? When I fell asleep?"

He turns me around again to face him. His pupils are so dilated that his blue eyes look as black as the night sky. Without breaking eye contact, he kneels before me. "Do you remember your first winter break home from college?"

He runs a single finger between my legs, from the apex of my thighs to my entrance, humming when he finds the fabric there already damp.

"Yes," I force out. "Tey said your parents were making you decide who you wanted to spend the holidays with, so you chose neither and stayed with us. I was so pissed."

He chuckles roughly, applying pressure. "No shit. When I left for college, you were just my best friend's sweet kid sister. Then years later, you walked through the door, and I kid you not, Joonie, when I saw you again, I felt like I'd been punched in the fucking throat. You marched in with all this beautiful black hair piled on the top of your head, your hands on your hips, and fury in your giant brown eyes. You hated me. Walked right past me without so much as a second look. And I was done for."

I run my hands over his silky buzzed blond head, his hair like strands of gold in the light of the streetlamps. "I promised myself that I'd act like you weren't there. Tey yelled at me for it."

"Yes." One hand undoes the button of my jeans, slowly pulls down the zipper. "It turned me on to see you get all fired up. You never gave me the time of day unless I ticked you off. So I began picking fights with you here and there. Nothing serious. Just enough to see your cheeks flush that crimson red. Like they're doing right now."

With one firm tug, my jeans and panties are pooled around my ankles. I whimper as the cool air brushes against the most sensitive parts of me.

"You've wanted me all this time?" His breath tickles my stomach. I bite my tongue so hard I taste blood. "But I was so mean to you. You were so mean to me."

"You fucking consume me, Joonie."

The stirring in my core is momentarily drowned out by the drumming of my heart.

"Tell me what you like," he whispers against my abdomen.

"Excuse me?" I've dated so many men, but not one has ever bothered to ask that question.

"Come on, Joon." He gives my ass a playful squeeze. "You're a romance reader. I know what that means. You've spent time exploring what turns you on. And that turns me on, too."

I grip his head like a steering wheel. The groan he lets out in response vibrates against my clit.

"Start slow," I whisper. "Tease me."

Nico doesn't hesitate. He leans in and parts my folds

with his tongue, not quite reaching the spot where I need him most.

"Like this?" He moans at the taste. "Fuck, you're so wet, Joonie."

He paints torturous, deliberate circles around my nerves, causing me to cry out.

"Fuck yes," he hisses. "I love that you know what you want."

His tongue circles my entrance, shallowly dipping in.

"Tell me what else you like." His eyes meet mine, heavy-lidded with lust.

"I've been looking for this. For you. You're the first to...to..."

"To what?" A finger replaces his tongue, edging its way inside me. I stifle a scream. "To make your legs shake? To make your entire body clench? Or to make you beg?"

A sliver of indignation passes through me. "I haven't begged."

"No." The finger inside of me begins to move. Slowly at first, then faster. Working up to a rhythm that I've only read about in books. "But you will."

Before I can protest, Nico adds a second finger, moving both of them against that hidden place deep inside of me that always makes me see stars. I close my eyes and throw my head back, a guttural sound leaving my throat that I don't even recognize. He continues to run his tongue back and forth over my slit, pausing to whisper words of encouragement that make me writhe. But as I squirm, a strong arm keeps my legs in place.

For the first time in forever, I don't compare the person I'm with to Ryke.

I don't think about Kyle.

In fact, I don't think at all.

There are only the sensations. Of Nico's fingers pumping in and out of me, stroking my inner walls. Of his hot tongue and lips, adding suction to that bundle of nerves. Of his racing pulse beneath my fingers, proving to me that he's enjoying this as much as I am.

"Is this real?" I hear myself whisper.

"This," he says, curling his fingers, "is as real as it gets."

And then, against my better judgment, I prove Nico right.

"Please," I hear myself say.

"Please what?" He removes his fingers entirely, and I immediately mourn the loss. "Use your words."

"Please, Nico." I shamelessly grind my hips against his face, seeking friction.

He laughs. "Please, Nico, what?"

"Please let me come, asshole," I practically bite, shutting my eyes tightly.

Then I hear the tearing of a wrapper, the sound of a zipper, and Nico's labored breaths. His hand touches my face, gently stroking my cheek. I hum as he cups my head.

"Look at me," he says softly.

He locks onto my eyes and draws in a short breath.

"Absolutely fucking perfect," he says.

And then, inch by inch, he works his way inside of me. Until the feel of him, fully seated, throbbing with anticipation, is almost too much to bear. I wiggle my hips, urging him to move, but he just stares at the place where we're joined, shaking his head.

"Hold on to my shoulders."

Then he is kissing me, owning my body, thrusting his hips in time with his tongue. And I feel so whole, so delightfully full, that I think to myself: *I couldn't write a better story than this.* Nico's hard body against my soft chest, his hands in my hair, his eyes on me. And the way he looks at me, like he cannot believe that I am here.

Like I am greater than any fantasy, any fiction.

His right hand moves between us, adding pressure, just as he nips at the crook of my neck. Suckling, and biting, then swirling his tongue to soothe the sting. Between us, his thrusts match the movement of his mouth.

My walls constrict around him.

"Where the hell did you learn that?" I manage to breathe, my eyes falling closed.

"I think it was in the fanfic where Ryke and Merriah return to the Ice Age to warn the mammoths right before—"

"Wait, what?" My eyes fly open, and my back straightens slightly, my climax building with every passing second.

"You read that fic? Before reading the source material? Wait. It was, like, a hundred thousand words. Did you read the whole thing?"

"Joonie." He kisses me on the forehead. "I've read everything you've ever written."

I detonate.

And like the skyline in front of me, I explode with a light so blinding, the city grows dark in comparison. Nico follows me over the edge, holding me through the aftershocks, kissing the top of my shoulder. He whispers to me, stroking my hair, that if tonight was the end of the world, this is the only place he'd want to be.

And later that night, when we go to sleep, I don't dream of the prince of Atlantia.

But I do dream.

When I open my eyes, I find myself sprawled out on a sand bed suitable for a king, staring at a shell-adorned ceiling and a gemstone chandelier. I hear the faint song of seagulls. The stillness of the sea around me makes me feel as if I am floating in midair, preparing to enter the heavens.

And maybe I am.

The image of Ryke devouring me, body and soul, enters my mind.

"Am I dead?" I whisper.

That is when I notice the objects lying at the foot of my resting place. A chest inscribed with ancient symbols, bearing the Trident of the Gods and the Conch of Hippios, along with two other golden objects I have yet to study. I long to hold them in my arms like newborn babes.

Real.

It was all real.

If I have not crossed over to the immortal gates, then I must be resting somewhere safe. Fort Caspian, perhaps.

And that must mean…

"My prince?" I call out. And then, quieter: "Ryke?"

A whirlpool rushes around the air bubble safeguarding me. A tail made of obsidian leather slaps against the safeguard, causing the entire room to shake. Screams sound as riptides break throughout the rest of the castle.

I draw in a sharp breath.

If Ryke's strength was incredible before, it is now unfathomable.

His body moves with an otherworldly grace, more deity than mer.

Exhaling slowly, I realize the implication of his rejuvenation.

"You were able to stop in time," I say, my voice suddenly timid. "I knew you would."

Memories of our joining flood my brain.

Ryke's lips kissing me.

Ravaging me.

Drinking from me.

I swallow and find my mouth completely dry. How ironic for a girl who supposedly controls the tides.

"Merriah," Ryke breathes. "I do not know how to thank you. The power your life force has provided me…I do not have the words for it. Not only am I healed, but I am more Herculean than ever. Furnace help me, I can move so fast that I am essentially in multiple places at once. The strength of my fist is enough to take out an army of mer. It is impossible to describe, but I feel limitless. For the first time since my family was deposed, I have true optimism. And that is all because of you." He blinks at me with incredulity, those golden orbs glowing. "You are magnificent."

I study his body some more. His senses do seem heightened. I can practically hear my blood rushing through his veins, see the organ trapped inside his rib cage throbbing. He is so utterly alive, moving with the vigor of a male in his prime.

On the other hand, I am bedridden.

"What happened to me?"

Ryke's tail folds so that he can nestle beside me on the sand bed. Immediately, my head finds the crook of his neck, and his arm wraps around my shoulders. I exhale into his chest.

"You fainted," he tells me. "After losing a lot of blood. I have to admit, we are both lucky you did. Your loss of consciousness was a jolt to my system. Your energy stuttered. It is what detached my life force from yours. I brought you here to heal, and you have been asleep ever since. How do you feel?"

"Tired," I admit. "A bit sore. I had the strangest dream that I was the descendant of some sort of sea goddess…"

He gives me a playful smile. "Now, now, my minnow. Let us not downplay it. You took out an entire army with a flick of your wrist."

I roll my eyes. "It was the trident that did so, not me."

"Do not do that," Ryke demands.

"Do what?"

"Devalue your power," he says, shaking his head. "Make self-deprecating comments. I will no longer allow it, Merriah. You may be the descendant of Amphitrite, but that is not what makes you special. Not what makes you mine."

Mine.

That single word has the ability to sink a thousand ships.

I look at Ryke and have the sudden urge to lock him up in this fortress and never let him go. To keep him here, safe from harm. I could use the trident to create deadly rapids around us, strong enough to pull even the most seasoned swimmer under. I would not have to share his attention with anyone else.

Blinking, I realize how barbaric my thoughts are. How senseless.

I raise my hand to my mouth in horror.

Did sharing my power with the prince create some kind of dependency?

I have never felt this strong a rush of possessiveness toward anyone or anything in my life. Like a starfish to coral, I have become inextricably attached to Ryke.

But does he feel the same way about me?

Has my blood made Ryke some kind of super mer and me a helpless barnacle?

He needed me to heal. To become whole once more.

I simply want him with every fiber of my being.

Those two things are not the same. What if our attraction is uneven? One-sided?

As if reading my mind, Ryke pulls my body flush against his. His hot breath ghosts across my neck, sending a shiver down my spine.

"I ought to take you again, fast and hard, to show my gratitude," he growls. "But we must wait."

"Why?" I protest, wanting that every bit as much as he does.

"We will wait until you are well, and that is final, Merriah," he says, kissing my collarbone. "I will not put you in harm's way again. Although I must say, it is a funny thing…"

"A funny thing?" I repeat.

He nods. "All this energy pulsing through my veins—it elevates every single one of my urges. My anger. My hunger." His eyes trail over my body. "My want."

My face falls. Is Ryke's desire for me fueled entirely by my energy flowing through his body? If I hadn't shared power with him, would he still be speaking to me in this manner?

Is it me he truly wants?

Or is it my blood?

"I can see now," he continues, "why the sirens convinced so many to trade their lives for just a taste."

I offer him a weak smile, but my heart nosedives to the very bottom of my chest until I am truly shipwrecked.

CHAPTER SIXTEEN

Sunlight pours through the window of Angel's Brooklyn enclave. In our hurry to get to bed, Nico and I must have forgotten to close the curtains. I let out a small groan. From the way the sun's positioned, barely peeking over the rooftops and fire escapes, it can't be later than 6 a.m.

Then all the details of last night come flooding back, destroying my brain's dental dam of denial.

Nico.

Nico touching me.

Nico touching me and feeling me and filling me—

I feel his breath, heavy against the back of my neck, before I see him.

He's partially on top of me, his arm thrown over my

waist and a leg sprawled over my thighs, holding me tightly against him in his sleep. Our night on the roof feels hazy, like a story I read when I was a child. The glow of the skyscrapers lighting our dilated pupils.

Nico's tongue against my pulse points.

My hands locked in his hair.

You have no idea, do you?

Absolutely fucking perfect.

I bite my tongue.

He had to have been exaggerating, right? There's no way Nico—grumpy, cynical, disaster-obsessed Nico—has been harboring an actual crush on me for a little less than a decade.

I mean, I would have noticed if he was.

But then again, they say the line between love and hate is thinner than a G-string.

Although Nico doesn't believe in love.

Just like that, my heart takes a back seat while my head takes the wheel. I need to be practical about this. Forward-thinking. I can't fall for Nico's dirty words or earnest promises, whispered like a quiet prayer after a few glasses of wine and some minor trauma bonding, and under the cover of night to boot. Our emotions were heightened, along with our stress levels. One night of good—okay, fine, incredible, best I've ever had, is that what you want to hear?!—sex with a man who practically brags about his commitment to not committing cannot derail my plans.

After all, Nico is here to chase some woman, not spend time with me. And I'm here for one reason and one reason only: to meet Ryan Mare. The real-life Ryke.

The potential love of my life.

Nico can't even be the love of my right now.

It's simple. Factual, even. Makes perfect sense.

So why does the idea of leaving the safety of this bed make me feel violently ill?

"Hey."

I'm startled out of my inner monologue to find those clear blue eyes staring at me. They're drowsy with sleep, slightly puffy from our eventful last couple of days, but there's an undeniable flicker of intimacy hidden in those baby blues. It's enough to make my insides melt.

"Hey yourself."

My voice comes out raspy and weird. I sound nothing like myself. Wincing, I attempt to run a casual hand through my hair, but it's knotted beyond belief after last night's, erm, activities.

"Gentle," Nico says. He props himself up on his elbow, then runs his fingers through the tangles slowly, combing with patience until my hand is free. The gesture feels oddly tender. Not what I need at present.

He gives me a cocky, triumphant grin before falling back onto his pillow.

I gulp.

"Thank you," I say. "Look, Nico. Last night was—"

"A revelation?"

"I was going to say satisfactory," I snap, unwilling to feed his oversize ego.

"Sure you were." His fingers dance up my neck, massaging my left shoulder, then my right. "You know, you're a lot less prickly when my tongue's between your legs."

My cheeks instantly heat. "Say one more word, and I'll cut off said tongue and use it as a bookmark," I grumble.

"Kinky," he says, winking.

Before I can get the last word, he grabs my torso and pulls me down until my chest is pressed against his own. We collapse back onto the mattress, soft and warm from our sleep, and he peppers my body with sweet, featherlight kisses. Against my better judgment, I giggle and exhale. Allow myself to enjoy this fleeting moment of bliss before my quest continues.

"We should really get going," I whisper, just as Nico nibbles on a particularly sensitive spot behind my ear.

"Oh yeah?" He laps at the spot, soothing the bite. "What's the rush? Does Angel host a leftist Pilates class here in the mornings or something?"

"Well, no." I swallow a laugh at that visual. "But I was planning on catching Ryan Mare outside his office. I figured I might show up before he starts work today. Intercept him and say hi. Introduce myself. Something like that."

Nico's body freezes. His hands tense so much, I worry they'll leave marks on my skin.

"You're not serious," he says. A statement and a question.

"Angel is lending me a couple hundred bucks, and Roy has a burner phone for some reason that he said I can use. It should be enough to last me a couple of days, then get us both back to Mystic. Unless, of course, it's love at first sight, and Ryan and I plan a shotgun wedding…"

I expect him to laugh.

Snort, at the very least.

He does neither.

Instead, he stares at me, blank-faced.

Waiting for me to add something.

A *Gotcha!* or a *Just kidding*.

Anything.

But I just lie in his arms like an idiot, blanketed by the silence.

"Okay," he finally says. "I'm going to take a shower, and then we'll go."

"Wait—"

But he doesn't wait. He practically throws off the comforter and stalks toward the bathroom, head hanging low, avoiding my gaze. He moves so fast that I hardly have time to appreciate his naked body in the daylight, all those firm lines and taut muscles. The trail of light hair leading down his abdomen.

I swallow, my thoughts transforming into that of a pre-pubescent boy.

Stop it, I chastise myself. *This is Nico. Nico!*

He showers for about five minutes, then returns to the room fully and unfortunately clothed. Gone is the low-slung towel from the motel, the playful look in his eyes. Was all of that intentional? An attempt to woo me?

Have I been so blind to Nico as a love interest that I've failed to consider him as a leading man?

Without so much as glancing at me, he begins to throw items into his backpack with so much force, you'd think his deodorant owed him money. When he gets to my copy of *A Tale of Salt Water & Secrets*, he looks down, face strained. Then he turns around and throws it at me.

"Here," he snaps with a glare. "I don't need this anymore."

"You didn't finish it," I say, scrambling to recover the book.

He doesn't respond, just keeps packing.

"Hey," I say to his back. "What's your problem?"

"I don't have a problem," he grumbles. "Drop it."

"You're obviously angry."

"And you're obviously delusional!"

My jaw drops; I'm taken aback by his aggression. Nico knows exactly how to get under my skin, but he rarely blows his lid at me like this. He normally wouldn't dare.

"You knew why I was coming here," I say slowly. "I've been up-front with you from the jump."

He drops his face into his hands. "I know."

The words come out muted against his palms.

"And you said you were okay with it," I continue. "That it was none of your business—"

"That was before!" He waves his hands around in the air.

I blink several times, caught off guard by this display of emotion.

He sighs, then lowers himself onto the bed. "Look, I'm sorry for yelling. I shouldn't have lost my temper like that."

"It's okay," I say. Then I take a deep breath. "Nico, last night was fun—"

"Fun?" He laughs haughtily. "Hockey games are fun. Ferris wheels are fun."

"But we both know that we're looking for different things," I continue. "I want to fall in love. Nail-biting, toe-curling, knock-you-off-your-feet love. And no matter how"—I don't have the words to describe what being with him in that way was like—"*special* last night felt, we both know you can't give me that. I need to hear the words. I need to see the actions. Feelings, sensations—they're not enough. It has to be…well, you know."

"Real?" His voice is back to that cold, distant tone.

"Yeah." I swallow. "Real."

"That's your problem, Joonie. It always has been. God, I feel so stupid. You're so focused on the image you have in your head that you miss what's right in front of you."

He laughs half-heartedly. "You say you want something real, but you're still living in a fantasy."

His words hit me like an anvil.

Just like that, I'm transported back to high school. I'm standing in that gymnasium, staring at Nico as he looks back at me with hollow red eyes. Holding Sam's hips flush against his, head hanging low. Reeking of gin and smoke and bitter regrets.

I wasn't enough.

I'm never enough.

When I look back up at Nico, my eyes are brimming with unshed tears. Instantly, I see the regret on his face, in the lines on his forehead.

"Shit, Joonie," he says, shaking his head. "I shouldn't have said that."

"You better go," I tell him. "That girl will be wondering where you are."

His eyes linger on me for a second.

Then he nods curtly, grabbing his backpack. With his hand on the doorknob, he turns his head a quarter of an inch back so that I'm in his periphery. Some taped-up, badly glued together piece of me cracks.

"I hope you get your happy ending," he says.

And then he walks out the door.

CHAPTER SEVENTEEN

I hate third-act conflict.

"So, as you can see, dear comrades," Ryke says, "with the combination of my enhanced strength and Merriah's considerable power, we might actually be able to stage a successful coup against the sirens. We will have to be methodical, of course. There is no room for error. But for the first time in ages, there may be hope."

He is speaking to a room full of mer rebels, who are eyeing me with raised brows and upturned noses, barely able to mask their doubt and disdain. We are gathered at Fort Caspian, no longer afraid the sirens will discover us after the exposure of our forces at the ball. The entrance to the castle is heavily guarded, although Ryke is certain the sirens will not strike again so soon. He claims that I caught them off guard with the trident. The queen will need time to recover and plan her next move.

"Commander Kai will come up with our battle plan," Ryke continues. "We shall make our move in a fortnight." He nods to Kai, who is seated to our left, along with Mira. Dylan and Guinn are perched on our right, watching the crowd carefully. Together, we appear powerful, the last stand against tyranny.

Nobody knows that my bowels have turned to liquid and not even the trident has the power to stop them.

"Forgive me, Your Highness," a white-haired mer with a long beard and frown lines interrupts. He points one long crooked finger at me. My stomach churns in response. "But are you suggesting that we put all our faith in a mere human? She is not our kind. Most of us have never once spoken to or even seen a human woman before. She can barely swim. How can someone so ordinary be our salvation?"

My hands start to shake.

I have similar reservations myself.

"That *ordinary woman* you speak of," Ryke snaps, "is the descendant of the goddess Amphitrite. All the potency of the ocean runs through her veins. She saved me from death, anointed me with her power. And you all heard the warning call of the ancient conch, felt the wave of sovereignty that rippled through our waters when she wielded the golden trident. She alone can command the trove of the gods."

I feel my face flush as the warmth of confidence explodes in my chest.

Ryke believes in me.

He trusts me.

He may even love—

"And she can command the trove at will?" the white-haired mer asks, smirking in my direction, one eyebrow cocked.

Ryke's eyes narrow. "No, Enochlo," he says. "Not exactly."

I swallow.

Earlier today, Ryke and I tried to test the extent of my power over the trove. I caressed the golden spear, closed my eyes, and tried to focus on my gifts. But nothing happened. I bit my tongue with concentration until it bled. Ryke insisted that I had not disappointed him, but I knew better. I saw the flicker of worry in his eyes.

"It appears that Merriah can only command the trident when her emotions are...heightened," he says. "Luckily, war tends to activate even the most passive sensibilities."

My stomach twists.

Heightened emotions.

The fear of losing my beloved to the murderous sirens.

The passion of being consumed entirely by the rightful ruler of Atlantia.

I think of the way my insides contracted around him and squeeze my thighs together.

"And what of the trove's other items?" the mer—Enochlo, some sort of noble—continues. "Have you confirmed that they answer to her and only her?"

Ryke clenches his fists. I can tell that he is only seconds away from losing his patience.

"Not yet," he grits out. "But we will. Soon."

I nibble on my lip. Perhaps Enochlo is right.

But perhaps not.

The other two items in the treasure trove, a dorsal fin carved with mysterious symbols and a golden whip, have thus far proved ineffective. When I held them, I felt no obvious pull, like I did when I somehow knew to lift the conch to my lips. Power surged through my body the moment I set eyes upon the trident.

Ryke insists that when the time is right, I will know what to do with each item.

I am not so sure.

"Pathetic human," Enochlo practically spits. "Can she even shift?"

My heart sinks. If only this mer knew how badly I wish I could do just that. But alas, the ability to grow a tail has thus far eluded me. My bloodline must be too diluted.

Out of the corner of my eye, I see Ryke open his mouth, prepared to take down Enochlo once and for all with his clever tongue. But it is Mira who stands before he can speak. Who looks the older mer directly in the eyes and says, "I would think twice before further insulting a deity of Atlantia." Her voice is ice cold, merciless. "Some might see it as sacrilege."

With that, Enochlo is silenced.

Ryke speaks again. "I have seen the strength of the almighty Merriah firsthand. Even without knowing the truth about our kind, she was summoned by the conch. Heard its ancient melody and felt possessed to blow it. The night of the Ball of Sinking Stars, when I was ambushed, Merriah single-handedly gutted the intruding sirens by boiling the very water inside their bodies. Her tidal waves and whirlpools outmatched those of the false queen Talassa. Where our fake sovereign draws her power from bloodshed and carnage, our goddess pulls from her birthright and her destiny. The sirens develop their abilities by killing humans. But Merriah wants only to save our race. She healed me with her energy, the natural potency of her life force, and kept me from dying, even when I brought her to the very edge of the afterlife. But those are not the main reasons you should put your faith in her."

I can barely breathe, can barely see. "Are they not?" I whisper.

He shakes his head, a smile playing at the corners of his mouth.

"No, my minnow. The people of Atlantia should rally behind you because you showed them kindness before they did anything to earn it." He turns back to face the crowd. "She was prepared to join our cause before she had any knowledge of her connection to Amphitrite. After surviving so much darkness in the human world, her spirit remains light and hopeful. She is every bit as much a queen as I am a prince. And only she can stand by my side as we liberate our people."

Then the crown prince of Atlantia sinks down on one knee and bows his head to me.

Dylan follows suit.

Then Guinn.

Kai and Mira.

Even Enochlo.

Before I know it, the entire room is bowing to me. A human woman.

I want to shout at them to rise. Urge them not to place their faith in me.

The pressure crushes my shoulders, my back, my mind.

What if I lead thousands of people to the slaughter?

I am no demigod.

I am just Merriah.

When I try to catch Ryke's gaze and silently communicate my panic to him, I find him already staring up at me.

Only he is not trying to look me in the eye.

He is studying my wrist. Seeking out the marks left by his teeth as he sucked the life force from me. As he claimed my energy when we became one.

Fantasizing about my taste.

Suddenly, I feel as if I might be sick. Ryke looks at me

with concern, and I know my face must have turned pale. But the truth settles over me like a strong current.

Ryke does not love me as I love him.

He is simply addicted to my power.

And I know then, looking out at the people I am meant to save, those who have pledged their allegiance to me, that I have to run.

CHAPTER EIGHTEEN

After a long, tearful goodbye with Angel, during which I may or may not commit to reuniting at a ski chalet in Zermatt (I can't ski) and a Sub-Saharan African safari that would require three new vaccines (I'm afraid of needles), I gather my belongings. As I pack my bag, I notice that Nico left a small notebook under his side of the bed, the very bed we shared just last night.

The ledger. It must have fallen out of his backpack when he left in a hurry.

Without thinking twice, I slip what feels like illegal cargo into my purse and embark on the next phase of my journey.

Armed with my brand-new, friend-provided

MetroCard, I descend the subway stairs, doing everything I can to focus on the image of Ryke that I have in my head and *not* the feeling of Nico's strong arms pushing my body down into the mattress.

Or the look of hurt on his face when he said I was still living in a fantasy.

Or the way something fundamental splintered inside me when he turned his back on me and walked away.

But you know what? Good riddance! Why should I care what a suddenly sweet-tongued Nico is doing? Or, you know, who he's doing it with? We spent one night together. Our tryst was merely a chapter, a footnote. Every romance protagonist needs a misleading blond-haired love interest before she finds her soul mate. Granted, they're usually patient and agreeable. Golden retriever boyfriends. Sunshine and roses. Everything Nico is not— and never has been.

But that's, you know, beside the point.

I just hope it isn't awkward the next time I see him at Sunday dinner.

I'm still mulling over these details as the train pulls into Grand Central and I scurry off with the rest of the commuters. It's still early enough that New York is hazy with a soft golden light. People are lugging their sleepy, sluggish bodies to the office in anticipation of their first cups of coffee. I take a moment to appreciate the ceiling of the terminal. Painted in a chipped bright turquoise and adorned with gold embellishments, Grand Central boasts an astrological skyscape featuring several Grecian constellations: Aquarius, Aries, and Cancer, along with Orion, the hunter, and Pegasus, divine stallion of the gods, sired by Poseidon, horse god of the sea. The latter reminds me so much of Ryke and Merriah.

Ryke.

Furnace help me. After years of obsessing and pining over my book boyfriend, I'm about to actually meet the man who inspired the myth. The legend. To shake his hand and feel that strong, calloused grip. To look into the golden orbs of his eyes.

Suddenly, nausea overtakes me. I run to a nearby trash can in case I actually hurl.

What if Ryan Mare doesn't like what he sees?

Will he think I'm too much? Too loud? Too different?

Pull yourself together, Joon, I hear Nico whisper in my head.

You're a force.

You are love.

I swallow, rolling my shoulders back and holding my head up high. Imaginary Nico is right. I have to do this, to see this through. If I turn around and give up now, I'll always wonder: *What if?*

According to the ancient iPhone Roy lent me, Ryan Mare works in a glass building on Fortieth Street and Park Avenue, one of those gauche new towers that takes up an entire city block and ruins the New York skyline. There's a hideous sculpture of a twelve-foot-tall pink balloon animal parked right in the middle of the lobby and turnstiles that remind me of going through security at the airport. The structure is cold and sterile, like the rest of the office buildings in the area.

Nothing like the warm charm of Mystic.

I station myself across the street like a certified stalker, sitting on the unassuming steps of a beautiful Gothic church, next to a Nuts 4 Nuts cart and a horde of pigeons. I'm nursing a one-dollar coffee in a paper cup that resembles a Greek ceramic urn and claims to be happy to serve me. I take this second nod to the Greek gods as a sign.

There's no doubt about it. This is what I'm meant to be doing, where I'm supposed to be.

So I sit and wait for Ryan Mare.

I flip through a few pages of a discarded old copy of *Vinyl* magazine before I get bored and check the Salty Girls group chat instead.

No Ryan Mare.

I take out my copy of *A Tale of Salt Water & Secrets* and start rereading my favorite passages, but my heart sinks when I see the indents where Nico dog-eared pages while he was reading. I put the book away.

Still no Ryan Mare.

I read an article by Rose Aslani about socialite grifter Poppy Hastings's recent escape from prison and their search for Aslani's missing partner, then a newsletter by my favorite writer, Noora, about Bernhardt Academy, the secretive school for nepotism babies that Angel mentioned they attended. Then I notice that the battery on my borrowed phone is dangerously low, and I have the horrifying realization that I forgot to ask for a charger.

Did I miss Ryan Mare?

At this point, it's almost noon. I've been sitting outside his building like an anxious-attached freak for so many hours, it's almost time for lunch. My stomach growls, and even the burned smell of the nut cart is starting to seem slightly seductive. Did Ryan call in sick today or something? Does he work from home? Did I get the address of his workplace wrong?

Or, worst of all, did I misread the signs?

I'm about to get up and trek back to Angel's apartment in defeat when the double doors fly open and a man exits the building in a hurry. His head turns ever so slightly, and I make fleeting, mindless eye contact with a familiar face. It's not actually familiar—I've never seen this man before in my life—and yet I know every single one of his features intimately.

Black hair, so thick and silky it almost looks wet, falls around his head and into his eyes, flirting with his long lashes.

His ironed white button-down hugs a well-defined

torso, powerful muscles, and the promise of veined fore-arms, all sculpted to perfection and primed for a fight.

His sun-kissed skin, a glowing tan color that makes no sense given the crisp fall air, shimmers in the late morning light.

A whisper of small indentations in his cheeks.

A strong jawline that could cut the glass of the building behind him.

And two hazel eyes, so bright they're practically blinding, so vibrant that I swear they contain flickers of molten gold.

My breath catches in my throat.

Holy shit.

Ryan Mare does not just look like Prince Ryke of Atlantia.

Ryan Mare *is* Prince Ryke of Atlantia.

My dream man. The subject of so many late-night fantasies. I've written thousands of words about the scar on the inside of his left wrist. I've bonded with friends over theories about which way his tail curves (I'm a right truther). I've broken up with countless men because they didn't measure up, in body or mind or soul, to the standard that this character set for me.

And now he's standing in front of me in the flesh.

All that's missing is an obsidian tail.

"Hi," I whisper under my breath.

Of course he doesn't hear me. Not only is he all the

way across the street; he's quickly weaving through the crowds, clearly in a hurry. Maybe to save the world from a dark unknown force. Maybe to grab lunch.

I wait for it to set in: the unbelievable feeling of rightness, permeating my skin all the way down to my bones. A clenching spasm in my gut and a lightness in my head. Shaking hands and sweaty palms. A pulse in my core. The unmistakable telltale markers of love at first sight as they've always been described to me in books.

But like the ancient, mythical maecena, it never comes.

All I feel, once the shock settles, is a sense of nostalgia. Of déjà vu. It's as if I've spied an old childhood friend with whom I've lost touch or a family member who has been exiled from Thanksgiving. Seeing them again is surprising—comforting, even.

But it doesn't send a tingle down my torso or make my breath catch.

Can this be it?

Could years of waiting for the perfect man culminate in such an anticlimactic moment?

A wave of panic washes over me as a new disturbing thought sets up camp in my brain: *What now?*

But you know what? No. I refuse to let this be the end of my story with Ryan Mare. I need to get closer. To engage him in conversation and hear the deep rumble of his voice. Maybe then, our bond will kick in.

My heart will recognize what it's been missing.

What if your heart has been whole all along? Imaginary Nico asks.

"Shut up," I mutter to absolutely nobody.

It's decided, then. I need to see this through.

Love at first sight is an overrated trope anyway. Who the hell likes reading instalove?

Resolute, I collect my things and follow Ryan Mare down a quiet side street before I can change my mind.

I wait until Ryke, his Upper Shoal, the rest of the sentries, and I have retreated to the main dining hall for dinner.

By the time they are on their second or third cups of ale, raucous laughter reverberates off the sand-papered walls, and someone plays the opening notes of a war ballad. This is when I excuse myself to my chambers. But instead of retreating to my waterbed and continuing to recuperate after my brush with death, I look behind me until I am sure I am not being followed, then slip out of the fort. Before I do, I grab the dorsal fin, the smallest and lightest item from the trove, and nestle it beneath my skirt. Then I swim as fast as my legs can carry me, as far as my air bubble can afford. Past the moat, away from the big pearly gates. I am not thinking clearly, moving without a plan of action.

All I know is that I need to get out.

Out of the palace. Out of the ocean.

I need to be somewhere I can finally breathe.

I cannot be molded into the mer's secret weapon. Not when I have barely begun to step into my own power, to understand my own strength as a human woman with the blood of a goddess, a sea ancestry. I have no idea what I am capable of and cannot fathom finding out for the first time on a battlefield.

Not that anyone has asked for my opinion.

In the eyes of the mer, my command of the treasure trove is a sign from the holy Furnace and its Fates. This fight is my destiny, regardless of whether I choose it for myself.

And Prince Ryke...my Ryke...

He may believe he loves me. Truly, down to his very bones.

But I know the truth.

I was willing to sacrifice everything, to forfeit my life, to help him regain his strength.

That is love.

I love him, body and blood and soul.

But he does not love me. He is merely confused. What he actually hungers for is my life force. He craves more of my energy. I saw the way he eyed my wrist, my neck, my veins, even as I searched for his eyes. The sparks between us must be the result of some kind of pheromonal release in the aftermath of our joining.

The only thing that I cannot account for is the tender way he held me. Declared me his. Looked at me with such adoration, so much worship, that I felt myself every bit the deity his people have declared me to be. I wanted to become the person he saw. To be worthy of him in that way.

What is that if not love?

But I was suffocating inside those walls. Even now, I feel the water all around me, ready to rush into my air bubble. I need to get out. To think. To let myself feel everything clearly, precisely.

I rush through the sand banks of Atlantia in a panic, not bothering to hover overhead, not caring whether I am seen. I fly by the theater where I first learned the truth of who Ryke is. Crowds of mer and merchants part as I move with agility and precision, a form of chaos upheld by the graceful movements of these great underwater beings. I care not. After the day I have had, my unhinged behavior feels like an outlet rather than a cry for help.

Turning into a side alley by the market, I find myself at a dead end. I sigh, turning around, when I hear the water rumble behind me.

"We have been looking for you," a voice says. "Did nobody tell you never to swim alone at night?"

And then everything fades into darkness.

When I come to, I have no way of telling how much time has passed. It could be minutes or days. My body is bound to a chair with rigid sea kelp and sailor's ropes, and I am in some kind of dark cavern.

"Good, you are awake," says the voice I heard on the street.

Nix, the false queen Talassa's younger brother, inches toward me. His bloodred eyes trail over my restraints with cruel delight. His white hair seems to glint, though there is little light in the cave.

"Here I thought kidnapping you would require some effort," he croons. "Imagine my surprise when the human heroine of the mer was spotted fleeing from her protectors, alone in the streets of Atlantia without even the magical items from the treasure trove to protect her."

He inches closer to me, his beautiful tanned skin smelling of rotting fish. "I owe you a great deal of pain. After all, you filleted my most seasoned marksman with a mere flick of the wrist. How do you plan to fight back now without your precious trident, my dear?"

I open my mouth to respond, only to discover—to my horror—that it has been sealed shut with some kind of gooey ink, the kind excreted by a squid.

I am trapped.

Despite all my training, my power, my abilities, I never stood a chance.

The sirens have abducted me.

It was never going to be a fair fight.

And now they will kill me before the coup even begins.

I will never learn the extent of my powers.

I will never discover whether I have the ability to shift.

And I will never get to tell Ryke that I am desperately in love with him.

Against my gag, I let out a small whimper.

Nix smiles at the sound, his teeth jagged and sharp as claws. "Let us begin, shall we?" he says. "When does the Prince of Atlantia plan to strike?"

I shake my head vigorously, unable to answer. If these are my last moments in this world, I will spend them with dignity, protecting those whom I have come to love. Kai and Mira. Dylan and Guinn. All of them.

I will take their secrets to my watery grave.

Nix raises a brow. "Very well, then."

He pierces my air bubble.

Water pours in, filling my shield from the bottom up. I pull violently against my restraints, attempting to move. If I can stand, I can hold the water off a moment longer.

But it is no use.

The water is pooling around my calves.

Soon it will be at my waist.

And after that...

"Allow me to ask you again," Nix muses, humor in his voice. "When does the Prince of Atlantia plan to strike?"

The water is at my neck now. I am gulping down all the air I can. Why did I not spend more time practicing holding my breath when I had the chance?

And that is when I realize the siren's true aim.

But it is too late.

All I can do now is close my eyes and pray for mercy as Nix begins to waterboard me.

CHAPTER NINETEEN

I follow Ryan Mare to an American restaurant in the East Thirties, careful to stay ten steps behind him, in constant fear of being caught. The entire walk, he speaks quickly into a wireless earpiece, punctuating his words with cackles and exclamations of "My man!" When we reach the door of the eatery, he checks the time on his phone. Satisfied with what he sees, he strolls in and waves to the hostess, a robust woman in her thirties whom he calls sweetheart. She blushes as he takes a seat at the bar and orders his what he calls his usual: a pint of beer and a Caesar salad with extra chicken, no anchovies.

A few minutes later, I take a deep breath and enter the restaurant after him.

The hostess greets me, color still staining her cheeks. "Table for one?" she asks, peering behind me.

I shake my head. "Any chance I can grab a seat at the bar?"

She hands me a menu, a knowing smirk playing on her lips. "Good luck with that."

"Thanks." I wink at her. "I'll need it."

But despite my false air of confidence, my palms are sweating.

Breathe, Joonie.

You've got this.

But holy shit.

I'm about to meet Ryan Mare.

My Ryke.

This is the moment. The one we might someday tell our children about.

I slide onto a stool next to him, smiling at the bartender in an attempt to mask my discomfort. He asks me if I'd like a drink, and I open my mouth to request a Shirley Temple, but instead I hear myself say the word *Chardonnay.* I guess my subconscious needs a little bit of liquid courage?

And besides, Ryan Mare is drinking at noon on a random weekday. Why the hell can't I?

The bartender pours my wine while studying me, but my eyes are glued to Ryan Mare's profile. The movement of his Adam's apple as he swallows down his IPA, the gold pendant that hangs from a delicate chain around his neck, the flex of his jaw as he checks his phone.

All so familiar, yet so novel.

Ryke.

I'm working up the nerve to say something to him when the waitress interrupts. "What do you want?" she asks, her tone a bit clipped.

"Um."

To fall in love.

To meet my soul mate.

To know that I'm worthy of a happy ending.

"Tuna club, please?"

"You got it."

She briefly gawks at Ryan Mare before scurrying off into the kitchen.

I turn my attention back to Ryan. If I was writing our meet-cute, how would I want it to go? Maybe I should accidentally knock over his glass (*Silly me, I'm so clumsy!*), apologize profusely, then offer to buy him another round.

Or maybe I should pretend to get a distressing phone call, burst into tears, and let him comfort me, wrapping one strong, muscled arm around my shoulders. And when I blink up at him through wet lashes and we lock eyes for the first time, I'll allow my breath to stutter. Later, I'll tell Tey and Ollie that he stole it away.

He could reach over and steal a fry from my plate when I'm not looking.

I could "accidentally" burp loudly and pretend to be embarrassed about it.

My phone could die, forcing me to ask to borrow his charger.

I shake my head. Why am I allowing myself to play out scenario after scenario in my head instead of just experiencing life firsthand?

Why am I *like* this, writing fanfic about myself in my mind instead of leaping off the page and making something happen?

"If you keep your mouth open like that for too long, you're bound to trap a fly," says a deep, throaty voice.

When I turn my head to the left, I find myself tumbling headfirst into golden headlights.

Ryke.

I immediately attempt to shut my mouth, swallowing my own tongue in the process, which sends me into a coughing fit.

"Now, now," Ryan Mare says, patting my back. "Water or wine?"

Ryke would say, It's your choice, I think to myself.

"It's your choice," Ryan Mare says.

I blink at him.

That was…eerie.

"I'll stick with my wine, thanks," I say, taking a big gulp to quell the oncoming hiccups. The drink tastes smooth, but it burns my throat.

Ryan Mare watches me, amusement spreading over his face. The corner of his mouth tugs upward in the exact way Evelyn G. Carter mentions more frequently than necessary.

I extend a hand. "I'm Joonie."

He takes my hand and shakes it, firm and strong. His palm is as rough as it is in fiction.

"Ryan," he says. "What brings a girl like you to a shitty tavern in Midtown, Joonie?"

I followed you here.

I traveled all this way to meet you.

I am hoping you'll sweep me off my feet.

"Just grabbing lunch," I say instead. "And what about you? Do you come here often? Do you work nearby? Are you meeting someone?"

So many questions, I think.

"So many questions," he says.

Whoa.

Every mannerism, every movement, is exactly like Ryke's.

It's honestly a little creepy.

He grins, his teeth white with elongated canines. Like he could drink from my wrist.

"Yep, I come here once a week. Truth? It's my hidden gem. Best salads in Manhattan. Asnd yes, I work a couple of blocks away at an environmental start-up called JUS. And yes, I'm meeting someone."

You.

"You."

I smile back at him, but somehow, it doesn't reach my eyes.

That line would have read *great* on paper. But in person, it feels a bit…lackluster?

"So, how does a pretty girl like you know about my best-kept secret?"

He does a slow scan of my body, from the curve of my waist to the swell of my breasts. When his eyes land back on my face, those golden orbs are swirling with mischief.

I wait to feel my pulse quicken.

Instead, I feel nothing.

"I'm on an adventure," I disclose, taking another sip.

"Is that right?" He runs a hand through his dark hair, mussing it slightly so that it falls perfectly into his face. "So mysterious, little Joon. But I'll crack you soon enough."

Little Joon.

He might as well have called me almighty Merriah.

But…Ryan Mare has no idea who I am. He has no idea I'm an avid reader of *A Tale of Salt Water & Secrets.* I mean, I'll tell him eventually.

Probably.

But this? This right here? It isn't an act. This is just who Ryan Mare is. It's uncanny. EGC captured him down to the very last detail.

I shiver.

"So, an environmental start-up, huh?" I break the tension with a question. Not that Ryan Mare noticed any tension. He's shoveling forkfuls of salad into his mouth, that intense stare glued to me. "You planning on saving the world, Ryan?"

I keep my voice light, full of flirtation.

But Ryan Mare doesn't pick up on that. Not at all.

"Absolutely," he says earnestly, his golden eyes growing wilder. "There's nothing I care more about than protecting our world, this planet we've been gifted. Where I come from, flooding and mudslides have ruined our land, destroying houses and tearing loved ones apart. I was eight years old when I lived through my first hurricane, which is why I've decided to dedicate my life to fighting acts of environmental terrorism, one rising water level at a time. That and puppies, of course."

He wiggles his eyebrows at me.

And I sigh.

Because Ryan Mare is saying all the right things.

He's perfect on paper.

But in real life? I feel like he's doing a weird Prince of Atlantia impression or something.

As Ryan Mare continues to talk about the threat of climate change and how inhumane dog breeding is essentially a multilevel marketing scheme, I allow my mind to drift. I take in the size of him—the way his forearms flex, the dimples in his cheeks.

317

Don't get me wrong. He's really fucking hot. And respectful. A real man.

But boy, can he talk.

I should probably cut him off, right? If Nico were here, he'd definitely cut him off. Make some quippy comment about disaster insurance and ask how Ryan Mare plans on single-handedly stopping West Coast flooding while sitting in a glass office building full of yuppies in Midtown Manhattan.

Nico.

Now, *he* always keeps me guessing. I never know what he's going to do next. He may get under my skin and piss me off to no end sometimes—like earlier, when he called me delusional—but he always manages to surprise me.

No, Joonie.

Bad.

You're with Ryan Mare now.

Ryan. Mare.

The real-life Ryke.

There's no reason for you to keep thinking about Nico.

But I wonder what Nico's doing right now. Is he with that woman in Harlem? Did he take her out for lunch? Is he lecturing her about 5G networks and long-term radiation or making fun of the way she holds her knife and fork? Or did they decide to forgo lunch altogether and stay in? Is he whispering dirty words against the small of her back, making her laugh and shudder in equal measure? Does his back-and-forth with every girl serve as foreplay, or am I special?

Suddenly, the idea of Nico touching another woman, calling *her* special, is enough to send my lunch back up my esophagus.

Why?

Why am I sitting here across from the man of my dreams, someone who literally feels too good to be true, thinking about Nico?

You know why, a voice in my head says. Nico's voice. *Because this is real.*

I snap out of my daydream, alarmed. Sirens blare in my head.

Do I have…real feelings for Nico?

My brother's best friend?

The man who, until this week, I considered my enemy?

"It's really nice to meet you, Joonie," Ryan Mare says, oblivious to the fact that I've floated so far outside of my body, I've nearly reached Maecanea. "You know, you are really beautiful."

"That's a very cool necklace," I blurt out, suddenly itchy.

He lets out one of Ryke's signature full-chested laughs. "Why, thank you. The pendant's an heirloom, actually. See?"

I inch closer so I can study the engraving.

Then my mouth drops open.

Because etched on the pendant?

The letters *MMC*.

This cannot be real life.

"What does that stand for?" I ask, unable to resist the urge to scratch my neck. My skin is on fire.

His cheeks flush with embarrassment. "It's my last name, followed by my first name. Mare, Marrion Chad."

I blink several times.

The universe is most definitely fucking with me.

"Your name is…it's…M-Marrion Chad?"

He squints. "Well, yeah. Ryan is short for Marrion. Marrion Chad. I'm actually fifth in a line of Marrion Chads. Hey, are you feeling okay? You look kind of green."

I just stare at him.

That tan skin and midnight hair to which I've dedicated thousands of words.

Those smile lines and full lips I've imagined so many times as I touched myself in the dead of night.

The gleaming light behind his eyes.

And I face a startling reality head-on.

"You know what? It was really nice meeting you, too, Ryan," I say apologetically, leaving some of Angel's cash on the counter and grabbing my bags. "But there's somewhere I've got to be."

And as I walk out that door and onto the sidewalk, I know one thing for certain.

Prince Ryke of Atlantia is good on paper.

But Nico?

He might just be better for *me*.

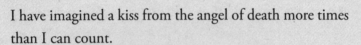

I have imagined a kiss from the angel of death more times than I can count.

The cold tickle of a dark lover's last breath.

A final foreboding peck on the forehead.

Lights in the distance beckoning me.

Children singing.

But I've never imagined it like this.

Death is not sweet, nor is it swift.

No, death is brutal and harsh.

It's the crack of a whip and the slap of a cheek. Death is iron fists clasped around your neck, squeezing the last remaining breath out of your body as time slows. Death is wet and frozen, in temperature and in time.

Death is a grave below the bottom of the ocean.

I am vaguely aware of my surroundings—the cavern where I am being held, the dark, murky waters in which I dwell. The kelp and knotted sailor's rope restraining my wrists and ankles. Ryke taught me how to escape from restraints for this very reason. He knew this moment would come, somehow. But he never showed me how to expel the water filling my lungs like a reservoir, pouring into my nose like warm blood.

"One more time: When does the Prince of Atlantia plan to strike?"

My body is limp, strands of my hair ripping from my head as if I am deteriorating in real time. Perhaps I am. I can no longer tell if I have been here for minutes or days. I can hardly muster up the energy to move, let alone speak.

Somehow, I manage to raise my chin an inch.

A refusal.

Nix sighs. "You are a stubborn little oaf of a human. I shall give you that, girl. Very well. Again."

He snaps his fingers, and it starts all over again.

Stolen life force flows through his veins. His red eyes illuminate, bright as rubies. Someone—another weak, defenseless human—powers those tiny vestibules. The water around us begins to drain away, then swell, filling the negative space without a second thought, the way air did moments ago. My mouth is forced open, and the liquid floods my lungs. I choke back a mouthful of salt water and pray to whatever sea god I am descended from to let me transform.

To let me grow a tail and gills.

To help me fight back.

And when the gods do not answer, I whisper a silent plea to them to end my suffering here and now. To allow me the dignity of a quick and quiet death.

But my luck seems to have run out.

My throat burns. The water is everywhere: wrapped around me, pouring into me, exploding out of me. I am suffocated by it, trapped by its particles. The ocean has turned its wrath on me, and there is nowhere I can hide from it. I know down to my very bones that I cannot survive this. I was always meant to succumb to its depths.

I cannot breathe, cannot think, cannot see. My eyes have begun to shutter, dark spots filling my vision. No blinding light from the heavens.

Only thick, unrelenting darkness.

My muscles seize up in pain as my vitals start to slow and my brain begins to shut down.

I am dying.

There is no mercy, no beauty in death. No forgiveness or redemption. I was silly to think of martyrdom as a hero's way to leave this plane. The truth is, there is no heroism in death, no bravery or sacrifice. What a fool I have been.

Death has no meaning, no purpose.

Only darkness.

"Tell me, you wretched bag of skin," Nix barks. "Reveal

your rebellious ways or be swept out with tomorrow's tides."

I think of my husband's wrinkled scowl. His limp, long, bony fingers.

I think of the treasure trove. The feeling of rightness the trident gave me. The call of the conch at the creek cottage. I never experienced true power before that. How naïve I was to allow it to plant seeds of hope inside my soul. But how sweet it was to believe in something larger than myself, even for a moment.

I think of Ryke.

His teasing remarks and terms of endearment. His eyes of gold and heart that matches. The stranger who saved me from the claws of my fate and gave me the adventure of a lifetime. The man I have come to revere.

To love.

I love Ryke.

But that secret will die with me.

After I am gone, my love will disintegrate into the salt and sand.

And there is poetry in that.

I smile to myself.

I can barely hear Nix screaming at me any longer, his voice merely a pleasant buzzing in my ear as I succumb to the darkness. My body no longer feels heavy but light as a lily pad. And the force of the water destroying me from the inside out evaporates into nothing.

It will not be long now.

My eyelids grow heavy. Behind them, a light flashes.

A sound buzzes below the hum of the darkness.

Then a whisper cuts through space and time, coming from far, far away.

"Little minnow," it hisses. "Merriah."

I reach for the voice, but I lack the energy.

And death pulls me in the other direction.

CHAPTER TWENTY

The second I leave the tavern, I feel like I can breathe again.

To confirm my suspicions, I inhale a big belly breath of polluted New York air and exhale slowly.

And you know what?

I have no idea what the fuck to do right now.

Me, Joonie, lover of plans. Flying by the seat of my perfectly tailored pants.

Do I message the Salty Girls? Give them the lowdown?

The idea of explaining to them that I went on this entire convoluted, semi-stalkerish (though admittedly epic) quest only to experience such an anticlimactic, lackluster finale is…unappealing at best. But now that I know them, I bet they'll just laugh it off and tease me.

Demand details and the next chapter of the fic I haven't updated since Miranda Sings made that terrible apology song video.

And I have to get to Nico. To talk to him.

Maybe even tell him how I feel.

Admitting that I've been wrong is possibly my least favorite thing on the planet (after the cheating trope), but if I can get him to hear me out, I'll do it. I'll tell him that I shouldn't have been so laser-focused on my checklist that I grew blind to what was unfolding in front of me.

Any good writer knows that even plotters get pantsed by their own characters sometimes.

Nico left in such a hurry this morning that we didn't even discuss how to get in touch again. I have no idea if he's obtained a burner phone or when he's planning on taking a train back home or if he's renting a car or a horse or a unicycle or what. The next time I see him could be at Sunday dinner.

In fifty years.

But he's probably with *her*. The girl who wasn't too stupid to dismiss Nico as a love interest. I don't even know her last name. It feels so beneath me to be this jealous of a stranger, and yet…

There's only one person I can call for help.

But I have *a lot* of explaining to do. And zero clue where to start.

I exhale, take out my dying burner phone, and do a

bit of Googling. A number pops up, and before I can talk myself out of it, I dial.

The phone rings twice before somebody answers.

"Kabobs 'n' Bits, Mystic's number-one hub for Middle Eastern cuisine—this *shish* is bananas."

Something in my chest cracks open in relief. "Tey?"

"Joonie?!"

My brother doesn't sound as happy to hear my voice as I am to hear his. He sounds, like, mega-pissed.

"Where the hell have you been? Did you turn off your location? I don't recognize this number. Whose phone are you using? Why are you calling me at the shop?"

"Well…"

"I thought you were dead. Are you dead?" I can practically feel the spit flying from his mouth on the other end of the line. "You better be dead, because if you're not, I'm going to murder you."

I pause for a second.

Remember what he said last week, a lifetime ago.

You could be kidnapped by an ax murderer.

He has no idea.

Then I can't help it.

A giggle escapes.

Then a larger sound. A snicker.

"Are you actually laughing right now?" he asks in disbelief. "Joon. My calls have been going straight to voicemail for *days*. I haven't been able to reach Nico, either. I didn't know if you'd even gotten to New York. Ollie had to talk me down from contacting the National Guard. Seriously, I was seconds away from heading to the city myself and checking all the major hospitals—"

"Thank you," I whisper.

I picture the way he's probably cocking his head before I hear his confusion.

"*Thank you?* I chew you out for going AWOL and you thank me? Did you hit your head or something?"

"Thank you for caring," I clarify. "You always look out for me, Tey. I know I give you a hard time about it, but I just want you to know I'm grateful. And that it doesn't go unnoticed. In case, you know...I don't say it enough."

For someone who is a true romantic, I don't do the whole earnest thing with my brother very often. He must notice, because when he asks his next question, his voice comes out kind of shaky and unsettled.

"Joonie, what's wrong?"

"Well, let's see..."

My phone dings, notifying me that my battery just hit 10 percent. I groan.

"Sorry, my phone's dying. Well, not *my* phone. My friend Roy's phone. He's one of my fanfic friends. I met them all in person for the first time. Here in New York. It was crazy. Nico and I had to crash with one of them— their name's Angel—because we didn't have any money, because a psychic stole our wallets after giving me this insane prophecy on the train. We had to take the train because the truck was totaled. Your truck. I'm so sorry about that. I'll figure out a way to pay for the repairs, I swear. I'm not sure where it is right now because we abandoned it in order to hitchhike with these two freaks—like, literal con artists—who ended up being bounty hunters for the Mob. They tried to kidnap us because Nico made some bad bets in an attempt to save the restaurant, which I know is in trouble. But I ended up getting us out of it. They took our phones, which is why you haven't been able to reach us. Nico wanted to turn around and go home, but I refused. I had to get to the city and find Ryan Mare. He's the real-life Ryke, from my books—like, the man the character was based on. There was never any writing workshop, by the way. I was always going to the city because I thought maybe Ryan was my soul mate, but then I met him, and even though he was exactly like I imagined, he just didn't make me feel…anything. There was no spark. Not like the one I feel with Nico. Oh yeah, that reminds me—I totally banged your best friend. Just, you know, FYI."

There's silence on the other end of the line for a whole minute.

"Tey? Did we get disconnected or—"

"What the actual fuck."

I gulp. "Which part?"

"Um, all of it? Are you okay, Joon? Are you safe?"

"Yeah, I'm safe."

"You don't have PTSD or anything?"

"The motel we slept in was a hellscape, but no."

"God forbid they don't have turndown service."

"Right?! Or chocolates on the pillows."

I hear a long exhale, followed by a groan. "I have no idea where to start," he says. "You got *kidnapped*? And *mugged*?"

"Yeah." I blow out a sharp breath. "But I know how to escape from restraints, plus a little hand-to-hand combat. Actually, I have my black belt. Also, I speak, like, five languages. Including Mandarin. And my Salty Girls have my back. So, yeah. I figured it out."

He whistles. "Even though that is thoroughly terrifying—and make no mistake, we *will* be filing a police report when you're back—I can't say I'm not impressed. How the hell did you become so resourceful?"

"Easy." I shrug. "By reading romance."

Tey lets out a laugh of disbelief. "Do I need to lecture you about the stalking?"

"No, not really?"

"So…your dream guy didn't meet your golden standards, huh?"

"Not exactly." I swallow. "He was a dream. I just woke up is all."

Tey clicks his tongue in thought. "Why'd you lie to me?"

I take a deep breath. "You already think I'm silly for holding everyone I date to standards set by a fictional character. Why would I confide in you about chasing down the man that fictional character is based on? You, Maman, Baba, Nico…after everything that happened in school, and then again with Kyle, you all think I'm just some stupid kid with her head in the clouds. Naïve. I didn't want you to think I was living in another fantasy world. Maybe if Ryan Mare had been The One, if we had shared something real, everyone finally would've taken me seriously."

The line is silent for a moment. Then Tey clears his throat.

"Is that what you think, Joonie? I remember what it was like for you when you were a kid. You were this ray of sunshine until those racist bullies dimmed your light. That Sam kid broke your spirit. And even though you never told me what went down between you and Nico after he stood you up for that dance, it was obvious that shit broke your heart, too. The darkness began to linger. I know you wanted to change in college to make everything easier on yourself, but that never sat right with me. And then when you started dating that asshole, Cole—"

"Kyle."

"Whatever. It was like he took the very last of your shine and stamped it out like a cigarette. You were a shell of yourself, and even though you never said anything to Maman and Baba, we could see it."

My eyes well up without my consent. "But I thought you liked him. You were always so nice whenever we came to visit. I didn't want to disappoint you guys after everything."

"We love *you*, Joon. Exactly the way you are. The day you left him, I was so relieved. Because I could see that your spark had never truly been extinguished. And I knew that over time, you'd grow back into the girl we all knew."

My heart feels so full, it might burst. "Then why do you always make fun of me?"

Miles away, I hear him buzz his lips. "At first, I was so proud that you finally saw how much you were worth, that you'd set your standards so high," he explains. "But after a while, I began to worry that you were using *A Tale of Salt Water and Secrets* and Rake—"

"Ryke."

"Whatever. That you were using Ryke as a crutch to keep people at an arm's length. If you didn't really let anyone in, no one could get close enough to hurt you again. Don't get me wrong, you dated some turds. And there's obviously real value in that series—I mean, it gave you a community and taught you how to pack a mean punch. But I think the fantasy of it all became an excuse. A reason to find fault with potential love interests because deep down, you still didn't think you were worthy of that kind of love. Because of what those asshole high schoolers said to you. Because of what that douchebag Kyle did to you."

The weight of his words settles right into that cavern in my chest. "Well, maybe there's a little bit of truth to that," I say quietly. "But I'm trying to change. Starting today."

"With Nico?" he asks, letting out a strangled laugh. "Can't say I'm surprised."

That comment catches me off guard. "What do you mean? Until forty-eight hours ago, I thought he hated me."

"Joonie." He says my name like it's the punchline of a joke. "Nico never hated you. When you started shutting him out when we were kids, he was devastated. He'd already lost so much when his folks split up, and you used to look at him like he'd hung the moon. Losing you was too much for him. It was like the whole night sky went dark, you know?"

"But we're always at each other's throats! You know how much we fought! Why didn't you ever say anything?"

"Wasn't my mess to fix." I can almost see him shrugging. "Plus, he was always finding some excuse to be near you, to spar with you. I figured it would come up organically sooner or later. Ollie was taking bets on when."

"You bastard!" I cry. Then, a bit carefully, "So, you're not mad that we, uh, hooked up, then?"

"Joon, if getting together with Nico means you force that grumpy asshole to crack a smile every now and then, I'll bankroll your relationship."

I let out a slow breath, my jaw tight with emotion.

"Yeah, well, I wouldn't break open your piggy bank just yet—and we *will* be talking about whatever the hell is going on with Kabobs 'n' Bits's finances when I'm back, by the way. I think I blew it with Nico, Tey. Before it ever really began. Pulled the ol' push-them-away-before-they-get-too-close thing you were just talking about. I even knew it was my MO. But now I've lost my chance. He's up in Harlem, finding that girl."

"What girl?"

"You know. The girl he hooks up with in the city every few months."

Tey grunts in disbelief. "Joon, Nico isn't visiting a girl in Harlem."

I don't think I've heard him correctly. "He's not?"

"Of course not. His mother lives in Harlem."

"His *mother*?"

I imagine Tey shaking his head. "He was just trying to rile you up. There was no way he was going to let you go on that road trip alone. I thought you knew."

My hands start to shake. Suddenly, it all makes sense.

"You wouldn't happen to have his mom's address, would you?"

This time, I hear the smile in my brother's voice.

"Got a pen?"

336

My eyelids flutter.

I gasp, choking, then throw up mouthful after mouthful of salt water. Finally I am empty and the darkness recedes.

Have I crossed over? Is this the afterlife? The sand feels granular and hard beneath my body. But my limbs are no longer heavy. A weight has been lifted from my shoulders, my waist, my ankles. I feel light, as if I could fly into the heavens or swim beneath the waves.

My eyes snap open, and I take my first real breath in ages.

My air bubble.

Someone has returned my air bubble to me.

I can breathe again. The water filling my lungs is gone. I am no longer drowning.

But how? Who revived me when I had all but embraced death as my eternal companion?

"Little minnow."

Awareness settles over me. Consciousness floods my mind, and sounds flare in my ears. I turn around and once again have trouble finding my breath.

For there he is.

Prince Ryke of Atlantia has come for me.

And his expression is one of molten fury, enough to bring an army to its knees.

I watch in awe as his thick obsidian tail whips around, a wrecking ball of his own making, parting the ocean and knocking Nix's goons out cold. His body emanates raw power—my power. And he channels that life force into raw, unadulterated strength. Just as he taught me to do when I was just a human willing to put her life on the line for a race of creatures she had only just learned existed.

He fights with purpose, clean lines and intentional blows. His heightened strength gives him extreme agility. I stare in awe as he moves through the water faster than even sirens can see. All five senses flare simultaneously, weapons in their own right. Ryke can now smell blood in the water. He can hear his opponents' smallest movements and knows where their blows will land even before they have made up their own minds. His fists deal in injury and death.

And vengeance is a thick serum on his tongue.

I know not how he found me.

Perhaps he followed the final tether I left in this world: my love for him.

Love.

I love this brave, kind, powerful mer. And if he does not feel the same way, it makes no difference. My words were almost stolen from me, but now I will have the opportunity to tell him the truth.

And that is enough for me.

My heart swells. I feel explosive, and warmth settles over me, fills me, moves through me, completes me. The sensation rushes through my head, making me delirious, dizzy in the most delicious way. I am faint once more. But this time, no darkness approaches to claim me. All I see in front of me is light. The light of the love inside my chest. The light that outlines Ryke's body as he fights for his land, his people.

And for me.

If my deep-seated fear was enough to call upon the power of the trident, this is the opposite. I allow the potency of my love to flow through me. To warm the water and sweeten its texture. My fingers pluck an object from beneath my skirt.

The dorsal fin.

I nearly forgot that I had an object from the trove with me. I took it because it weighed less than the trident and was less conspicuous than the whip. As I have not yet unearthed its purpose, thus far the fin has served as little more than a trinket. A souvenir piece of the trove to remind me of my place. A token and nothing more.

Now confidence washes over me, mixing and mingling with the love that flows through my blood. The love is pure, unadulterated power. It gives me a calm certainty.

The answer before me is clear.

My love for Ryke is more potent than fear.

Tonight, I will fight Nix and the sirens with that love.

I rub my thumb over the strange symbols covering the dorsal fin. Spirals and ripples. Etchings in a language I do not understand. And yet I hear words falling from my lips, foreign but familiar, hearkening back to a time when I was not yet born.

Ryke whips around and inhales sharply. "Merriah."

"Ryke," I call out to him, my voice unlike anything of this realm. "I have something to tell you. I—"

Just then, Nix emerges from the mouth of the cavern, both fists clenched. The water around him bubbles with rage.

"Behind you!" I shout.

Ryke turns around and throws a punch into Nix's pristine face, but Nix wraps a fistful of water around his wrist, forming handcuffs. Ryke struggles against them, unable to move his hands.

Nix laughs, shaking his head. "Good luck getting out of this bind, prince," he sneers.

A high-pitched cry sounds from outside the cave.

Both Ryke and Nix turn around to face the noise, their faces twin with shock.

Several more sounds follow the first.

Battle cries.

An army coming to the defense of its prince.

But these noises are not mer.

They are not human.

In fact, they sound like—

"Dolphins," Ryke breathes.

Sure enough, an entire infantry of the mammals storms the cavern, whinnying with defiance. They bare their teeth with a vengeance, their fins so sharp they slice through flesh and bone. I always thought of dolphins as adorable creatures of the deep, but these dolphins are anything but. They are warriors of the highest degree, merciless in their pursuit of blood.

The remaining sirens flee like their lives depend on it.

And they do.

Ryke points directly at me.

My jaw drops. Could I be commanding this army of dolphins with the force of my love?

"How?" Nix demands. "You did not kill the human. A life did not end as one was created. You should not be able to command this kind of power. Unless…"A slow smile creeps over his face. "How long have you known?"

"Stop talking," Ryke grunts.

"Known what?" I whisper.

Ryke shakes his head. "Please."

I look at the mer I love.

My prince. My protector.

But Ryke avoids my eyes, refusing to answer.

"Known what?"

CHAPTER
TWENTY-ONE

I stare down at the crinkled piece of paper in my hand, then back up at the giant brick condominium building in front of me.

"Oh well," I mumble to myself. "Here goes nothing."

Biting my lip, I buzz the apartment number Tey gave me.

Static sounds on the other end. Then a lovely high-pitched voice.

"Come on up!" a woman sings.

The door buzzes open, and I hurry inside.

Nico's mother's apartment is on the second floor at the end of the hall. I prepare to knock, but she beats me to it. "Door's open!" she calls from the other side.

I take a deep breath and turn the handle.

The apartment is tiny but charming. It's a studio with

one big window lighting up the space and a view of a big oak tree outside. There's a small kitchenette, where a teakettle heats on the stove. The wallpaper is peeling slightly, but the crown moldings are in excellent shape. She's replaced all the light fixtures with ceiling fans. Even standing in the entryway, I can tell this isn't merely an apartment.

This is a home.

A safe space to start over.

To get to know yourself again.

Nico's mom sits cross-legged on a cushy love seat. She's as beautiful as I remember—big eyes, a blue so light they're practically gray, and Nico's blond hair flowing down her back. But now, more than a few strands of white mingle with those honey locks, and those eyes are creased with well-earned wrinkles. When she sees me, her face breaks into a wide smile that I've seen on her son only once or twice.

"Joonie Saboonchi, is that you? I haven't seen you since you were small enough to hide under my skirts! Nico, come—look who it is!"

At the sound of his name, Nico steps out from behind the curtain separating his mother's bed from the rest of the space. He's dressed in the same clothes he was wearing this morning, but his normally neat hair looks messy. As if he's been pulling on it the way he tends to do when he's stressed. Or like a lover ran her hands through it.

I swallow back the bile making its way into my mouth and put on a brave face.

"Hi," I squeak.

Nico looks at me as if I'm a mirage, his eyes wide with disbelief. "What are you doing here?"

"Tey sort of gave up your whereabouts."

"Shouldn't you be with your soul mate?" Nico's voice is hard, relentless.

My stomach drops about twenty stories.

"About that… Nico, I need to talk to you. I'm so—"

"Not now," he says, clenching his jaw as if the words require effort. "I'm with my mom. You should go."

I nod, trying not to let my insides splatter all over the floor. "Okay. I'll go."

"Nonsense," Nico's mom says, turning around to scowl at her offspring. "I can barely get you to visit me once in a blue moon, and now that I've got a special visitor, you're trying to scare her away?" She walks over to the kitchenette and opens a cabinet, pulling out mugs. "Come, Joonie. Stay for a cup of tea. Fill me in on the last decade and a half of your life. Of course Nico keeps me updated on the basics, but I want all the juicy details."

I walk over to the love seat and allow myself to sink into the cushions. "He does?"

She laughs. "Are you kidding? I practically know your schedule by heart. I swear, you should hire him to write your newsletter. It's always *Joonie said this the other day* or

You won't believe what Joonie did this time. I've never seen someone burrow their way under Nico's skin quite the way you have."

"Mom!" Nico yells, his cheeks flushing in a manner I'm all too familiar with.

"Oh hush, honey. It's just a little bit of girl talk. Don't be so sensitive. Honestly, the way you go on and on about her, I never know whether you want to kill her or kiss her. But since blood has always made you a little queasy…"

"Isn't that the truth," I mutter.

Nico looks up at the ceiling. "Okay, I'm ready for the apocalypse to start anytime now."

His mother looks between us and frowns. "Why are you two sitting so far apart? And avoiding eye contact? You're acting strange."

She squints at us, and I squirm in my seat.

Nico takes a sip of tea.

His mom's hand flies to her mouth. "Oh my God, you've had sex!"

"What? No!" I shout.

"How could you possibly know that?" Nico groans.

"Mother's intuition." She beams. "So it's true? Oh, this is so wonderful! I've always thought you two would make the cutest couple. Joonie, you had the most adorable crush on Nico when you were little. You were always coming up with silly excuses to follow him around, to play with him, to ask him questions."

I feel all the blood rush to my head.

"Now, now. That's nothing to be embarrassed about. You two were kids. It was so sweet. I remember one time when he was in the bath, you—"

"I would really, really like to stop having this conversation," I interrupt rather rudely.

"Finally, we agree on something," Nico mumbles.

"Never thought I'd see the day," I retort.

His mother just giggles, her voice like the ringing of a bell. "Oh, you two are too much. What banter! Finally, someone who can keep up with his witticisms and call him on his bullshit. I mean, bull crap."

"Mom, I'm almost thirty," Nico says. "You can curse in front of me."

"Hush," she says again, pulling him to her chest and planting a big wet kiss on his forehead. "You'll always be my baby. My boy. So strong, even when you didn't have to be."

Her lower lip quivers.

Those gray-blue skies darken.

Oh God—the waterworks are about to start.

"The truth is, I'm relieved," she says, turning to face me once again. "Nico hasn't brought a girl home to meet me…well, ever. He hasn't talked about anyone but you for the last decade. I was starting to worry that he'd never let anybody in. You were so young, you probably don't remember, but my divorce from his father was messy. It really did a number on all of us, Nico most of all. It wasn't fair."

Nico shakes his head, sucking in his cheeks. "No, Mom. What wasn't fair was Dad cheating on you. Over and over again. And with your *sister*. You always say we can choose love. Well, he had a choice. And his decision was to walk away from us. His son and his *soul mate*."

He spits the last word as if it's a curse.

"Honey, I won't pretend your father's actions didn't hurt me. They wrecked me. But we didn't have a perfect marriage. Not even close. We saw the world differently—he was always worried about the things he couldn't change, and I was so caught up in the small changes I could make. We bickered to avoid talking about the big stuff. It's one thing when someone who doesn't really know you tries to hurt you. It's whole different situation when the person who knows you best in the world takes a shot. We both knew where to aim our cruelest comments. How to dig the knife in and really make each other bleed."

Nico rubs his hand down his face like he can't believe what he's hearing.

"But you two were the perfect couple. Next-door neighbors, high school sweethearts. Fated in the womb…" says Nico.

"Well, we were so young when we met. We didn't know yet that you're a new version of yourself every day. Which means that every day, you're in a new relationship with a new person. You have to keep checking in. And we stopped doing that."

I think about this. Using Nico's mom's logic, many different versions of ourselves can love many different versions of someone else. Like alternate realities. Different dimensions.

Or second-chance romances.

"Even so, I wouldn't take back loving him for the world. I grew into myself while falling for him. Our love painted my world with color. And loving him led to loving you, Nico. I'll always have love in my heart for him. But love isn't a bucket, baby. It's a well. And I have so much more love left to share."

I smile to myself. "Love isn't a bucket; it's a well," I repeat. "I love that. Mind if I use that in one of my fics?"

Nico's mother puts a hand on her chest. "Why, it would be an honor! Nico told me you're a writer." She smiles at me. "You always did love happy endings, even as a little kid."

I turn to look at Nico, swelling with pride. But he's quiet, his fingers twined together. Contemplative. Processing all this information and thinking it through.

"How can you still believe in happy endings when your story ended in tragedy?" he finally asks. "How can you still believe in love?"

She takes a long sip of her tea, then hums quietly.

"Because, sweet cheeks, love is matter. Love is the stuff

the world is made of. Love is the reason to get up in the morning and the way to sleep soundly at night. My marriage ended, but that wasn't the end of love. It was an evolution. Because love doesn't just disappear into thin air. No, sir. When I got divorced, I took all that love I had for your father and put it into myself."

Nico stares at her, his eyes growing misty. "You never told me any of this."

"I know. And that's on me, kid. After the divorce, you were so angry. Anytime I tried to talk about your dad, about love, you changed the subject. You'd bring up climate change and the end of the world and all that. I gave up trying. And I'll always regret doing that."

Nico swallows hard, as if he's trying to will his face to remain neutral.

"But I'm telling you now," says his mom. "Hopefully I'm not too late."

My cheeks feel damp. I raise a hand to my face and discover I've started to cry.

What would my life look like if I stopped looking for love outside of myself and summoned the love inside me instead?

"Plus, the best stories have tons of plot twists." Nico's mother turns to throw me a wink. "Isn't that right, Joonie?"

Nix looks at me. His sandpaper laugh scrapes against my cheek.

"She has no idea, does she?" he asks Ryke.

Ryke's answering glare sends a chill down my spine.

I clench my fist around the dorsal fin, and my band of dolphins circles the siren in a predatory dance. Nix grimaces, then quickly regains his composure.

"Of course she does not. Why would she? For she is only a human. She lacks the sight."

"The sight?" I repeat. "What is the sight?"

"One more word," Ryke says, "and I will not wait for these vicious creatures to rip out your throat. I shall do it myself."

"Ah, yes. With your enhanced strength. Funny." Nix

turns around and cocks his head at me—a challenge. "And how is it, do you think, that your fair prince gained this enhanced strength without repercussions?"

I gulp, my vision blurring. I am still faint. "We… power shared."

"And yet you remain alive," Nix says.

A statement, not a question.

Ryke grunts in warning.

I shoot him a look. "I need to hear this," I tell him. Then to Nix, "Go on."

"Do you not find it odd that centuries of mer have attempted to do precisely what your prince did in order to heal and grow strong, but all of them lost the battle and paid a steep price? Did it not occur to you that sirens would not exist if all mer had the same level of restraint as your lover?"

The blood pumping through my veins pauses. In fact, the entirety of the ocean seems to still.

I ponder his query.

The truth is, these things did occur to me. I questioned Ryke about this very matter. But he dismissed my concern outright, told me that he was able to take enough blood without killing me and then stop because of me. That my reaction was enough to signal him, to wake him from his power-hungry haze. And I accepted that, took his words at face value.

What a childish, naïve woman I am.

I must think very highly of myself. Me, a mere human, able to control the actions of the prince of Atlantia? Of course there is another explanation.

"Since drinking your blood, the prince has evolved into a strange creature, an amalgamation of sorts," Nix muses.

Behind him, my dolphins whine and whinny. An intimidation tactic.

"What do you mean?" I ask before I can stop myself.

Nix's lips twitch. "Well, he is clearly no longer your average mer. Although you could argue that his royal bloodline has always afforded him certain…privileges. Advantages that we sirens were not given at birth but rather had to take by force."

"By murdering innocents?" Ryke growls.

Nix shrugs. "You say *innocents*. My sisters and I say *collateral damage*. I am surprised by you, Your Highness. I really am. You know better than anyone that the best way—the only way—to gain power is to take it."

My insides start to churn. What is he talking about it? What could that possibly mean?

"No, the reason you two were able to power share, to gain strength without giving up your humanity and live to tell the tale—or rather, the tail—is simple. Rare, but simple. One word, really."

Ryke charges forward, the veins in his forehead popping. "I will cut out your tongue—"

"Lochs."

The dolphins cease their snarling as the current around us slows.

A satisfied smirk graces the false prince's face.

Devastation suffuses the face of the true prince from chin to brow.

I, however, remain confused.

"Locks?" I repeat, tasting the word on my tongue. "What do they have to do with anything?"

Ryke's next sentence comes in a whisper. "I did not want you to find out this way." He starts toward me, but Nix blocks his path. "You were never meant to feel forced by anyone's hand, even the Furnace and its Fates. It was always meant to be your choice."

I shake my head, still not understanding. "What was meant to be my choice?"

"Why, him, of course." Nix purses his lips. "You see, lochs are ancient bonds predating the written word, the mer, and perhaps even this universe. They are lore and they are law. But they are so uncommon that it is highly unlikely one will come across their own in their lifetime. Most mer do not consume themselves with looking, with wondering, or with wishing. It has been centuries since I have seen one myself."

I store the information that Nix is hundreds of years old in the folds of my brain for another day.

"Lock," I repeat to myself. "Like the mechanism that safeguards a door or trove?"

"No, you fool." Nix shakes his head. "A loch is the very arm of the sea. The backbone of the tide. The intersection of the water and the earth."

The intersection of the water and the earth.

I cannot think of a more apt description of Ryke and me.

"But in the case of the mer, your loch is your fated mate, forged by the Furnace, predestined for you at birth by the North Star. Your entire life, the North Star tries to guide you toward your loch, even when you are not aware of it."

I look over at Ryke, whose eyes brim with unshed tears.

Ryke—my stranger, my lover, my friend—is my destiny?

My loch?

Chosen for me by the North Star itself?

I need not ask the siren for confirmation. I can see it in the eyes of my prince.

Regret.

Betrayal.

And pure, unconditional longing.

"You knew?" I whisper, needing to hear the words aloud. "All this time, you knew I was your loch, and yet you said nothing? You never thought to tell me?"

He hangs his head, unable to look at me.

"How did you know?"

I think back to the first time we met at the creek cottage.

The night he saved me from the abuse of my husband.

Was he merely claiming what was rightfully his?

I had fancied him my liberator, not my captor.

"Your light," Nix answers for him. "When two people become interloched—that is the term for when two lochs converge, their fated journey completed—they begin to glow faintly with the light of the North Star, a blaze that grows even brighter when they are together. You cannot see your own light because you are a mere human. You do not possess the sight. But the first time our sweet prince laid eyes on you, you began to glow, and he immediately knew that you were his loch. If, that is, he had not already felt the tugs of fate, the watchful North Star, leading him to you before that day."

I look to Ryke, a mix of horror and wonder mingling in my mind.

"I suspected," Ryke admits to the ocean floor. "But I did not know for certain until then."

Every hair on my body stands up straight, the muscles in my abdomen, which Ryke has helped me to develop, clenching as I fight the urge to burst into tears. "So everyone—Dylan, Guinn, the others—they all know?"

Ryke grits his teeth and nods. "The people who have not seen us together know only that I am interloched. But yes, our friends know."

Our friends.

Not his friends. Not his Upper Shoal.

Ours.

And somehow, that makes the truth sting all the sweeter.

"They never said a word," I mutter.

Then an even more paralyzing thought strikes me.

"Of course—the night of the ball. You knew the risk of us attending together. Everyone present knew that were interloched. We must have been glowing more brightly than the moon."

Ryke grimaces but does not contradict me.

"Oh, Furnace help me," I mutter as the pieces begin to fit together. "That is why you caught the attention of the false queen Talassa. That is why the battle ensued and all those mer died. Because of me."

"No," Ryke says sharply. "Because of me. Not because of you. I let you go into that situation blind. I put you in danger because I was afraid that if you knew, you would feel obligated to be with me. And I wanted you to choose me of your own accord. To fall…"

I wait for him to finish his sentence.

But all that follows is silence.

I shut my eyes and hear the bloody cries of the siren attack. Think of the sirens whose organs I boiled, their bodies exploding.

It is horrifying, even if they deserved it.

I killed all those creatures because the North Star decided Ryke and I were destined for each other even before I took my first breath.

Everything I have been through.

The suffering of my village.

The abusive hand of my husband…

Oh, tides. My husband.

A man who made my light dim instead of glow.

I married him, not knowing that the Fates were laughing at me.

My head throbs as I fight another wave of nausea.

As if he can read my mind, Ryke cuts in. "Please, my minnow. Allow me to explain. I was so afraid of losing you, of hurting you. Of behaving like…him."

He does not dare utter my husband's name.

"You needed to realize your own power. Your own strength. Merriah, you are the only living descendant of Amphitrite, the sea goddess. The ocean bends to your will. The conch calls to you. You even command a dolphin fleet." He gestures to the battalion behind me. "You are so more than my loch. You are Atlantia's salvation."

I cannot bring myself to ask Ryke why he does not believe I can be both.

CHAPTER TWENTY-TWO

Nico and I walk out of his mother's apartment in charged silence. The sun is starting to set, casting a golden haze over the row of brownstones and older tenement buildings. Across the street, an elderly woman pushes a shopping cart while humming a song I don't recognize. A dog barks in the distance, followed by a loud curse. Nico is holding a plastic bag of Tupperware containers full of about six months' worth of leftover casserole. I've got a rice cooker and a phone charger in my hands. The latter is because I mentioned I needed one. The former? Nico's mother heard I was cooking rice the old-fashioned Persian way and immediately insisted I take hers off her hands. That's just the kind of woman she is.

I turn to face Nico. He still looks boyishly disheveled. I resist the urge to touch his hair.

"Why did you lie to me?" I ask quietly.

Nico inspects something fascinating on the concrete sidewalk. "How was your date with Prince Charming?" he deflects. "Please, don't hold back the gory details. The anticipation is killing me. Did he sweep you off your feet?"

I roll my eyes, studying his profile. A week ago, I would have taken his rude brush-off as an obvious sign of his vehement hatred for me. I would have met his vitriol with a retort of my own, and we would have gotten into a sparring match that would have resulted in us not speaking for three to five business days.

But that was then.

Now that I've gotten to know Nico, to really understand him, I can see the obvious layer of hurt nestled beneath his words. The vulnerability he feels talking to me about his mother. He goes on the offensive so he never has to open up.

I can't believe I ever missed that about him.

Now I want to spend every day making sure he knows he can lower his guard around me.

I want to be the kind of person he feels comfortable talking to.

"He was perfect." I take a step toward him. "I really think he might be The One."

Nico lets out a sharp laugh and backs away. "Good. I hope you guys are really, really happy together."

"You didn't let me finish, asshole," I say. "I said he *might* be The One. For Evelyn G. Carter. For Merriah. And maybe for some other lucky person out there."

He turns a quarter of the way to glance at me, his breathing shallow. "But not for you?"

I shake my head. "No, not for me."

Nico's eyes widen for a second, and then he dons his mask of feigned boredom again.

"I'm so sorry to hear that," he says carefully. "I know you had a lot riding on meeting him. So what are you going to do now that even your perfect guy didn't live up to your standards? Join the Peace Corps? Become a nun?"

"Shut up, dickwad," I snap, even though I'm grinning from ear to ear. Truth is, I'll take Nico teasing me over Nico giving me the silent treatment any day. "You still don't get it, do you?"

He quirks a brow. "Get what?"

"Ryan Mare met my standards, Nico. Every box was checked. That wasn't the issue."

"Did you bring up Ryke and totally freak him out?" he asks, biting his lip. "Did he call you out for stalking him or something?"

I shake my head. "The issue is that my standards have changed. They've imploded, actually. Totally turned on their head."

"Is that right?"

"Yeah. That's right." I huff out a laugh. "Here I thought I was attracted to dark-haired good Samaritans with hero complexes. But as it turns out, pessimistic blond conspiracy theorists are more my speed. Who knew?"

Nico finally turns to face me fully.

He narrows his eyes.

"What are you saying, Joonie?" he asks. "Spell it out for me."

"I realized I have feelings for someone else, idiot," I say. "Someone unexpected. But the thing is, I think I may have ruined things before ever giving us a real chance."

Nico rubs his chin, glancing sheepishly at me before looking away once more. "This mystery guy have a name?"

I grin. "You wouldn't know him."

"Well, this is just a shot in the dark here, but I'm guessing that if you explain yourself to him, apologize, and prepare to do a little bit of groveling, he'll probably forgive you."

"Oh yeah?" I ask, my insides swelling with hope.

"Yeah." He smiles back. "Call it a hunch."

"And what would this groveling entail?"

"I'd prepare to get on your knees," he says. "Maybe even beg."

Suddenly, the twisting in my gut is replaced with burning heat.

We maintain eye contact for three seconds, then look away, laughing awkwardly.

"I guess we better get to Grand Central, huh?" My voice sounds practically falsetto. "And we'll have to figure out which auto shop Tey's truck is at sooner or later. Preferably before he yells so loud he blows out Oliver's eardrums."

Nico groans. "Don't remind me. Maybe we should go on the run instead?"

I throw my head back and cackle. Nico watches me closely.

"What?" I ask. "Do I have something on my face?"

Then Nico—confident, bullishly stubborn Nico— does something totally out of character.

He stumbles over his words.

"Look, I didn't tell you about my mom because I don't talk about my mom with anyone," he confesses. "She moved here after the divorce because she wanted a fresh start. Said she couldn't take running into her family at the grocery store or my dad at the car wash. I was mad at first that she was so far away. It felt like she had abandoned us, abandoned me. You know? But now that I'm grown, I realize how good it's been for her. She really does have a new lease on life. So I try to visit her every few months. It's…new. But we're trying to get to know each other again."

He's rambling so fast, I can barely make out every other word.

And you know what? It's adorable.

"Nico." I reach for his hand and squeeze. "Thank you for sharing that with me. I know talking about your family isn't easy for you. So it means a lot."

He gives me a shy half smile, and I feel like I may melt into the pavement.

"For what it's worth, it seems like your mom really cares about you," I add. "More than my parents care about me, honestly. And they're still happily married."

"Who needs parents breathing down your neck when you have Tey?" Nico jokes.

He opens his mouth to say something else, then hesitates.

Closes it again.

"Were you going to say something else?" I prod.

"Well, there's a small, tiny chance that I told you I was coming to see a girl because I wanted to make you jealous," he finally says. "Minuscule, even. Can you blame me? You were going on and on about how perfect this guy was going to be. It was driving me insane. I just wanted to give you a taste of your own medicine."

My heart starts pounding so loudly, I think it's connected to a car speaker.

"Well, there's a small, tiny chance that it worked," I tell him. "Minuscule, even."

He lowers his head so close to mine, his breath ghosts across my cheek.

"You were jealous?" he asks.

"Maddeningly so," I answer.

Two pigeons sitting on a wire above us choose that very moment to squawk at each other, breaking the tension between us. We spring apart, giggling like schoolgirls.

"We better get going," he whispers, never once taking his eyes off of me.

Then I hear a familiar drawling voice behind me.

"Leaving so soon?"

"The reason we were able to successfully power share is because we are interloched?" I ask.

Nix nods. "That is the working theory. Of course, there is no record of an interloched couple attempting such a feat. You two might very well be the first."

I turn to look at Ryke. His fists are clenched, his body writhing with the need to go to me.

To hold me. To comfort me. To protect me.

There are shadows below the golden orbs of his eyes, dimming his light. Even his skin looks unusually pale. He has been driven to sickness by this truth. And I believe in my very core that he did not enjoy deceiving me.

But I also know he does not regret it.

He just has to live with it.

For however much longer we get to live.

"I will allow you the opportunity to tell your story," I say to him, ignoring Nix's greedy eyes and the whinnying of my dolphin horde. "You may explain, and I will listen. Then I will decide whether I can forgive you or if I will return to the surface."

To land.

To live among the humans.

Among my own kind.

I watch Ryke's throat work as he swallows.

"Thank you for this kindness," he says. "I promise to be worthy of it."

"Go ahead," Nix chuckles. "Let us see you get your tail further into a twist."

Ryke glares at Nix, who smiles in return. He is enjoying this. Us, divided. Distrusting each other.

Ryke sighs, running a hand through his midnight hair.

"I have already told you that my family has ruled over Atlantia for millennia. That I was born into this fight, given little choice about my path in life. And that this birthright was an isolating, lonely one. Even my brothers and sisters in the Upper Shoal could never quite understand the burden bestowed upon me at birth. And then the sirens staged their coup, and I escaped Atlantia with the conch, destined to remain onshore until the time finally came for the resistance to strike."

Ryke pauses, searching my eyes. I nod. We have already discussed this. I am familiar with his history.

"What I never told you was that I was in hiding for centuries. Three, in fact."

Three centuries.

Three hundred years, concealed in my tiny village.

He had moved there when my ancestors were but babes.

The uprising of the church. The poverty of my people. Burning houses and famine.

He had witnessed it all, a creature in the shadows.

And that meant Ryke was…

I could not even fathom how old he might be.

We lock eyes, and I signal for him to continue.

"Those first few centuries were some of the most difficult years of my life. I mourned my parents and siblings. The days were dark, the nights endless. The ocean beckoned to me, but I knew I could not risk answering the water's call. There were several times when I considered succumbing to the dark thoughts that swam inside my head. In those moments, I pictured Dylan and Kai's faces, remembered the lilting laughter that sprang eternal from Guinn and Mira's mouths. My salvation was my thirst for vengeance. I longed to be the one to wring Talassa's neck, to watch the life drain from the false queen's eyes. I knew I needed to swim in Atlantia's waters again, but the longer I lived on land, the less likely that felt. I was beginning to run out of the one resource I needed to survive above the surface."

"Fish food?" Nix mocks.

"Hope," he continues, unfazed. "Then one day nearly one and twenty years ago, I awoke in the dead of night. Hovering above my bed, I saw what can only be described as a tiny dancing light. Not quite a flash or a flame—more like a flicker, a shimmering tendril. The light twisted and sparkled above me, a living, breathing entity. The sight was so beautiful it brought me to tears. It was moving, clearly attempting to lead me somewhere, and I felt compelled to rise and follow it. And do you know where it brought me?"

The air seizes inside my lungs.

"To me?" I ask.

He smiles, small and sad. "I could barely see you through your father's window. But I could sense you. Your bones were so breakable, your breath so shallow. You were completely, utterly human. I did not know at first what it meant that the light had led me to you. I had never come across two interloched mer before. No one had ever described to me what the pull of Fates' strings might feel like. I had only the lore to go off of. Stories my mother told me before she rocked me to sleep."

I choke on my next exhale.

Ryke was no stranger when I met him, then.

In a sense, he had known me all my life.

"But sensing you—so small and innocent, glowing with that tendril of light, of life—returned to me that shred of hope I'd lost, as if you had been holding on to it for safekeeping. It reminded me what I was fighting for: the future of not only my world but the human world as well. In fact, the very idea of a siren one day sucking the life force out of you, stealing that light…it was enough to encourage me to embark on my journey the very next day."

"Where did you go?"

"Everywhere. All over the continent, seeking mer dissenters and shifters living amongst the humans and maecenas. I found ways to get messages to my Upper Shoal, then established a method of communicating with many individuals at once, sending out rallying cries to the rebels. Most knew I had the conch in my possession, that it had been missing from the treasure trove for centuries. It became a symbol of the resistance. It gave my people courage. But even then I knew, somewhere deep in the crevices of my soul, that I would not be the one to make it sing."

For it was my destiny to call the mer to war. Not just as a descendant of Amphitrite, but as the true loch of the crown prince of Atlantia.

"When I returned to the creek cottage decades later, after establishing pockets of a rebellion militia across several territories, I immediately felt that tug toward you again. Your light, which had once been a mere dancing flicker, a tendril, had grown. As had you. When I saw you for the first time, I felt as if I had been punched in the gut. You were the most beautiful creature I could imagine. And you were glowing, Merriah—glowing with the light of the North Star. I knew then and there that you were my loch, that the Fates had chosen you for me. The runes on my back are the proof. A male mating mark."

A tear slides down his cheek, matching the ones that now streak down my own.

"But I was too late."

Another tear.

"You were already betrothed. To him, a human man. He was years your senior, and yet you appeared besotted by him. Happy with him."

We were happy together for years before his accident robbed him of his manhood. And then the foundation of our married life shattered like his leg.

"So I made a promise to myself to stay away from you and allow you a chance at a peaceful life, free of warfare and court scheming. I would not force you to be with me. I would accept your existence for what it was: a small gift that had restored my faith. I was able to convince myself that knowing you were alive, happy, and loved would be enough to sustain me."

Even on our happiest days together, I never loved my

husband. Not the way I love Ryke. What he saw that day was a mere illusion. We were content in each other's company at first, but our joining had been a duty. There was no passion, no feeling that if we were parted, the world would cease to spin, that my lungs would fail to fill. For loving and interlocking are not one and the same.

There is a difference between living on the world and living in it.

"But then you came to me."

Ryke's voice cracks, his words as shaky as my hands.

"I could not believe it when you brought that conch to your lips that day in the creek cottage. Could not believe you could hear its call, master its song. At first, I thought maybe I was dreaming. Then I tricked myself into believing that you were a shifter and I had somehow never spotted the signs. Later, I laughed at the cruel twist of the Fates. Of course my loch would be the lost descendant of the sea goddess herself. Only destiny would have such a sense of humor. When I followed you that day, I was driven primarily by curiosity and a desire to retrieve the conch. But when I saw how your husband looked at you with such vitriol, when I understood the shambles your marriage was in, my restraint snapped. You were my loch, godsdamn it. I would not have you living in pain as this man dimmed the light given to you by the North Star itself. And when we were together, our blood sang. We shone with the blaze of a raging fire."

How he had winced at the insinuation that he was my captor, my kidnapper.

"Taking you was the most selfish act of my life. By bringing you to my safe house, I immediately put you at risk. I loathed myself for it. And after I got to know you, my sweet, strong, sassy little minnow, I knew that if you found out we were interloched, you would hand yourself over to me. You have a strong sense of duty. But I did not want a subservient. I wished for a true partner. So I kept the truth from you, hoping that one day you would choose me as I had chosen you."

Although I didn't learn to swim until recently, I have always felt drawn to the water.

Perhaps it was not the water that called to me but the mer underneath it.

The one who dwelled there, shining with the light of a star.

My prince.

My loch.

My destiny.

My love.

Ryke's next words are so soft, I can hardly hear them above the breaking waves.

"I love you, Merriah. With everything that I am, I love you. You do not need to say anything. I do not need to hear those words back. I just want you to know that before we were interloched, I was in love with you. In love with everything that you are."

"Well, is that not the sweetest sentiment you have ever heard?"

The waters around us part. The sea starts to twist and bubble like a potion in a witch's cauldron. Tidal wives crash against the surface. A whirlpool pushes me away from Ryke even as I call out for him. I reach for him, but to no avail. The dolphins scream and scatter, terrified by the water's movement.

A mighty wave to end the world as we know it.

The false queen Talassa swims out of the watery vortex.

And smiles.

CHAPTER TWENTY-THREE

I can remember only three times in my life when I have felt bone-chillingly, life-flashing-before-my-eyes, shit-my-pants scared.

The first was when my parents took me into the city to see Cirque du Soleil when I was six. It was my first time at Madison Square Garden, and the number of people in the stadium, sucking the life out of the room, overwhelmed me. I felt like I couldn't breathe. By the time the contortionists took the stage and began bending their bodies backward, I was throwing up into my popcorn.

The second was in high school, when some wiseass who believed the Middle East was monolith and couldn't tell the difference between Syria and Serbia spray-painted

Bombs Away! on my locker. When I entered my combination, a ticking sound filled my ears. For about thirty seconds, I actually believed that some idiot bully had the gall to bring an explosive device to school. Turned out it was just a kitchen timer. But the scare tactic worked all the same.

The third was a year after I graduated from college. It was a Friday night, and Kyle had discouraged me from going out with my friends. We were curled up on the couch, my head nestled into his chest, watching a movie. An actor came on screen, and before my brain could catch up with my mouth, I murmured, "He's so hot," under my breath. Without warning, Kyle's right hand stopped caressing my hair and wrapped around my throat. And squeezed. Lightly. Then a bit harder, until I felt the oxygen leaving my lungs. When he released me, he insisted I apologize to him for being insensitive.

Three times in my life.

Three incidents that made me feel like the rug had been pulled out from under my feet, like my days on this Earth were numbered, like my limited time here was precious.

All three times, I was immobilized by my fear.

But that version of Joonie?

She had never heard of EGC.

That Joonie had never met the Salty Girls.

And that Joonie hadn't read *A Tale of Salt Water & Secrets* upward of seven times.

So when I turn around and come face-to-face with one of my foes, a tiny voice in my head whispers: *Not this time*.

"Good to see you, sugarplum." Thomas's smile is menacing. He makes his way around the block on the right-hand side, still dressed in that same gaudy velour tracksuit. "We were so sad when we returned to find y'all missing. Didn't your folks ever teach you that it's rude to leave a party without saying goodbye?"

Nico takes a casual step in front of me, adopting a protective stance. "Apologies for our etiquette," he says, his voice steady. "We were looking for more…comfortable accommodations."

Thomas clicks his tongue. "And after we were so welcoming, too. Giving you two stragglers a lift. What ever happened to gratitude?"

Clarisse turns the corner opposite from her partner, approaching us from the left, her blue hair billowing behind her like a rogue wave. She blows out a cloud of smoke from her vape, her red lipstick smeared all over her face and teeth like she has a bloody nose.

I feel Nico stiffen next to me, fighting the urge to panic.

Think, Joonie. What would Merriah do?

Well, she'd fight back, that's for damn sure. She'd call upon the powers of the treasure trove. Too bad I don't have an ancient conch to call Tey with or a dorsal fin to rub, signaling a horde of bloodthirsty dolphins to come to my aid.

I do, however, have a borrowed phone.

Without breaking eye contact, I reach into my pocket and find Roy's burner. I type a message without looking at the screen and press send, dispatching it to my few contacts.

A Hail Mary.

And now I need to keep these circus freaks distracted.

"How did you two even find us?" I ask, buying time. "Did you put trackers on our bags or something?" Nico suggested we ditch our stuff, and I called him paranoid. Insisted that there was no way two amateur thugs with what was surely a paint gun and a taser would be able to pull off such CIA-worthy tomfoolery.

"It wasn't easy, I'll tell you that much," Thomas says. "We had to phone a friend."

The door of a punch buggy parked on the street opens.

I hear the chiming of thick gold clanging together first.

Then I see the fine leather shoes.

The slick, gelled-back hair.

The receding hairline.

And the...surprisingly youthful face? Like, this guy moisturizes. I want to know about his skin care routine. He looks way too young to be the notorious Harry "the Hug" Lester.

"I'm sorry," I say. "Who are you supposed to be?"

The man bristles. "They call me Little Lester, or the Shrug. I'm Harry's nephew."

"Nephew?" I wrinkle my nose. "Harry didn't want to come himself?"

He lets out a loud, exasperated sigh. "You don't think the head of a crime syndicate does this kind of dirty work, do you? Give me a break. The Hug's at the spa."

Of course this juvenile in need of a toupee is waving a gun in my face while the real villain is getting a cucumber facial.

"Do they really call you the Shrug?" I ask.

The mobster grins. "Where's my shrug at?"

"Is that supposed to be, like, half a hug?"

"Enough with the questions," he snaps. Guess I hit a nerve? "They're just nicknames. My real name's M.C."

If that's short for Marrion Chad, I'm literally going to kill myself.

I stare at him. When I don't move, he pulls me against his chest with a touch too much force. There's a threat in that embrace. He pats my back, his hand wandering for a disrespectful moment. Then he pulls back and winks.

"Pleased to make your acquaintance."

Beware the goat dressed as a lamb. Where have I heard that phrase before?

"We all work the same circuit," the Shrug continues, gesturing to Thomas and Clarisse. "Last year, we met while running a long con on the coast. Now I send them to retrieve items that belong to me and have a habit of running away. Your friend Nicholas is one of them. And from what I've heard, you have something valuable of ours as well. Luckily, I've got eyes and ears all over this city. So this meeting was somewhat inevitable, wouldn't ya say?"

Clarisse holds up our phones between two fingers. "Plus, once we charged your phones, this number kept calling. Of course we wrote it down and gave it a ring from a burner. Super sweet, your mother is. Big talker, too. A bit gullible, though. We've been staking out the neighborhood ever since. Figured you'd show up eventually."

They must have claimed they'd found something of his and offered to return it out of the kindness of their hearts, like the good Samaritans they are. Why wouldn't she share her address? Especially since we conveniently forgot to tell her that we're on the run from the literal Mob.

Um. Oops?

"I'll cut right to the chase," Thomas says. "You two are coming with us. One of you stole something from us, and it made, uh, a very important person unhappy."

The ledger Nico took.

The one we accidentally-on-purpose never turned in to the police.

The one that's now hidden in my purse.

And now this trio of freaks has us surrounded.

Thomas is on our right.

Clarisse covers our left.

M.C. "the Shrug" Lester stands in front of us.

We are a little too far away from Nico's mother's

apartment for her to hear us scream. All around us, locals pass by, unbothered by the spectacle. Minding their own business. Fucking New Yorkers.

For all intents and purposes, we are trapped.

It's Nico who speaks first, his voice clear and curt. "I have what you're looking for. Let her go, and I'll consider giving it to you."

A bluff.

I know that the notebook is nestled somewhere inside my bag.

He's sacrificing himself to protect me, just as Ryke would.

"Aw, how sweet," Clarisse coos. "Looks like these two lovebirds finally figured their shit out. Fly, little birds. Fly!"

"That don't make any sense, Rissy," Thomas chuckles. Then, to Nico, "Too little too late, kid. Lester Senior wants a return on his investment—with interest. And you're going to give it to me, even if I have to break every bone in her body."

The sound Nico makes at his threat isn't human, somewhere between a growl and grunt.

His chest puffs up. He bares his teeth.

I watch as he transforms into something more animal than man.

Practically primal, lethal.

And when he opens his mouth, his voice is a low, forbidding warning.

"If you lay a hand on her," he says, "you will lose that hand."

I hold my breath.

If he says, *Touch her and die*, I will lose my goddamn mind.

"Touch her and die. Simple as that."

Holy fucking shit.

"How romantic," Clarisse whispers to Thomas.

He glares in response. "An empty threat. Do you want to do the honors, or should I?"

I stare at M.C., who's watching the scene with interest.

I try to communicate my desperation to him with my eyes.

"Take the ledger and go," I plead with him. "Nico doesn't have your money. We have nothing left to give you."

He shakes his head, the corner of his lips curling into a half smile.

We know too much. I mean, we've *seen* too much.

Do not use your mind or your eyes to guide you. Follow the moonlight of your heart.

It all clicks into place—the prophecy the fortune-teller gave me on the train. Of course. Why didn't I think of it sooner?

Three men emerge from a shallow pool of damnation.

My journey to find true love.

One made of tree sap and ink.

Ryke. The hero of my favorite series.

The second, hallucinations and the fog of the mystic.

Ryan Mare. The perfect man, but only in theory.

And the third, flesh, fire, and the truth of the histories.

Nico. The boy of my past and the man right in front of me.

When the squatting bird chants twice, go forth to the fallacies of your soul.

The pigeons. They chirped twice just moments ago.

Do not use your mind or your eyes to guide you. Follow the moonlight of your heart. Beware the goat dressed as a lamb. Only then will you defeat the fool and the red-painted maiden and land in the arms of the steady tide.

I have already underestimated Harry Lester, his nephew, and his band of thieves. The only way I can defeat Thomas the fool and bloody Clarisse is to follow the moonlight of my heart. To look inside myself and let that truth guide me.

For what you seek, you hold in the marrow of your shrouded words.

I am a reader. A writer. Words have always shown me the way.

They will not fail me now.

I know what I have to do.

"Well, well, well," the false queen coos. Her voice is honey-coated granite, as if she has not yet spoken today. "What do we have here?"

I can hardly hear her over the vibration of the water all around us.

Through the churning sea, I see Ryke. He is on bended knee, his brow knitted, doubled over in pain. Straining with every muscle in his body to fight his way closer to me.

Talassa raises a powder-white brow. And Nix, the horrid creature who laughed at my suffering—who tortured me for hours, taking joy in it—flinches under the heat of his sister's gaze. Pure stolen power radiates from her taloned fingertips.

"If I recall correctly, I gave you strict orders to grab the girl and do whatever it took to extract information about the rebellion from her *without* alerting the prince and his merry band of insurgents." She bares her canines, as impossibly white as her hair. "Or am I mistaken?"

Nix gulps. "That is correct, sister," he says quickly. "I mean, Your Majesty."

Her red eyes narrow until they are mere droplets of blood leaking from sliced skin.

"Then why have I intruded upon what appears to be a heartwarming scene of reunited lovers?" she snaps. "Why is the girl the picture of health? Did your villain monologue really last long enough for the two to reconcile?"

Behind her, someone snickers. Naia emerges from the darkness, her nose curled. She sneers at her twin brother.

"Did you, at the very least, obtain the intelligence we were after?" Talassa asks.

Nix grits his teeth. "No, Your Majesty."

In an instant, a collar of bubbling water chokes the next breath out of him.

"Then what exactly are you good for?" Talassa barks.

Naia claps her hands, delighted.

"It is not what you think." Nix struggles to speak through her chokehold. "The girl and the prince—they are interloched! I could not take her without alerting him. They are drawn to each other like plankton to the light.

Prince Ryke is able to draw life force from her without killing her or putting his own health at risk."

"And why should I give a flapping fin about that?" The queen's dark cheeks burn scarlet to match her eyes. "Do you think you are smarter than me? One step ahead?"

She spits in Nix's face, the moisture turning into a searing concoction that stings his eyes. He cries out, blinded.

"You fool!" she shouts. "Everyone in this ocean with eyes could see that the two were interloched at the Ball of Sinking Stars. They were glowing as bright as the moon! My pupils practically burned." Talassa shakes her head in dismay. "Although the power bit is…interesting. Curious. I suppose it makes sense that lochs would be able to recharge one another's life force. After all, they are rumored to share one soul."

She looks into the distance, thoughtful.

I steal a glance at Ryke.

My loch.

The other half of my soul.

His eyes are shut tightly, as if he is focusing entirely on maintaining consciousness.

"There is more," Nix says as the iron grip on his throat finally loosens. "The girl has powers."

The false queen's gaze locks onto mine. "Powers?" She inches closer to me, sniffing me. Inspecting my energy. "Is that so?"

I wince as she pulls a lock of my hair from my head.

Nix nods emphatically. "I saw her command an entire battalion of angry dolphins. They bowed to her, were loyal to her. Not the prince. It was…peculiar."

The dorsal fin hidden in my hand beats as if it has a pulse. I clench my fist around it in an attempt to conceal it, a move that is not lost on the false queen.

"And what is this?"

She pries my hand open. And when she sees the fin upon my palm, her face drains of color.

"But that is impossible," she sputters. "That fin is part of the treasure trove. But the chest has been locked up in my palace for centuries. It refused to open for me…"

She shakes her head again and again, an attempt to knock the notions out of her mind and onto the floor of the ocean.

"You." She points at me. "You were the one to sound the stolen conch of Amphitrite, the missing item from my treasure trove. Not the crown prince of Atlantia. But you are a mere mortal. That should not have been possible."

She taps her talons on her chin, lost in thought.

"Unless, of course, you were able to access the rest of the trove, including the Trident of the Gods. That would have given you command of the oceans. The ability to, say, detonate my soldiers with a mere thought."

Ryke lets out a muffled cry.

He is inching toward me.

And in his unblinking eyes, I see true fear.

"How can a human command the treasure trove when it will not bow to me?" she asks her siblings. "Merriah, your kind has not even entered our waters for millennia. How have you gained such strength? The power you call upon belongs to an immortal. Not just siren or mer. But that of a god."

She hums under her breath, a seductive siren song.

Then her fangs drag over her lower lip before her mouth falls open.

I know the moment she stumbles upon the truth.

Her voice cuts like a blade. "Of course. A descendant of Amphitrite."

For the first time since arriving in the cavern, the false queen of Talassa looks truly shocked. "I should have seen it before," she murmurs. "You were foretold."

Ryke pulls himself an inch closer, using only his elbows and the tip of his tail.

"Amphitrite's heir, the loch of the prince of Atlantia." Talassa laughs in disbelief. "The Fates have quite a sense of humor. Of course, this makes you an invaluable weapon in the war to come."

I imagine what it would mean to be a tool in the arsenal of the sirens.

A weapon to be wielded by the false queen in battle.

My stomach churns.

"Let her go, Talassa," Ryke growls, nearly below us now.

"An object this powerful?" the false queen cackles. "Now, why would I do that?"

"Because if you do, I will hand myself over to you. Grant Merriah her freedom and take me as your prisoner. You can hurt me all you like. Torture me for information or sport as you wish. Or you can kill me and end this war, the rebellion, here and now. Take my life, but give Merriah back her own."

All the blood rushes from my head to my heart.

No, only half of my heart. Because the other half is offering his wrists to the siren queen so she can shackle them.

"No!" I scream. "Ryke, if you feel any love for me, I beg of you, do not do this."

For he means to sacrifice himself to free me.

Does he not know that a world without him is just another prison?

"Minnow," he says quietly. "It is because I love you that I must."

The false queen swishes her tail back and forth as she considers his proposal. Tears fall from my eyes, evaporating the second they hit the air in my bubble due to the heat of Talassa's anger.

"It is an interesting proposition," she says. "But one question remains."

"Ask me anything," Ryke pleads, desperation dripping from his voice. I yearn for the days he taunted me with that signature phrase of his: *So many questions.* "I will tell you whatever you want to know."

The corner of the false queen's lips curls upward.

"Why would I torture you when we both know the very best way to hurt you is by hurting your loch?"

Naia creeps toward me, her white hair blowing behind her in a phantom wind.

"Do you really believe," Talassa continues, "that I would allow your power source, a weapon that could kill me if it were to fall into the wrong hands, to live even a moment longer?"

With one strong slap of her tail, my air bubble pops.

Distantly, I hear the faint music of Ryke's screams.

As Naia grabs my shoulders.

And cracks my spine.

CHAPTER TWENTY-FOUR

Before I can open my mouth to scream, Thomas punches Nico square in the nose. He goes down instantly, his body hitting the pavement with a loud smack.

"Nico!" I cry, reaching for him.

He looks up at me, blinking rapidly. There's already the ghost of a purple bruise forming below his right eye. When he attempts to speak, he coughs twice, then pulls his hand away from his mouth.

Blood.

My stomach sinks. At the very least, he's concussed.

"Bind his arms and legs," Thomas tells Clarisse, who spits out her bubble gum in response. "Then tape his mouth shut. And no weird ranting this time, okay? I'll search his things. Once we find the book and hand it over to Little Lester, I say we knock this loser out and go. Doubt anyone's going to care if we rough up this pretty face. Plus, we're shit kidnappers. Let's stick to thievin' from here on out, leave the rest to the Shrug."

Clarisse inclines her head in my direction. "What about the mouthy chick?"

"Leave her. She's too dumb to understand what's going on. Darlin', she's the one who got in our car in the first place. We've already got the brains behind this operation."

And even though I fear for Nico's life, even though I'm furious that these people won't leave us the hell alone, I can't help but smile.

Because these C-list villains? They're underestimating me, just like I knew they would. And that'll be their downfall.

I continue to shake and shudder by Nico's body, pretending to weep. But from where he's lying, he can easily see that my face is dry as my vagine during sex with Job.

"What are you doing?" he mouths.

All I can do is wink.

"Get back, girl." Clarisse shoves me away, using the same rope as before to bind Nico's ankles.

Good. I hope Nico remembers everything I taught him about escaping from restraints. And he soon proves me a capable teacher. Behind me, Clarisse is ripping duct tape.

And Thomas is too busy tearing apart Nico's backpack to notice anything amiss.

I creep up behind him and tap him on the shoulder.

"What?" He continues rummaging, tossing a pair of Nico's boxer briefs onto the street.

"S-sir," I stutter. "There's…there's something you should know."

He turns around then, his face bored. "What is it, sweetie?"

First, I kick him in the balls.

He immediately doubles over.

Next, I crouch and elbow him in the gut.

He tips his head back and howls in pain.

Opening up the perfect opportunity for me to stick my fingers in his eyes.

"Don't mess with the heroine." I step on his abdomen as he collapses on the ground. "Or the man she loves."

I knew my black belt in tae kwon do and those self-defense classes I took at the YMCA after reading the second ATOSAS book would come in handy. At first they were just for fanfic research, but then I really grew to love the feeling of getting stronger, of being able to defend myself from bullies like Kyle. I swore to myself that I'd never feel helpless again. But the last time we crossed paths with Thomas and Clarisse, they tied us up before I had a chance to show off my skills.

Not this time around.

Not with Nico's life at stake.

The entire thing happens so quickly that Clarisse misses the action, turning around at the last minute and gaping in pure shock. When she sees Thomas doubled over on the sidewalk, clutching his junk, she lets out a shriek so shrill, I think it's an ambulance siren.

"Baby!" she cries. "What did she do to you?"

She abandons Nico's half-bound wrists in order to fall over her nearly passed-out partner, fussing over his injuries. While she's distracted, I use Angel's key to scoop up the gum she spat on the sidewalk.

And dispose of it in her bird's nest of blue hair.

"You witch!" she wails, as if I've done more damage to her than Thomas. "What did you just do to me? To my hair?!" Clarisse clutches her chest with dramatic flair. "I've been hit!" She claws at a nonexistent bullet wound, falling next to Thomas on the sidewalk. "I'll have to cut it all off!"

I run over Nico, who is already rotating his hands, attempting to loosen his ropes so he can slide his wrists out. Without hesitation, I move to his ankles, freeing his legs from the restraints. We move in tandem, as if our movements are choreographed, rehearsed.

When I'm done, I rip the duct tape from his mouth, wincing at the sound of it tearing away from his flesh.

"Behind you!" he shouts the moment he's free.

I feel a cold object press against the back of my head.

Slowly, I turn around to face M.C. "the Shrug" Lester.

He's holding a small pistol, now pointed directly between my eyes.

The worst part?

He's smiling at us.

"Very good," he says. "Poetic shit, that stuff you were mumbling under your breath about the *marrow of shrouded words* or whatever the fuck. That really was a pretty line. But you see, gunpowder beats paper."

He cocks the gun, and I hear it click, just like they do in the thrillers.

Ugh. I hate thrillers.

"Just give me the notebook and get on your knees," he says. "I know you have it. It's easy to see this guy cares about you. You'll be good collateral until I collect what I'm owed. I'm real good at reading people."

Sure he fucking is.

This guy? He hasn't read a day in his life.

Maybe if he had, he'd be able to see what's coming next.

But still, with Nico beside me and a pistol pointed at my face, I forget how to breathe. How to think. The Shrug has the advantage here, and he knows it.

"Hand me my bag," I say.

"You," he nods toward Clarisse, keeping the gun and his eyes trained on me. "Will you stop rolling around on the ground and bring me her purse, please?"

Clarisse sniffles but obeys.

He's the false queen Talassa to their Nix and Naia.

And I think we have *his lackey's* ledger.

There's no way that one muscle man's notebook has the power to take down an entire organization, but there has to be something incriminating enough in there to make Little Lester travel all this way, right? Maybe we hold more chips than we realize. And once he takes the book back, he's going to get away with everything.

But at least Nico will be safe.

And then I hear footsteps, and a voice says, "Not so fast."

I recognize that voice.

Roy stands across the street, dressed in a giant fur coat and bare legs that can't be comfortable in the cold, holding what appears to be a bedazzled pink can of mace.

Next to him, Kalli is demonstrating her most intimidating scowl, a taser in one hand and a phone in the other. When I look closer, I realize she must be filming. Live streaming, if I'm not mistaken. That familiar blinking red light taunts the Shrug, who squints in confusion.

And in front of them, Angel grins, walking toward us and swinging a baseball bat—signed by Babe Ruth, no less. They're wearing an elaborate top hat and raincoat. Purrtha Mason hums at their feet.

My very own Upper Shoal.

They're here to defend me.

Fight for me.

With me.

To remind me, once for all, that I am not in this alone.

I hear police sirens swelling in the distance.

Angel's smile only grows.

"Don't screw with the Salty Girls," they say.

The Shrug hesitates, lowering his gun in surprise.

And then Angel takes a big swing.

I hear the sound first, deep in my eardrums.

The crackling of burning wood.

Bound paper torn at the seams.

My spine, split in two.

My spirit floats above my body, untethered from my corporeal form.

Funny, I think. It took dying to move freely beneath the waves.

To swim through the tides effortlessly like the mer.

I watch, a silent shifting observer, as Ryke lets out a guttural noise. A primal scream, loud enough to wake the creatures sleeping deeply under the sand. His eyes shut tight for a moment, and when they fly open, his golden orbs are melting down his very cheeks. A single finger points in the direction of the false queen.

A brutal promise of death to come.

His muscles begin to thrum with power, as if my life force has somehow poured out of my body, traveled through the water, and entered his soul.

From one broken half to another.

I do not allow myself to think of the pain he must feel.

Of that loch shattering in real time, on his plane.

He screams again, and even Nix and Naia have the good sense to look afraid.

The former begins to gather power with his fingertips in preparation for a fight. The latter just smirks, red eyes piercing.

But that crimson blade quickly dulls as Ryke cuts through the water in a millisecond, places one large hand on either side of her head, and rips it clean from her neck.

Nix cries out at the sight of his decapitated sister, as if a bond between them, an invisible string connecting the siblings, has snapped. His tail bends in two as he barrels to the bottom of the ocean to collect her skull.

The false queen does not show an ounce of the compassion her brother displays, the same mer who took pleasure in torturing me for hours. Instead, she looks to Ryke and says, "Very well. A life for a life, prince. A debt has been paid. And now our slate has been wiped clean ahead of the war to come."

A snarl sounds from below me, where Ryke swims, gathering energy in his palms.

My life force.

Whatever the false queen sees in Ryke's eyes must frighten her. As he approaches her, his fists clenching in a silent threat, she gathers her siren power and uses it to ride a current out of the cavern.

I expect Ryke to go after her. To finish what he started. The way he pointed at her was clearly an oath to end her life, one that I imagine he does not plan to break.

But no, it seems he will return to collect the false queen's life another day. Now, he hurtles toward my broken body. Salt streams down his cheeks, mixing with the ocean water.

"Merriah," he whispers, his voice cracking. "Merriah."

I do not move. My chest does not rise and fall like the tides. The sun does not shine once the moon rises. And mine has permanently set. Now it will be night for the rest of his days. Forever.

His tears tickle my unfeeling lips, but he licks away the moisture.

Then he leans in and lightly lays his lips upon mine.

Stiffening at the coldness of my flesh, he pulls away and buries his face in my chest. His back shakes as he sobs.

A strange sensation overtakes my spirit. It is almost as if I can feel his tears melting into my bloodstream, sending oxygen back into my vital organs. Ryke must feel something, too. A tug, perhaps, on our interlocked limbs. Because he pulls away and studies my face as if waiting for my eyes to open. And when they do not, he leans in and kisses me in earnest. A real, lasting kiss. To say goodbye, I realize.

The prince of Atlantia is letting me go.

"I love you," he whispers.

The strength of his kiss sings in the oxygen now flowing through my blood, resurrecting my brain and paying a visit to my heart. The water around me grows taut, a quiet vibration that no human could ever hear.

But I can.

I should not be able to.

But even in death, I can.

Ryke lets out a quiet yelp, backing away just as lightning strikes from above, where my spirit lingers. The water all around my slain body begins to gurgle like a pot beginning to boil, blurring his view of me. I feel the electricity answer the call of my blood, dancing with the oxygen and the energy from Ryke's kiss. Together, they dance down my body, repairing my bones one by one. My skin melts and hardens and twists until I am as tough as leather: scales. An elegant, muscular new appendage extends from my once-human spine, a straw-like yellow, as golden as Ryke's eyes and as potent as the sun.

For I am the sun, ready to rise again.

Somewhere in between the land of the living and the resting place of the departed, where I sit and watch, entranced, another being appears. A female. Tall and strong, with a mind of steel and energy unlike anything I have ever felt before. Though I cannot see her, I feel her take my spirit in her arms. She lightly traces my face with her fingers, allows her breath to fill my lungs. A faint drumming sound begins.

My own heart, learning to beat once more.

"Light of my light, blood of my blood," Amphitrite says, her voice overpowering the noise. "You carry the line. The line cannot die. The line lives on in you."

Her power kisses my own, then disappears.

And when I awake, sitting upright with a sudden breath, it is not as a mere human.

But as a mer.

CHAPTER
TWENTY-FIVE

I sit on the sidewalk, my ankles crossed and a blanket around my shivering shoulders, as two cops haul Clarisse and Thomas into a police car. Clarisse is still blabbering about the gum stuck in her hair, her cheeks streaked with melted mascara and her red lipstick still smeared all over her teeth. Thomas still has his eyes closed, no longer able to rub his temples, thanks to the silver handcuffs around his wrists.

Serves him right.

Let's see how he likes restraints.

Nico is across the street with his arms around his mother, talking her down. When she saw on the news that her son had been involved in an armed assault a block away from her apartment, she came running.

In front of me, a third officer struggles to shackle Little Lester, who is screaming in a foreign language, a slightly unhinged gleam in his eyes. Every few seconds, he points at me and lets out a string of profanities as the cop tries to wrestle him into submission.

His partner turns to me and groans. "Just got off the phone with FBI Director Simon Fischer. Apparently, the feds have been trying to track these three down for months. Those two have been going from town to town all over the Northeast, swindling innocent people and tracking down bounties. Apparently this one"—he indicates the mobster—"got into a bit of trouble in Yorktown. Owes the Rudaj Organization an ungodly amount of money."

I raise an eyebrow. "The Rudaj Organization?"

"Albanian Mafia. Traffickers—arms, drugs, girls. You name it. This guy appears to have severely pissed off one of the bosses by screwing him out of a considerable payday. They tracked him down a few months back, and he blackmailed these two idiots into helping him collect from your boyfriend to pay them off. And when that didn't work…"

I swallow the lump forming in my throat. "Let me guess. He figured kidnapping and ransom might do the trick?"

The cop snaps his fingers. "Bingo. And those two bozos have done a pretty terrible job of covering their tracks. We have footage of them pulling what appears to be a toy gun on a cashier. And they keep leaving empty liquor bottles with their prints in the cars they ditch. I assume the alcohol might be a little bit to blame for their slippery fingers. But for amateur con artists, they sure do move fast. And when criminals cross state lines as quickly as they've been doing, it leaves our people with a lot of paperwork and a nightmare headache. Hence why it's taken so long for the feds to nail 'em." He shudders, shaking his head. "I knew there was a reason I avoided casinos. Sad, sad places. Always been afraid of unhappy endings."

"Me too!" I say, choking on a laugh.

The cop leans forward and high-fives me. "Well, we can't thank you enough. If your friends hadn't called this in, we'd still be chasing these three around in circles."

My cheeks flush with pride at the memory of my Salty Girls coming to my rescue.

My very own Upper Shoal.

My dolphin horde.

My treasure trove.

"It was all them," I say.

This time, it's the officer's turn to raise his brows. "It looks like you landed quite a few punches yourself. Don't sell yourself short—you incapacitated your attacker and distracted the woman long enough to free your man. And your friend Angel told me that you were the one to make the rescue call."

I bite my lip. "That is true," I admit. "But I blame

my career as a copywriter for my thumb's stellar muscle memory. Apparently, I don't need to see to type an SOS."

The officer grins. "Well, Ms…"

"Saboonchi."

"Right. Well, Ms. Saboochy—"

He butchers it.

But I let it slide.

Just this once.

"—it sounds to me like you saved yourself."

I smile up at him, straightening my shoulders under the blanket. "Thank you, sir."

"Of course," he says, his face turning as red as the sirens. "What brought you to New York, anyway? You have a Connecticut license."

"Looking for true love," I tell him.

"Did you find it?"

"I think so." I bite my lip, studying Nico. "But not in the place I expected."

He clears his throat and turns his attention back to his partner and the man in cuffs. "Okay, no more funny business. There are a lot of people who can't wait to sit you down and ask you some questions. You have the right to remain silent. Anything you say can and will be used against you in a court of law. You have the right to an attorney. If you cannot afford an attorney…"

As he tells M.C. "the Shrug" Lester his rights, Lester locks eyes with me one more time. He holds up his wrists with a crooked grin. The playful fire in his eyes hasn't dulled a bit. And as he lowers his body into the cop car, joining a gobsmacked Clarisse and Thomas, he doesn't once break eye contact with me. A silent promise that he'll see me again.

Even if only in my dreams.

A shiver runs through my body like an electrical current.

And off in the distance, I swear I hear a siren call.

You have fulfilled your destiny, a voice says inside my head. *Do not waste it.*

Wasn't planning on it.

"What the hell was that all about?" Nico asks as he takes a seat next to me on the curb. Across the street, his mother has joined Angel, Roy, and Kalli, who appears to be reading something aloud from her phone. I close my eyes and say a silent prayer that it isn't an excerpt from my latest fic.

"Oh, you know." I look up into the pools of his eyes and get momentarily distracted. How did I ever think they were gray? They're so obviously the lightest, truest blue. "The NYPD was just thanking me for my great act of heroism. I thought about chewing them out for their history with stop-and-frisks, but I'm pretty sure Angel already read them the riot act, so…"

Nico leans forward and tucks a piece of my hair behind my ear.

I momentarily forget how to breathe.

"You are a hero, Joon," he says. "You saved my life, do you realize that?"

"I'm sure we can come up with some kind of repayment plan," I try to joke, but it comes out all weak and strangled.

"Seriously. Thank you, Joonie. You were amazing. Like Merriah, but better. You never needed a Ryke or a Ryan Mare or"—he swallows—"even me. You've always been the smartest, most badass person I know. Maybe now you can finally believe that, too."

Warmth spreads through my stomach. "You know what? I think I might actually be starting to."

"Good."

He leans in for a second, his eyes searching mine, before pulling away again.

Unsure.

"Nico?"

"Yeah?" His voice is barely a breath.

"Just because I don't need you"—I cup the side of his face, using my thumb to trace the edge of his stubbled jaw—"doesn't mean I don't want you."

He doesn't blink.

He doesn't even breathe.

"You called me the man you love."

Suddenly shy, I turn away, biting the inside of my cheek. "I did."

"Look at me, Joonie."

I do, and what I see steals all the oxygen from my lungs.

Nico's cheeks are flushed, his eyes wide with adoration. With hope.

"Did you mean it?" he asks.

I nod. "You were right. I was too focused on my fairy-tale ending to see what was right in front of me."

I lift my lips to his forehead and kiss him lightly there.

"Even though I'm not your Prince Charming?"

His body is so still. It's as if he's worried he might spook me.

I bring my lips to his ear. "Especially because you're not my Prince Charming."

"I'm still the same guy, Joon," he warns. "Once the adrenaline wears off, you might not want me. I'm still a grouch and a cynic. Like, I'm fully investing in space travel in case the Earth runs out of natural resources and we need to start a colony on another planet. I can be an anxious mess sometimes. And mean to myself. And to others. Even when I don't mean it, when I don't want to be. What if I say something wrong and accidentally break your heart? What if we fight and resent each other and never speak again? I don't know if I could live with myself if my darkness absorbed all your light. Because that's what you are, Joonie. Pure, radiant light. Always have been."

"Nico?"

He stops ranting long enough to look at me.

And the moment he does, I lean in and kiss him.

His lips are soft against mine, and he tastes both sweet and smoky and so incredibly like himself that I almost cry out. And when his tongue teases the seam of my mouth, I open up, and our tongues tangle. He nibbles on my lower lip, and I can't hold back a groan.

I try to convey everything I want to say with my kiss. That I was wrong to pursue someone I'd never even met, convinced he was my soul mate. Because it doesn't matter if my relationship with Nico isn't perfect. I'm not looking for smooth sailing anymore, but someone I want stuck on the ship, who will weather the storms alongside me. We can argue and disagree, and as long as we respect each other, we'll communicate our way through it.

I am ready to earn my happily ever after with Nico.

When I pull away, panting, he's studying me with disbelief. As if I'm a revelation.

The fanfic writer in me whispers, *He's your loch.*

And at that exact moment, I swear to the holy Furnace, to the Fates, to Amphitrite herself, that Nico begins to glow.

When he sees the wonder on my face, a small smile tugs at the corner of his mouth.

As if I am glowing, too.

"Nico." I take his hand in mine and squeeze tightly.

"Hm?"

"If you're getting on that rocket ship to Mars, I want you to save me a seat."

He laughs. "Consider it done."

And then he kisses me again.

I look out into the crowd, the assembly of dissenters and revolutionaries, and raise one arm.

Within seconds, everyone in the room quiets.

Stills.

Lifts their faces to stare at me.

At my brown hair, now a glossy, deep chestnut hue. At my pale skin, cleared of any lines and shining like the sun upon the sea. When I gained my immortality, I went from plain to striking in a moment. My very presence has the ability to command a room, to turn heads and demand respect. And beyond my beauty, my power has emerged as a mighty force that can no longer be denied.

My tail swishes, holding me in place, upright and steady. The amber scales shine like nuggets of gold, layered like a cake, weaving the most beautiful tapestry from my tapered waist to my elongated fins. I inhale deeply, drinking in the salt water around me, and exhale with nary a bubble in sight.

In my left hand, I hold the Trident of the Gods, the symbol of my lineage, of my birthright. Not that the mer need to see it to know whose blood flows through my veins. Amphitrite's power pulses with every flex of my fingers. Around me, the ocean pulls apart and twists like a whirl pool. A low, thrumming tension radiates into the water from my skin. Behind me, a loyal cadre of dolphins stands by, watching my every move. They act as my personal guard and menace any mer who dare defy me. The dorsal fin I use to call them is hidden, nestled between my breasts.

And in my right hand, I clutch the golden whip, an object of brute force that began to respond to me the second I shifted into my true form. With the flick of my wrist, I can call my chariot pulled by ancient hippocampi, seahorses older than Atlantia itself. They whinny in greeting, ready to escort me wherever my heart desires if the newly formed muscles in my tail give out, not yet accustomed to constant use.

Beside me, my loch swims with his head held high.

Ryke's strength is its own weapon, although we agreed to be careful when, where, and how he wields his pure energy now that he cannot draw life force from me. A mer cannot power share with another mer, and since I shifted in death, not life, we do not know how much of my humanity remains. A hybrid of my kind has never, to our knowledge, been seen before, below the water or onshore. When we hold hands, an explosion of light radiates from our bodies: our interloched bond, the glow of which I could not see when I was merely human. Its shine has amplified tenfold since I shifted into a mer, lighting up the sea and sky.

Our rebel army shields its eyes, in awe of our shared energy. The power of our love for each other.

Upon my head is a tiara of golden trident spikes and spiraling seashells, encrusted with rare gems from sunken ships and sea glass smoothed by the waves for centuries. A matching crown adorns Ryke's wavy midnight-black tendrils, elevating my loch from a fallen prince to what he was always destined to become: a true king.

And I his holy queen.

Lifted up by the Fates and anointed by the Furnace.

The heir of a goddess.

Ryke clears his throat, and every mer in our company bows their head in reverence.

Beside our royal seats, the Upper Shoal hovers proudly. Their hands are intertwined, and looks of wonder and admiration decorate their faces.

Above our heads, our new sigil flies: a woman with half a tail and a single leg, holding a conch to her lips.

Shutting my eyes tightly, I hear the crackle, the snap of my spine. A reminder of the trauma I survived to be here on this stage. The miracle I represent.

My eyes flutter open, and I take in the masses. The people it is now my duty to protect.

I lower the trident, and they meet my gaze.

Power sings as my lips twist into a smile.

"Shall we begin?"

EPILOGUE

But that's not how it happened!"

Nico is hovering. He's studying my laptop screen, reading over my shoulder, even though he knows that's my pet peeve. But he's also got my coffee in one hand, lingering by his waist. And if he leans any farther forward, that scalding liquid is going to spill all over the crotch of his pants.

That'll teach him a lesson.

"I did *not* whimper when Clarisse and Thomas locked the car door," he argues. "I growled. It was, like, a very manly sound."

"Funny," I say. "I seem to remember you being near tears."

Nico pouts. "Baby, don't get me wrong: I'm so happy

you're writing this story. But do you have to make me sound like such a fucking loser?"

"Would you prefer a *masculine* whimper? Or perhaps a macho sniffle?"

He rolls his eyes. "Fine. Write whatever your heart desires. Just make sure it has a happy ending."

I grin, spinning around to plant a kiss on his lips. "That's a given. But this is fiction, remember?"

"Whatever you say, Joon."

I shake my head, looking out the window. It's late summer in Mystic, and tourist season is in full swing. The smell of ice cream and fresh fudge floods the cobblestone streets, along with selfie sticks and T-shirts featuring the drawbridge. There's a troubadour playing his guitar on the corner outside of Sift, his song drifting up the road to the countertop at Kabobs 'n' Bits, where I'm seated. I can't see him from all the way up the hill, but I do have a spectacular view of the old church, empty parking lots, and the new apartment I now share with Nico—a renovated loft above an old print shop.

When I first told Nico that I felt ready to take a stab at writing a novel, he asked what story I planned on telling. I had no clue. At first I wanted to write a fantasy, like Evelyn G. Carter. After all, I had been writing high fantasy romance fanfic for years. I figured I could take everything I had learned and apply it to building a world of my own, then transfer my audience to boot. At the very least, I could pick my most successful fic and adapt it into something that was actually publishable, like all the hottest indie authors are doing these days. But after Kalli's video went viral and everyone started asking for my side of the story, Nico convinced me to write that instead. I was hesitant to try literary fiction, but he assured me that what we'd gone through, our adventure, was more unbelievable and fantastical than any fantasy novel he'd ever read. Including *A Tale of Salt Water & Secrets*.

And you know what? He wasn't wrong.

As it turns out, the reason Nico's mom saw our story on the news and came running is because Kalli live streamed the entire incident on Twitch. Local news channels like NY1 picked up the footage, which promptly went viral on X, TikTok, and Instagram. At first, I really fucking hated the idea of everyone forever associating me with the worst thing that has ever happened to me, but my Salty Girls made me feel a lot better about it. The ATOSAS community has been so supportive of my author journey, and I quickly learned that some good can come from the darkest periods of your life. It's like stepping on a rock, cracking it open, and finding gold.

Not only did the road trip from hell provide some much-needed inspo for my first full-length novel, it also saved the family business from going under. When Nico made that bad bet, Teymoor was more than worried about our last quarter's numbers and was considering selling the joint and cutting our losses. Ollie came into town to draw up legal documents. Tey asked the two of them to keep it from me because he didn't want me to worry—he knew how much I loved Mystic and that I considered the restaurant my true home. But he never expected me to go viral for kicking my kidnapper in the nuts. And he *definitely* didn't think I'd do it while wearing an oversize Kabobs 'n' Bits sweatshirt.

Now the restaurant has become a tourist destination for true crime junkies. Six days a week, we've got a line out the door. Some travel websites are even calling us the new Mystic Pizza, and we are not above milking it. We're selling prophecy-embroidered sweatshirts and **Don't Mess with the Heroine** mugs, and I come over once a week to sign them, much to Tey's annoyance. He's grateful that I saved the shop and all, but the amount of shit I give him every time I autograph merch is enough to make him reconsider.

Last week, I requested that he feed me grapes as I worked.

"Maman and Baba want to know if we'd be willing to drive up to port over Labor Day and cruise with them for a couple of days," Tey shouts from the kitchen. "And before you ask: yes, Nico can come, and no, we will not be sailing to the Caribbean. This will be half family hang, half business meeting. They want to look over my expansion plans before I meet with that CEO in September."

The national interest in the restaurant has investors knocking down Tey's door, begging him to consider franchising. He always says he'll think about it, but I know a part of him has no interest in leaving Mystic or Nico and me. He's content here, and I can't say I'm too mad about that.

"I'll think about it," I tell him. While a long weekend on my parents' houseboat sounds nice and all, I know from personal experience that the lack of boundaries gets really old after day or two.

Not to mention the lack of walls.

Tey nods, reading my thoughts on my face. "Nico!" he yells from behind the counter. "Your order is getting cold, asshole. We've got paying customers waiting, *ghologh*!"

My boyfriend shoots him a cocky smirk, grabbing his plate and plopping down next to me. "Why don't you want us to go sailing off into the sunset with your family?" he asks, popping a piece of crispy rice into his mouth. "Worried you'll get sick of me?"

"Worried I'll feed you to the sharks?" I ask sweetly, stealing a bite from his plate.

I watch out of the corner of my eye as he does his best to take a peek at the laptop screen without moving his head. "FUCK OFF," I type in big, bold letters. He chokes on his next bite and starts coughing up his Kabob. I pound on his back until he's breathing again.

"That'll teach you to stop back-seat driving. Or back-seat writing, if you will."

"You sure you don't want to give my character a tail?" he jokes.

I bite my lip. "Maybe a teeny-tiny one."

He raises his hand to his heart. "You wound me, woman."

"You love it."

"I love *you*," he says, leaning in to punctuate his words with a kiss. Then he looks out the window and frowns. "Is it supposed to rain today? I didn't bring an umbrella."

"Who cares?" I shrug. "I love sun-showers. They're romantic."

"They're wet," he protests.

"We can dance in the rain."

"Or get hypothermia."

"Maybe after the storm, there will be a rainbow." I sigh dreamily. "I fucking love rainbows."

Nico leans down and presses his lips to my forehead. "Never change, Joon," he whispers.

I break away suddenly, squealing. "Oh my God, you're brilliant. That's the perfect ending for my book."

He raises his hands to his ears. "Even though you fully just blew out my eardrum?"

I beam up at him.

"Don't worry," I say. "I'll make it sound better on paper."

And they lived happily ever after.

The End.

READ ON FOR A SNEAK PEAK OF IMAN HARIRI-KIA'S NEXT NOVEL!

A DAY IN THE LIFE OF LAIA GRACE @LAIABILITY

Morning Routine

I start my day by rubbing whale semen into my pores. The key is to do it right when you wake up, which for me is 5:30 a.m., under the cover of darkness, right before the sun rises. Massage delicately, never rub or pat. Whale semen is full of multivitamins and proteins that will keep your skin hydrated all day long. Now, I know what you're going to say—"Laia, it's too expensive. Can you suggest a more accessible alternative?" I totally get where you're coming from, but to be honest with you guys, I prefer my semen sustainably and ethically sourced from whales that aren't raised in captivity. That's just my preference. I feel like you can tell when the mammal in question consented. You know?

After doing my skincare, I meditate for fifteen minutes while lying down with my legs extended vertically against a wall to increase blood circulation and boost brain activity. Once my synapses are firing on all cylinders, I light a candle, take out my daily affirmations journal, and write out my manifestations for the week. I only manifest using natural light because I read an article once that said that the energy of a living flame is supposed to bring you one step closer to the elemental wavelength of your wishes. You guys, I know I'm going to sound like a broken record, but it's crucial that you repeat your manifestations three times aloud, or they likely will not reach their intended energy source. Trust me: It's life-changing. Try this hack at home and let me know if it works for you. I have been able to manifest so many of the best, most beautiful parts of my little life, from my dream man to my cozy, two-bedroom New York City apartment.

By now, the sun has risen, filling my newly renovated, rent-controlled third-story walk-up with the most stunning golden light. I put on a plush striped robe, slippers, and matching headband, and wade over to my open-concept kitchen. If you haven't checked out my vlog on how I used stick-and-peel emerald tiles to DIY the hideous backsplash, definitely watch that after this video. I turn on my espresso machine to make my daily iced latté. You guys, this recipe... I'm obsessed. Two shots of fair trade, finely ground espresso beans. A splash of nondairy vanilla oat milk creamer. A sprinkle of cinnamon. A teaspoon of plant-based protein powder. And a handful of collagen peptides, which I swear you can barely taste beneath all the frothy goodness. I literally go to sleep dreaming about my morning coffee—it's that delicious.

Once I'm finished in the kitchen, I make my bed, throw on a matching activewear set and Uggs, and sit down at my vanity. I have a busy day ahead of me—shooting content, grabbing lunch with a friend, and dropping off some returns. But first, I'm going to morning Pilates. That means I need to apply glam that's both long-lasting and light enough to survive my class. Nothing too heavy. Just a little bronzing primer, concealer, and liquid foundation. Then contour, cream blush, and a touch of highlight. And mascara. Also, a tiny bit of eyebrow gel. And Freck. I'm obsessed with fake freckles lately—I just feel like they pull my entire look together, you know? I add a little setting spray, and I'm ready to start my day.

My Workout Regimen

I always walk to my local studio in the East Village because I like to get at least fifteen thousand steps in a day. In New York, that's honestly not that hard—everyone walks everywhere here, so much so that I don't even notice the calorie burn anymore. I swear, I get, like, ten thousand steps in before lunch without even trying. On my way to class, I always stop and say hi to my local homeless man who lives outside of Whole Foods. I don't know his name, but I see him every day, and I always make sure to give him a crisp dollar bill. I know how privileged I am to live in New York and have the best job in the world—and make no mistake, content creation is hard work, you guys—so I believe it's really important to give back to my community whenever and however I can.

Pilates always kicks my ass, but somehow, I never manage to break a sweat. Not to be a pick me, but I seriously hate sweating, you guys. I have always preferred to say, "I'm glowing," rather than "I'm perspiring." Plus, as most of you know, I've been bleaching my hair platinum for the past few years, ever since moving to the city, which means that I have to be really careful about my wash cycle and oil exposure. Anyway, I have been beyond obsessed with low-impact exercise lately. I don't know what it is about running and weightlifting, but I just felt like it was making me bulky. Pilates, however, leaves me feeling snatched and energized all day. And it's, like, really hard, you guys. I'd pay to see a football player attempt to operate a reformer.

What I Eat in a Day

After class, I meet up with my colleague, fellow content creator Harlow Belle, also known as @TheHarlowdown, to grab protein smoothies from this new, viral spot in the West Village. You guys, I'm not even kidding: These are a near-perfect dupe for the Hailey Bieber smoothie. And this time, we only had to wait in line for forty minutes. Anyway, Harlow Belle usually brings a duffel bag full of outfit changes, a ring light, a tripod, and the new Nikon Z FC 4K, so we spend the next few hours shooting content. I like to have designated shoot days so I can record content in bulk, then edit and schedule it out in advance. Lucky for me, Harlow Belle feels the same way, so we usually just team up and help each other with our brand deals. This industry can feel super isolating and competitive, and I am beyond blessed to have met Harlow Belle early on at an influencer event. We instantly clicked. And I can truthfully say that now, she's no longer just a coworker—she's one of my best friends.

Get Ready with Me

Once we wrap, I spend the rest of my afternoon doing errands: dropping off clothes at the dry cleaner, picking up pieces from my tailor, Alejandro, and doing some returns at Sephora, Ulta, Love Shack, and Free People. After I dump everything back at my apartment, I head back out to the salon to get a wax from my girl, Sherry, and touch up my acrylics with my nail tech, Lucy. This time, we decided to do something crazy and try out the double-glazed, jelly-filled cronut trend that everyone and their mother is raving about. This takes three hours, but honestly, you guys? Look how cute they came out!

Such an real reminder that in life, it's important to take risks.

While I was getting a matching pedicure, I received a heartfelt text from my long-distance boyfriend, Harrison. Believe it or not, we are actually coming up on our three-month anniversary. Time really does fly. As a lot of you guys know, we had the sweetest meet-cute: Harrison was visiting New York from Boston on a work trip for the week and decided to download Hinge when he was bored at a conference. We matched pretty much right away—he responded to my "I'm looking for" prompt (my answer was "A man who is either taller than six feet or can fund my extra dirty martini habit") and said, "What about 6'4?" But here's the funny part: When I messaged him back, he somehow accidentally blocked me! We probably never would have gotten together if I hadn't run into him later that weekend in line at Common Grounds. (The bar, not the coffee shop.) I called him out, and he explained the entire debacle. Of course, I immediately forgave him, and he offered to buy me a drink to make up for it. You guys: Never forget that if he wanted to, he would. We got to talking and realized that we had a lot in common. For example, he works in private equity, and I've been thinking of maybe potentially investing in cryptocurrency sometime soon. We shared our first kiss that very night, a sloppy dance floor make out. And he asked if he could take me home, but I told him that I don't do it on the first date, which majorly bummed him out. So much so that he insisted that I buy a train ticket to Boston the very next weekend so we could rectify the situation immediately. I did. And the rest is history.

Lately, our relationship has been getting really serious. For example, he left a box of condoms at my apartment after his last visit, which he said I should save for "next time." Um, okay. Obsessed with me much? Also, he told me a little bit about his family vacations to St. Barths growing up, which is actually a very big deal because he is a Scorpio and doesn't open up easily. (Long-time followers will know that I am a Pisces and have always been very in tune with my emotions.) I know you guys are dying to know what he looks like, but can I be vulnerable for a sec? I don't know if I'm ready for that step yet. Right now, we're still really enjoying getting to know each other offline. So, I think I need to keep my relationship private but not secret, for the time being. But the moment that changes and we're ready to hard launch, you guys will be the first to know.

Anyway, back to my day. After I leave the salon, I rush home to shower and change because I'm already running late to a brand dinner in the Meatpacking District. The dress code said, "floral Phantasia," so I opted to keep it pretty casual: black tights, mini leather shorts, an oversized floral patchwork coat, and heeled knee-high boots. For the glam, I throw my hair into a slicked-back bun because it wasn't a wash day and do a quick, thirty-minute no-makeup makeup look that leaves me with rosy cheeks and freshly bitten lips.

Come with Me to a Brand Event

In the Uber ride over, I give my mom a call. She doesn't pick up, so I leave her a voicemail, then spend the rest of the drive catching up on emails and editing photos. Guys, you know I believe everybody is beautiful, and I 100 percent don't endorse going on a diet or getting anything done to your face to change your appearance because, at the end of the day, nothing will make you happy unless you love yourself first. And true love and beauty come from within. That said, I'm really considering getting a chin job. I would probably do it with atmospheric sculpting, which is different from getting actual plastic surgery because you use air to burn off your fat rather than sucking it out. Again I am in no way, shape, or form encouraging you to get this procedure. Most of you know that I've never gotten any work done, with the exception of my nose job, which I was forced to undergo at eighteen because I broke my cartilage. But if I end up going through with the operation, it will be a little treat to me, from me.

Then I get to the event, and oh my god, you guys: Phantasmic is absolutely killing it. The vibes of the tablescape were immaculate. Phantasmic is a BV Suppository

Company that I've been working with over the past few weeks. I don't know if you guys know this, but roughly one in four women will experience BV at some point in their lives. It's literally an epidemic. Luckily, boric acid exists. Basically, it's a natural compound that can regularize your vag's PH. And Phantasmic makes suppositories that are not only adorably pink and bedazzled, but they come in different floral scents. That's right: You can now clear your cooch from infections while smelling like literal roses. Use my code LAIAS SNATCHED SNATCH for a 10 percent discount off your next Phantasmic purchase.

After I walk the VIPussy (their genius slogan) red carpet, I sit down to dinner in this beautiful back garden that actually used to be a slaughterhouse but has all of this gorgeous, exposed brick. The tables are covered in dried lavender and false flowers made of organic tampons that we all get to pose for pictures with. Phantasma's owner, a sixty-year-old white man named Gary, gives an amazing toast, while the rest of us munch on three courses of vegan delights. I don't care what anyone says: Portobello mushrooms do taste exactly like ground beef, and you cannot tell the difference when you order a meatless burger! After Gary's speech, a modern dance company does, like, an interpretive dance inspired by the spring equinox, and we are all encouraged to go around and share what we are planning to "spring clean" from our lives, our closets, and our vaginas.

You guys, I'm not going to lie: This guest list was stacked. Jade Aki, former digital director of *Vinyl* and host of the new podcast *Deconstructing from Digital Media*, was seated at the head of the table, and she looked seriously stunning. She spent the entire night talking to Cat Christie, the deputy editor of *The Shred*, who was recently promoted to oversee all content strategy for the *New York Dweller*. Even though my job means I'm often in the presence of some smaller-scale celebrities, I was feeling pretty starstruck. I actually studied writing in college—well, screenwriting—and really look up to women like Jade and Cat. They're actual icons.

Daily Debrief

After dessert, I decide to walk home, a task that proves to be pretty difficult in my heels against the cobblestone, but whatever. I try my mom again, then Harrison, but both calls go to voicemail. They're probably already asleep. I look up at the sky. It is a clear night, and the moon is full and tinged orange, a real solar eclipse. I'm sure you guys already know this, but when the moon, Earth, and sun align, crazy things can happen. Solar eclipses can be transformative, catalyzing change and bridging hidden issues to the surface, where they can no longer be concealed from the light. So as I head home to get ready for bed (I need at least ten hours a night or I get really puffy), I shut my eyes and whisper a wish to the cosmos. It is so important to voice your gratitude at every opportunity. I feel so lucky to have the life I've always dreamed of—and most importantly, you guys in my corner. Thank you for spending my perfect day with me.

I am nothing, no one, without you.

ACKNOWLEDGMENTS

My debut novel was the book I needed to write. My second was the book I wanted to write. This book practically wrote itself. I truly had so much fun working on this story, and I hope that joy and passion permeate the pages. These characters mean the world to me, and I feel so grateful for and indebted to them for helping me fall back in love with the creative process.

First and foremost, this book would not exist without the Romance community. A huge thank you to the Romance authors whose books line every surface of my apartment and whose words have sat with me in the quiet moments of long days and guided me through dark periods toward the light. You are pure magic. I am so grateful you are here. And to the Romance readers: Thank you for embracing me so wholeheartedly. I wrote this one especially for y'all. I figured, after the last two, I owed you. I love you. I'm sorry. Forgive me?

Taylor Haggerty. Give her the Pulitzer. Give her the Nobel Peace Prize. Give her the damn EGOT! Taylor, you hold so many people together with both a firm, steady hand and a gentle, tender touch. You have the mastermind of a genius and the patience of a saint. Thank you for all that you do, day in and day out—from championing my work to listening to me rant for hours at a time. You are the best of the best. And to the rest of the Root Literary team, especially Gabrielle, Holly, and Jasmine: Thank you for holding down the fort this year and creating an agency that feels like found family.

Kate Roddy: Can you believe we've worked with each other for *five years?!* I wouldn't want to be on this roller-coaster ride with anyone else. Thank you for always immediately understanding me and my characters and my ideas (especially the chaotic, unhinged ones). I can't tell you what a relief it is knowing that you're in my corner, advocating for these narratives that we carefully craft together. It's been such a thrill to watch your hard work and brilliance pay off ten-fold, and I am so proud to be your author.

Cristina Arreola: You really did your big one. Thank you so much for bringing all of my fantasies to life. I feel like the luckiest girl in the world to be a recipient of your talent and instincts. And to the rest of the Sourcebooks team, I can't thank you enough for continuing to believe in me, both as an author and as a person. In an industry that can be incredibly isolating, I've never felt less alone—and I know that I have the community you've created to thank. A big thank-you to Brittany Vibbert and Kelly Lawler for ensuring that we get this one right; Alison Cherry, Sanjana Basker, and Tyler McCall for their thoughtful edits that prioritized the safety of my readers. Emily Mahon and Austin Drake, thank you for designing the cover of my dreams. Pam Jaffee, thanks for inviting me places and introducing me to my idol. And Dominique Raccah, thank you for continuing to take a chance on me. It's a privilege that I do not take for granted.

Team Cosmo: You can take the girl out of the magazine world, but you can never take the magazine world out of the girl… From the bottom of my heart, thank you. For choosing to take this colossal step in tandem with me, for all of your support over the past six months, and, above all else, for loving my words. I am so proud to be a Cosmo girl.

Willa Bennett, I would have followed you to the end of the earth—but this is much better. When I left media, I never dreamed that we'd be able to work this closely together again. Our paths are truly star-crossed, and I don't know what I would do without you. Thank you for your counsel, advocation, and friendship. We fucking did it.

Addison Duffy: Everything you touch turns to gold. Thank you for all that you do. I'd trust you with my life, but my characters mean much more.

Bahman Kia and Gisue Hariri, thank you for always asking questions and sharing in my excitement. You make writing books feel like a team effort. Ava Hariri-Kia, thank you for picking up when it matters and humbling me when it doesn't. You're my favorite person in the world. Mojgan Hariri, I am officially appointing you the title of Rose 3.0. Karim Hariri, thank you for being the nucleus of our family. Christine, Martin, Alexandra, and Max Falkner, thank you for welcoming me into your family and supporting me unconditionally. James Banbury, you too. And Angie Tinto: Just, thank you. Seeing you alive and happy and healthy is the greatest gift.

Simone Rivera and Ariel Matluck, I literally could not make a single decision without consulting you first. Thank you for existing. Melanie Mignucci (WB, I already thanked you), thank you for always reminding me what matters most. Katie Duncalf, let's be honest: You weren't really involved with this one, but I love you so much that I wanted to write your name anyway.

Louisiana, thank you for always making me look good—and for being the eyes to my ears.

To all the authors who took the time to blurb, thank you so much for your kind words and for taking the time out of your busy days to read my work. Because of you, I highly recommend meeting your idols.

To all the book bloggers, BookTokers Bookstagrammers, and BookTubers who took the time to read my last two books, post a review, share a picture, recommend to a friend, attend a tour stop, or send a kind message: Please know that you are constantly making my day. You are the bedrock of this entire industry and the reason I get out of bed in the morning excited to put pen to paper. Thank you, thank you, thank you! Also, I legit get all of my book recs from you.

Cherry Pickers: Shit, I love this community so much. Thank you for making me smile every week and for allowing me to pay the rent with my words. I feel so honored to have helped foster the smartest, sweetest readership on the internet. I hope to continue to pay it forward for as long as I can.

Mrs. Mass: Sorry you caught a stray in the author's note. Can I send you a book, and we'll call it even?

Matthew Falkner, I always save the best for last. Our first year of marriage has been the happiest of my life. I love you so much. Thank you for being my happily ever after. I'll save you a seat on that rocket ship to Mars.

ABOUT THE AUTHOR

© Louisiana Mei Gelpi

Iman Hariri-Kia is a writer born and based in New York City. A *Forbes* 30 Under 30 honoree and award-winning journalist, she covers sex, relationships, identity, and adolescence. Her work has appeared in *Vogue*, *New York Magazine*'s The Cut, *Harper's Bazaar*, *Cosmopolitan*, and more. She is the author of *A Hundred Other Girls* and *The Most Famous Girl in the World*. You can often find her writing about her personal life on the internet, much to her parents' dismay.